THE BURNT ORANGE SUNRISE

FOR THE ONE AND ONLY BLACK CANARY,
MY FAVORITE SONGBIRD

THOMAS DUNNE BOOKS.
An imprint of St. Martin's Press.

THE BURNT ORANGE SUNRISE. Copyright © 2004 by David Handler. All rights reserved. Printed in the United States of America. No part of this book may be used or reproduced in any manner whatsoever without written permission except in the case of brief quotations embodied in critical articles or reviews. For information, address St. Martin's Press, 175 Fifth Avenue, New York, N.Y. 10010.

www.minotaurbooks.com

Library of Congress Cataloging-in-Publication Data

Handler, David, 1952–
    The burnt orange sunrise / David Handler.—1st ed.
        p. cm.
    ISBN 0-312-30735-7
    EAN 978-0312-30735-6
    1. Berger, Mitch (Fictitious character)—Fiction. 2. Mitry, Desiree (Fictitious character)—Fiction. 3. African American police—Fiction. 4. Film critics—Fiction. 5. Policewomen—Fiction. 6. Connecticut—Fiction. 7. Ice Storms—Fiction. 8. Parties— Fiction. I. Title.

PS3558.A637B87 2004
813'.54—dc22

2004049404

First Edition: October 2004

10 9 8 7 6 5 4 3 2 1

THE BURNT ORANGE SUNRISE

DAVID HANDLER

THOMAS DUNNE BOOKS
ST. MARTIN'S MINOTAUR
NEW YORK

THE BURNT ORANGE SUNRISE

PROLOGUE

"I AM ONLY GOING to tell you this one more time," she said to him in a quiet, determined voice. "That mean old woman just has to die. You know it, I know it, we both know it. Do you get what I'm telling you?"

"I get it," he responded irritably. "I've gotten it every single time you've said it, and this is, like, the third time."

She watched him carefully as they idled there in the Old Saybrook train station parking lot, hearing the icy pellets go *tappity-tap-tap* on the roof of the car. "Well, what do *you* say? That's what I want to know."

What he said was, "We should get back before the roads get any worse." Though he made no move to put the car in gear. Just sat there behind the wheel, his gloved hands gripping it loosely. "We'll be missed."

"Not until we talk this out," she insisted, staring out at the floodlit rail platform, which gave off a ghostly yellow glow in the frigid night.

The dashboard clock said it was only a few minutes past nine. It might as well have been three in the morning. Absolutely no one else was out. It was a weeknight. The wind was blowing. A steady frozen rain was falling, and it was supposed to turn to snow overnight. There were only a half dozen cars in the parking lot, left behind by Amtrak passengers who would be real unhappy when they returned in a day or so to find them encased in an impenetrable shell of ice. The station was a tiny one, situated almost exactly midway between New York and Boston on the Northeast Corridor. The much-hyped high-speed Acela did not even stop here. Only the occasional local train, none this time of night. The station office was shuttered. Old Saybrook was a shoreline town popular with summer people. During the warm, sun-drenched months, this parking lot was a joyous, bustling place, a place for animated hellos and rushed, giggly good-byes.

Tonight, it was a cold, dark place to talk about murder.

A few businesses were clustered around the parking lot. A dry cleaner, newsstand, a health club. And the Chinese restaurant where they had just eaten. They had been the only customers in the place. She'd had beef with broccoli. He'd had moo shu pork. Also two beers. She could smell the beer on his breath as they sat there with the engine running, the car's interior growing warm as the heater took hold.

He had been maddeningly quiet all through dinner. She was the one who did all of the talking. And all of the thinking. This was not something new.

"More than anything, I hate what she does to you," she said, trying a new approach.

"Me? What does she do to me?"

"It's what she doesn't do. She doesn't appreciate you. Doesn't listen to you. Doesn't *know* you. She just takes you for granted, like you're her loyal hound."

He stuck out his lower lip like a hurt little boy. Sometimes he seemed so very young to her. Except, God knew, he wasn't anymore. Neither of them was. "That's something I'm used to. Doesn't bother me. I don't expect her to respect me."

"Well, you should. And you shouldn't have to put up with her. Neither of us should." Her eyes studied him expectantly. Still no reaction. *Nothing.* "Look, I'm just being honest, okay? Once the old lady's gone, we'll have everything we've ever wanted. And that's a good thing, isn't it?"

"True enough," he allowed, following her lead at long last.

Always, it was up to her to take the lead. Always, it had been this way when it came to men. And she was fine with it. Really, she was. Way back when she was a schoolgirl, she'd been utterly floored when her class had read *Pride and Prejudice* by Jane Austen. What an impression that awful book had made on her. Those five sisters sitting there all pure and dewy-eyed and silly in their white frocks, tender young breasts heaving as they read their sonnets and waited and waited for some kind, handsome young lord to ride up on his horse and sweep them away, one by one. *Not going to happen to me,* she remembered saying to herself as she whipped through the pages, shaking her head in disbelief. *Never, ever going to happen to me. Whatever I am going to get in this life I will get because I go out and get it myself.*

Especially men. Men didn't decide things. Women did. This was something she had known since she was very young, and saw how they would respond to her. How she could get anything she wanted if she simply smiled at them a certain way. Men were easy. Men were slow. She'd made the first move with virtually every one of them she had been with in her whole life. If she'd waited for them to make the move, she'd still be waiting, book of sonnets in hand. And she had zero tolerance for those women who complained that they couldn't "find" a man. Bull. Any woman who really, truly wanted a man just had to go and get him. So what if he wasn't, strictly speaking, available at the time? If there was one thing she'd learned in life, it was this: No man who is genuinely worth having is ever actually out there on the open market. He always belongs to someone else when you first meet him. You just have to take him away from her, that's all. He isn't going to be handed to you.

Life isn't going to be handed to you.

Which was what brought her to here and now—this car, this night, this move. Because time was running out for her. She wasn't getting any younger. She still hadn't gotten everything she deserved, and it wasn't fair. No, it wasn't. Especially when she thought about how many opportunities she'd let slide on by because she was waiting for something better, *someone* better. Especially when she looked at what all of her friends had. Compared to them, her life still constituted a total failure. And the window of opportunity was sliding shut faster and faster. And when she allowed herself to think about it, she felt an overwhelming sense of desperation that bordered on outright panic.

She needed this. This was her chance. Maybe her very last. And she was not about to let it pass her by. Trouble was, she couldn't do it alone. She needed him on board. Him thinking it was going to be about the two of them.

"Once the old lady's gone," she repeated slowly, "we'll have everything we've ever wanted."

"I don't disagree." After a brief silence, he added, "As long as there's a we."

So that was it. He sensed something.

"Why wouldn't there be?"

He looked over at her, swallowing. He did not have an intelligent face. He did have a gentle one. He was really very sweet. Not many people knew this. "You tell me."

"What's bothering you?"

"Money changes everything, that's what."

"Well, it won't change us. We're together in this. We'll always be together."

"How do I know that?"

"Because I just said so, that's how. Have I ever once lied to you?"

"No, you've never lied to *me*."

Meaning he thought she had lied to other people. Okay, maybe she had. But never him. *Or* herself. She was always honest with herself, and that was crucially important. Because the people who lied to themselves were the ones who did the real damage in this world and ought to be punished. As long as you were straight with yourself, you could look right in the mirror and say, *This is not wrong.*

"What about *him*?" he wondered, gazing at her accusingly.

"Not to worry, I can handle him. That poor man thinks he's in love."

"And you?"

"What about me?"

"Do you love him?"

"God, we've been over this a million times," she said, her voice rising with exasperation. "I don't even like him—you know that. He's just a means to an end."

"How do I know that's not what *I* am?" he demanded. "How do I know you don't say the exact same things about me when you two are in bed together? How do I know that?"

"Everything I do, I do for us," she responded patiently. "You know this."

"Do I?"

She reached for his gloved hand and squeezed it. "There's only one man in my life, and that man is you. This won't change us, I swear. We're for keeps."

"So what'll you do about him?"

"I can manage him."

"How?"

She saw a glow now coming from the west, growing brighter and still brighter. And then a sleek, low-slung silver Acela rocketed past on its way to Boston. As it shot by, she could make out snapshot glimpses of figures seated at the windows, snug and warm. People who were going somewhere while she idled here in this car, going nowhere. And then the train had gone by and there was only the silence and the darkness and them.

"That's no concern of yours," she said, chewing fretfully on her lower lip, terrified that he was getting cold feet. He had to feel right about this. Since he was a man, that meant he had to feel it had all been up to him to decide. Only then would he get behind it.

"Well, what if they catch us?"

"They won't. Why would they? She's old and sick."

"They won't do tests or anything?"

"You mean like an autopsy? They only do those if there's something fishy about how a person dies, which there won't be. Trust me. Or if the family requests it, which they obviously won't."

"Why not?"

"Because everyone's *waiting* for her to die, silly."

"So why don't *we* just wait?"

"Because we can't."

"Why not?" he persisted.

"Because she can't get away with what she's doing to us."

He sat there in silence for a long moment. "Well, no one lives forever," he finally conceded, his voice hollow. "We're all going to die soon enough. Each and every one of us. We'll just be kind of easing her along. I guess that's one way you can look at it."

"Please don't get all gloomy on me. You know it makes me crazy."

"I'm not, I'm just . . . We're talking about taking another human life."

"Not human. *Her*."

"Will she feel any pain?"

"Not one bit. She'll never even know what hit her."

He ran a gloved hand over his face, distraught. "I don't know, it feels so wrong."

"There's no such thing as wrong. There's bold and there's frightened." She studied him carefully in the dimly lit car. "Which are you?"

"Right now, I'd say you have balls enough for both of us."

She let out a soft laugh. She had a delicious laugh. She had been told this by any number of men. "It's the right move. We need to do this."

He gazed at her pleadingly. "How do I know for sure that you love me?"

So that was it. She relaxed now, knowing what he wanted, knowing that everything was going to be okay. Turning in her seat, she reached over and gently unzipped his pants, searching for him with her deft sure fingers, caressing him, squeezing him, feeling him grow under her touch.

"There, there . . ." she whispered lovingly.

He drew his breath in but remained stone-still, as if he were afraid she'd stop if he so much as moved a muscle.

"There, there . . ."

She wriggled sideways and knelt before him, taking him deep into her mouth, teasing him with her lips and tongue. Slowly, she moved her head up and down on him, up and down. Steadily, his breathing grew more rapid.

It bothered some women, performing this particular task on a man. A couple of her friends disliked it so intensely they flat-out refused to do it, even for their own husbands. Her it had never bothered. In fact, she found an open-mouthed kiss to be infinitely more off-putting. Some guy jamming his tongue into her mouth, forcing his spit and his gastric juices down her throat. That was supposed to be romantic? No, for her this was nothing. Besides, when she had a man's zipper down, she was in charge of him. And she was always happiest when she was. She knew this about herself.

He climaxed in no time, his hands gripping her head tightly, feet kicking out at the floorboards, that strange gurgling noise of his coming from his throat. Then she zipped him back up, gave him an affectionate pat and sat back in her seat.

He stared straight ahead, waiting for his breathing to return to normal. "I love you," he said, his voice painfully earnest. "You do know that, don't you?"

"I do," she said. "And I love you back."

He put the car in gear and eased it out into the darkness of the parking lot, away from the floodlit platform.

"So what do you say?" she asked, gazing at him.

"I say the mean old woman's in our way," he replied solemnly. "And she has to die. She just has to."

Delighted, she leaned over and kissed his cheek and said, "So she'll die."

Next Morning

CHAPTER 1

IT WAS MITCH'S FIRST stay on the Connecticut Gold Coast in February—the official off-season. As in a lot of Dorset, locals shut off their water, bled their pipes and headed somewhere—anywhere—else. Mitch was discovering that there was a very good reason for this. Those refreshing summer sea breezes off of Long Island Sound were now howling thirty-five-miles-per-hour arctic blasts that never let up. Especially out on Big Sister Island, where Mitch's quaint little antique post-and-beam carriage house offered very little in the way of insulation. Make that none. His big bay windows, with their breathtaking water views in three different directions, offered so little wind resistance that they might as well have been thrown open wide. It was very difficult to keep the temperature inside his house above a gusty fifty-five degrees, even with the furnace running non-stop and the fireplace stoked with hickory logs.

And then there were the storms.

Like the wicked Nor'easter that blew in on the last day of January, flooding his kitchen and crawl space, ripping half of the roof from his barn and, for good measure, washing away a section of the quarter-mile wooden causeway that connected the forty-acre island to the mainland, rendering it unsafe for vehicular traffic. The only way Mitch could cross it now was on foot.

All of this plus it happened to be the snowiest winter anyone under the age of ninety could remember. It seemed as if every three days another six inches fell. Mitch had personally measured seventy-eight inches since the first flakes appeared back on Thanksgiving Day. The banks of plowed snow that edged the town roads had to be ten feet high.

In spite of these rigors, Mitch Berger, lead film critic for the most prestigious, and therefore the lowest-paying, of New York's three daily newspapers, stayed on. This was his off-season, after all. The season when the studios released only what was officially known in the movie trade as "Post-Holiday Crap." Nothing was due out until Memorial Day that didn't star either Martin Lawrence or David Spade. Or, God forbid, Martin Lawrence *and* David Spade. Besides, Mitch was finding the beach a surprisingly beautiful place to be in the winter. He had never seen a full moon shine so brightly as it did on a cover of pure white snow. He had never seen sunsets such as these; the crystal-clear winter sky offered up such awe-inspiring pink-and-red light shows that he'd taken to photographing them many afternoons. Honestly, he couldn't understand why anyone would want to leave such a winter wonderland.

So he stayed. He also had his responsibilities, after all. He'd promised the other islanders, all of whom had migrated south to the Peck family compound in Hobe Sound, that he'd keep an eye on their houses for them. Plus three of Dorset's elderly shut-ins were counting on him to deliver their groceries. This, Mitch had learned, was part of the social contract when you lived in a small town. Those who were able-bodied looked out for those who were not.

And Mitch was not exactly idle professionally. He was busy making notes for *Nothing But Happy Endings,* a book he wanted to write about the pernicious influence of Hollywood escapism on contemporary American politics. Washington and Hollywood were one and the same, Mitch felt. The nation's halls of power nothing more than sound stages, its politicians merely actors mouthing carefully scripted, substance-free dialogue, its journalists nothing more than compliant pitchmen eager to peddle that day's feel-good story line. Every policy issue, no matter how knotty and complex, was now being reduced to a simplistic, highly commercial morality tale. Even war itself was nothing more than just another cable entertainment choice, complete with blood-free battles, awesome computer-generated graphics and soaring background music. As Mitch had watched Hollywood's escapist mind-set steadily engulf and devour the nation's public discourse, he'd found himself growing more and more alarmed, because if there was one thing he knew, it was this:

Life is not a movie.

And so he wanted to write about it. At age thirty-two, Mitch had written three books so far, all of them lively film encyclopedias that were popular with armchair video and DVD fans. But he had never written a serious book, a book that required a lot of long walks on the beach and solitary evenings spent before the fire, searching his soul while he squeezed out notes on his beloved sky-blue Fender Stratocaster. It was something he needed to do. Mitch wanted his career to be about something more than a mountain of film trivia. Sure, he could readily provide the answer to a question like, say, "Who is Sonny Bupp?" (Sonny Bupp was the child performer who played Orson Welles's son in *Citizen Kane*.) But so what? Mitch was a critic, not a game-show contestant. Partly, his desire to write *Nothing But Happy Endings* was fueled by the new, socially involved life he was leading in Dorset. Partly it was the influence of Dorset's tall, gifted and babe-a-licious resident trooper, Desiree Mitry, whose commitment to her art and her work was boundless.

The only problem was that he really couldn't seem to get started on it. Oh, he had lots of ideas. Just no coherent structure or vehicle for them. No outline. No plan. No, well, book. Possibly, he didn't have it in him. Possibly, he was out of his league. Such thoughts had occurred to him. But he would not give in to them. Just kept on walking the beach and making more notes, believing that his breakthrough would soon come.

Mitch also had a certain matter weighing on his mind that he needed to get straight with Des. It was something heavy, something unavoidable, something he had to tell her. And he would, when the time was right. But to date, beyond one oafish attempt that he desperately wished he could take back, he still hadn't gotten it done. And it was beginning to create some tension between them. Because anytime he edged anywhere near the subject, a melon-sized lump would form in his throat. Sensing his discomfort, Des would immediately morph from his green-eyed sweet patootie into a taut, six-foot-one-inch predatory cat. Her Wary, Scary Look, he'd taken to calling it.

Quickly, he would change the subject. She did carry a loaded semiautomatic weapon, after all.

Still, Mitch looked forward to each winter day out on Big Sister with great enthusiasm. All except for this getting-out-of-bed part, he had to admit as he lay there listening to the early-morning snowflakes patter softly against the skylight over his head. Mitch's sleeping loft happened to be unheated, aside from the open trapdoor in the floor. During the summer the trapdoor helped to ventilate the loft. Now it allowed the heat from the kitchen below to waft upward at suppertime, warming the loft just enough so that Mitch didn't have to look at his breath when he climbed into the feathers. Trouble was, by morning it was a meat locker—and Mitch was just so nice and warm buried there under two Hudson Bay blankets, a goose-down comforter, a Clemmie and a Quirt. Quirt, who was Mitch's lean, sinewy, outdoor hunter, had taken to sleeping on his chest. Clemmie, his lazy meat loaf of a house cat, lay on Mitch's belly. The cats assumed these same sleeping positions every night, by some territorial arrangement that they'd worked out between themselves. They never varied.

Reluctantly, Mitch awakened them, and the three musketeers shared a huge morning yawn. First Clemmie, who passed it to Mitch, who passed it to Quirt. Then, as they began stretching and washing themselves—the cats, that is—Mitch got up and coaxed his pudgy self down the steep, narrow stairs to crank up the heat, shivering in his gray sweatpants and complimentary red sweatshirt for Rob Zombie's *House of 1,000 Corpses*.

Mitch had one very open, good-sized room to live and work in downstairs, with exposed, hand-hewn chestnut posts and beams, a big stone fireplace and views—views everywhere. He had a kitchen and bath. And, upstairs, his sleeping loft. It was a tiny house by most people's standards. But it was everything Mitch had ever wanted.

There was still a good warm bed of coals in the fireplace. He fed the fire and got it going again, then put his coffeemaker on, first preheating the pot with hot tap water. If he didn't, the boiling water would shatter its ice-cold glass on contact. Mitch had learned this the hard way.

The thermometer outside his kitchen window said it was a balmy two degrees this morning. An oil barge was heading for the big tanks in New Haven, riding low. No one else was out on the water. Even though it was snowing pretty steadily, there was a thin sliver of burnt orange sunrise layered in between the waterline and the cloud cover. Mitch had never seen such a sunrise phenomenon before. He went and fetched his camera, but by then it was already gone—all that was left was a faint orange glow on the water. Red sky at morning, sailor take warning. What did orange mean? Was this a good or a bad omen?

He turned on the Weather Channel, which was something he'd taken to doing no more than twenty times a day since winter had arrived. The National Weather Service was predicting three-to-five inches of new snow on the Connecticut shoreline this morning, tapering off to flurries by afternoon and followed by—surprise, surprise—gale-force winds. And this was actually good news. What they were experiencing was the relatively harmless northern edge of winter storm Caitlin, which was heading out to sea south of Long Island by way of the Delmarva Peninsula.

He shaved and drank his coffee while he made himself a large bowl of Irish oatmeal topped with dried cranberries and Vermont maple syrup. Oatmeal was Mitch's main form of cold-weather sustenance before noon. After that, he moved on to his world-famous American chop suey, which he cooked up by the vast pot load, reheating the pot again and again until it had formed a truly magnificent crust.

Mitch had owned a good, arctic-weight Eddie Bauer goose-down parka for years, but out here it was not nearly enough protection. Not without layers and layers underneath it. First a T-shirt, then a cotton turtleneck, then a wool shirt, then a heavy wool fisherman's sweater. He'd never needed long johns when he'd lived in the city. Now he wore a pair made of itch-free merino wool under beefy twenty-four-ounce wool field pants. He'd never bothered with a hat either. Now he owned a festive red-and-black-checked Double Mackinaw Wool number complete with sheepskin earflaps. His socks were heavy-duty wool. His boots were insulated Gore Tex snow boots. His gloves were lined with shearling. Much of his new winter wardrobe he'd ordered from C.C. Filson and Company, the Victoria's Secret catalog of foul-weather geeks the world over.

Properly swaddled and insulated, earflaps down, collar up, Mitch slogged his way out into the two-degree snow, feeling very much like the Michelin Man's heavyset Jewish cousin. The snowflakes stung his cheeks a bit. Otherwise he was plenty warm. Three or so inches of fresh powder had already fallen, the snow creating a wondrous muffled silence, as if cotton batting were wrapped around everything. There had been some frozen rain last night before the snow came. His boots crunched hard against it as he plowed his way toward the barn, where he filled his wheelbarrow with firewood. He rolled it back to the house and stacked the wood by the door under the overhang. Then he trudged down the narrow path toward Big Sister's beach. Each and every tuft of tall, golden meadow grass was swathed in white. Snowflakes dusted the sharp green of the cedar trees and clung to the gnarly, iron-gray bare branches of the old sugar maples.

Mitch walked Big Sister's beach every morning, no matter the weather. There was a desolate, windswept beauty to the beach in the winter. And he felt it was a precious gift to be here. After he'd lost his beloved wife, Maisie, to ovarian cancer, Mitch had promised himself he would never again take a moment of happiness for granted. And he'd kept that promise.

The water was choppy this morning and the tide was going out, leaving a crust of ice behind on the sand. Blocks of ice as big as manhole covers had floated down the Connecticut River and washed ashore like so many pieces of a giant jigsaw puzzle. Mitch had to navigate his way through them as he made his way along the water's edge. A dozen or so giant tree trunks had washed up, too, encased in ice, looking very much like dinosaur bones. A few hardy gulls and mergansers were poking along for their breakfast. Supposedly there were eagles around, although Mitch still hadn't seen one. As he passed the old lighthouse, he came upon the broken remains of a Hobie Cat that someone with too much money and too few brains had left behind on the town beach at summer's end. Each morning now, it turned up in a different place out on Big Sister's beach, its mast long gone.

Mitch shared Big Sister with the surviving members of the blue-blooded Peck clan, who had held title to it since the sixteen hundreds. There were five houses in all, not counting the decommissioned lighthouse, which was the second tallest in New England. When he reached Bitsy Peck's mammoth shingled cottage, he dutifully climbed the snow-packed wooden steps to her door and poked his head inside to make sure her furnace was running. Then he retraced his footsteps and continued on to Evan Peck's stone cottage. The Pecks didn't believe in shutting their island houses down over the winter—sometimes they felt like using them. The furnaces had to be kept running or their pipes would freeze, so someone had to keep an eye on the places. A caretaker, in other words. Mitch had happily volunteered.

His daily rounds completed, Mitch arrived at the island's highly compromised wooden causeway, which had so many planks and railings missing it reminded him of a suspension bridge in an Indiana Jones movie. As he stepped gingerly across it, mindful of the frigid, choppy surf directly below, he hoped that his cottage's 275-gallon fuel tank didn't run dry before he was able to get the causeway repaired. Because no oil truck could make it out there right now. If he was careful, he had enough oil to last him for another month. But if he ran short in March, he'd have to tote emergency supplies out in five-gallon cans.

His bulbous, kidney-colored 1956 Studebaker pickup was parked by the gate under a blanket of snow and ice. Paul Fiore, Dorset's plowman, hadn't been by yet, so the dirt road that curved its way back through the Peck's Point Nature Preserve to Old Shore Road was invisible save for the slender guide poles that Paul used. The Preserve was a windswept peninsula that jutted right out into the Sound at the mouth of the Connecticut River. The Pecks had donated it to the Nature Conservancy for tax reasons. During warm months, it was very popular with local bird-watchers, dog walkers and joggers. There were footpaths along the bluffs. A meadow tumbled down to the tidal marshes, where osprey, least tern and the highly endangered piping plover nested.

Mitch kept a scraper, an ice pick, a can of W-D 40 and a shovel in the back of the truck under a tarp. He scraped the snow and ice from the windows, grabbed hold of the driver's side-door handle and tried to yank it open. No chance—it was frozen solid shut. He carefully chipped away at the ice with the pick, sprayed W-D 40 in the crack and tried again, putting every ounce of his considerable weight to the task. The top third of the door pulled open, the bottom two-thirds remained stubbornly shut. More W-D 40, more big boy pulling . . . and success. Mitch jumped in and tried the ignition. The engine kicked right over on the first try. The battery was brand new, plus his Studey was steadfast and true, aside from the fact that it had no heat. He stamped his feet on the floorboards to warm them up, found first gear and went roaring off, skidding on the sparkling blanket of virgin white snow as he slalomed his way between the guide poles. He did have snow tires, and two sixty-pound bags of sand over each rear wheel. But when there was ice under the snow, traction was not easy to come by.

Old Shore Road had been plowed and sanded already. But the Dorset Street historic district, with its majestic 250-year-old colonial mansions and towering sugar maples, still had not. Mitch chugged his way slowly through it, windshield wipers swatting the snowflakes to one side as he gazed out in wide-eyed wonder at the steepled, white Congregational Church, at John's barbershop with its antique Wildroot sign, the old library, town hall, the Dorset Academy of Fine Arts. He could not believe how beautiful, how *calm* it all was. And how much he felt as if he'd been magically transported to a place far, far away from the real world. A kindly place where no crazed suburban commuters were scrambling their way to and from their snap-together modular homes built around a cul-de-sac one-half mile down the road from the newest on-ramp to nowhere. A contented place, a place where people led happy, meaningful lives.

Paradise, in other words.

Not that Dorset was. Mitch had been here long enough to know that a lot of good, generous people lived inside the village's picture-postcard colonial mansions. But they were real people leading real lives, lives that routinely spun out of control. In short, Dorset was just like everywhere else, only prettier.

Because there was no such place as paradise. Not if people were living in it.

School had been canceled. As Mitch rounded the bend by Johnny Cake Hill Road, he saw that dozens of pink-cheeked neighborhood kids were already using their freedom to sled down the hill by way of the Dorset Country Club's third fairway. Mitch could hear their joyous laughter as he drove past. Part of him, a big part, wanted to pull over and join them. But he was all grown up now, or at least his body was, so he kept on going toward the Big Brook Road shopping district, watching them wistfully in his rearview mirror.

He stopped first at the post office to pick up his mail and that of his three elderly charges—Sheila Enman, a retired school teacher well into her nineties; Sheila's girlhood friend, Tootie Breen; and seventy-eight-year-old Rutherford Peck, a distant cousin of the Big Sister Island Pecks who had recently dozed off behind the wheel and lost his driver's license. Mitch honestly didn't mind running errands for them. It was no trouble. Besides, Mrs. Enman made him chocolate chip cookies, Mr. Peck supplied him with bottles of his excellent home-brewed stout and Tootie paid him each and every day with a shiny new quarter. Already, he'd earned almost six dollars this winter.

During the summer, when Dorset's population doubled to nearly fourteen thousand, the A & P would be packed with hyper, sun-burned fun-seekers shouting into their cell phones and scratching at their mosquito bites. The aisles were utterly deserted now as Mitch clumped his way along, earflaps up, shopping lists in hand. His grocery cart, which hadn't been serviced since the Ford administration, kept driving hard to the left and slamming into the shelves. Elton John's "Benny and the Jets" was playing over the store's tinny sound system, a bit slooowwer than usual, it seemed. It sounded way more like a lullaby than it did a rock anthem. Actually, the scattered handful of aimless store workers seemed to be living in slo-mo as well.

Yesterday's leftover rotisserie chickens were on sale—he got one for each of his elders. A box of Pilot crackers and three cans of chicken noodle soup for Mr. Peck. Clamato juice and Cream of Wheat for Mrs. Enman. A one-week supply of butter-pecan-flavored Ensure for Tootie. For himself Mitch collected the closely guarded secret ingredients to his American chop suey: one large jar of Ragu, one pound of ground beef, one pound of spaghetti, an onion, a green pepper and a package of frozen mixed vegetables. Garlic salt to taste.

It was in the frozen food aisle that Mitch ran smack into a local innkeeper named Les Josephson, who was not exactly Mitch's favorite Dorseteer right now—for reasons that had to do with this upcoming weekend and with Les's famous mother-in-law, Ada Geiger. Les, who operated Astrid's Castle with his wife, Norma, had talked him into participating in something that Mitch would never in a million years be caught doing were it not for the fact that Les had, well, lied to him.

"Mitch, I am so glad I ran into you," Les exclaimed, smiling at him radiantly as he stood there, cradling a gallon jug of milk under one arm. "I was *just* going to call you."

"Is that right?" Mitch noticed that Les was not only blocking his path but had a firm grip on his left-leaning grocery cart as well. "What about, Les?"

"I want to throw myself on your mercy. I feel as if I got you involved under false pretenses."

"Only because you did, Les."

"You're absolutely right," he agreed readily. "You couldn't be more right."

He was a most agreeable fellow, Les Josephson was. Outgoing, friendly, helpful—everything you could ask for in an innkeeper.

Although, in fact, he had been one only since he latched on to Norma a few years back. Les was actually a retired Madison Avenue advertising executive, which Mitch felt explained a lot about him. Because this was a man who was always selling something, always on, and never totally on the level. Les was in his early sixties, not quite five feet nine but very chesty and broad-shouldered, with a big head of wavy silver hair that he was obviously very proud of since he never wore a hat, not even in the snow. Taking good care of himself was clearly important to Les. He held himself very erect—shoulders back, chin up, feet planted wide apart. His smooth, squarish face had a healthy pink glow to it, his teeth looked exceedingly white and strong. He wore a Kelly-green ski jacket with the Astrid's Castle tower insignia stitched on its left breast, corduroy trousers and L. L. Bean duck boots.

"I'm hoping I can make this up to you, Mitch," Les went on, as the sound system segued into "Born to Run" by Bruce Springsteen, the funeral dirge re-mix. "I'd really like to, if you'll let me."

Mitch tried to pull away, but Les wouldn't let go of his cart. "If you don't mind, Les, I really have to get these groceries delivered."

"But Ada really wants to meet you. *Before* this weekend, I mean."

Mitch immediately felt his pulse quicken. "She does?"

"Absolutely. She's most insistent. After all, you're the man who dubbed her The Queen of the B's."

"No, that wasn't me. That was Manny Farber, years and years ago."

"Ada's very grateful to you, Mitch. She wants to thank you personally."

Norma's legendary ninety-four-year-old mother, Ada Geiger, was one of the twentieth century's most illustrious, controversial and remarkable cultural figures. Also one of Mitch's absolute idols. It was safe to say that Ada Geiger was the only person, living or dead, who had been a colleague of both Amelia Earhart and the Rolling Stones. The beautiful, fiercely independent daughter of millionaire Wall Street financier Moses Geiger, Ada had captured America's imagination back in the Roaring Twenties when, at the age of sixteen she became the youngest woman ever to fly solo from New York to Washington. That feat earned her a charter membership in the Ninety-Nines, a group of daring young female pilots whose first president was Earhart. After brief stints as a socialite, fashion model and Broadway actress, the spirited young Ada bought herself a Speed Graphic and stormed the rollicking world of New York tabloid journalism as a crime scene photographer. Soon she was writing the news copy that went with her uncommonly lurid photos. By 1934, she'd moved on to penning politically charged plays that were being staged by a band of upstarts called the Group Theatre. Among the Group's founders were Harold Clurman, Lee Strasberg and Clifford Odets. Among its discoveries was the brilliant young Brooklyn playwright Luther Altshuler, whom Ada would marry.

When World War II came, Ada Geiger served as a combat correspondent for *Life* magazine: Her collected dispatches and combat photographs, *To Serve Man,* became America's unofficial scrapbook of the war. Practically everyone who made it home owned a copy. It was the top-selling book of the post-war era, an era that found Ada and Luther out in Hollywood raising a family and producing low-budget movies together. Ada directed several of the films herself, making her the only woman besides Ida Lupino and Dorothy Arzner to crash through the industry's concrete gender barrier. Her films were reminiscent of her photographs—shadowy, gritty, and unfailingly bleak. And while they attracted only very small audiences at the time, she began to develop an ardent cult following through the years among critics and film buffs. Mitch stumbled on to her work at the Bleecker Street Cinema when he was a teenager and was totally blown away. For him, *Ten Cent Dreams,* her taut, twisted 1949 love triangle about a conniving dance hall girl (Marie Windsor), a consumptive bookie (Edmond O'Brien) and a crooked cop (Robert Mitchum) ranked right up there with *Out of the Past* as one of the greatest noir dramas ever filmed. And he thought that her seldom-screened 1952 melodrama about big-city political corruption, *Whipsaw,* totally eclipsed the universally overrated *High Noon* as a parable about the dangers of the Hollywood blacklist. When he became a critic, Mitch championed it as a lost American classic. And hailed

Ada Geiger as "the greatest American film director no one has ever seen."

She might have achieved genuine Hollywood greatness had it not been for that blacklist. Both she and Luther were called before the House Un-American Activities Committee to testify about their Communist Party affiliations back in their Group Theatre days. They refused to name names. Both were jailed for a year. Upon their release in 1954 they fled the country for London, where they wrote and produced plays, and where Ada went on to direct documentaries for the BBC, including *Not Fade Away,* her electrifying 1964 Rolling Stones concert film. Later, she and Luther moved on to Paris. Ada's films had long been beloved there. Her work was a huge influence on Clouzot, Melville and Godard. François Truffaut called her his favorite American director. She acted in a pair of Truffaut's films, scripted another with Luther, and spoke out loudly against the Vietnam War. When Luther died, she retired to a solitary villa on the Amalfi coast.

Now she was back in America for the first time in fifty years.

Back in Dorset, actually. It turned out that Ada had a local connection and that connection was Astrid's Castle, the colossal, turreted stone edifice that had been erected back in the Roaring Twenties as a love shack for Ada's father and his longtime mistress, Astrid Lindstrom, a leggy Ziegfeld Follies girl. Eventually, the mountaintop castle became an inn. Now it belonged to Norma and her second husband, Les.

Ada's return was proving to be a triumphant one. America had "discovered" her. Steven Soderbergh had just finished the principal photography on his stylish remake of *Ten Cent Dreams* with Julia Roberts, Kevin Spacey and George Clooney. A digitally re-mastered print of her original film was due for theatrical release in March. And a retrospective of her tabloid crime scene photos was slated for April at the International Center of Photography on Sixth Avenue, accompanied by a lavish coffee-table book.

It had been Les's idea to host a small tribute for Ada at Astrid's Castle upon her arrival. When the innkeeper had contacted Mitch about it a few weeks back, Mitch was thrilled to participate in the event. He'd always wanted to meet the great lady. And Les had promised him that it would be a dignified, low-key symposium for a select group of film scholars, critics and authors. However—and here was the really big surprise—Les hadn't been totally straight with Mitch. It turned out that he had much, much bigger plans for Ada's tribute. An entire delegation of Panorama Studios heavy-hitters was en route to Astrid's Castle for a weekend-long blitz of cocktail parties and testimonial dinners, accompanied by Soderbergh, his star-studded cast and a bevy of celebrated Geigerphiles like Quentin Tarantino, Oliver Stone, Martin Scorsese and the Coen Brothers. The likes of Jodie Foster, Meryl Streep, Susan Sarandon and Tim Robbins were coming. So were assorted supermodels, rap music stars and high-profile professional athletes. Camera crews from every media outlet in America would be on hand. This was going to be a major, major celebrity gala—everything short of velvet ropes, klieg lights and Joan Rivers standing at curbside, hissing at all of the skanky outfits.

And it was just the sort of event Mitch hated. He was furious. But he was also trapped. By the time he'd found out what Les's true intentions were, it was too late to back out. Which was, without question, exactly what Les had counted on.

"Honestly, Mitch, this weekend completely got away from me," Les apologized profusely. "The studio took control. It's their money, their publicity machine and you know how they like to make everything splashy. I was powerless to stop them. You can understand that, can't you?"

"Well, yes," Mitch allowed, because it did sound plausible. Just not wholly true.

"You must let me make this up to you," Les pleaded. The man seemed genuinely upset.

Mitch wondered why. Was Les afraid he'd bad-mouth him around town? Or was something else going on here?

"Norma and I would love to have you up for dinner this evening, if you can make it. Just a low-key family meal, word of honor. Ada will be there. And Norma's son, Aaron, is up from Washington with his wife. They're staying through the weekend. Do you know Aaron?"

"I know *of* him. Kind of surprised he made the trip."

"As was I," Les agreed, nodding his head of hair vigorously. "But I suppose family ties are stronger than their . . . differences. Shall we say six-thirty?"

"I'll be there," promised Mitch, who was not going to pass up this opportunity.

"That's terrific, Mitch!" Les said excitedly. "And I hope you can bring your lady friend along. Any chance she can get free on such short notice?"

"A good chance, yes. Things are very slow for her right now. She was saying so just the other day."

CHAPTER 2

WHEN THE RACCOON LET out a screech and came charging right at her across the garage floor, Des opened fire. Her first shot tore through the rabid animal's chest. The damned thing kept right on coming, snarling with crazed fury, leaping at her as Des put two more rounds into its snout, her shots echoing loud in the enclosed space. It landed at her feet, where it scrabbled and twitched before it died, emptying its bladder directly onto her black lace-up boots.

Des kicked it aside, holstered her SIG-Sauer and checked herself over thoroughly to make absolutely certain the raccoon hadn't managed to penetrate her uniform trousers. There was no torn material, no broken skin. Her thick wool socks were good and dry. She was fine, unless you counted her ruined boots.

She shoved her heavy horn-rimmed glasses up her nose and covered the dead animal with a tarp. Then Dorset's resident trooper strode back out into the weak late-afternoon sun, leaning her body into the mighty wind that had blown in around lunchtime.

The lady of the house, Gretchen Dunn, was watching her from the kitchen window, eyes wide with fright. Des smiled at her reassuringly as she headed across the snow-packed driveway to her cruiser, where she radioed Jane Shoplick, Dorset's Animal Control officer. It was Jane who had called Des about a possible rabid raccoon sighting at Dunn's Cove Landing. Jane was up near Devil's Hopyard at the time and couldn't get there for at least an hour. That had left it up to Des.

She got there in five minutes, although she'd needed directions from Jane on how to get there. Dunn's Cove Landing was not on any local map. Des hadn't even known it existed. She was discovering that there were quite a few such hidden blue-blooded compounds in

Dorset. Unless you knew the people, or had business with them, you would have no idea where they were. This was something entirely new for Des, who came from the outside world where those who had it, flashed it. Not so in Dorset. Here, they did not wish to be found, period. No street sign. No mailboxes. Just a turn-in on Route 156 up by Winston Farms with a tiny, discreet wooden placard that said "Private." And a long, narrow driveway that twisted its way back through old-growth forest, where she saw half a dozen wild turkeys and a family of deer, then across a ten-acre meadow blanketed with snow. A stone bridge took her over a frozen river. There must have been a patch of open water because she spotted a mighty pair of bald eagles circling the river in search of food. Finally, Des had arrived at a cluster of a dozen Revolutionary War–era mansions and cottages that overlooked the Connecticut River.

The house she wanted was a rambling shingled place with a Subaru wagon parked in the driveway. A big golden retriever was locked inside it, barking furiously. The detached two-story garage had once been a barn. There were two big doors for vehicles, both closed. Also a people door, again, closed. This one had a cat door in it.

Gretchen Dunn had come out to greet her, wearing a duffel coat and stretch pants. She was a young mother with tiny girlish features and a blond ponytail.

"Is everyone okay?" Des asked as she climbed out of her cruiser.

"Just a little shaken," responded Gretchen, who seemed pretty calm under the circumstances. "Make that a lot shaken. Ginny, my ten-year-old, was out in the garage putting down food for Herbert. He's our outdoor cat—real tough guy, won't come inside no matter how cold it gets. And Ginny walked in on this great big raccoon eating Herbert's kibble. It screeched at her and chased her right on out of there. Fortunately, Casey was on the porch and he chased it back inside. He has a mighty big bark, and he's real protective of the girls. I called Jane right away, then checked every single pore on Ginny's body. She hasn't got a scratch on her. She's just fine. We're having cocoa now."

"I can see Casey. Where's Herbert?"

"He took off across the meadow. What do you think, is it rabid?"

If a raccoon showed itself during daylight and behaved aggressively, then it most likely was rabid. Everyone in Dorset knew that. Just as Des knew what to do as soon she got the call from Jane.

"I think we can't afford to take any chances. Please go back inside now."

And with that, Des had moved stealthily into the garage, her SIG drawn and her eyes searching for the animal. She didn't have to search for long—it came right at her from behind the trash barrels.

"Is it dead?" Gretchen Dunn asked her now, when Des was finished reporting in to Jane.

"It won't bother you anymore." Des popped her trunk, donned a pair of latex crime scene gloves and untied her ruined boots, which she bagged and tossed into the trunk along with the gloves. Then she stepped into her spare boots and laced them up. "Jane will be along soon. She'll take it in for tests. Is Herbert up-to-date on his rabies shots?"

"I just double-checked my records. He had his last vaccine over the summer."

"That's good," Des said, since the raccoon had been eating out of the cat's dish. Rabies could be transmitted from one animal to another through their saliva. An alarming number of local people didn't know this and didn't bother to inoculate or, for that matter, neuter their outdoor cats—thereby explaining why Des and her friend Bella Tillis were constantly rescuing so many sick, sad kittens from the Dumpsters behind nearby markets and restaurants. They tried to find good homes for the ones they managed to nurse back to health. Presently, eighteen bright-eyed imps were bunking in Des's garage and basement. "I'd throw out Herbert's food and water dishes. And change his bedding, too."

"I absolutely will," Gretchen promised, wrinkling her cute little nose. "Can I offer you a cup of cocoa? We're making ginger snaps, too."

"Yum, sounds wonderful. But I have to be somewhere." The Troop F Barracks in Westbrook, to be specific. Anytime she discharged her weapon, she had to file an incident report immediately.

Two grave, adorable little blond girls were waving to her now from the kitchen window. Des waved back at them.

"I should have been able to handle this myself," Gretchen confessed, gazing at them. "But Shawn and I don't like having guns around. I felt so helpless."

"Don't second-guess yourself. I've been trained to handle this kind of deal. You haven't. Say you did have a gun, okay? Chances are, that raccoon would have taken a piece out of you by the time you got your shot off. And you'd be on your way to the emergency ward right now. You did right, Gretchen."

"Well, thank you. And thanks for being such a, you know, good neighbor."

This was the ultimate compliment in Dorset—to call someone a good neighbor. It was a compliment that no one had paid Des before. Gretchen Dunn was her very first.

Beaming, Des climbed into her cruiser and started her way back down the private drive to Route 156, positive that she could smell raccoon piss on her, although she could not imagine how this was so. As she lowered her front windows, freezing air be damned, it did occur to her that she'd just experienced her first genuine action of the entire winter. Until now, about all she'd been doing was filing one-car accident reports—weather-related, alcohol-related or both. Crime was way down from the peak summer months, when she'd had her hands full with bar brawlers and shoplifters. In fact, winter was so quiet here that Dorset scarcely needed a resident trooper at all. But it did need one, of course. Home break-ins would be rampant if she were not around. And the drug dealers would set up shop. And then Dorset wouldn't be Dorset anymore.

It was past four now, and the sun had already passed behind the trees, leaving puddles behind on Route 156 where the sunlight had warmed the plowed, salted pavement. Those puddles would freeze back over real fast, so Des took it nice and slow, her hands light on the wheel, foot steady on the gas. She was a patient, humble driver when she was around ice. She did not tailgate. Did not make sudden stops or starts. She respected the ice.

But she hadn't gone a mile down the narrow, shadowy country road before she came upon yet another fool who didn't respect it. No, he'd been too busy listening to those TV commercials instead of his own common sense. And now he and his super-duper, manly-man's Jeep Grand Whatever had gone skidding off the road into the ditch, where he was trapped inside a three-foot ice bank, his wheels spinning furiously as he tried to power his way out of there, pedal to the metal. God, how Des wished those damned commercials would stop showing SUVs conquering Mount Everest in third gear. In the real world, SUVs performed no better on ice than any other vehicle. But their dumb-assed owners flat-out refused to believe that. And so they disrespected the ice. And so Des spent half of her time rescuing them. In addition to the jumper cables and spare fuses that she carried year round, she had a winter ditch kit consisting of extra scrapers and blankets, two jugs of sand and a pair of eight-pound Snow Claws with hardened-steel teeth to slide under those spinning rear wheels. As she pulled over and got out, squaring her big Smokey hat on her head, she decided she just ought to go ahead and become a tow-truck operator. She'd make a lot more money.

He was young and burly and absolutely positive that if he just pressed down a little harder on that gas pedal, he'd be able to blow his way out of there. As she approached, he rolled down his window, glowering at her.

"Well, you're good and stuck, aren't you?" she called to him pleasantly over the angry whine of his spinning wheels. "If you'll just ease off of the gas, I'll see if I can help you—"

"Just leave me be," he snapped at her irritably. "I already called Triple-A on my cell. I'm fine, okay?"

Des had encountered this before. A certain species of young male who refused to be helped by a woman, especially one of color. A point of pride with them or some fool thing.

"Suit yourself, sir," she said, hoping the auto club was all backed up and he had to spend the next two hours sitting there. "But please put on your flasher, okay? We wouldn't want anyone to plow into you."

She climbed back in her cruiser and continued on to the Westbrook Barracks, reflecting on just how far she had managed to come in so short a time. It seemed like only yesterday that her smile had lit up the cover of *Connecticut* magazine. Back then, she had been the state's great non-white hope, youngest woman in state history to make lieutenant on the Major Crime Squad, and the only one who was black. Within a year she'd moved right on up to homicides. Always, she had produced.

And now here she was, Master Sergeant Des Mitry, getting dissed by stranded mesomorphs.

This was the price she'd paid to pursue her dream, and she was willing to pay it. Happy to pay it. But there were moments, like right now, when it was growing dark and she was driving along in the middle of snowy nowhere, swearing she could still smell raccoon piss, that Des missed the action.

Even though that action had nearly torn her apart. Mostly, it was the faces of the murder victims. She could never seem to forget those faces. Especially the babies. The fact that her marriage to Brandon was falling apart certainly hadn't helped. In order to cope with it all, she had brought home crime scene photos and started making drawings of them. Transferring the horror from her nightmares to the page, line by line, shadow by shadow. Injecting the images with fearsome emotional power. Turning them into one gut-wrenching portrait after another. Thanks to the twist of fate that had barreled her headlong into Mitch Berger, Des's therapy became her salvation. Her portraits had gained her admittance to the world-renowned Dorset Academy of Fine Arts, where she was presently studying long-pose figure drawing two nights a week, thereby shining a light on every single weakness in her game. Still, a pair of her most recent victim portraits had been included in this month's prestigious student show, and that was not shabby for a freshman. Des still had much more to learn, and she knew this. Yet she'd found herself getting itchy in class lately. Anxious to move on. She wasn't sure where. She wasn't sure why.

She wasn't sure about Mitch, either. She could not imagine her life without him in it, even though they made no sense at all together.

None. But lately her beloved, exceedingly chatty doughboy had grown strangely quiet and remote on her. Something was eating at him. He would not say what. All she had to go on was the lone grenade he'd lobbed at her across the dinner table a few weeks back—a cryptic, highly unsettling question that had instantly filled her with a million doubts. Doubts that Mitch had, thus far, done squat to assuage. Anytime it seemed that he was about to spill his guts he'd swallow hard and out would come . . . *nada*. His Great Big Fat Nothing Gulp, she'd taken to calling it. Des was terribly thrown by his behavior, more than she could have thought possible. In fact, Mitch's strained silences were making her so tense that she was experiencing the recurrence of a dreaded nervous thing that she thought she'd said good-bye to back when she was a gawky, vision-impaired giraffe of a high school girl.

Still, she had to admit that he'd sounded like his bubbly old self on the phone this morning when he called to tell her they'd been invited to dinner at Astrid's Castle. More excited than she'd heard him in weeks. So maybe it had passed, whatever the hell it was.

Then again, maybe it hadn't.

She was tied up at the barracks for well over an hour filling out her incident report, requisitioning a new pair of boots from the quartermaster, and responding to one smirky male query after another about that pungent new perfume she seemed to be wearing. It was already six o'clock by the time she started home to her cottage overlooking Uncas Lake. Mitch was expecting to pick her up in twenty minutes. No way. She phoned him on her cell to say she'd have to meet him there. No problem. Mitch was used to her unpredictable work schedule.

Bella Tillis was busy whipping up an apple cake in the big open kitchen when Des got there. A round, fierce little Brooklyn-born widow in her mid-seventies, Bella Tillis was bunking with Des while she looked for a place of her own. Bella had been her next-door neighbor in the New Haven suburb of Woodbridge back when Brandon had ditched Des for Tamika, a U.S. congressman's daughter with whom he'd started sleeping back when he and Tamika were classmates at Yale Law School. In fact, Brandon had never stopped sleeping with Tamika, not even after he'd married Des. Which had taught Des one very valuable lesson in life: *Don't ever trust lawyers.* And caused her to make one very solemn vow to herself: *I will never get married again for as long as I live.* Because no man on this planet was ever going to get the chance to hurt her that bad again. Never. Utterly shattered by Brandon's betrayal, Des had stopped going to work, stopped leaving the house and stopped eating. Until, that is, Bella came barging in one morning, Tupperware tub of stuffed cabbage in hand, and recruited Des for her feral stray rescue program. They were best friends now. When Des relocated to Dorset, Bella unloaded her own big house and followed her. As far as Des was concerned, she could stay as long as she wanted. Bella was good company and a dynamite housekeeper and it was nice to have her there when Des felt like staying over with Mitch.

"Oy-yoy, Desiree, what is that awful smell?" she demanded when Des came charging through the back door into the laundry room, shivering from the wind.

"It's raccoon urine," Des replied as she stood there on the mud rug, unlacing her spare boots. Not an easy proposition when she had five house cats studying her socks with keen, busy-nosed interest.

Bella appeared in the laundry-room doorway, scrunching up her face. "Forgive me, it sounded like you just said—"

"You asked, I answered."

"Take those socks off at once, tall person. I will not have you tracking that-that smell all over my clean floor."

"Um, okay, I like to think of it as our clean floor."

"*Off!*" she roared, hurling herself in Des's path. Des towered over her, but Bella was as wide as a nose tackle.

"All right, all right." She yanked them off and tossed them out the door into the snow. "Feel free to burn them."

"Oh, I shall. Believe me."

Barefoot, Des hurried across the kitchen toward her bedroom. When she'd bought the place she'd torn out walls so that her kitchen, dining room and living room all flowed together. Her studio was in the living room, which had floor-to-ceiling windows overlooking the lake. "Bella, I am feeling *so* not glamorous right now. And I am late, late, late. Tell me what to put on."

"Well, for starters, forget glamorous." Bella went back to work on a Granny Smith with a paring knife, slicing it rapid-fire into a mixing bowl. "You're not about glamour."

Des stopped in her tracks, hands on hips. "Was that supposed to be a compliment?"

"No, that was honesty," she replied, hurling cinnamon, brown sugar and nutmeg into the bowl with the apple slices. She made cakes just like Des's granny did. Never measured, never used a recipe. Hell, there was no recipe. "Glamour is a facade, Desiree. Strictly for *tsotskes* who are trying to hide something. You don't have to hide a thing. You're the real goods."

"Does that mean I should or shouldn't wear a dress?"

Bella puffed out her cheeks in disgust. "Covering your *tuchos* with a dress is like putting a veil over the Mona Lisa. I forbid it."

"Girl, I don't know what I'd do without you."

"I don't either, quite frankly."

Des whipped off her uniform en route to her bedroom and jumped into the shower, toweling off while she searched frantically through her closet. She was not what anyone would call delicate. Des knew this. She was broad-shouldered, high-rumped and cut with muscle. Nor was she a girlie-girl. She kept her hair short and nubby, and wore no war paint or nail polish. But she did have alluring almond-shaped pale green eyes, and a dimply wraparound smile that could melt titanium from a thousand feet away. And Des knew this, too. She settled on her black cashmere turtleneck, gray flannel slacks and black boots with chunky two-inch heels.

By now it was a quarter to seven. She'd already reloaded her weapon at the barracks. She tossed it and her shield into her shoulder bag. Her cell phone and pager she wore on her belt. On her way out she shoved her gloves into a pocket of the hooded, buttery-soft shearling coat that she'd bought in Florence on her honeymoon. She loved that damned coat so much she'd worn it around their hotel room naked. Brandon hadn't exactly minded. God, that was ages ago.

"Yum, what am I smelling?" she wondered, pausing in the kitchen to say good-bye.

"I already had the oven going, so I figured I may as well do my brisket, too. When I thawed it this morning I didn't know you had plans."

"Sure, we can have it tomorrow. Mitch loves your brisket."

"Of course he does. This is a man of discerning tastes."

"If that's the case, then how do you explain his American chop suey?"

"This is also a man," Bella replied, glancing at her. "What's with you tonight? You nervous about meeting Ada?"

"Should I be? I don't know her films."

"She was one of my heroes when I was a girl," Bella recalled, her face creasing into a smile. "So smart and gutsy and beautiful. Her husband, Luther, was a very fine playwright. The two of them were hounded out of the country by those thugs during the McCarthy era. That was a terrible time, Desiree. A girlfriend of mine whose father wrote for the radio, he ended up committing suicide." She peered at Des shrewdly. "What is it then?"

"What is what?"

"You're acting *meshuga* tonight."

"Am not. I'm just in a rush."

"Whatever you say," Bella said doubtfully. "Have fun."

"I'll do my best." Des was halfway to the door, car keys in hand, before she came back and said, "It's Mitch. I think he has a problem with our relationship."

"Tie that bull outside, as we used to say on Nostrand Avenue."

"Bella, I have never understood what that expression means."

"Well, what's the problem—is it the lovemaking?"

"God, no. He's still the Wonder from Down Under. But the man has something serious on his mind, Bella. He keeps getting all quiet and far away. Which I'm, like, he is never."

"Maybe it's that book he's been trying to write. How is that going?"

"It's not, near as I can tell."

"Then that's probably it. Men can get very strange when their work isn't going well."

"Men can get very strange come rain or come shine. But it's not the book, Bella. His words say otherwise."

"Why, what did he say?"

Des took a deep breath before she replied, "He said, and I quote, 'I wonder if we're getting in too deep.'"

Bella's face dropped. "Oh, I see . . . And what did you say?"

"I said, 'Why, do *you* think we are?' To which he replied, and I quote, 'It could certainly appear that way.' To which I said, 'Appear that way to *whom*?'"

"Hold on, you actually said to *whom*?"

"I did. This girl's got herself a proper education."

"And what did Mitch say to that?"

"Jack. Not one damned word."

Bella considered this carefully. "Desiree, I'm not necessarily hearing qualms here. Mitch could simply be trying to engage you in a dialogue about *your* feelings."

"No sale. If he's not getting cold feet, then why raise it at all?"

"You do have a point," Bella admitted, sticking out her lower lip.

"Besides, when we first got together we swore we'd never do this."

"Do what?"

"There are two subjects we agreed that we'd never, ever obsess about—our slight cultural differences and our future. That's written in stone, Bella. It's a rule."

"Tattela, we're talking about a relationship here, not a nuclear non-proliferation treaty. Rules like that are made to be broken."

"Not by me they're not."

"Okay, here's a kooky idea—have you tried talking to him about it?"

"I can't. I get all uptight and then I start feeling this horrible panic thing coming on that I haven't had since I was fourteen. And, excuse me, but *kooky?*"

"So I'm not hip. Shoot me." Bella furrowed her brow. "What kind of panic thing are we talking about?"

"We're not talking about it."

"Why not?"

"It's incredibly embarrassing, that's why not."

"If you can't tell me, who can you tell?"

"No one, I'm hoping." Des stood there jangling her keys. "He's met someone else, must be. Someone who he has more in common with. Maybe it's another movie critic. No, no, that can't be it. They all look like nearsighted mice. At least, that's what he told me once. But maybe he was lying to me about that. Maybe they all look like Cameron Diaz. Or maybe he *likes* nearsighted mice. Or maybe he . . ." Des stopped and came up for air. "I don't know who she is, but when I find out I am going to hurt her."

Bella shook her head at her. "Desiree, that man absolutely adores you, and he'd never give another woman so much as the time of day. He is *not* Brandon."

"I do know that."

"Do you? I don't think so. If you ask me, you're still schlepping your baggage around with you like Willy Loman with his sample cases."

Des shot a hurried look at her watch. Past seven now. "Okay, then how do you explain the dead shark?"

"The dead *what?*"

"He made me watch *Annie Hall* with him last week—I'd never seen it before."

"Did you like it?"

"It was okay, if you like watching white people whine for two hours. But there's this scene with Diane Keaton on the airplane, when Woody says that a relationship is like a shark, it has to keep moving forward or it dies. 'What we have on our hands is a dead shark,' is what he says."

"I remember the scene," Bella said, nodding.

"Why did Mitch pick *that* movie for us to watch?"

"It's a classic."

"World's full of them."

"It's very romantic."

"Bella, it compares true love to a killing machine."

"He screened *Psycho* for you a couple of weeks ago, did he not?"

"And your point is . . . ?"

"Has he proceeded to hack you to death in the shower with a big knife?"

"No," Des admitted. "Not yet, anyway."

"Desiree, I want you to stop and listen to me very carefully," Bella said sternly. "You *have* to believe in him. You *have* to believe in the two of you. If you don't, you're going to sabotage the best thing that's ever happened to you, and you won't have anyone to blame but yourself."

"Bella, I'm not sabotaging anything," she insisted. "And I'm not playing a head game. I know the signs. I know the man. I know where this is heading." Des drew in her breath, her chest tightening. "Mitch Berger is getting ready to break my heart. And when he does, you may as well just dig me a hole and shove me in, because I am not going to survive. Not this one. I will die. Hear me? I will absolutely die."

CHAPTER 3

ASTRID'S CASTLE WAS PERCHED high atop an exposed granite cliff that overlooked the Connecticut River about ten miles upriver from the village of Dorset. For drivers heading north to Boston on Interstate 95, the immense stone replica of a medieval fortress was hard to miss, looming there as it did above the river, so majestic, so improbable, so floodlit. Many people, especially those who wrote travel brochures for the state's tourism office, thought Astrid's looked like something straight out of a fairy tale.

Mitch thought it looked more like the main attraction of Six Flags Dorset. If such a place existed. Which, happily, it did not.

A gate with stone pillars marked its entrance on Route 156. During the summer, when tourists flocked to the castle by the thousands, there was an attendant in a kiosk there, collecting admission. Now there was no one. Inside the gate, the private drive forked almost at once. The left fork was for visitors who had come to ride Choo-Choo Cholly, the castle's whimsical, brightly colored narrow-gauge steam train. From May through October, Cholly was a big attraction for day-trippers with kids. It made a couple of stops at scenic overlooks and hiking trails as it chugged its way up the mountain to the castle.

The right fork, which was for guests of the inn and deliveries, led to a private road that climbed for three miles through heavily forested grounds. Mitch's old truck labored as it made the ascent. The road was steep, twisty and very narrow, especially with the plowed snowbanks crowding in on both sides. Finally, he came around a big bend and crested at the top, and there it was before him in the floodlights, framed by a pair of giant sycamores that flanked the end of the road like sentries. Astrid's was eye-poppingly massive from close up—wide, vast and three stories high, not counting its trademark tower. There was a moat. For arriving and departing guests, a circular driveway passed over it on a drawbridge to the castle's main entrance. For Choo-Choo Cholly riders, there was a miniature train station with a platform that was roofed in copper and illuminated by Victorian lamps.

Mitch eased into the guest parking lot in between a silver Mercedes wagon with Washington, D.C., plates and a rental Ford Taurus from New York. The temperature had moderated since morning, up close to 30, but when he got out he discovered the wind was absolutely howling off the river, especially up on this exposed hilltop. Mitch could see the lights of Essex directly across the river. Yet he could not make out the moon or the stars, which he found a bit peculiar. When it blew this hard it generally meant the sky was clearing. Tonight, it was not.

The moat was solidly frozen. Mitch clomped his way over it on the wooden drawbridge, half expecting to run into Errol Flynn and Basil Rathbone locked in a sword fight.

Instead he encountered a short, powerfully built young guy hunched over a snow shovel, clearing the remains of the day's snow from the blue stone path that led to the front door. He wore a heavy wool lumberjack shirt over a hooded sweatshirt. The stocking cap he had on was pulled low over his eyes. His jeans were baggy, his boots scuffed. He wore no gloves. His hands were chapped and red, nails blackened with grease. He halted from his labors to glance up at Mitch. He had a thick reddish beard that grew up unusually close to his eye sockets. Very little skin showed, especially with that knit cap pulled so low over his eyes. Mitch thought it gave him the Lon Chaney, Jr., look, as in when the moon is full, as in *Wha-oooo* . . .

"Get your bags . . . you, sir?" the Wolfman asked him in a voice so faint that Mitch could barely hear him.

"I'm not an overnight guest, thanks. Just here for dinner." Mitch realized on closer inspection that he recognized this particular lycanthrope. "I see you at the hardware store all the time, don't I?"

"Could be," he replied shyly. "I'm in and out of there a lot."

"Mitch Berger," he said, sticking out his hand.

"Oh, sure. You're looking after things out on Big Sister. I'm Jase Hearn," he said, gripping Mitch's hand. His was so rough it was like grabbing a chunk of firewood. "You're a brave soul, man, wintering over out there," he added, his voice growing stronger as he got more at ease.

"Or possibly just crazy," Mitch said, grinning at him.

"They usually just hire some poor doofus to do it."

"No need to—they have me for free."

"Me, I keep things running here," Jase said, leaning his weight on his shovel. "Me and my big sister, Jory. She's head housekeeper, I'm maintenance."

"That must keep you pretty busy," Mitch said, his eyes taking in the hugeness of the place. "Especially this time of year."

"She's a beauty and a beast," Jase admitted, scratching at his furry face. "Took twenty men five whole years to build her. She's all native fieldstone. And, man, does she eat up the fuel. Three furnaces, two hot-water heaters, forty-eight guest rooms with forty-eight wood-burning fireplaces. Windows everywhere, on account of the views. You wouldn't believe what it costs to heat her. Winters, they got to close down the third floor entirely. Lay off most of the staff, too. Me and Jory are the only full-timers."

"Business is slow this time of year?"

"Dead slow, unless we get like a corporate retreat or a wedding. Tonight, we got no paying guests at all. This thing for Mrs. Geiger is huge for us. All kinds of Hollywood celebrities will be staying here. Movie studio's picking up the whole tab. A hotshot, Spence Sibley, is already here, job-bossing the whole thing. Better him than me. I just keep the fires burning and the road clear." Jase resumed his shovel-ing. "Watch out for black ice on your way back down tonight. It can be a real bitch."

"Will do," Mitch promised, continuing up the footpath toward the castle's big slab of an oak front door. Hand-painted wooden signs marked the paths leading off across the courtyard to the rose garden, wisteria arbor, lily pond and greenhouse. There was also a service path that led to the caretaker's cottage and adjoining woodshed.

Les was waiting for him with the front door opened wide. "I saw your lights," he explained cheerily as he ushered Mitch into the cavernous three-story entry hall, where the lights from the chandeliers glowed golden on the yellow pine floors. A pianist was playing something jazzy and up-tempo in a nearby room, filling the hall with vibrant tones. "So glad you could make it."

"Glad to be here," said Mitch, thinking that Les really played his ruddy New England innkeeper role to the hilt. He even dressed the part in his Viyella tattersall shirt, cable-stitched sweater vest and gray flannel slacks. His head of lush silver hair was brushed so wavy and lustrous it reminded Mitch of plumage.

"Where's our resident trooper?"

"Running late." Mitch realized that he recognized what the pianist was playing—it was the theme song to the TV sitcom *Will and Grace*. He was not proud that he knew this. "She'll be along as soon as she can."

"Mitch, you'll have to refresh my memory. Have you been with us before?"

"No, I haven't," Mitch replied, gazing up, up, up at the intricately carved, winding three-story center staircase.

"That's solid cherry," Les said proudly. "It was imported from a castle in Wiltshire, England, as was a lot of the woodwork and molding. The paneling and upstairs doors are native oak. Would you believe that the local gentry were in a dither about Astrid's when it was first built? They thought it was vulgar. Now it's Dorset's most famous landmark, known the world over."

There was a coatroom where Mitch deposited his hat, scarf and parka. Underneath, he wore his standard corduroy sports jacket, V-neck sweater and Oxford button-down shirt, along with baggy wide-wale cords and Mephistos. Mitch didn't own a tie. Refused to. Just as he'd refused to rent a tuxedo for Saturday night's big tribute bash. They could take him as he was, or not at all.

There was a glassed-in gift shop, closed now, that sold things like postcards and a wide array of Astrid's Castle merchandise. There was a reception desk with wall-mounted racks filled with tourist brochures and maps. Doorways led off to the morning room and dining room. Also the taproom, where Mitch could hear voices and polite laughter.

Les led him through a wide doorway toward the music. "We call this room the Sunset Lounge because the windows face west. We're famous for our sunsets up here, Mitch. You can see Long Island Sound, the boats on the river. The view's really quite extraordinary, actually."

Actually, the Sunset Lounge was more like a ballroom in Mitch's estimation, with a twenty-four-foot ceiling, shimmering chandelier and a stone fireplace big enough to walk into. A fire was roaring in it. Leather sofas and armchairs were grouped there. And a radiant oil portrait of Astrid Lindstrom hung over the mantel—beautiful, pink-cheeked Astrid in an elegant silver gown, gazing over one bare ivory shoulder at the artist, her eyes bright with amusement. The one-time Zigfeld Follies girl bore more than a passing resemblance to Mary Pickford, or so the artist had portrayed her.

The elegantly dressed older gentleman at the Steinway grand piano had moved on to "They All Laughed," a Gershwin brothers number from *Shall We Dance,* which was Mitch's favorite of the Fred Astaire–Ginger Rogers musicals. In this he was alone. Every other film critic on earth thought *Top Hat* was Fred and Ginger's best.

"Come meet Teddy Ackerman, Mitch. Teddy is Aaron's uncle. His brother, Paul, was Norma's first husband."

Teddy was in his early sixties, slender and pale to the point of wan. In fact, his complexion closely resembled the ivory of the key-board before him. Teddy had a long, narrow face, finely chiseled features and a high forehead with receding steel-wool hair. He wore his navy-blue suit very well. He had on a burgundy tie with it and a sparkling white shirt with French cuffs. His cuff links were of gold with sapphires.

"Say hello to Mitch Berger, Teddy," Les said.

Teddy paused from his playing to offer Mitch his hand. It was a very cold hand, the fingers long and smooth. "Glad to know you, Mitch."

"You play beautifully," Mitch said, because he did. Teddy had a touch so natural it was as if he and the piano were a single organism.

"Thanks much. You'll have to come hear the whole gang this weekend. We're playing at the cocktail mixer Saturday afternoon. We call ourselves the Night Blooming Jazzmen because all four of us have held on to our day jobs. Much better off that way, Mitch." Teddy spoke with a wistful air, his voice tinged with loss and regret. "You should never, ever try to make a living doing the one thing you care about most. You'll only get your heart broken. I came up a couple of days early at Norma's invitation," he added, with just enough emphasis on "Norma" to suggest some tension between him and Les.

If it was there, Les didn't acknowledge it. Just beamed at the two of them, the genial host.

"Too bad you never got a chance to meet my brother, Paul," Teddy said to Mitch, sipping from the goblet of red wine that was set atop the piano. "Big Paul was a living hero. Graduated top of his class at Columbia Law School, turned down every single big-money offer to go to work for the American Civil Liberties Union. Paul fought for the underdog. Tilted at windmills. Me, I just tilt at wineglasses. He dropped dead of a heart attack in 1992. Seems like it was just last week."

"I'm sorry," Mitch said.

"Say, Les, where were *you* in '92?" Teddy asked him mockingly. "Still writing trenchant ad copy for Preparation H?"

"Something like that," Les responded shortly, not wanting to mix it up with him, although it was obvious from his clenched jaw that he disliked the guy. Just as it was obvious that Teddy resented him for wooing and winning his beloved brother's widow.

"The rest of the boys are coming up tomorrow, Mitch," Teddy said, launching into a bluesy version of "Stardust." "We're a diverse bunch. We've got an eye doctor, an accountant, a pharmacist and me—I sell suits at Sig Klein's Big and Tall Man's store."

"On Union Square? Sure, I know that place," Mitch said, smiling. Sig Klein's had been advertising on New York radio since Mitch was a little boy. Any number of second-tier Knicks big men had done spots for Sig's over the years, going all the way back to Kenny "The Animal" Bannister.

"I'm surprised I haven't seen you in there," Teddy said, checking Mitch over with a professional eye. "You're a good, healthy-sized boy."

"I'm mostly wearing insulated goose down these days."

"Still, I could fit the heck out of you. You ought to stop by, buddy."

"Right now, let's go get you a drink," Les offered, clapping Mitch on the back.

"Will you join us?" Mitch asked Teddy.

"I'm fine right here, thanks. Any requests?"

"No Billy Joel?"

"No problem," Teddy responded, chuckling.

"The family ne'er-do-well," Les explained under his breath as he and Mitch moved back toward the entry hall. "Real, real sad case. Still lives with his mother in an apartment in Forest Hills. Never got married. Loses every dime he makes playing high-stakes poker. It was Norma's idea to throw some work his way this weekend. She's always felt sorry for him, I think. Aaron can't stand him. Although, near as I can tell, Aaron can't stand any of his relatives. Remarkably enough, the feeling is entirely mutual."

Les was steering him toward the taproom when a rather pillowy woman in her sixties came bustling out of a service door and very nearly collided with them.

"Ah, here she is now," Les said with a jovial laugh. "Mitch, have you met my lovely wife, Norma?"

"No, he has not," Norma said briskly, swiping a loose strand of gray hair from her eyes. "A pleasure, Mitch. I'm sorry if I seem to be run ragged. It's only because it so happens I am."

Ada Geiger's daughter spoke in a clipped, precise manner. And she most definitely had an English accent, which made sense since she would have been a little girl when Ada and Luther fled there in the fifties. Norma was plump, heavy-bosomed and rather slump-shouldered. She had soft, dark eyes and a kindly face, a face that once might have been very smooth and lovely, Mitch felt. Right now she just seemed worn and tired. There was a sheen of perspiration on her forehead, and her breathing seemed quite labored. Mitch could actually hear the air bellowing in and out of her lungs. She practically sounded like Choo-Choo Cholly trying to chug its way up a hill. Norma wore her gray hair cropped at the chin. She had on a dark blue cardigan sweater over a light blue turtleneck, blue slacks and red kitchen clogs.

"There will be a huge kitchen staff arriving tomorrow," Norma explained to him. "But tonight, there is no one. Unless, of course, one counts Jory. As I do. She's a gem. I'd be lost without her. I am accustomed to the grind, naturally. But it's always just a bit harder when one's mother is around. Especially *my* mother. She's having a nap right now. She tires easily. Where's Des? She *is* coming, isn't she?"

"She'll be along soon," Mitch assured her.

Back in the Sunset Lounge, Teddy segued from "Stardust" into a heartfelt rendition of "More Than You Know."

Norma seemed to melt as soon as she heard it, a fond, faraway smile creasing her face.

"Are you okay, dear?" Les asked, peering at her.

"Why, yes," she replied, coloring. "Fine. I've just always loved this song."

An efficient young woman with curly ginger-colored hair came barging through the service door. "We can plate the main course whenever you're ready, Norma," she announced.

"I'm afraid we're still minus one, dear," Norma told her.

"No problem. I can keep it warm." She gave Mitch a quick, bright smile and said, "You must be our movie critic. I'm Jory Hearn. Welcome to the castle."

Jase's big sister was in her late twenties and not conventionally pretty. Jory had a bit too much bulldog in her chin, and her nose was a good deal broader and flatter than the beauty magazines would have liked. But she had creamy, lovely skin, an inviting rosebud of a mouth and an eager vitality that was very appealing. Jory was by no means a frail little thing. She was about five feet nine, big-boned and ripely, head-turningly *zaftig*. Her curves were hard to miss even in her sober dining hall uniform of black vest, white blouse and black slacks.

She was also available. Very available. Her eyes gleamed at Mitch invitingly.

"I just met your brother outside," he said to her. "He seemed real nice."

Jory and Norma exchanged a confused look before Jory said, "Jase *spoke* to you?"

"He seemed a little quiet at first, but once we got going about the castle, he was very talkative."

"Normally, our guests can't get one single word out of him," Les said. "They think he's a mute. The little kids even call him Igor."

"He's a good, hard-working boy," Norma spoke up. "And he takes wonderful care of this place. He's just a bit delicate, poor thing."

"Our mother died in childbirth," Jory explained to Mitch. "And Jeremy died three days later."

"Jeremy?"

"Our brother. Jase's twin."

"That must have been very hard for you," Mitch said to her quietly.

"It's still hard, sometimes," Jory admitted, swallowing.

"Well, he sure seems to love this place."

"Believe me, Mitch, we both do," Jory assured him. "It's round-the-clock hard work, but it's rewarding. And it's home. The drinks are in the taproom. May I pour you something?"

"No need to worry about me. I'll manage."

"Oh, I'm sure you will," she fired back, showing him her dimples before she headed back to the kitchen, her hips moving with just a little extra oomph. Definitely for Mitch's benefit. Although, as she passed on through the staff door, he couldn't help notice that Les was missing none of the show.

If Norma was aware of this, she didn't let on. Just said, "I'm still relatively new here myself. My brother, Herbert, ran the castle until 1993, when he was killed by a drunk driver. I had recently lost Paul.

Aaron was off in Washington. I was lonely, lost, too much time on my hands. And so I took the plunge. And then one weekend Les showed up here as a guest . . ."

"And I never left," he said happily, squeezing her hand. "I know a good thing when I see it."

"Mind you, it's a small miracle that this place has survived at all," Norma said. "When Grandpa Moses died back in 1948, he left the castle to his dear protégée, Astrid, for as long as she lived. Which turned out to be until 1980, as it happens."

"I didn't realize Astrid stayed on here for so many years," Mitch said.

"Local legend has it that she still haunts the place," Les revealed in a low, guarded voice. "That is, if you can dismiss it as a legend. Strange noises have been heard in the night, Mitch."

"You've actually heard them?"

"Oh, heck no," Les said, winking at him. "But we hold a séance for her every Halloween. Our guests get a real kick out of it. A couple of young actresses from Yale Drama School come up for the occasion. One plays Astrid, the other summons her."

"The sad reality is that poor Astrid became quite decrepit in her later years," Norma said. "And the castle fell into terrible disrepair. Plumbing, wiring, everything. Herbert went to the bank, hat in hand, and restored it from top to bottom as an inn. He got Choo-Choo Cholly up and running again. He also arranged for some three thousand acres of grounds to be donated to the state in exchange for historic landmark status. If he hadn't, well, the property taxes would totally cripple us."

"And, hey, some years we actually break even," Les said gamely. "Well, almost."

"Such a far, far cry from the castle's glory days," Norma said nostalgically. "Grandpa Moses was quite the theatrical impresario. And Astrid, his greatest stage discovery, blossomed into the reigning society hostess of her day. There were truly remarkable weekend parties up here, Mitch. San Simeon East, Dorothy Parker famously dubbed it. The Marx Brothers stayed here. Lunt and Fontanne, Mae West, Cole Porter, Scott and Zelda Fitzgerald. They all had grand, giddy fun at Astrid's. She was a great lady. After Grandpa passed away, she converted the place into a private club for his Wall Street friends. They used to motor up from the city to hunt and fish and—"

"Jesus Christ, Norma, what a load of simpering, G-rated crap!" a voice erupted from somewhere upstairs. It was an elderly woman's voice, raspy but strong. It was Ada Geiger's voice. Evidently, she'd been eavesdropping on Norma's historical retelling. Evidently, there was not a thing wrong with her hearing. "Moses Geiger was a god-damned bootlegger and racketeer!" the ninety-four-year-old director thundered as she descended the hand-carved staircase, tall, regal and so remarkably light on her feet that she seemed to waft. "Astrid was his succulent lemon tart on the side, and she turned this underheated pile of rocks into the fanciest cathouse in New England. What is this, Norma, kiddie hour?"

"Why, no, Mother." Norma reddened under her mother's rebuke.

"Then tell this poor man the goddamned truth. Tell him how the entire New York Yankees team used to get laid here after a weekend series up at Fenway Park." Ada Geiger had been famous throughout her career for her bold, savage directness. Clearly, she had not changed. "Tell him how Astrid always had to keep silk sheets around for DiMaggio because Joe D wouldn't sleep on anything else. I swear, Norma, by the time I'm gone you'll have turned this place into a for-mer convent. And Moses into, well, *Moses*. Don't try to cover up the truth. Revel in it. It's your heritage, dear."

"Yes, Mother," Norma said, lowering her eyes.

When Ada reached the bottom of the stairs she glided slowly toward them, her aquiline nose raised high in the air. She reminded Mitch of an ancient bird of prey. An osprey, perhaps—proud, fierce and defiantly alert, her hooded eyes sharp and keen. Ada combed her pure white hair straight back. Her face was still beautiful. It wasn't an old face. It was a lived-in face. Her hands shook slightly, but she stood strong and straight. She wore a pair of eyeglasses on a chain around her neck. No makeup or lipstick. She was dressed in a bulky black turtleneck, wool slacks and sturdy walking shoes. A tweed jacket was thrown over her shoulders like a cape.

"Besides which," she continued, "Astrid was a great dame in her own right. Somebody ought to be getting her life story down on paper instead of trying to 'summon' her every year with a crystal ball and a bad Romanian accent. True story: My mother never even knew Astrid existed. Hell, I didn't meet her myself until I was forty. But people knew how to keep secrets in those days. Not like now. Now everyone wants to *share*. What fun is that?" Ada turned her piercing glare on Mitch. "You must be this Mitch person. Well, speak up. Are you or aren't you?"

"I am," Mitch responded, a bit awestruck. "How are you, Mrs. Geiger?"

"First of all, the name's Ada. Second of all, don't ever ask someone my age how they are. They might actually answer you, individual organ by organ, and it will consume the entire evening's conversation. I have health problems. They're not very interesting problems. Now let's leave it at that, shall we?" She took him by the arm and pulled away from Norma and Les, her grip surprisingly strong. "I'm glad you could make it, Mitch. I know you had zero to do with this freak show they're putting on for me. Or I prefer to think you didn't."

"I didn't, actually. And meeting you this way is an incredible honor for me."

"Nonsense. It's entirely due to your efforts that today's young people have so much as heard of my movies. I wished to thank you."

"I was just doing my job."

"Hah! You say that as if most people actually *do* their jobs. Your lady friend is the one who draws dead people, am I right?"

"Why, yes. She's very talented."

"Of course she is, of course she is," Ada said impatiently. "Where is she? I need to speak with her."

"She's running late," Mitch said, wondering why the grand old director wanted to speak to Des.

50

Jory reappeared now to see to her. "How about a nice cup of your herbal tea, Mrs. Geiger?" she asked, raising her voice.

"You needn't shout at me, tootsie," Ada barked. "I'm not deaf."

"I'm sorry. I just wondered if you'd like a cup of your Lemon Zinger."

"I would. With a generous slice of fresh ginger . . ."

"And a half teaspoon of honey. I know, ma'am."

"I can't abide most American tea," Ada explained to Mitch. "It tastes like monkey piss to me. I'll make it myself, if you don't mind," she told Jory. "It's not that I don't trust you, it's that I, well, don't trust you."

"At least let me help you," Jory offered.

"If you must, Dory," Ada said imperiously.

"It's *Jory*, ma'am," she pointed out as the two of them started for the kitchen.

Norma let out a suffering sigh as soon as they'd disappeared through the service door. "I love the old dear, Mitch. But, as you can see, she is absolutely impossible. Not that she's any different now than she was when I was a girl. She's just more so."

"I like her," Mitch said admiringly. "She's real."

"Ada's one of a kind, all right," Les agreed. "Thank God."

"I don't know *how* I shall ever make this up to poor Jory," Norma fretted.

"Have she and Jase worked here long?"

"Their whole lives. Their father, Gussie, was caretaker here going all the way back to Astrid's days. He raised the two of them on his own out in the cottage. When they were old enough to work, they stayed on. Now if you'll excuse me, I'd best see to dinner—*and* rescue the girl."

"Come on, let's get you that drink," Les said, steering Mitch toward the taproom.

The castle's taproom was paneled, cozy and clubby, as in the Union League Club, circa 1929. There was a hand-carved hardwood bar with half a dozen stools before it. Behind it, an antique wall clock seemed to be keeping perfect time. There were tavern tables and card tables, and comfy leather armchairs parked before the fire that was crackling in the fireplace. There were Rex Brasher Audubon Society prints hanging from the walls, built-in bookcases filled with hardcover volumes of literature and history. A vintage Brunswick pool table with ornate carved legs and hand-sewn leather pockets anchored the middle of the room. An amber glass light fixture was suspended over it, casting a warm glow over the green felt. The sound of Teddy's piano was fainter in here, but Mitch could still hear it—just as he could hear the howl of the wind through the chimney flue.

A slender, striking blonde with very long straight hair was standing over by the fire in a sleeveless black dress and stiletto heels, sipping a martini and looking rather sulky. The great Aaron Ackerman sat gloomily at the bar, both hands wrapped around a snifter of single malt Scotch, a bottle of twenty-one-year-old Balvenie parked at his elbow.

A second couple, both in their twenties, were working away at a tavern table in the corner. She was busy inputting notes in a laptop computer. He was busy negotiating with someone on his cell phone: "I understand you perfectly—Oliver wants a limo from JFK. But I can't give him one. If Oliver gets a limo, then Quentin will want one." Spence Sibley from Panorama Studios, evidently. "I swear, *no one* is getting a limo. This is not the damned Golden Globes!"

"Now what can I get you, Mitch?" Les asked as he bustled around behind the bar.

"Whatever you have on draft will be fine."

Les drew a Double Diamond for him in an Astrid's Castle pilsner glass and set it before him on an Astrid's Castle bar coaster. Mitch began to wonder if he'd be seeing that damned logo in his sleep tonight.

"We've never had the pleasure, Mitch," Aaron spoke up, sticking his hand out toward him. "I enjoy your work thoroughly."

Mitch shook Aaron's hand, which was limp and sodden. "Thanks, glad to meet you," he said, even though he was far from it. As far as

Mitch was concerned, Aaron Ackerman was one of the most despicable figures in modern American journalism.

If you could even call what Aaron Ackerman did journalism. Mitch didn't. Aaron specialized in skewering public figures for fun and profit, a brutal form of personal destruction that had come to be known in media circles as Ack-Ack. Ada Geiger's grandson got his start during the Monica Lewinsky scandal as a member of what Mitch called The Young and The Damp, that perspiring, attention-starved legion of bow-tied baby neo-conservatives who began popping up all over the cable news channels to pummel Bill Clinton and tout their own right-wing agenda. Aaron had two things going for him that quickly set him apart from the others. He had a very famous left-wing grandmother and he had a giddy, unabashed love for toxic tirades. The man became a full-fledged star with the publication of *Incoming Ack-Ack*, a collection of his most outrageous diatribes, which spent a dizzy twenty-eight weeks atop the *New York Times* Best Sellers list. Among his targets: tax-and-spend liberals, mealy-mouthed moderates, yuppies, gays, feminists, environmentalists, New Yorkers, Hollywood political activists, the French—anyone and everyone whose world vision didn't march in lock-step with his own.

Aaron Ackerman spared no one—not even his own grandmother. He'd gone so far as to Ack-Ack her just this past weekend on *Larry King Live,* labeling her "a misguided paleo-leftist relic." He'd even called Ada's films "objectively, tragically awful."

He was in his early thirties and had the blinky, nose-twitchy look of someone who used to wear thick glasses before the advent of laser eye surgery. He had a jiggly, shapeless body and an extremely big head. Not in the sense that it was swollen, though it was, but in the sense that it was just a really big, meaty head. Mitch couldn't imagine what size hat the man wore. Aaron had a rather simian shelf of bone where his eyebrows were. One brow, the right, was often arched in a manner that reminded Mitch of pro wrestler turned movie star The Rock—minus the calculated irony. Aaron did have an affluent surface shine. His curly black hair was neatly trimmed, teeth bleached camera-ready white, fingernails buffed and polished. And he was impeccably dressed in a navy-blue blazer, pink shirt, polka-dot bow tie and charcoal flannel slacks. But the man still had the word *shlub* stamped all over him. He lacked physical ease, reeked of insecurity.

"I'm surprised you're here for Ada's tribute," Mitch said to him, sipping his beer. "After what you said about her on television, I mean."

"That happened to be a great deal of nothing," Aaron said with a dismissive wave of his hand. He had an orotund style of speaking, a manner so pompous and self-satisfied that he practically cried out to be mocked—which he had been to devastating effect on a recent *Saturday Night Live* by guest host David Schwimmer. "And it was by no means personal, merely something that I needed to do so as to create space between us in terms of the public Aaron. Naturally, the private Aaron is an entirely different matter. I love my grandmother dearly." He paused, peering in Mitch's general direction without actually looking at him. It was more as if he were looking through him. "Surely you can understand that, can't you?"

"No, I'm afraid not. I only have the one me."

Aaron seemed shocked by this. "Really? How very disappointing." Now he turned in his stool to face the slender blonde over by the fire. "Mitch, allow me to introduce my lovely wife, Professor Carly Cade. Carly, say hello to Mitch Berger."

"Pleased to meet you, Mitch," she said in a voice that was well-bred, lightly Southern-accented and quite mature. As Mitch moved toward her outstretched hand he realized that Carly was not as young as he'd first thought. Not that he could tell how old she was, but she sure wasn't in her twenties. She parted her shiny blond hair in the middle and combed it straight down like a teenaged girl, framing her face like half-closed curtains. It was a face that seemed peculiarly expressionless, almost as if she were wearing a mask over it. She was petite, maybe five feet three, and looked terrific in the little sleeveless black dress she had on. Her arms were toned and taut, her legs shapely and smooth.

"Your hand is absolutely frozen," Mitch said as he released it.

"If you think my hand is cold, you should feel my toes right now," Carly said, shivering. "I feel like we're in the real Dorset tonight, don't you?"

"The real Dorset?"

"In England," she said. "Where they have no central heat."

"We have central heat," Les said defensively, throwing another log on the fire. "But when it gets this windy, it just goes flying right out the windows."

The wind was definitely howling. In fact, Mitch thought it might even be picking up.

"They do have such things as sweaters, you know," Aaron said, looking his bare-skinned wife up and down in a most proprietary fashion.

"Aaron, I can tell you don't know one thing about women," Les said.

"You are so right, Les," Carly agreed. "I have spent a fortune on this dress. I have huffed and puffed for two hours a day at the gym so I can wear it. And I'll be damned if I'm going to throw some old sweater on over it."

"I think you look great in it," said Mitch.

"Why, thank you, kind sir." She treated Mitch to a dainty curtsy. "I like this man, Aaron. I just may have to run off with him."

"Sorry, I'm taken," said Mitch, who was trying to figure out how Carly Cade had ended up married to a mean-spirited weasel like Aaron Ackerman. She was pretty. She was classy. She wasn't dumb—Aaron had gone out of his way to identify her as a professor.

"Mitch, you're probably wondering what a major babe like Carly is doing with a beltway wonk like me," Aaron said, gazing through Mitch.

"Not a chance," Mitch smiled, sipping his beer.

"Believe me, everyone in Washington does," Aaron assured him, his tone suggesting that the subject of their marriage was Topic Number 1 wherever people of power and influence gathered. Senators, cabinet secretaries, Supreme Court justices—they all talked about Aaron Ackerman and his comely blond wife. "They call us the beauty and the beast. You can guess which one I am. All I can say on my own behalf is that I'm the luckiest schnook in town."

"And don't you forget it, Acky," Carly said tartly, tossing her blond head. "It's like I always tell people, Mitch. I believe in equal opportunity. I've already been married to two handsome, athletic men with impeccable social skills. Now it's Aaron's turn."

"He *doesn't* need to hear about your other marriages," Aaron grumbled at her peevishly.

She held her empty martini glass out to him. "Acky, will you get me a refill?"

He snatched it from her and took it to the bar, where Les did the honors.

"So how did you two meet, Professor?" Mitch asked her.

"God, don't call me *that*. Every time I hear the P-word I think of some old hag with a mustache and a hump. Make it Carly, okay? I was up in D.C. for a symposium on U.S. global hegemony at the American Enterprise Institute. I live in Charlottesville, teach modern political history at Mary Baldwin College over in Staunton. Anyway, the two of us were seated next to each other. I knew Aaron's work, of course. We started talking, and I ended up inviting him down as a guest lecturer. After that, he just swept me off my feet."

"Translation: I got into her sweet little pants my first night there," Aaron boasted, returning with her refill.

"Acky, he really doesn't need to know that."

"You told him I swept you off of your feet. I was merely elaborating."

"You were not. You were being disgusting."

Over at the tavern table, the young man from Panorama was still negotiating on his cell phone: "I understand you perfectly—*Quentin* wants a limo. I'm just a little taken aback, because *Oliver* has already agreed to a town car. His people don't want to make this into a big glitzy deal. This is *not* the damned Golden Globes. Those were Oliver's exact words."

His companion bit her lip as she continued to labor at her laptop.

"Feel like a game of eight-ball, Mitch?" Aaron asked, blinking at the vintage pool table.

"You're on."

Les racked the balls for them while Mitch and Aaron chose cue sticks from the rack mounted on the wall.

"How about a small wager just to make it interesting? Say, a hundred dollars?"

"Let's make it ten," Mitch countered. "So there won't be any hard feelings."

Aaron let out a derisive snort. "What are you, short on nerve?"

"Acky, he's *trying* to be a gentleman."

"Really? I never realized that 'gentleman' was synonymous with 'wimp.'"

"Actually, why don't we make it five?"

"What *is* your problem?" Aaron demanded.

"He's trying to spare your feelings, if you ask me," Les said.

"I don't recall asking you," Aaron snapped.

"Why don't you break, Aaron?" Mitch offered, chalking his cue.

"Don't you want to flip a coin or some such thing?"

"That's okay. Go right ahead."

"Suit yourself. But, frankly, you carry this nice-guy act a bit far. It's somewhat embarrassing." Aaron broke thunderously but to no avail—he sank nothing.

Mitch promptly went to work. "Three-ball, corner pocket," he said, dropping it crisply.

"Kindly explain something to me, Mitch," Aaron said as he watched him line up his next shot. "Why don't you get an honest television job instead of writing for that biased liberal rag of yours?"

Mitch's newspaper was by no means biased. It was scrupulously even-handed, and Aaron knew this. He was just trying to get a rise out of Mitch so he could show his pretty blond wife how devastatingly clever he was.

"Nine-ball, side pocket," he said, sinking it.

"Seriously, you need to get your face on TV," Aaron persisted. "The air time will double your book sales."

"I'm a journalist, not an entertainer," said Mitch, who had turned down a number of offers to review movies on television.

"God, that is so beneath you, Mitch. Those labels are demonstrably obsolete. We are *communicators,* nothing more or less. Accept it. Take advantage of it. You're well-spoken, make a nice impression. And compared to Roger Ebert, hell, you're Brad Pitt." Aaron let out a big, booming laugh. "I like that line. I'll have to use it."

"You just did, Acky," Carly pointed out tartly.

"I meant on the air," he growled at her. "Mitch, I'm privileged to know any number of prominent people at CNN, Fox News . . . I'd be happy to put out some feelers for you."

"That's very nice of you, Aaron, but I'm fine right where I am."

"But how can you be? That's not possible."

"I assure you, it's very possible."

"Acky, you're doing it again."

Aaron arched his eyebrow at his wife. "Doing *what?*"

"Laboring under the misapprehension that someone is unhappy because he's not you," she said. "Mitch is a smart man. Good at what he does, successful at it. If he wanted to be doing TV, he'd be doing TV. Since he's not, that means he doesn't want to. So shut up about it, okay?"

"Couldn't have said it better myself, Carly. All except for the shut-up part." Mitch scoped out the table, observing that Aaron was glowering at her, red-faced. Acky did not like to be spoken to that way. "Seven-ball, corner pocket." It was a long rail shot, but Mitch sank it.

By now the man from Panorama was done with his calls and charging toward Mitch with his hand held out. "Spence Sibley, Mitch," he exclaimed. "Sorry about all of this studio business. You must think I'm ultra-rude."

"No, not at all."

"I've just got so many last-minute details coming together at once. The studio's West Coast contingent jets into Teeterboro in the morning, filled to the overhead luggage rack with heavy-hitters. Plus I've got carload upon carload of people coming out from New York. Many of these people are directors who, believe me, have egos that are roughly akin to Afghan warlords. Stars are cupcakes in comparison." Spence Sibley was about twenty-eight, boyishly handsome and innately self-assured. He had an open, clear-eyed face, a good strong jaw, and possibly the cleanest shave Mitch had ever seen. In fact, he was clean all over. Clean blond crew cut. Clean symmetrical features. Not particularly tall, but he looked as if he were a runner or maybe a swimmer. He practically hummed with good health. He was also exceedingly polished in that way successful corporate people so often are—upon closer inspection, his open face revealed not one thing about the man inside. Spence wore a camel's hair blazer over a burgundy cable-stitched crew neck, perfectly creased tan slacks of heavyweight twill and polished chestnut-colored ankle boots. "Mitch, may I introduce you to Hannah Lane? Hannah is Ada's personal assistant."

"Pleased to meet you, Hannah," said Mitch, thinking her name sounded familiar.

Hannah clambered awkwardly to her feet, nearly knocking over the tavern table. "Yeah, right, back at you," she blurted out nervously. Hannah was about the same age as Spence, tall, coltish and incredibly ill at ease. Her features were striking. She had deep-set eyes, terrific cheekbones and a long, straight nose. Her look was even more striking. Hannah resembled a saucy 1920s Parisienne with her schoolboy-length henna hair, jaunty beret and bright red lipstick. The glasses she had on were thick and round and retro. She wore a bulky turtleneck and tweed slacks, a matching tweed jacket thrown over her shoulders the same way Ada's was. In fact, it was as if Hannah had patterned her entire style after an old photo of the great director. Mitch couldn't help wonder if she ordinarily looked completely different. "I just love your work," she said to Mitch effusively. "Especially your weekend pieces. You're part of my Sunday ritual. First church, then Mitch. I always read you. Always."

"Why, thank you."

"Same here, Mitch," echoed Spence. "I've been reading you since I was at New Haven."

Mitch, a Columbia alum, had to smile at this. Somehow, Yalies never failed to shoehorn their academic pedigree into the first sixty seconds of a conversation. It was one of the few things he could count on in life.

"Mind you, I'll have to start reading you on the Web next month," Spence said. "They're moving me out to the Coast. I've been promoted to vice president of marketing. Still hasn't quite sunk in, actually. The whole picking up and moving thing. I've never lived more than ninety minutes from New York in my whole life. But I'm plenty psyched."

Jory entered the taproom now with a tray arrayed with pâté, cheese and crackers.

"How on earth did you know I was starving?" Spence asked her as he helped himself to brie.

"Growing boys are always hungry," she answered lightly.

Mitch and Hannah sampled the pâté, which was excellent.

"I've been up here since Tuesday, trying to pull everything together," Spence went on, chomping on the cheese. "Kind of a nostalgia trip for me, really. When I was a kid, the whole Sibley clan used to descend on Astrid's during leaf-peeping season—my aunts, uncles, cousins. We always had a blast." Spence reached for more brie from Jory's tray. "In fact, I spent some time in this area when I was in New Haven." Again with the Yale. "A classmate of mine belonged to the Dorset Yacht Club. We used to hang out on his dad's Bertram. Is that outrageous diner still there on Old Shore Road?"

"McGee's," said Mitch, nodding. "Sure is."

"Great fried clams."

"The best," Jory agreed, moving on to Aaron and Carly with the tray. Neither of them wanted anything. She set it down on the bar and returned to the kitchen.

"Hannah, it must be a thrill working with Ada," Mitch said. "How long have you and she been together?"

"Less than a week," she replied. "To be honest, the two of us are not exactly . . . What I mean is, she doesn't even know my name yet. Won't let me lift a finger to help her, *or* listen to one word of my pitch. So I'm basically just helping Spence out. I'm not complaining, the Lord knows. It's just that I'm really desperate to make a documentary about Ada's life. See, I-I'm a filmmaker myself."

Spence said, "Hannah produced and directed *Coffee Klatsch,* that documentary about the old-time character actresses who hang out in the coffee shop of Sportsman's Lodge. They ran it on Bravo a few months ago."

"Oh, sure." Mitch recognized her name now. "I saw it at Sundance last year. It had real heart. I loved it."

"I know you did," Hannah said, her eyes puddling with tears. "I wept with joy when I read your review."

"And now you want to film Ada?"

"If she'll let me. And if I can get the financial backing. Which, as you know, is no sure thing." Hannah cleared her throat uneasily. "Mostly, I've been kind of regrouping back home in D.C. for the past few months."

"Hannah's name came up when the studio suggested that Ada hire an assistant," Spence said. "We've actually known each other for years. We went through Panorama's internship program together."

"So you put the two of them together?" Mitch asked him.

"No, that was me, actually," Aaron interjected from behind Spence.

Mitch thought he noticed Carly stiffen slightly. She turned to face the fire, tossing her long golden hair.

"Hannah approached me a few weeks ago in Washington through mutual friends," Aaron explained. "It seems she wants nothing more than to follow the old girl around with a camera."

Now Carly darted out of the taproom, her high heels clacking on the entry hall's hardwood floor.

Aaron paid no notice to her departure. He was busy talking. And when Aaron Ackerman was talking, self-absorption took on a whole new dimension. "Quite frankly, I was impressed by the depth of

Hannah's interest, and by her passion for her subject. She seemed the ideal candidate. By the way, Mitch, it's still your shot," he pointed out, tapping his cue stick against the floor.

Mitch returned to the table and immediately drained his last ball. Called the eight-ball and dropped that, too. Game over. Aaron hadn't sunk a single shot—and Mitch had actually been going easy on him.

"I guess this means I owe you ten dollars." Aaron reached for his wallet.

"I thought we agreed on five."

"No, it's definitely ten."

"Forget it. I don't want your money."

"Sure, we're all friends here," Les agreed from behind the bar.

"What are you, kidding me?" Aaron demanded. "The instant Mitch gets home tonight he'll e-mail every liberal he knows that Aaron Ackerman stiffed him on a bet. By morning, it will be all over the Internet. Mitch and his New York media cronies just love to trash me. It's what they live for." Aaron started to hand over a ten-dollar bill, then stopped, glancing slyly at Mitch. "Of course, we could go double or nothing."

Mitch smiled at him. He was going to enjoy this immensely. Really, he was. "Aaron, you talked me into it. Rack 'em up."

CHAPTER 4

DES COULD FEEL THE rear end of her cruiser shimmy on the curves as she made the climb up the long private drive to the castle. Black ice had formed on the pavement. Plus some windblown frozen rain was starting to come down, tapping against her windshield like BBs. She'd even heard rumbles of thunder. Just to play it safe, she'd checked in with the Westbrook Barracks on her two-way radio, but the National Weather Service was issuing no new watches or warnings for tonight. Their forecast called for flurries, diminishing winds and overnight lows in the teens. Nothing, in other words.

So why does it feel like something?

She parked near Mitch's old truck. Grabbed her shoulder bag, got out and headed over the moat on the drawbridge, burrowed deep inside of her hooded coat, the frozen rain pelting her, the bare winter trees groaning and creaking against the wind.

She was just about to ring the bell when the castle's massive front door swung open and there stood her doughboy in the warm glow of the lights, wearing a big happy smile on his round face. He looked like an eight-year-old boy who'd just gotten a new bicycle for Christmas. Make that Chanukah.

"You must be this new resident trooper I've been hearing so much about," he said solemnly as he ushered her in. "Desiree Mitry, right?"

"That's correct, sir." She raised her chin at him sternly. "And you are . . . ?"

"Berger. Mitchell Berger. I'm in vinyl siding. You need any durable, low-cost protection for your home, I'm your man."

"I'll be sure to keep that in mind."

"I hope you won't take this the wrong way, Trooper Mitry, but nobody told me you were a total hottie. Would you slap my face if I tried to kiss you?"

"Sweetness, you'd better do a whole lot more than that before this night is over," she murmured, brushing his lips with hers. "It is getting *nasty* out there."

He immediately put her in his big teddy-bear hug, making her feel more adored and cherished than she'd ever thought possible.

So why does he want to break up with me?

Des had been to Astrid's Castle before. Les and Norma often hosted meetings of the Chamber of Commerce, of which Les was currently president. Still, she could never quite get her mind around how immense it was. And she had never been here at night, when the chandeliers were all lit. It was positively grand. Someone was even playing show tunes on the piano in the Sunset Lounge.

Les and Norma came to greet her. Les wore a welcoming smile on his face. Norma looked positively worn ragged. "Glad you could make it, Des," he said. "How are the roads?"

"Getting a little slick, actually."

"Sorry to hear that. If you have any qualms about driving home, we've got dozens of warm empty beds you can choose from."

"So good of you to join us, dear," Norma said with a bleary-eyed smile. "May I help you off with your coat?"

Before Des could respond, a tremendously self-important windbag started throwing himself a fit at the top of the staircase. "She is *not* in our room!" he shouted, clomping down the stairs toward them. He was a pear-shaped windbag possessing an exceedingly large head. "She is *not* in the morning room! She is *not* in the kitchen. She is *not* anywhere else!"

Des glanced over at Mitch. "And this is . . . ?"

"Norma's son, the great Aaron Ackerman."

"Refresh my memory. What's he great at?"

"Not to worry, he'll let you know."

"She *must* be found!" Aaron Ackerman roared. "I demand that she be found!"

Now an imperious old white-haired lady appeared in the dining room doorway. "Aaron, stop this appalling display at once," she hollered at him. "You're behaving like an overwrought little thumbsucker."

"That would be Ada," Mitch whispered to her.

"Good evening, Ada." Des reached a hand out to the old woman. "I'm Des."

"Of course you are." Ada's grip was firm and dry. "This is a genuine honor, Des. I've been so very anxious to meet you."

"You have? Why is that?"

"Hel-*lo*, can I get some attention here?" Aaron cried out. "I can't find Carly!"

"It's a big place, Aaron," Les pointed out mildly.

"And Carly's a big girl," Norma said. "If she wants to be found, she'll be found."

"But what if she's thrown herself off of the tower? What if she's lying dead out there in the snow at this very minute?"

"Do you have any reason to believe this is what's happened?" Des asked him.

"And who are you?" he huffed, arching an eyebrow at her.

"I'm the resident state trooper, Mr. Ackerman."

"Well, good. Maybe *you* can do something about this. Carly is missing, and absolutely no one gives a damn."

"And Carly is . . . ?

"My wife, of course. I *demand* that you find her."

The pianist had stopped playing. Des could hear footsteps starting toward them across the hardwood floor.

"Mr. Ackerman, I think you need to calm down," she advised Aaron, unsure whether she was dealing with a genuine situation or a genuine nut. Possibly she was dealing with both.

"It's true, Aaron, this gorgeous lady doesn't even have her coat off yet," the piano player said as he breezed in from the Sunset Lounge. He was an older man, tall and elegantly dressed. "And a very nice coat it is," he observed, fingering her sleeve expertly.

"Des, this is Aaron's Uncle Teddy," Mitch said. "Teddy's in the clothing business during daylight hours."

"Glad to meet you, Des." Teddy turned to his nephew and said, "What is all of this?"

"Yes, darling, why such a fuss?" Norma asked Aaron. "Has something happened between you two?"

"What's happened," Aaron answered, clenching and unclenching his fists, "is that she's missing and needs to be found."

"What are you driving these days, Mr. Ackerman?"

"A Mercedes wagon. Why is that of the slightest significance?"

"Silver, with Washington plates?"

"It is. I repeat, *why?*"

"Because it's still parked out there in the lot—meaning she hasn't left the premises. Les, do you keep the unoccupied guest rooms locked?"

"Yes, we do," he replied, nodding.

"Meaning she's either in one of the common rooms or she's outside. Mr. Ackerman, did you notice if her coat was missing from your room?"

"I-I don't remember."

"Then let's go have a look, shall we?" Des started for the stairs.

A lushly built redhead appeared in the dining room doorway, clad in a staff outfit of black vest and slacks. "Les, I can have Jase look around outside, if you'd like," she said.

"That might be a good idea," he said to her.

"Trooper, shouldn't you be calling someone else?" Aaron asked Des rather pointedly as he led her up the grand curving staircase.

"Such as who?"

"Such as someone who deals with this sort of thing on a regular basis."

"Mr. Ackerman, let's assume I know how to do my job and we'll get along just fine, okay?" she said politely. "Only, I can't help you unless you help me."

"Absolutely. Tell me how."

"By explaining to me why you are so freaked out."

They'd reached the second-floor landing. Aaron hesitated there. "Well, okay," he allowed, lowering his voice. "But this has to be in the strictest confidence. I can't allow some media outlet to get a hold of it."

"They won't."

"I have your word on that?"

"Spit it out, Mr. Ackerman."

"Carly overdosed on Prozac a few weeks ago when we were at our farm in Virginia. I had to rush her to the emergency room. She almost died. *Now* do you see?"

"Yes, I see."

"I thought you might," he blustered, starting down the second-floor hall.

The corridor was softly lit and quaintly old-fashioned. The doors were of polished oak. The carpet had a floral pattern, the wallpaper a water-fowl motif. Vintage photographs of yesteryear's celebrities lined the walls. At the end of the hallway there was an outside door, the top half of it glass.

"Where does that go?" she asked Aaron, motioning to it.

"Up to the tower."

"Did you look for her there?"

"Well, no," he had to admit.

Too busy huffing and puffing, Des thought as she made straight for it, digging her gloves out of her coat pocket. There were twenty-four rooms on the second floor, twelve on each side of the hall. Halfway down the hall there was a housekeeper's closet. Also a fire-proof steel door that led to the staff stairway. Next to that was an elevator for transporting wheelchair-bound guests and freight. When Des reached the end of the hall, she pushed open the outer door, or tried. She could feel the wind fighting her. She fought back and ventured out onto a snow-packed, floodlit observation deck. Wind gusts buffeted her and ice pellets smacked her in the face. The deck was surrounded by a three-foot-high stone parapet topped by an iron safety railing. A narrow iron staircase led up to the third floor, and from there on up to the castle's trademark tower, which was lit up bright enough for the drivers way down on I-95 to see. Des felt certain that on a balmy summer evening this would be a breezy, terrific place to be. Right now it was intensely uninviting.

The great Aaron Ackerman remained behind in the warm, dry hallway.

Des could make out several sets of footprints in the deep snow just outside the door. Someone had been out here since early that afternoon, when the snow had tapered off.

"CARLY?" she called out. "ARE YOU OUT HERE, CARLY?"

She heard nothing in response, just the howling wind.

There were more shoe prints on the iron stairs up to the tower. It was hard to tell how many sets since these prints had turned to partial slush in the weak afternoon sun and then iced back over. The handrail was coated with a shimmering layer of ice. She clutched it tightly as she started climbing, her boots slipping and sliding under her.

"CARLY?"

There was no outside door leading into the dimly lit third-floor corridor. Just a window, which was locked. She continued on, making her way up the final exposed flight of stairs to the tower, her shoulders hunched against the wind gusts.

"CARLY?"

The cement floor of the enclosed tower was damp but free of ice and snow. There were narrow vertical slits in the tower walls for people to peek through. Hundreds of these people had carved their initials in the mortar between the stones. Quite a few had left cigarette butts behind.

But there was no sign of Carly.

Aaron was waiting down there in the doorway for her with an anxious expression on his face. She gave him a thumbs-down sign as she shook the ice pellets from her coat. Then she followed him to room five, the third door from the center staircase. That door was not locked. It was a lovely room with a fireplace, ornate wooden molding, a big oak bedstead. It was also a mess. Dirty clothing was strewn all over the floor, up to and including underwear and stockings. Newspapers, books and magazines were heaped on the nightstands and dresser and desk. The bathroom was no tidier.

Carly's black leather Il Bisonte handbag lay on the bed. So did her full-length mink.

"Did Carly bring another coat with her besides this one?"

"No, she did not," Aaron replied.

Meaning that she wasn't out taking a stroll. Not that any sane person would in this weather. "Which of you is the smoker?" she asked, noticing the butts in the fireplace.

"Carly is," he sniffed. "Dreadful habit. It reeks of human weakness."

"Okay, it's time for the real deal, Mr. Ackerman," Des told him, standing there in the middle of the room with her arms crossed. "Did you two have a fight tonight?"

"Perhaps a small misunderstanding," he admitted, clearing his throat. "She seems to have gotten it into her head that I'm being unfaithful to her."

"And are you?"

"What business is that of yours?"

"Mr. Ackerman, you've *made* it my business. I came here this evening to enjoy a pleasant meal. Instead, you've got me traipsing all over the place. Now you can tell me what's going on or you can go look for Carly yourself. The choice is yours."

"Point taken," he acknowledged, running a hand over his neatly trimmed black hair. "I love my wife. I would never do anything to hurt her. And that's the absolute truth."

The classic non-denial denial. Des had heard it from every cheating husband she'd ever met, including her own. "I see," she responded. "Let's head back down with the others, shall we?"

They were gathered in the taproom. All of them looked up at Des with tense anticipation when she and Aaron strode in.

"Any luck?" asked Les.

"Not one bit," Aaron replied, his voice cracking with strain.

"Let's try to relax, okay?" Des suggested, shrugging out of her coat. "There's no cause for alarm at this point."

"Jase is still looking around outside for her," the curvy redhead told Des as she took her coat from her.

"And Jase is . . . ?"

"My brother. Oh, I'm so sorry, we haven't met. I'm Jory," she said, smiling at Des just a bit too brightly. Jory had an artificially ingratiating manner, the kind that men never saw through and women always did.

"Glad to know you, Jory."

There were two others in there whom Des didn't know yet. He was a squeaky-clean young corporate type. She was a lanky, jittery thing all tricked out in a beret and retro tweeds.

Mitch introduced them to her as Spence Sibley and Hannah Lane. "Spence is with the studio," he explained. "And Hannah's with Ada."

"She is?" Ada frowned at this, confused. "Since when?"

"Des, why don't you warm up in front of the fire?" Les said. "May I pour you something?"

"A glass of red wine would go down pretty nicely."

"Coming right up," he said, scooting around behind the bar.

Des felt a tug at her sleeve and discovered that Ada was standing right beside her now. She could have sworn that the old filmmaker was over on the other side of the taproom not one second ago. She moved fast for someone of her years. Fast and quiet. "Perhaps you'd like to powder your nose first," she said to Des under her breath.

"Something wrong with my nose?"

"I just thought you might wish to freshen up a bit," Ada persisted quietly, her gaze positively piercing. "The ladies' lounge is just off the dining room, second door on your right . . ."

It was lavishly appointed with mirrored makeup tables and plush chairs. Des could hear the sniffling as soon as she walked in. It was coming from the farthest toilet stall. She could see the black stiletto heels under the stall door. "Carly . . . ?"

"What do you want?" a voice mewled in response.

"I want you to come out."

"No!"

"Will you at least open the door?"

Carly flung it open. She was a slender, pretty little thing in a skimpy black dress. Her blond hair was long and shiny, her eyes puffy and red from crying.

"Now come on out of there," Des said to her gently. "Let's have us a talk."

She came along willingly enough. They sat in two of the little chairs in front of the makeup mirrors, Carly dabbing at her swollen eyes with a tissue. She wore false eyelashes, a ton of eyeliner, mascara. And not one bit of it was any the worse for wear. Forget the Internet—as far as Des was concerned, the most amazing technological breakthrough of the past twenty years was stay-on eye makeup.

"Everyone has been looking for you, Carly. What's going on?"

"I'm miserable, that's what," she snuffled. "And I'm a fool. And I'm . . . I'm sorry, do I even know you?"

"My name is Des. I'm with Mitch."

"Of course. You're the state trooper, are you not?" Carly had finishing school manners and a slight Southern accent. "You don't look like a trooper. I always picture a dull, beefy boy with a crew cut who adores things like motorcycles and hunting."

"I hit what I aim at. Aaron is very upset, Carly. He was afraid something had happened to you."

"Something *has* happened." Carly let out a huge, ragged sob. "My marriage has fallen apart. That man, he . . . he brought his born-again whore here with him!"

"His born-again who?"

"Hannah," she said angrily, her fists clenched. "Little Miss Christian Virtues. Acky's been squiring her around D.C. for weeks. Taking her to cocktail parties, to dinners, to bed. My best friend saw them coming out of the Hay-Adams together on Christmas Eve. She wants to make a movie about Ada, you see, and it's thanks to Aaron that she's here this weekend. He got her this job because she, because

71

they . . ." Carly broke off, tossing her long blond hair. "I am not a nut, present evidence to the contrary notwithstanding. I actually saw the two of them kissing out on the observation deck this afternoon."

Which would explain the footsteps Des had found there in the snow.

"Hannah's not even pretty, is she? This is not a pretty girl. But she's young, and that's all that ever counts with Acky."

The closer Des studied her, the more she became aware that Carly was not as young as she'd first appeared. Her figure was very good, her hair to die for. But her face had the cushioned, expressionless look that suggested collagen replacement therapy, Botox injections and possibly even surgical work. This woman was well into her forties. Aaron she'd pegged as being in his early thirties.

"It's the young ones who hang on his every word," Carly added bitterly. "They laugh at his jokes, puff up his ego for him."

"Seemed to me he can do plenty of puffing on his own."

"No, no, that's just an act. Acky's self-esteem is actually very low. He needs constant reassurance and mothering. He's completely helpless. And he can be so sweet and dear." Carly sniffled, blushing slightly. "I happen to be somewhat older than he is. Thirteen years, if you must know. And I am *so* terrified of losing him."

"He mentioned something about you overdosing on pills."

"I was just trying to get his attention."

"Have you tried doing anything else?"

Carly frowned at her. Or tried. That stuff she was wearing in her forehead wouldn't allow for much more than a faint, sub-dermal pulsation. "Such us what?"

"Such as counseling. You two ought to consider it."

"I don't recall asking for your advice," Carly said, climbing up onto her high horse. "In fact, I'm quite certain I didn't."

"You're getting it anyway. You need help. Swallowing pills, disappearing into thin air—this is not mature adult behavior."

"You're right, it's not," she admitted. "I don't even know why I love him. Truly, I don't. What I ought to do is divorce him. Find myself a man who'll treat me like I deserve to be treated. The dean of students has always had a thing for me. Well, not *me,* but my legs. They're still . . . what I mean is, I'm reasonably good-looking."

"Shut up, you're a bombshell."

"I'm smart, I'm tenured. And if I wanted to descend into total blond bitchdom, I could be plenty rich, too."

"Descend how?"

"By hiring myself a shark lawyer, the kind who'll produce photos of Aaron and his whore together. Then I'd get it all. The townhouse in Georgetown. The farm in Virginia. The stocks, bonds, every last penny he's made from his books."

"You two didn't sign a pre-nup?"

"Pre-nups are for cynics," Carly replied, her blue eyes twinkling at Des devilishly. "I'm a romantic. Maybe the last one left on earth. Mind you, Acky resisted. He even held out for a few weeks. But in the end, he married me on my terms. He wanted me." Carly admired herself in the mirror, her chin up, her self-confidence returning with a vengeance. "And now the bastard's got me, for richer or poorer."

Des took this particular display of spunk 'n' sass as her own cue to get up out of her chair and say, "Ready to join the others now?"

"*God,* no!" Carly flew right back into total panic. "I can't face them after this. They all think I'm a menopausal hysteric."

"Are you planning to hide in here all evening?"

"I'll go up to bed in a little while. Don't worry, I'll be fine."

Des stood there thinking it over. "I may have an idea. Stay put, okay?"

"Believe me, I'm not budging."

Des stuck her head out the door. She could hear voices coming from the taproom, but the coast was clear. She darted up the castle's stairs to Aaron and Carly's room, fetched Carly's mink and purse from the bed, and started back down with them.

Her gallant, pudgy white knight in rumpled corduroy was planted there at the bottom of the staircase, waiting for her. "What's going on, Master Sergeant?"

"Just a little aiding and abetting," she said hurriedly. "It's a girl thing."

73

"Is Carly okay?"

"She's perfectly fine. Can't say I care much for her taste in men, though."

"You'll get no argument from this reporter. Anything I can do?"

"There is, baby. Go back in the taproom with the others and play dumb."

"I can definitely do that."

"Oh, and please don't say anything about Carly's shoes."

"Her shoes? Why would I do that?"

"No reason." She kissed him on the cheek as she slipped by on her way back to the lounge.

Carly was sitting right where she'd left her. Hadn't moved a muscle.

"Here, put this on," Des commanded her, handing over the big fur. "You were outside having a smoke. Act completely surprised by all of the fuss."

"Actually, I could kill for a cigarette right now." Carly dug a pack of Marlboros out of her purse and lit one with a gold lighter, dragging on it deeply.

"You see? It's not even a fib."

"But no one will buy it," Carly pointed out. "The weather's absolutely awful. And only a streetwalker would wear these heels out in the snow. Besides which, look at them—they're completely dry."

"Trust me, those folks will buy whatever you sell them. And Aaron will back your play. He wants this to disappear just as much as you do. You can pull this off, Carly. Just breeze on into that taproom with your head held high. Anyone tries to smart-mouth you . . ."

"I can sink my teeth into them." Carly smiled, showing Des her teeth. They were nice and white, and looked exceedingly sharp. "It's something I'm good at."

"There you go. I'll stay here a minute before I join you. We were never in here together. Never met. Got it?"

Carly took one more pull on her cigarette before she flicked it into the nearest sink and climbed into her big mink coat. She looked like a million bucks in it and she knew it. "Why are you being so nice to me?" she wondered, narrowing her eyes at Des suspiciously.

"Just doing my job."

"Patching up my mess of a marriage is your job?"

"I do whatever needs doing in Dorset."

"Well, I owe you one. And I hate owing anyone anything. You see, I'm really not a nice person." Carly took a deep breath, steeling herself. Then she said, "Wish me luck," and darted out of there.

Des sat herself back down in front of the mirror. She hadn't been there for more than ten seconds when the door flew back open and in came Ada Geiger, a goblet of red wine clutched in her thin-boned, translucent hand.

"I believe you ordered this, my dear," she said, gliding over toward her with it. The old woman had an uncanny way of moving, almost as if she had a cushion of air under her. Or maybe that tweed jacket she wore over her shoulders doubled as a set of wings.

"Why, thank you," Des said, taking the glass from her. "You knew Carly was in here this whole time. Why didn't you say anything?"

"Because it was obvious that she did not wish to be found. I respect that. I respect what another woman needs to do. Besides, my grandson is an ass. He's cheating on her, isn't he?"

Des sipped her wine in discreet silence.

"Of course he is," Ada went on, undeterred. "They're terribly ill-suited for each other, you know. He's needy and selfish, and she's a fading debutante with a post-graduate degree in bullshit. I assume they're drawn together by their mutual weakness. That is, after all, what passes for love among most couples—unless they happen to be very lucky. Are you lucky, Des?"

"I'll have to get back to you on that one."

Ada eased herself slowly down onto the plump little chair next to Des and turned her penetrating, hooded gaze on her. "I wish to have a word with you. It's rather important."

"All right." As Des studied Ada's face in the mirror, she found herself recalling something her granny had told her once: Everyone gets old, but a rare few *grow* old. Ada Geiger was one of those—

someone who had seen it all, done it all and, most significantly, savored it all. There was no regret in her proud, deeply lined face. No fear. Only wisdom. "What's it about, Ada?"

"You, my dear. You need to be rescued."

Des frowned at her. "Rescued from what?"

"I happened to take in the student show at the Dorset Academy yesterday," she replied. "It invigorates me to see what young artists are doing. Mostly, what I saw them doing was dreck—lifeless, passionless, highly derivative. There was only one artist in the whole exhibit who genuinely moved me. I asked about this artist. I said, 'Who draws the murder victims?'"

Sitting there, Des could feel her pulse quicken.

"I can't begin to tell you how excited I was to learn that *you* would be Mitch's companion this evening."

"Well, that's life in a small town."

"Spare me your modesty, okay?" Ada shot back. "We are kindred souls, you and I. When I was your age, I did the very same thing you're doing—except with a camera. Ever hear of an old-time tabloid photographer named Weegee?"

"Are you kidding me? I *love* his work."

"I thought so," Ada said, nodding to herself in satisfaction. "I knew him well."

Des gaped at her. "God, tell me about him. What was he like?"

"A horrible, unkempt little man. He lived in cheap rooming houses, reeked of body odor and awful cigars. 'Crime is my oyster,' he used to say. It became mine, too, Des. I followed him around like a puppy. Drove the streets of New York City with him, night after night, listening in on police calls on his two-way radio, hightailing it to murder scenes. He kept a key to the darkroom at the *New York Post,* where he'd develop his pictures at two, three o'clock in the morning. Then he'd head right out to peddle them to editors around town. He tried repeatedly to get me to go to bed with him," Ada remembered fondly. "As if he had a prayer—I was a gorgeous broad in those days. And yet, I was utterly fascinated by the man, Des, because he *understood.*"

"*Understood* what?"

"That we are all victims in the end. That's why his work needs no captions. No critics to 'explain' it. It's all right there in front of you. Because the very best art isn't 'art' at all—it's reality. That's what I've always tried to accomplish with my own work. That's all I've ever tried to do."

"Me, too, I think," Des said gingerly. Unlike the other students at the academy, she was not comfortable talking about her work. It felt very raw and personal to her, and she sure didn't know what any of it *meant*.

"Which is precisely why you need to get out of that place," Ada said to her urgently. "Des, you must stop taking classes at once."

"But I'm learning so much. Why would I want to stop?"

"Because if you stay they will steal your soul from you. Don't let them do it. Don't let them mold you into one of *them*. That's what they do, Des. That's how the competent take their revenge against the truly gifted. It's their sole satisfaction in life. It's what they live for. Do you hear me?"

Des fell silent for a moment, floored by the old woman's ferocious intensity. "I'm sure listening . . ."

"You're already beginning to feel a bit restless there, am I right?"

"Now *how* on earth did you know that?"

"I already told you," Ada said impatiently. "We're kindred souls. Listen to your heart, Des. Get out before it's too late."

"And do what?"

"Go your own way—wherever that way takes you. But it will be *your* way, not theirs. I happen to be a cranky old woman. I know this because I was a cranky young woman. But if there's one thing I've learned after all of these years, it is this: If you possess what other people want, and can't have, then they will try to destroy you." Ada paused, gazing around at the opulent ladies' lounge. "It's just like with this place."

"Astrid's Castle? What about it?"

"They will never, ever get it," she said insistently.

"*Who,* Ada?" Des asked, wondering if the old lady was totally with it mentally. She seemed sharp enough, full of fire and strongly held views. But she also seemed to be up to her ears in paranoia.

Or was she?

"Promise me you'll think about this," Ada said, clutching Des by the wrist now. "Promise me you will never forget this conversation. Will you do that for me?"

"Ada, I will never forget this conversation. Count on it."

"Thank you. I feel much better." Satisfied, Ada Geiger released her grip on Des, then got slowly to her feet and glided back out the door.

Des stayed put for a while, staring at her reflection in the mirror as she sipped her wine. It was better this way. She was alone in there and no one else could see just how badly the goblet was trembling in her hand.

CHAPTER 5

"WE CARED NOT ONE bit about studio politics," Ada told Mitch as she nibbled regally at the food on her plate. Dinner was a flavorful beef bourguignon, roasted root vegetables and good, crusty bread. "All we cared about was making our movies. We wrote them together. My dear Luther produced them. And I directed them, which the studio boys didn't like at all. I was a broad. Broads are for sleeping with. Broads are for shutting up. I wouldn't do either of those things. Nor would I back down, because I saw them for the complete boors that they are, and . . . Lester, *must* I compete for attention with this New Age crap?" Ada meant the vaguely Eastern-sounding music that was playing on the dining hall's multi-speaker surround-sound system, something with tubular bells and wind chimes. "I feel as if I'm at one of those touchy-feely retreats where they stick needles in your feet."

"Sorry, Ada. Force of habit." Les hurried over to a wall control by the kitchen door and flicked it off. "We turn it on to signal our guests that it's mealtime."

"What are they, lab rats?"

The dining hall of Astrid's Castle was even vaster than the Sunset Lounge. It had three chandeliers, walk-in fireplaces at either end, both ablaze, and enough tables to accommodate a hundred or more guests. Right now, only their lone table by the windows was set, complete with twin candelabra. Les and Norma were at either end. Ada sat on Norma's left, Teddy on her right. Mitch was next to Ada, with Des directly across from him. Aaron was next to her, facing Carly, who sat in between Mitch and Spence. Carly seemed very subdued. She'd said nothing since they sat down to dinner. Just kept staring across the table at Hannah, who was next to Aaron.

Outside, the frozen rain pattered loudly against the windows, and the wind continued to howl.

"You say the boors that they *are,*" Mitch spoke up. "That sounds like you think the movie business hasn't changed much since the fifties."

"It hasn't," Ada said. "Oh, sure, they come out of Harvard Business School now instead of the rag trade. But they're still the same boors. And the movies are the same dumb crap. Mitch, there are so many amazing people out there leading amazing lives. So many fascinating stories to tell. Instead, they keep churning out their same tired kiddie stories about flying saucers, Santa Claus and the Tooth Fairy. Mind you, the movies are louder and shinier than they used to be, and they can do things with computers that we never even dreamed of. But no matter how you dress them up, they're nothing more than fake, sickening bedtime fables."

"Here's what I keep asking myself," Mitch said. "And maybe you have the answer, Ada. What is this steady diet of fantasy doing to us?"

"Nothing good," she replied flatly. "We're turning into a nation that cannot cope with reality. We no longer deal with any of our genuine social ills. We merely pretend to be—*more* fantasy. And that is a very dangerous thing, Mitch. Because people who cannot accept reality are generally considered to be insane."

Jory appeared at Mitch's elbow now with the serving dish of beef bourguignon. He helped himself to seconds. Across from him, Des was still pushing her food around on her plate. She was not at ease at dinner parties with people whom she didn't know well. When she felt tense, her appetite vanished. Mitch was entirely the opposite. Hence their entirely different body shapes.

"I don't agree with you about our movies, Mrs. Geiger," Spence said, ladling seconds onto his own plate. "True enough, we put out our share of youth fare. But I'd still stack up this year's slate of mature-audience films against any in Hollywood history. We are talking about many, many Oscar-worthy films."

"They pass out those awards as easily as they do condoms—and for much the same purpose," Ada sniffed, peering down the table at him. "And you are . . . ?"

"That's Spence, Mother," Norma reminded her. "He's with the New York office."

Ada curled her lip with disdain. "Ah, yes, the New York office. Let me ask you this, Mr. New York Office. And do think hard before you answer: Have you ever performed one single spontaneous act in your entire life?"

Spence didn't respond. It wasn't a question that called for a response. He went back to his dinner, reddening.

Hannah took a quick, nervous gulp of her wine, clanking the glass against her teeth, and blurted out, "How did the actors take to it? Being directed by a woman, I mean. Was that hard for you?"

Ada sat back in her chair, dabbing at her mouth with her linen napkin. "Actors *want* to be directed. I had no trouble with my casts. Not even Bob Mitchum, who everyone told me would be difficult. He wasn't. He was a pussy cat. He always wanted me to teach him how to fly a single-engine plane. I told him, 'Bob, you stay out of two-seaters and I'll stay out of whorehouses,'" she recalled fondly. "It was the crew that was my real challenge. They had to know I was in charge of that set, knew what I wanted, knew when I'd gotten it. Because if your crew thinks you're at all unsure, you'll never make it."

"I think today's women would be thrilled to hear how you did it," Hannah plowed ahead. "What you had to go through, how you coped, how you came out on top . . ." She was deep into her movie pitch now, no question. "You should share some of this with women my age, Ada. You're such an inspiration."

"What I did fifty years ago doesn't interest me at all," Ada responded stiffly. "I don't care to look back. Looking back is strictly for people who think their best days are behind them."

"You don't miss the old days?" Mitch asked her.

"Never even think about them," she insisted, in spite of the glow that had come over her deeply lined face when she'd mentioned

Mitchum. "There's so much that is new and fascinating to talk about. Why look back?"

"For any lessons that might be learned," Carly said. "As historians, that's what we are always trying to do."

"Like with the blacklist," Mitch said, sopping up the last of his gravy with a chunk of bread. "People are interested in how we let that whole, awful episode happen. And they should be. Because if we forget, it could very easily happen again."

"It *has* happened again," Ada said sharply, glaring at Aaron. "Because fear never goes away. Nor do the self-proclaimed patriots who fan that fear and twist it and profit from it." She paused, wetting her thin, dry lips with a pale tongue. "Were they right about Luther and me? Of course they were. Not only were we active in socialist causes in the thirties, we were proud of it. I'm still proud. This country was falling apart. Capitalism was *failing*. Millions were out of work. Spain was falling. Hitler was on the rise. My God, we almost didn't make it in this country. And if it hadn't been for Franklin Roosevelt, we might not have. But we pulled together. We fought. And we prevailed."

"And then Roosevelt gave half of Europe away to Stalin," Aaron cracked. "Just a little parting gift from one comrade to another."

"Franklin Roosevelt was a great president, Aaron," Norma objected. "He saved this country, whether you wish to admit it or not."

"He can't admit it, Norma," Ada said. "He and his so-called friends are too busy trying to dismantle the government that FDR worked so hard to build. Let me tell you something, Aaron. You people were wrong about the New Deal seventy years ago and you're still wrong now. But you won't let up, will you? Not until you've destroyed every single public agency that exists for the common good in this country."

Des's napkin slipped from her lap onto the floor. She bent down to retrieve it, briefly ducking her head under the tablecloth. Mitch could have sworn she'd done this on purpose. When she sat back up, napkin properly restored, he looked at her curiously. Her face betrayed nothing. She was a lovely, impassive sphinx.

"You've been out of this country for too long, Grandmother," Aaron lectured her. "You've lost touch with average people. I am simply espousing mainstream American values."

"What in the hell do *you* know about mainstream Americans, Aaron?" Ada demanded. "For your information, mainstream Americans will be living out of mainstream garbage cans after you and your band of greedy jackals have your way. Besides, I am *not* out of touch. To live overseas is to see us for the bullying, rampaging hypocrites we really are. We are positively awash in self-delusion. We steal peoples' lands and tell ourselves we're 'liberating' them. We lecture other countries about human rights even as we stage public, state-sanctioned executions of our own mentally handicapped. We preach equal opportunity, yet we've never, ever practiced it. Just ask anyone of color." Ada glanced at Des. "No offense, dear."

"None taken," Des said quietly, as the frozen, windblown rain continued to pelt the windows.

"Now you just hold on one second, Grandmother," Aaron countered. "I have allowed you your say—"

"You have *allowed* me nothing, you little twit."

"But I don't believe I should have to apologize for living in the greatest country in the history of the earth."

"I think that we in the studio audience are now supposed to clap our hands like seals," Ada jeered.

"This is the land of opportunity," Aaron pronounced, his voice resonant and assured. "Everyone is free to make his or her own way, however they choose. The only thing holding them back is their own damned government robbing them blind to pay for bloated bureaucracies such as Social Security, which is nothing more than a spectacularly failed Ponzi scheme that was forced upon us by dreamers and fools."

"Dreamers and fools," Ada said, nodding her head. "That's what we were. Some of us still are. Not you, though. You are a true, red-meat American, Aaron. And good for you, I say. But do me a small favor, will you? Give me an example of one moment of pure joy that it's brought you in your entire adult life. One moment that wasn't based on the manipulation and misfortune of others."

Aaron sat there with his mouth open, at a loss for words. Which Mitch felt had to be a first.

"You can't, can you?" Ada went on. "And that's terribly sad. Because I can think of a hundred moments, a thousand moments. We had passion, Aaron. We cared about other people. You don't. All you care about is sounding clever on national television." She raised her chin at him, her eyes fierce. "My God, if your father could see you now . . ."

"My father was a loser," Aaron snapped.

Norma let out an astonished gasp.

"You are *way* out of line, buddy," Teddy said angrily. "My brother was a great man, and you're not going to run him down—especially in front of your mother. Try that again and I'll take you outside and pop you one."

"Oh, go play your stupid piano, Teddy," Aaron said to him savagely. "No one is interested in what you have to say."

From across the table, Des locked eyes with Mitch. Behind those heavy horn-rimmed glasses, hers were wide with amazement. She had a few months of service in Dorset under her belt, but she still could not get used to this—wealthy white people behaving badly.

"Hey, come on now," Les interjected, forcing a cheery smile onto his smooth pink face. "Let's all relax and enjoy our meal, okay?"

Carly stayed out of the line of fire entirely. Just kept staring balefully across the table at Hannah. Mitch wasn't sure why. He did know that Hannah was growing very uncomfortable under her gaze.

"I feel bad for you, Aaron," Ada went on. "You're my grandson, and I love you, and you have no idea how they're exploiting you."

"And just exactly who is *they?*" he demanded, seething.

"Why, the ruling class, of course. You're not one of them, Aaron, and you never will be. You're merely their court jester, all dressed up on television in your little bow tie. Should you displease them, they will unplug you. And you will cease to exist. You do know this, don't you? You are such a realist you must realize this particular fact of—"

"Why did you even come back?" Aaron erupted at her. "You're a horrible hateful woman! I wish you had stayed in Europe. And I'm sorry I schlepped all the way up here to see you. Carly made me. She said I'd be sorry if I didn't. Well, guess what? I *am* sorry. I am really, really—" Aaron jumped to his feet, kicking over his chair, and fled from the table.

"Does the truth frighten you that much?" Ada called after him as he went charging across the dining hall, his footsteps heavy and clumsy.

"Leave him alone, Mother," Norma pleaded. "He's very young."

"He's an ass," Ada shot back.

Teddy shook his head at her in amazement. "You haven't changed a bit, have you, old girl?"

"And why should I?" she demanded.

"No reason," he said, smiling at her. "No reason at all."

The commotion brought Jory out of the kitchen. She righted Aaron's chair, then refilled the wineglasses with the last of the Côtes-du-Rhône they'd been drinking.

"We'll be needing another bottle, Jory," Les said. "Would you mind getting one from the cellar?"

"Be happy to," she said brightly, heading back through the kitchen door.

"I'd better see to dessert," sighed Norma, massaging her temples with her fingers.

"You seem tired tonight, dear," Les observed. "Let Jory take over."

"I'm quite all right," she insisted.

"Always the steady little plugger, my Norma," Ada said, needling her. "Always the one to keep her troublesome personal feelings bottled up inside."

"*Yes,* Mother," Norma said irritably. Ada had pricked a tender nerve.

Mitch was wondering what that particular nerve might be when a tremendously powerful gust of wind rattled the dining hall windows, followed almost at once by a sharp, frighteningly loud crackle somewhere outside—and then by a thud that practically shook the castle to its foundation.

"My God!" Hannah cried out in alarm. "What in the hell was that?"

"That, my dear, was the sound of a very large tree coming down," Les responded quietly.

Hannah shook her head in disbelief. "But why did it . . . ?"

Another crackle interrupted her—and a second tree crashed to the ground. This one seemed even closer.

This one also plunged the entire castle into darkness.

Or something sure as hell did. The only illumination in the cavernous dining hall came from the candelabra on their table and from the flickering, amber glow of the fireplaces. The doorway to the entry hall was nothing but a black void. Likewise the kitchen door.

"Just a localized blip," Les assured them. "Our power goes off like this all the time when there's a storm. It usually comes back on again in a second."

But it didn't come back on again in a second.

Des went over to the windows and looked outside, shielding her eyes with a hand. "I don't want to alarm anyone, but I don't see a single light on anywhere in Dorset. Or across the river in Old Saybrook or Essex."

"It's the ice storm," Mitch said. "The trees can't handle the extra weight, not when there's this kind of wind. It can split them down the middle."

"And right down onto the power lines," Des added grimly. "This looks bad. Very bad."

"Poor Jory is stuck down in the wine cellar," Norma suddenly realized. "I'd best take her a flashlight."

"I can do that," offered Spence.

"You'd better let me," Les said. "Those old cellar stairs are tricky, Spence. You might fall and hurt yourself."

As Les started for the kitchen, candelabrum in hand, Norma began lighting the candles that were set on the other tables.

Over by the windows, a pager started beeping.

"That's me," Des said. "I need to check in."

"I'm afraid the phones will likely be out, too," Norma told her.

"It's okay, I've got my cell." Des grabbed a candle, excused herself and retreated in the direction of the taproom.

Now Mitch heard a door slam somewhere, followed by heavy footsteps. Someone with a powerful flashlight came clumping into the dining room from the kitchen. It was Jase. The shy caretaker was covered with ice and panting so hard for breath that the key chain on his belt was jangling like a tambourine. "There's . . . there are . . ." He could not get the words out, he was so agitated.

"What's happened, dear?" Norma asked him gently. "Go ahead and tell us. Speak right up."

"It's the t-trees!" he stammered. "They're coming down all over the place!"

"Why, it's a miracle," Carly exclaimed in mock astonishment. "The furnace monkey spoke an entire sentence." She didn't say this to anyone in particular, but she did say it loud enough for Jase to hear. The offhanded cruelty of her remark stunned Mitch.

Jase, too. He peered at her with a surprised, hurt look on his furry face before he turned back to Norma and said, "Is . . . Jory okay? Where is she?"

"In the cellar, dear. She was fetching a bottle of wine when the power went out. Les has gone down with a light to find her."

They heard footsteps in the kitchen now and Les appeared in the doorway, candelabrum in hand. "You'll never guess who I found wandering around in the laundry room."

"Where is she?" Jase asked him anxiously.

"Right here, sweetie." Jory appeared next to Les in the candlelight, giggling. "I seem to have taken a wrong turn somewhere."

"But you're okay?" Jase moved over toward her, acting very protective.

"Of course. Not to worry."

Outside, another tree landed with a thud.

"Folks, we may be in the dark for a while," Les informed them. "There's a supply of hurricane lamps and flashlights at the front desk. If you'll follow me, I can hand them out."

"We're all yours," Teddy said gamely. "Lead on."

"Mitch, may I borrow your elbow?" Ada asked, clutching him by his right arm.

"Absolutely," he said, as someone else grabbed his left hand.

"I'm afraid of the dark," Carly explained, her hand small and cold in his. "It turns me into a snarling bitch. I hope you don't mind."

"I don't. But Jase might beg to differ."

The three of them followed Les and his candelabrum through the blackened entry hall. As they passed the taproom, he could hear Des in there talking on her cell phone.

At the front desk Jory produced a tray filled with kerosene lanterns. She swiftly fired up enough of them for everyone, bathing the three-story entry hall in a golden glow. She also pulled out a carton of flashlights. Les, meanwhile, checked the telephone at the reception desk. The line was dead.

From upstairs, a male voice roared, "Will someone kindly tell me what the devil is going on?! It's pitch-black up here!"

"That would be our red-meat American," Ada observed dryly.

"The storm has knocked out our power, Aaron!" Les hollered up to him.

"I have no lights up here!"

"No one does!" Norma called out. "It may get a tad nippy, too, but we'll just have to muddle through!"

Muddling through was something that Mitch had gotten quite used to. Out on Big Sister, he lost power pretty much every time they had an electrical storm. On at least a half dozen occasions, he'd gone without power for twenty-four hours. And the darkness was actually the least of it. Without electricity the well pump couldn't produce water and the fuel pump couldn't feed the furnace. That meant no water, hot or cold, and no heat—which was why Norma had said it might get a tad nippy. Try frozen.

"Stay where you are, son!" she called to Aaron as he started down the stairs to them. "I shall bring you a light!"

"Surely you have a back-up generator for this type of situation," Aaron blustered as Norma met him on the winding stairs, clutching two lanterns. "They sell the damned things at Home Depot."

"We did have a diesel generator," Les acknowledged. "But our guests complained about the stink and the noise. They prefer to go without. We've got plenty of firewood. The kitchen stove runs on gas. And our stereo system can run on batteries."

"Oh, goodie," Ada cracked.

"Besides, it's a bit of an adventure," Les added. "People think it's fun."

"*Fun?*" fumed Aaron. "Freezing to death in the dark is *not* my idea of fun!"

Mitch went over to the big front door and flung it open, shining his flashlight out into the blackness of the howling night. What the flashlight beam revealed was a shimmering, bejeweled world unlike any he'd ever seen before. A gleaming layer of ice had coated every single exposed surface. Every branch, every path, every stone. And the frozen pellets continued to hammer down as the raging winds whipped and tossed the trees out beyond the parking lot, snapping their frozen limbs like bread sticks and slamming them to the ground with horrifying force.

"God, how I wish I had this on film," marveled Ada, gazing out at it in wide-eyed wonderment.

Des appeared behind them now in the doorway, wearing her game face.

"What have we got, Master Sergeant?" Mitch asked.

"A T-1 emergency, that's what," she reported crisply. "Power lines down all over the state. As many as a half million people are without electricity. Most surface roads are impassable. The major highways are skating rinks. They're shutting the airports down. The governor's about to declare a state of emergency."

"I don't get it," Mitch said. "The weatherman said that this storm would be passing out to sea way south of us."

"Mitch, the weatherman was wrong."

"Any idea when it's supposed to let up?" Spence asked her apprehensively.

"By dawn. It's supposed to get very cold. And *then* it's supposed to snow—another six to ten inches."

"But I've got Hollywood celebrities flying in tomorrow," Spence protested.

"I very much doubt that anyone will be flying in tomorrow," Des told him.

"You mean the entire event might be *canceled*?" Les was utterly distraught. "This can't be. It just can't. We've ordered tons of food and liquor. We've taken on extra staff . . ."

"You'll be reimbursed," Spence promised him. "The studio will make good on it."

"It's not the money," Les insisted. "Ada was really looking forward to this."

"I was not." She growled. "*You* were."

"We *all* were," Les said. "This is a big, big event for us."

"Les, if people can't get here then they can't get here," Norma said to him patiently. "We must accept it."

Des fetched her shearling coat from the coatroom, climbed into it and started for the door, her hood up, a flashlight in hand.

"Wait, where are you going?" Mitch asked her.

"When there's a T-1, every available trooper goes on emergency assistance detail. That's why they paged me. I have to find out whether I can get out of here or not."

"May I come, too, Des?" Ada asked excitedly.

Des looked at the old woman in surprise. "Why would you want to do that, Ada?"

"I want to be out in it."

"You'd better not. You might slip and fall."

"Nonsense."

"Please, Mother, it's not safe." Norma took her firmly by the arm and ushered her away from the door. "Just think what would happen if you broke a hip."

"Such a frightened little mouse you are," Ada sniffed at her. "But you always have been, haven't you?"

"Whatever you say, Mother," Norma responded wearily.

"Hang on, *I'm* coming with you," Mitch told Des as he went for his parka.

"No, you absolutely aren't," she insisted. "This is a work thing, Mitch. I can't put you or anyone else at risk. But send out the dogs if I'm not back in five minutes." She flashed her mega-wattage smile at him, then headed out, her long lean body hunched into the howling wind.

Mitch watched her make her way down the icy stones of the front path. She slipped and slid but stayed on her feet. She was lithe and nimble. Careful, too. Still, he kept watch over her, her flashlight growing steadily dimmer as she made her way farther and farther out into the stormy darkness.

"I've never been in a blackout before," Hannah said, her voice quavering with fear. "It feels kind of like the end of the world."

"It's certainly the end of mine," Spence said heavily. "I don't know *what* to tell the West Coast."

"You Americans are so spoiled," Ada said reproachfully. "It's a power outage. The French get them so often they don't even bother to light candles. They just find someone to make love to."

"Typical French behavior," Aaron said sourly.

Des had made her way across the drawbridge now. Mitch could just make out their iced-up cars in the distant beam of her flashlight.

"Why do you right-wingers all hate the French so much?" Ada wondered. "Is it because they know how to enjoy life and you don't?"

"No, it's because they're spineless."

She let out a mocking laugh. "You didn't exactly sound like Monsieur Spiny yourself just now when the lights went out. You sounded like a scared little girl crying for her mommy. Norma had to come rescue you."

"Grandmother, I've had just about enough of you tonight," Aaron shot back. "Kindly leave me the hell alone, will you?"

"No, please don't, Ada," Carly begged her. "This is the most fun I've had in months."

"Me, I've been through three New York City blackouts," Teddy said. "Know what? They've checked out the birth records, and it's amazing just how many babies were born nine months to the day after each of them. Which is to say, old girl, that the French don't have the market cornered on l'amour."

Des's flashlight beam was growing brighter now. She was starting back across the drawbridge toward them.

As she made her way closer, Mitch called out, "How is it?"

"We can't get out!" she called back, darting under the castle's covered entryway. Her hood and shoulders were crusted with ice. Droplets of water had beaded on her face and glasses. "There are two huge trees down right at the top of the driveway, completely blocking it."

"Those must be Astrid's sycamores," Norma said, her voice heavy. "She planted them there more than seventy-five years ago. They were quite lovely and spectacular, poor things."

"How are the power lines?" Les asked.

"Don't know. Couldn't see them." Des shook the ice off of her coat outside, then came back in, slamming the big door behind her.

Mitch took the coat from her and gave her his handkerchief for her glasses. "What are you going to tell the barracks?"

"That they'll have to cover for me. I'm stranded up here."

"They can't send someone to come get you?"

She shook her head. "They'll be stretched thin for bodies as is. Can't spare other troopers just to come get me." Clearly, Des was not happy about this fact. She wanted to be out there doing her job.

"Well, that settles that," Spence declared decisively. He yanked his cell phone from the breast pocket of his camel's hair blazer and hit the speed dial button. "Hi, it's me . . . No, everything is *not* okay. We've got a natural disaster here."

"I'd better warn Wolf Blitzer's people," Aaron said, reaching for his own cell phone. "I was supposed to do his show tomorrow. They're sending up a cameraman."

Des got busy phoning in as well. The sudden flurry of cellular activity reminded Mitch of a herd of commuters at Grand Central after Metro North has announced a train delay.

"Mitch, I was kidding around with you earlier," Les said. "But it looks like you and Des *will* be staying over with us."

"Looks like. Not a bad place to be stranded for the night, if you ask me."

"We're happy to have you. And just so there's no confusion, you're our guests, not paying customers." Les pulled him aside, lowering his voice discreetly. "But being an innkeeper does mean you have to get rather personal sometimes. What I mean is, one room or two?"

"One, please."

"Fine, fine." Les went behind the reception counter, poked around and presented him with a pair of keys to room six. "Norma can fix you kids up with toothbrushes. And Jase will fetch you extra fire-wood and blankets. You should be cozy enough until morning. I'm sure the power will be back on by then."

"Dunno, Les," Jase said softly. "Last time this many trees came down it was three, four days before the crews got to us."

"Did your pipes freeze?" Mitch asked him.

"Would have, if I hadn't bled them," Jase replied.

Les said, "Mitch, if you'd like a nightcap, the taproom should stay pretty snug for a while. But if I were you, I'd go up and get a fire started in your room."

Mitch glanced at his watch. It was not yet ten, but the darkness had a way of making it seem a lot later. "Sounds like a plan."

"I'll clear the table," Jory informed Les briskly. "I can cram every-thing in the dishwasher until morning." To Jase she said, "Sweetie, you'd better . . ."

"Firewood, right." Jase went tromping back toward the kitchen, lantern in hand.

By now Des was done phoning in. Norma unlocked the gift shop for them and filled an Astrid's Castle tote bag with travel toothbrushes and toothpaste, bottles of mineral water and matching Kelly green Astrid's Castle flannel nightshirts, size extra large. Also a disposable razor and shave cream for Mitch in case there was hot water by morning.

"If you need anything else, anything at all, do let us know," Norma said. "Shall I show you up to your room?"

"We can find it, thanks," Des said.

They said their good-nights and started up the winding staircase together, their lanterns casting a soft glow in the darkness. Des had her shoulder bag thrown over her left shoulder. Mitch had been involved with her long enough to know that her SIG-Sauer and her shield were in there. She had to keep them with her at all times. If she left them unattended somewhere, anywhere, they could be stolen. Mitch remained amazed that he'd gotten mixed up with a woman who was always armed.

"Sorry about this," he said to her as they climbed. "I know you want to be out there, making sure people are safe. And instead you're trapped in this castle with a family of feuding crazy people."

"No big. It reminds me of Thanksgiving dinner at my Aunt Georgia Mae's. The only difference with this bunch is that nobody's throwing punches. Not yet, anyway."

"Still, it's my fault that you're stuck here."

"Mitch, I'm glad I came. And way glad I met Ada. She's special. But you're right, I do feel like I ought to be out there."

"Same here. I'm worried about Mrs. Enman and Tootie and Rut. They all live alone. They could freeze to death and nobody would know."

"I just spoke to First Selectman Paffin. The Center School emergency shelter will be up and running by midnight. We have a plan in place for dealing with the elderly. I'll make sure your three are on the watch list. The fire department can get them to the shelter if they have to."

"Thanks. I'd hate for anything to happen to them."

"It won't. I promise."

"Did you reach Bella?"

"Our phone's out, and she refuses to get a cell. I'll keep trying her."

"I put down plenty of food for the cats. They'll be okay by themselves, right?"

"They'll make you pay for being somewhere else, but they'll be fine."

"I wish I felt as confident about my houses out there. All I keep thinking about is trees crashing down, roofs caving in, pipes freezing. I'm responsible for that whole island."

"Mitch, you're not responsible for the weather. Besides, Big Sister has withstood a lot of pounding over the years. Compared to a hurricane, this is nothing."

The darkened second-floor hallway felt genuinely spooky as they started their way along it with their lanterns, the carpeted floorboards creaking softly underfoot. Those old photos of the celebrated long-dead looming there on the walls certainly didn't help.

"I am starting to get definite vibes from *The Shining,*" Mitch had to confess. "If I see a pair of identical twin girls standing together at the end of the hallway, I'm spending the night out in my truck." In fact, all he could make out was a glass-paned door reflecting their lantern lights back at them. "Where does that go?"

"To the tower, and please don't tell me you want to go up there."

"Not even a chance."

"Could you believe Ada wanted to go outside with me?"

"Des, she flew a plane solo when she was sixteen. That's who she is. If she ever changed, she'd shrivel up and die."

Their room was the third door on the right. Mitch unlocked it and set his lantern on the mantel, gazing around. It was cozy and charming, with a huge old oak bedstead. Des took her lantern into the bathroom and deposited their gift-shop loot in there. The room was already plenty cold, so Mitch immediately got busy building a fire.

"I wonder what they use for kindling around here," he muttered, pawing through the wood basket in vain.

Someone tapped on their door. It was Jase, wearing a hiker's headlamp over his knit cap so that both hands were free to hold canvas carriers of firewood. He looked like a miner standing out there in the darkened hallway.

"Just the man I wanted to see," said Mitch, as the squatly built caretaker dumped more logs in their wood basket. "I can't find any kindling."

"We don't use it here. Too much of a fire hazard. Here . . ." Jase reached a rough hand into the pocket of his wool overshirt and gave Mitch a sealed plastic packet of something called Firestarter 2. Inside, there was a shapeless blob that distinctly resembled earwax. "Don't open it. Just light the whole packet."

"What's this stuff made out of?"

"Man, you don't want to know. You folks need any extra blankets?"

"You won't hear me saying no," Des answered sweetly.

Jase went and opened a vacant room and came back with two heavy wool ones. Des thanked him and got busy piling them onto the bed. Outside, another tree gave way under the weight of the ice and crashed to the ground.

"Will you and Jory be okay tonight?" Mitch asked Jase, who'd retreated back out into the hall.

"Shoot, yeah. Got us a couple of kerosene space heaters out in the cottage. We'll be fine. Have yourselves a good night."

"Back at you, Jase," Mitch said, closing the door after him. "He's a nice guy. I couldn't believe Carly called him a monkey right to his face."

"She called him a *what?*"

"What's that woman's problem anyway?"

"Aaron brought his mistress here for the weekend. She's totally bugging."

"Are we talking about Hannah?"

"We are."

"So that explains the evil eye Carly was giving her during dinner." Mitch set the packet of Firestarter 2 under the logs he'd stacked in the fireplace and lit a match to it. The waxy blob flamed blue, much like a can of Sterno. Actually, it smelled a lot like Sterno. Whatever it was, it worked—the logs caught quickly and began to crackle. Mitch sat back on his ample haunches and watched them. "Carly's a lot more crush-worthy, if you ask me."

"She's also a lot older than Aaron," Des said from the bathroom, where she was already brushing her teeth. She got ready for bed faster than any woman he'd ever known.

"Really? How much older?"

"Sorry. Girls never tell on each other."

"Why is that?"

"Because we have to trust one another. We sure can't put any faith in our husbands."

"Hey, I resent that. It so happens I was a husband once."

"My bad. But that woman has taken just about all she can handle, Mitch. Aaron's a total raw dog."

"He's a mess is what he is," Mitch said, piling two more logs onto the fire. "A classic case of the Pip Syndrome."

"The wha-a-a . . . ?" She was gargling with mineral water now.

"His dad was a real dynamic person, sounds like. And we know his grandmother is. So he's always carried around this weight of great expectations. Aaron is desperate to prove to everyone, particularly Ada, that he matters. But, believe me, when he looks in the mirror he doesn't see a man who matters. He sees an overweight geek who couldn't get a date to the prom. I feel sorry for him, actually. That is not a happy camper."

"Your toothbrush awaits you, m'lord," Des informed him, padding back barefoot from the bathroom in one of their Astrid's Castle nightshirts, her trousers thrown over one arm.

Mitch gaped at her as she moved around the room. He couldn't help it. The merest glimpse at the way that flannel was clinging to her incomparable booty was enough to send his engine racing right into the red zone. His mouth went dry, his palms tingled. A vein began to throb in his forehead. "Tell me," he croaked, "why did you drop your napkin on the floor?"

"I was checking to see if Aaron and Hannah were playing footsie under the table," she replied, draping her trousers neatly over the desk chair.

"And were they?"

"*They* weren't."

"Interesting. You don't suppose Carly's imagining this whole thing, do you? Because Hannah hardly seems like . . . Freeze frame, was someone *else* playing footsie?"

"As a matter of fact, yes." Des pulled back the covers on the bed and dived in, shivering and whooping. "God, it is *freeeezing* in here!"

"Well, who was it? Give it up."

"Not until you get your hot bod in here with me. Come on, move your pink butt. Your girlfriend needs warming up."

Mitch needed no more in the way of encouragement. Quickly, he brushed his teeth, tore off his own clothes and joined her. Des's teeth were chattering, her hands and feet like ice. She snuggled close, one incredibly long, smooth leg thrown over him, her head on his chest. As Mitch held her there under the mountain of covers, warming her, he watched the reflection of the flames dance across the ceiling and walls. He listened to the storm rage outside. And he remembered to be happy. Happy he was sharing this moment with her. Happy that she was such a big part of his life.

And here is what Mitch was thinking: *If only we could stay like this forever. If only things didn't have to change. If only WE didn't have to change. But we do, we do . . .*

"So talk," he said to her. "Give it up."

"It was Norma and Teddy."

"No way."

"Yes way. Norma's stocking toes were in Teddy's lap."

"So the two of them are . . . ?"

"You now know as much as I do."

"Des, can I tell you something I'm not very proud of?"

Her eyes met his slowly in the firelight. "Mitch, you can tell me anything."

"I have trouble picturing two people that age having sex together. I mean, they're as old as my parents."

"Well, you'd better start picturing it," she chided him. "Because you're going to be that age yourself one day, and I expect you to be having sex with me regularly and with great . . ." She drew back from him suddenly. "God, shoot me right now. I can't believe what just came out of my girl hole."

"Which was . . . ?"

"That what we have going is . . . that we might still be together in thirty years. Or thirty days. Make that thirty minutes. I had no business going there. Forget you ever heard it. Erase it from your hard drive, will you?"

"It's a duh-deal . . ." Suddenly, Mitch had great difficulty swallowing. That same damned melon-sized lump had formed in his throat. "You're awfully funny sometimes, know that?"

"Oh, yeah. I'm a regular Henry Youngman."

"It's *Henny* Yuh-youngman," he gulped.

Now she was glaring at him in the firelight. Here it was—Her Wary, Scary Look. "Mitch, have you got something you want to say to me?" she demanded stiffly.

"Absolutely not. Why would you suh-say that?"

"No . . . reason." Her eyes widened with alarm. She'd started breathing in ragged, uneven gasps. Plus her entire body was clenched tight.

"Des, is something wrong?"

"Absolutely . . . not. Why would . . . you . . . ask me that?"

"No reason."

"It's just . . . I'm still cold, that's all." She raised her nightshirt over her head and flung it aside. "Why don't you see what you can do about it?"

"You sure you're . . . ?"

"I'm fine," she purred, her naked body taut and elastic against his, her flesh satiny.

He closed his eyes and buried his nose in the long, sweet hollow of her throat, inhaling the spicy fragrance that made him dizzy with longing.

"Ada likes my work," she whispered after a moment, her breath warm on his face. "She thinks I'm gifted."

"She's right, you are."

"But she wants me to get out of the academy. She thinks they'll try to control me."

"She's right again."

"How will I know when it's time to go?"

"You just will. It's an instinct, kind of like this . . ." He kissed her gently on the mouth, feeling her lips soften and flower under his.

And so they made love together like a couple of eskimos, burrowed deep under all of those covers as the fire warmed their room and the wind howled and the ice pellets smacked against the windows. It was a different kind of lovemaking from what Mitch had ever experienced with Des Mitry. She clung to him with a passion that very nearly overwhelmed him with its urgency. He wasn't sure whether it was to do with the storm, being trapped here. Or if it was about him and that damned lump that kept clogging up his voice box every time he tried to tell her the thing he needed to tell her. They didn't discuss it. Didn't talk at all after that. Just drifted off to sleep, safe and snug together.

The sound of another big tree coming down woke Mitch sometime during the night. He didn't know what time it was, but the fire had burned down to glowing coals by then, and the room was frigid. As he lay there, Des fast asleep next to him, Mitch thought he heard footsteps up above them on the third floor. The floorboards creaked. But it must have been the castle itself creaking in the wind. Because who would be walking around up there in the middle of the night in the dark?

He slid out of bed and piled more logs on the fire and made sure they caught. Then he dived back in, shivering.

Des stirred, semi-awake. "Wha . . . ?"

"Just feeding the fire. Go back to sleep. I'm sure the power will be back on by morning."

But he was wrong. When they woke up in the morning, the power wasn't back on.

And there was one other development that was even more troubling:

Not everyone in the place woke up.

CHAPTER 6

NORMA LAY IN BED with her hands clasped on top of the covers.

Her nightgown was buttoned to her throat, her hair neatly combed, skin and lips slightly blue. Her hand, when Des felt it, was cold to the touch, the fingers beginning to stiffen. Rigor was setting in, which meant that Norma had likely been dead for several hours. Although it was hard to be certain since the room was so chilly.

Des had her shearling coat on, hands stuffed in her pockets as she stood there studying Norma. More than anything else, there was an incredible stillness about death. A stillness that she was never quite prepared for even though she'd seen it many times. Too many times. "This is how you found her?"

"Yes, it is," Les said hoarsely, standing there next to her. It was Les's anguished cries that had roused her shortly after dawn. Roused them all. "It was her heart, Des. She'd had a lot of trouble. A serious attack three years ago. It was just a matter of time, really."

Les and Norma were in the first room at the top of the stairs on the left, room one. It was practically identical to the room Des and Mitch had shared, just slightly smaller. Outside, the morning sky was clear and blue. The sunlight that streamed through the tall, granite-ledged windows seemed impossibly bright after the darkness of the night. The thermometer that was mounted out on the sill said it was three degrees below zero. And that didn't factor in the wind that was still howling. Des could hear the angry whine of a chain saw outside. Jase was trying to do something about those two big sycamores that had come down at the head of the drive. Mitch and Spence were helping him. The others had retreated to the relative warmth of the taproom in stunned silence.

Except for Ada, who lingered there beside Les, staring down at her daughter with a shocked, hurt look on her ancient face. The old director had on cream-colored silk pajamas under a belted robe of heavy navy-blue wool. Her beautiful white hair needed brushing.

"My poor, sweet Norma," she lamented, bending down to kiss her daughter's cold forehead. "I nursed you at my breast while you gazed at me in innocent, trusting wonder. Now look at you, you sad thing. Ran out of time, didn't you?" Ada glanced at Des, a deep, moist sadness in her hooded eyes. "She was just like her father. Luther had it, too."

"Had what, Ada?"

"Heart disease. He died young himself, sixty-three years old. Not a day goes by that I don't miss him."

"She had a valve blockage," Les spoke up. "Her heartbeat was irregular as a result. Cardiac arrhythmia, they call it. She was on medication, and bypass surgery had been strongly recommended, but she wouldn't hear of it. Apparently her father . . ."

"Luther died on an operating table in London," Ada said. "It was supposed to be a routine heart procedure. It wasn't routine. Not unless you consider death routine. Norma was convinced the same thing would happen to her if she went in, so she refused to even . . ." Ada's voice broke, a jagged sob coming from her. "That's my baby girl lying there. A mother isn't supposed to outlive her children. I've outlived them both. First Herbert, now Norma. There is no one left. They're gone. All gone." Ada lingered for a moment longer, then shook herself. "I'll join the others downstairs, if you don't mind."

"That's fine, Ada."

"Des, we need to talk some more, you and I," she said with sudden urgency. "It's vitally important. Later this morning, okay?"

"Sure, if you'd like."

Ada touched her fingers to her own lips, then to Norma's. "Good-bye, my dear. I shall always love you."

"She loved you, too, Ada," Les said softly, as the old lady glided from the room. Then he slumped heavily into the armchair by the bed, his eyes red and pouchy. He was unshaven, his wavy silver hair disheveled. He had dressed hastily in a rumpled Astrid's Castle fleece top and baggy flannel-lined jeans. "She carried too much weight around. Her cardiologist in New Haven, Mark Lavin, kept after her to lose more. She did try, but she just had so much trouble keeping it off."

"Les, I'll need a list of the medications she was on."

"Whatever you say. I used to pick them up for her at the pharmacy, so I ought to know. She took the digoxin for her heart. She also had an underactive thyroid. She took Synthroid for that."

Des glanced at Norma's nightstand. She saw a water glass, half empty, reading glasses, a book. No pills. "And they'd be where?"

"The bathroom. She was also on a couple of different, you know, female drugs—in spite of the negative press they've been getting."

"You mean hormone replacement therapy?"

He nodded. "Prometrium and one other one. Can't remember the name. She swore they made her feel more energetic. She took too much upon herself for a woman in her condition. Long, hard days. Loads of stress. I begged her and begged her to slow down, but she wouldn't. I-I knew there was a chance that this might happen some-day. I just . . . I wasn't ready."

"We never are, Les. Was she feeling poorly yesterday? Did she complain at all?"

"She absolutely never complained. But I did think she looked tired at dinner."

"I remember you mentioning it."

"No question she was under an added strain with this big tribute coming up—Ada being here, not to mention Aaron. I guess it was just too much for her."

"Did she get up at all last night?"

"I wouldn't know. I sleep like a log. You can set off dynamite next to me and I won't wake up. That's the worst of it," he said, ducking his head.

"What is, Les?"

"I was lying right here next to her, snoring away like a big dumb clod, while Norma was fighting for her very life. I wasn't here for her, Des. In her last moments on this earth, she was all alone. I just feel so . . ."

"Responsible? You're not. Don't go there, Les. I'm sure she didn't suffer." Besides which, Des reflected, what could he have done? No ambulance could have made it up there. Not even a Life Star helicopter could have come to the rescue. Not in this kind of wind. And even if they had, chances were the lady would have already been gone. "Don't beat up on yourself. Try to remember the good times."

"We were happy together," he said mournfully. "We only had a few short years, six this coming May. But we were so happy."

Des went over to the window and looked out at the morning sunlight. The world had never looked quite this way before. The sky had never been so blue, the snow so white. The clean hard coating of ice that covered everything positively shimmered. Many, many of the castle's trees, especially the slender, pliable birches, were so bent over from the weight of the ice that their tops had actually frozen to the ground. When they thawed—assuming it ever got that warm again—they would very likely be severely damaged. For now, the sight was simply a breathtaking one. So was the panoramic mountaintop view. The Connecticut River was entirely frozen over. Downriver, where I-95 crossed over on the Baldwin Bridge, not a single car could be seen. The highway was deserted. Beyond that, she could see steam rising off the salt water of Long Island Sound.

"What do we do now, Des?" Les wondered. "I can't imagine Fulton's Funeral Home will be able to make it up here today, can you?"

She turned and faced him and said, "Actually, you're getting a little bit ahead of yourself, Les. I have to phone this in first."

"You do?" His eyes widened in surprise. "What for?"

"It's a state law. Norma didn't die in the presence of a physician. She was unattended. That makes hers what they call an untimely death. It's just a formality, but I have to report it to my commanding officer. Also the medical examiner."

"The medical examiner?" Now Les looked truly aghast. "They're not going to cut her open, are they?"

"I highly doubt that. Not if Dr. Lavin confirms that her death wasn't unexpected. But that's entirely up to the medical examiner. His people will have to come up here and take a look at her. Road conditions being what they are, Norma may have to stay put for a while. Why don't you move some of your things into another room? I need to close this one up."

"Whatever you say," Les said woodenly, getting up slowly out of his chair. "But I'm going to join the others down in the taproom right now, if you don't mind. I can't stay in here with her any longer."

"That's fine, Les. By the way, did you tidy Norma up before the rest of us came in?"

"I did. I wanted her to look nice. Is that okay? I didn't mean to do anything wrong."

"Not at all. I was just curious. Go ahead and go downstairs with the others."

Once he'd left, Des got busy on her cell phone. As she'd suspected, Norma wasn't going anywhere for the next twenty-four to thirty-six hours. Connecticut was officially locked down, its highways and roads closed to all but emergency vehicles. Most residents were still without power. Phone service was spotty. All of this plus the bright blue morning sky was merely a cruel tease—the National Weather Service was still predicting that same six to ten inches of snow later in the morning.

First Selectman Bob Paffin told her that the Center School emergency shelter was up and running, complete with food, cots, blankets and kerosene heaters. Three hundred very cold people were already making use of the facility. Members of Dorset's volunteer fire department and ambulance corps were making sure that anyone else who needed to get there could do so. Des gave him the names of Mitch's three elderly charges. Bob assured her they'd be seen to. Des was pleased that folks in Dorset were so on top of things. And damned frustrated that she couldn't be with them, pitching in.

She tried calling Bella again. This time she got a ring instead of a busy signal. Also a thick, drowsy "Wha . . . ?" from the other end of the crackly line.

"Girl, I don't mean to be a Jewish mother," Des said, greatly relieved to hear her friend's sleepy voice, "but you don't call, you don't write, *nothing*."

"Everything is fine, tattela," Bella assured her, yawning. "The house is fine, I'm fine. Although I must tell you that I am not alone in this bed."

"Shut up! Who's . . . ?"

"All five cats are under these covers with me."

"Oh, I see," Des said, smiling.

"I find this very intimate, also lumpy. And, feh, I have someone's tail in my face. Spinderella, move over, will you? Where are you, Desiree?"

"Stranded up at the castle. The way things look, I may never get out of here. When did you lose power?"

"About nine o'clock. And, believe me, we were very, very lucky. A big oak came down right next door and flattened George's sun porch. But don't worry about a thing. I can make a fire, and I've got enough brisket to feed the entire block. We're okay here."

"Bella, that's the best news I've heard in a while. And I sure can use it."

"Desiree, I don't like what I'm hearing from you. Are you okay?"

"Aside from the fact that our hostess died in the night, I'm just dandy."

"Who, Norma? What happened?"

"Heart attack."

"My God, that's awful. I'm so sorry." Bella paused, clearing her throat. "From your tone of voice, I was thinking it might be something else."

"Like what?"

"Like that other matter we discussed, regarding a certain Semitic gentleman who shall remain nameless. Mitch Berger is who I'm talking about."

"Yeah, I kind of caught that."

"*Nu?* How are you two?"

"Okay, I guess. Maybe you were right. Maybe this stuff's all in my own mind."

"And what does that tell you about yourself?"

"That I'm a whack job, totally demented." Which she totally wasn't. There was still something heavy going on with him. She'd felt it the second he'd made with his Great Big Fat Nothing Gulp in bed last night. Just as she'd felt her own sheer desperation when they'd made love together, her hunger for him so insatiable that she'd nearly bounced the big guy off the ceiling. "But, hey, we already knew that about me," she put in dryly, hearing the creak of a floor-board out in the hallway.

Teddy Ackerman stood there in the doorway in his topcoat, look-ing pale, teary-eyed and utterly grief-stricken.

"I have to go now, Bella. I'll see you as soon as I can. Take care of yourself."

"You, too, tattela."

"How can I help you, Teddy?" she asked him as she rang off.

"Sorry, I didn't realize anyone was still in here," Teddy snuffled, swiping at his eyes. "I just wanted to say good-bye to Norma."

"Come right on in."

He sat on the edge of the chair by the bed and reached for Norma's cold dead hand, gripping it. Outside, Des could still hear the whine of Jase's chain saw.

"You two knew each other a long time, didn't you?" she said, studying him.

"Forty years," Teddy said quietly, gazing at Norma. "That's how long I've loved her. I've always loved her. You see, I'm . . ." He hesi-tated, glancing up at Des uncertainly. "I'm the one who met her first, not Big Paul . . . I'd dropped out of City College. Was bumming my way around Europe, playing the piano for my keep. Not a care in the world." The words were starting to tumble out now. Teddy needed to talk, to tell someone. "Ada and Luther were living in London in those days. That's where I first met Norma. She was home visiting them for the summer. She'd just finished her second year at Barnard. A buddy of mine back in New York told me to look her up because she'd grown up in London, knew the place. She was . . . She was the kindest girl I'd ever met. Not the prettiest. There were always prettier girls. But none sweeter. We spent that summer together in London. When she headed back to school in New York come fall, I followed her. Took classes again myself. Thought about getting my degree, making a life with her. I was going to marry this girl, Des. I even invited her to lunch one day to meet my big brother, the crusading young ACLU lawyer." Teddy paused, swallowing. "The girls always took to Paul. He had those broad shoulders and that curly black hair. I'll never forget when she walked into that restaurant and saw him for the first time. And he saw her. They couldn't take their eyes off each other, Des. From that moment on, I knew she wasn't going to be my girl any longer. She was going to be Paul's. Two weeks after she graduated, she became his wife."

Des found herself studying Norma, trying to see her as Teddy obviously still saw her—not as a jowly, gray-haired older woman but as a lively, smooth-cheeked young girl. She couldn't see it. Hadn't been there, hadn't known her. "Did you ever tell Paul how you felt?"

Teddy heaved a sigh of regret. "No, I bowed out very graciously— told him she and I were just good friends and the coast was clear. There was no point in doing otherwise. You can't stand in the way of such things. Besides, Paul made a better husband than I ever could have. No one ever knew how I really felt. Aside from Norma, that is," he said, gazing at her lovingly. "She always knew. I've never married. Never even had a steady girl. My mother needed taking care of. At least that's always been my excuse. The real reason was Norma. We had a bond. We were soul mates. No other woman could ever come close to her in my eyes. The two of us . . ." Teddy's mouth tightened. "I wouldn't want this to get back to Les, but she and I had been in touch a lot lately."

Des kept her face a blank. "I see . . ."

"We talked on the phone almost every day. Sent each other e-mails. And she came into the city whenever she got a day to herself. We'd spend a few stolen, glorious hours together. She'd listen to me play. I always played "More Than You Know" for her. She loved that song. It was *our* song. I made a tape of myself playing it and gave it to her so she could listen to it here. She told me she listened to it often."

"Teddy, how was her state of mind lately?"

"Not good," he said. "She was unhappy with her marriage. Les had lost interest in her. She put it all on herself, of course. Felt she was no longer desirable, as if such a thing could be possible."

"Is Les seeing someone else?"

"Apparently. But don't ask me who the other woman is, because Norma wouldn't tell me. She wasn't the type to gossip. Took no pleasure in it. She was too busy looking out for others. She *never* looked out for herself. That's the truly tragic part of all of this, Des. You see, last night it was finally, at long last, going to happen."

"What was, Teddy?"

"We'd never made love together. Beyond a few furtive kisses in taxicabs, we'd never done anything about how we felt. Too damned proper. But we'd talked it through and agreed that she was going to come to my room last night, once Les had fallen asleep."

Des wondered if Ada knew about this. Wondered if this was what the shrewd old bird wanted to talk to her about.

"She assured me Les would never notice. Once he's out, he's out. She told me she often got up in the night without disturbing him. Norma was not a sound sleeper. The responsibility of running this place weighed on her, I think. She often made herself a cup of hot cocoa in the night and sat up in the taproom, reading John O'Hara. Her favorite novel of his was *Ten North Frederick*. She must have read it twenty times." Teddy cast a sidelong glance at the book on Norma's nightstand. It was a rather worn hardcover, missing its dust jacket. "I gave her that copy of it last year. It's not the least bit valuable, but I'd like it back if you don't mind. For personal reasons."

Des studied him. He seemed anxious about this. Exceedingly so. "I'd rather not disturb anything just yet."

"Of course. As you wish." Teddy looked back at Norma and said, "I sat up all night waiting for her. I waited and I waited. It was supposed to happen, Des. The one thing I've yearned for my entire adult life. Norma in my arms. Norma mine, all mine. Only, it never did. She never came to my door. I . . . I was crushed. Disappointed beyond belief. You can't even imagine."

Des looked at this thin, pale man in his topcoat, thinking she felt sorrier for him than she'd felt for anyone in a long time. "What did you think when she didn't show?"

"That she'd changed her mind about me," he said morosely. "The only other possibility I could think of was that Les hadn't fallen into his usual deep slumber, what with this storm and all. Maybe he was up and down, feeding the fireplaces. As it turns out, I was wrong on both counts."

"Did you know she had heart trouble?"

"I did," he replied. "Although it was my own feeling that there was nothing physically wrong with her."

"Les said her doctor wanted to operate."

"Doctors always want to operate. That doesn't mean they're right. It's simply all they know. I know better. I know that Norma loved me. I know that she died of a broken heart. I will go to my own grave knowing that."

Outside, the chain saw ceased. Male voices hollered to each other briefly, then it fell silent in the dead woman's room. Eerily so.

"Teddy, may I ask you something that's none of my business?"

He looked up at her curiously. "What is it?"

"If you were so in love with Norma, then why did you let Les move in on her after Paul died? Why didn't you marry her yourself?"

"That's a fair question," he admitted. "The simple answer is that she'd already gotten married again—to Astrid's Castle. And I could never fit in up here. I'm a no-good bum of a piano player. I drink too much, gamble away every penny I make. I could never be an innkeeper, coping day and night with other people's problems, always keeping a smile on my face. No, Les was the right man for her. And they were right for each other, or at least they were for a time. He's just a guy who can't stay married to the same woman for long. Norma was his third wife."

"Does he have children?"

"I believe so, with his second wife. She lives outside of the city somewhere. Nyack, maybe." Teddy stared down at the love of his life, his eyes filling with tears. "But the honest answer to your question is that you're absolutely right—I should have made my move after Paul passed. Grabbed on to this woman and never let her go. But I couldn't. I . . . I was afraid."

"Afraid of what, Teddy?"

"That it would turn out badly. That I couldn't cut it. I lacked the courage, Des. And that's my single greatest regret. Because we all die in the end. Everybody dies. It's the one sure bet we've got going. And if you haven't gone after what you want, *who* you want, if you haven't really, really tried . . ." Teddy trailed off, his chest rising and falling. "Then you've never really lived at all."

CHAPTER 7

"OKAY, THAT MAKES IT official," Spence Sibley announced, shoving his cell phone back in the pocket of his persimmon-colored Patagonia ski jacket. "This weekend's gala tribute is now one hundred percent toast. They were fine with the highways and airports being shut down, no heat, no hot water. That stuff never fazes studio people. They just figure they can throw enough money at a problem and it's solved. But when I told them that there'd been a death in Ada's family, that was pretty much a deal breaker."

"Awfully darned inconvenient for the family, too," Mitch said, breath snorting out of his nostrils as he worked away at a sycamore branch with the heavy-duty pruning saw.

Both of the majestic old sycamores had pitched right over onto their sides, giant root balls and all, leaving craters in the ground big enough to lose a pair of United Parcel Service vans in. Their massive trunks were doing a handsome job of blocking the only way in or out of the castle. A nearby sugar maple had crashed down onto the roof of Choo-Choo Cholly's depot, crunching its snow-capped roof as if it were made of papier-mâché and shaving cream. Farther down the drive, dozens of smaller trees had come down, taking the power lines with them. Once Connecticut Light and Power gave the go-ahead, Jase felt he could horse many of these trees off to the side with the plow blade on his big Dodge Ram 4×4. For now, the three lumberjacks were not going anywhere near them.

"Mitch, I don't mean to sound like an insensitive prick," Spence said, his voice raised over the *varoom* of Jase's chain saw. "It's just that I've been working eighteen hours a day on this for weeks and weeks—twisting people's arms, pleading with them. And now they're not coming. Not Oliver, not Quentin, not anybody."

"Will Panorama reschedule?" Mitch asked as he sawed, sawed, sawed. The blade had wicked jagged teeth that cut right through the pale speckled bark and deep into the wood.

"Oh, who gives a damn," Spence replied, snapping off a two-inch-thick, ten-foot-long branch with Jase's ratcheted tree loppers. They had razor-sharp jaws, and he was working them with intense fury. The young, clean-featured marketing executive was no more Mr. Upbeat Guy. He was Mr. Pissed-off Guy. "It's not like *I'll* be around to see it. *I'll* be frozen solid by the time breakfast is served. They'll find my cold stiff body right here, stuck to the pavement."

Spence wasn't exaggerating by much. It was absolutely frigid out there. The arctic wind gusts cut through every layer of clothing Mitch had on. He'd wrapped his scarf around his head and face so that only his eyes and nostrils were exposed to the elements, and they stung like crazy. His eyes wouldn't stop tearing up. His nose kept running—and then freezing. Under his earflaps, his ears ached. His arm and shoulder muscles cried out in pain. His feet were numb. And the solid ice underfoot was incredibly slippery, even though Jase had laid down a heavy coat of sand and rock salt.

They'd quickly developed a routine. Mitch and Spence stripped away as many small limbs as they could with the pruning saw and loppers while Jase tackled the bigger limbs with his chain saw. Which suited Mitch just fine. He felt roughly the same way around chain saws as he did around loaded handguns. Much of this had to do with the fact that he sat through *The Texas Chainsaw Massacre* seven times in one weekend back when he was in the fifth grade.

Jase had thrown himself into the job with a manic form of abandon. He was obviously very upset about Norma's death, yet when Mitch tried to engage him in conversation about it, Jase had purposely moved away from him, not wishing to share his heartfelt grief. Hard work was Jase's way of dealing. He seemed tireless. Also impervious to the bitter cold. He did have on a pair of buckskin work gloves, but no coat. Merely that same heavy wool shirt he'd worn last night.

Mitch's gloves were suitable for outdoor work. Not so Spence's kid-leather dress gloves. Before they'd gotten started, Jase had led them across the courtyard to his cottage, where he'd fetched Spence a pair of work gloves. It was a low-ceilinged little cottage, smelling of mold and the kerosene space heaters that Jase and Jory had used in the night. Spence had seemed fascinated by the place. His eyes flicked eagerly around the cramped, dingy parlor as if he were taking in the sights of a preserved dwelling at Colonial Williamsburg.

"Well, at least you got your promotion," Mitch reminded him as he kept on sawing, the icy air knifing in and out of his lungs.

"You're right. I got my damned promotion."

"You don't sound so happy about it."

"Right again."

Jase halted his chain-sawing and barked out, "Okay, hold up a sec!" He jumped in his truck and used his plow blade to shove aside the heavy sycamore logs they'd produced. Then he backed up and got out, staring down the frozen, tree-strewn drive with an alarmed expression on his bearded face. "Man, it'll take the crews *forever* to get here. And the more it blows, the slower it goes."

The wind did seem to be picking up new strength, Mitch observed. It was positively roaring its way through the trees that were still standing, making them creak and groan most ominously under the weight of their ice coatings.

"We'll be okay, Jase," Mitch said confidently, even though he himself was quite unnerved to be standing out there under so many trees. He also couldn't help noticing that the bright blue sky was starting to give way to dark storm clouds.

"I could hike my way down to the front gate," Jase volunteered. "It's only, like, three miles. I could make it."

"And do what?" Spence asked him. "Where the hell would you go?"

"He's right, Jase," Mitch agreed. "It's another eight miles to town from there, and no one's out on the road. Besides, it's going to start snowing again."

"I just, Norma wouldn't . . ." Jase broke off, fumbling helplessly for the words. "Norma wouldn't *like* this. How everything looks, I mean."

The young caretaker seemed genuinely distraught. Mostly, it was his grief over Norma, Mitch felt. Partly, it was that Astrid's Castle was his baby. Seeing all of this damage to its grounds was upsetting to him. Mitch understood the feeling. He felt the same way about Big Sister.

"We're going to be fine, Jase," he said, patting him on the shoulder. "We'll get through this."

Jase shook himself now, much like a wet dog, and said, "Enough jawing. Let's get some work done." And with that he clomped on over to the other sycamore and began attacking it with his chain saw.

"Actually, I've been seriously rethinking my move out to L.A.," Spence told Mitch as they returned to their own labors. "The promotion, the whole thing."

"Is that right—how come?"

"The young lady who I'm presently involved with has roots here in the East, and she doesn't want to relocate out there. Not right now, anyway. It's . . . kind of complicated."

"Life can be," Mitch said, working the pruning saw back and forth.

"It didn't used to be. Not for me. I've never let any woman get in the way of my career. They're strictly around for recreational humpage, nothing more. But now that it's *turned* into something more—Mitch, I'm not even sure I know how to describe how much different this all is."

"I'm partial to food analogies, if that's of any help."

"Okay, then here it is," Spence offered. "It's like the very first time you taste fresh store-made mozzarella from one of those delis down in Little Italy. Once you've had the real thing, there's no way you can ever go back to those blocks of bland pale cheese food that you get at the supermarket. Does that work for you?"

Mitch's stomach promptly began to growl. They'd eaten no

breakfast, and he was burning off a ton of calories. "Sure does. How long have you two been together?"

"We've known each other off and on for a number of years. But it's only blossomed into a romance quite recently. She's in the media."

"Anyone I might know?"

"It's . . . kind of complicated," Spence repeated.

"Complicated," said Mitch, who wondered why Spence was being so vague.

"I think about her day and night, Mitch. When I'm not with her, I miss her so much I can barely function. I will be miserable out in California without her—absolutely none of which was part of my plan. I never intended to get this involved."

"Sometimes you have to come up with a new plan," Mitch said, his own thoughts turning to Des and what he'd tried, and failed, to tell her in bed last night. He'd choked, no two ways about it.

Jase had powered his way through a massive log, the two pieces splitting apart. He paused a moment to catch his breath, the chain saw idling in his hands.

"The awful truth is that other women just don't matter anymore," Spence confessed. "Mind you, I'm not about to kick someone soft and warm out of bed on a cold winter night, but the whole time I'm with another woman I'm thinking about *her*."

"You dudes going to work for a living or just talk puss?" Jase growled at them.

"Keep your shirt on," Spence growled back. "We're working plenty hard."

Jase let out a derisive snort, then went back at it.

Spence glanced over his shoulder at the castle, his cheeks puffed out. "Norma dying in her sleep like this, it gives you pause, that's all."

"It does." Mitch's mind paused on Maisie and how quickly he'd lost her. One day they were young and in love, everything sunshine, everything ahead of them. The next day he was a lonely widower sitting by himself in the dark. "And it should, Spence. That's healthy."

"Believe me, what I'm thinking about right now is not healthy.

Not career-wise. But I'm so nuts about this woman that I'm seriously considering turning it down. The very job I've been fighting for these past five years. Totally insane, right?"

"Not if it will make you happy."

"But it'll make me damaged goods, as far as the job is concerned."

"Jobs come and go."

"Mitch, what would you do?"

"That's hard to say, since I don't know the woman." He looked at Spence pointedly. "Or do I?"

"She's in the media," Spence repeated stubbornly. "And it's kind of . . ."

"Complicated, I got that," said Mitch, wondering why Spence wouldn't provide any more details about this woman. Wondering if it was because she was none other than Hannah Lane. Hannah worked in the media. Hannah was living in Washington, D.C. And Spence had known her off and on for years through the Panorama internship program. Toss in that she was presently hooked up with Aaron Ackerman and, well, that sure qualified as one hell of a complication, didn't it?

Question: Was it possible that the talented young filmmaker was romantically involved with both men?

Answer: Hell, yes.

CHAPTER 8

"THIS IS ABSOLUTELY THE best cup of coffee I've ever had in my life," Des exclaimed, because it absolutely was—hot, strong and flavorful. She gulped it down gratefully as she huddled there next to the stove in her big coat, both hands wrapped around the mug for warmth.

Jory had gotten two big kettles of bottled water up and boiling on the kitchen's battered old six-burner propane stove, enough to fill a pair of Melita drip coffeemakers and a ceramic teapot for Ada's Lemon Zinger.

"Coffee always tastes better when it's cold out," she said, smiling faintly at Des.

"Not to mention cold *in,*" added Hannah, who was lending Jory a hand with breakfast.

Actually, Des had barely recognized Hannah without her bright red lipstick and jaunty beret. She also had on a different pair of glasses—slender, contemporary wire rims instead of those heavy round ones she'd worn last night, when she'd seemed to Des like an effete, rather useless trendoid. But stripped of her war paint and Left Bank costume, Hannah looked a lot more useful than she'd first appeared. Narrow-shouldered, yes, but broad through her hips and flanks, with strong wrists and large, knuckly hands that were no strangers to scullery work. She also seemed a good deal younger to Des, not so much a polished young professional as a college girl with chapped lips and a pink runny nose.

"I hate being cold," Hannah confessed, shivering in her navy-blue pea coat. She lit a match to another burner and began laying strips of bacon out in a well-worn cast-iron skillet. "I hate it more than just about anything."

"Once a stone house gets cold, it stays cold," said Jory, who had on a bulky ski sweater, a down vest and fleecy sweat pants. Her curly ginger hair was gathered into a top knot. She seemed very in charge of things in Norma's absence. Her bulldog jaw jutted with determination. Her eyes were still puffy and red, though. She'd done a lot of crying after they'd found Norma. "And it's way hard to warm it back up. I must be wearing six layers."

"I'd settle for one pair of long johns," Des said.

"I can loan you a pair of mine," she offered. "They'd be too short, and kind of huge in the waist, but they'd keep you warm."

"I may take you up on that," Des said, glancing around at the kitchen as she drank her coffee.

Astrid's Castle had two kitchens, actually. There was the one they were in, a homey old tiled farmhouse kitchen, with its double porcelain sink and six-burner range. There was a long cluttered trestle table where the innkeepers grabbed their meals and did their paperwork. There were windows over the kitchen sink. Through them, Des could see across the frozen courtyard to the caretaker's cottage. A door led directly out to the courtyard. Next to the door was a gun case.

Des went over for a closer look. There were two deer hunting rifles in it, a Remington Model 700 bolt-action with a side-mounted thumb safety and a Winchester Model 70 Classic. "Do much shooting up here?"

"We find it necessary from time to time," Jory answered cautiously. "We get foxes and coyotes. City folks with small children don't much care for those. A few years back we even had a bobcat. We always make sure the case is kept locked, and Les keeps the ammunition upstairs."

"He's the hunter?"

"No, Jase is. But Les likes to join him. It makes him feel like the lord of the manor or something."

A mudroom was just off of the old kitchen. There was a deep work sink in there, jackets on hooks, work boots, a five-gallon bottled-water dispenser. The service stairs ran their way through the mudroom—the narrow staff stairs up to the second and third floors as well as the steps that went down to the wine cellar.

The second kitchen, which had been added on in the past few years, was a charm-free stainless-steel restaurant kitchen designed for high-volume, high-speed output. It had multiple stoves and prep stations, a walk-in pantry and freezer, a separate entrance for kitchen staff and deliveries.

This kitchen was not in use. Not a soul was in there.

"When we just have a few guests, we do breakfast ourselves," Jory explained, her gaze following Des's. "The kitchen staff doesn't arrive until later. Of course, today they won't be coming at all. I thought we'd do a big breakfast, get some fuel into everyone. Eggs and bacon, a big pot of oatmeal, bread and jam. Sound good?"

"Like heaven," said Des, helping herself to more coffee.

"I agree," Hannah said as she turned the bacon, which was starting to sizzle and smell sensational.

Jory got a box of Irish oatmeal out of the cupboard and put another pot on the stove. "One good thing I can say about Astrid's is we're always prepared for bad weather. Plenty of food and clean dishes, plus we have gallons of bottled water. That's all we ever pour at the table."

"You folks have trouble with your well?"

"Not usually, no," Jory said, filling an eight-cup Pyrex measure from the water dispenser. "But the coliform bacteria can get a bit iffy during the rainy season, and you don't ever want to send sixty paying guests home with a dose of the trots. You can't afford to take that chance. It's like Norma always says . . ." Jory's voice caught, the emotion welling up in her. "Every guest is our most important guest. Which reminds me. Is Mitch on any kind of a special diet?"

"Yes, he is. It's called the I Never Get Full Diet."

Jory let out a soft laugh. "And how does he take his eggs?

"Any way you cook them, as long as they're good and hot. Mitch hates cold eggs, especially if they're scrambled. He's been known to hold forth for twenty minutes on the subject of cold scrambled eggs and how they taste exactly like . . . Damn, will one of you kindly stick a fork in me? I'm starting to sound just like June Cleaver."

"You are not," Hannah said. "You sound sweet. I wish someone knew my likes and dislikes that well. I wish someone *cared*."

"Me, too," sighed Jory. "That's all I ask for. A man who cares." She stood there with her brow furrowed, taking stock of their progress. "Let's see . . . bacon's going good, and the oatmeal won't take long once this water's boiling. I'll slice up some bread. We can scramble the eggs last, okay?"

"Anything I can do to help?" offered Des.

"We're on it," Hannah said briskly, breaking the eggs into a bowl as she tended to the bacon.

"You seem very at home in a kitchen."

Hannah let out a horsey bray of a laugh. "I should. I started waiting tables when I was sixteen. I've worked short-order, slung beers. You didn't think I was some rich kid, did you? Because I am totally not. My dad works for the U.S. Postal Service. Mom's an OR nurse at Bethesda Medical."

"Is that right?" Des took a seat at the table, keeping her company.

"And do you want to talk lack of cool? When I was at George-town I lived at home in my same old room in my parents' same old tract house in Falls Church. Commuted to and from campus every day in my ten-year-old Honda Civic. Even so, I'll *still* be paying off my student loans until I'm forty. Not that I'm complaining, but nothing ever comes easy for me. Just the good Lord's way of testing me, I guess. Like after I got *Coffee Klatch* made, you know? I figured it was all going to be lollipops and balloons. Development deals left and right. I was *applauded* at Sundance, you know? But you girls can't imagine how hard it is out there in Movietown, U.S.A. How ambitious everybody is. How deceitful." Hannah shook her head as she stood there turning the bacon. "When my internship ended, there was nothing. Nobody wanted me. I was desperate to stay out there, but I couldn't afford to. Before I knew what hit me, I couldn't even scare up my rent money. So I came home with my tail between my legs, moved back in with my folks. I honestly didn't know what I was going to do until I met Aaron. He's been the answer to my prayers. Working with Ada this way is such an incredible opportunity, and Aaron's been . . . you wouldn't believe how sweet he's been."

"Well, you *are* doing him, right?" Jory said. More a statement than a question.

Hannah whirled, gaping at her in shock. "You just said *what* to me?"

"Sorry, I guess that came off a little blunt. But we don't have any secrets in this kitchen. Long-standing castle rule."

"You could have warned a person. And why on earth would you . . . ?"

"I saw you two sucking face on the observation deck yesterday."

Hannah reddened immediately. "Oh . . ."

"As did Carly," Des said. "She mentioned it to me last night."

"This is awful, just awful," Hannah gasped, horrified. "I feel like some kind of steamy Jezebel. And I'm not, I swear. I'm a deeply religious person, and nothing like this has ever happened to me before in my whole life. It's wrong. I know it's wrong. It's just that we're so, well, good together."

"You're actually *into* him?" Jory seemed flabbergasted. "I figured it was strictly business on your part."

Hannah said, "Look, I feel kind of funny talking about this, okay?"

"Sure, whatever." Jory's pot of water was boiling now. She dumped in the oatmeal and started stirring it. "I'm not judging you. We all do what we have to do. Besides, it couldn't happen to a nicer girl. This is me being facetious."

"You don't like Carly?" Des asked her.

"What's to like? She treats people like dirt. Yesterday morning, she *ordered* me to iron her silk things for her—like I'm her personal maid or something. Who the hell does that old bitch think she is? And who does she think she's fooling? She's got so much collagen in her face you can practically hear it sloshing around in there. She didn't so much as thank me when I did do her ironing for her, let alone tip me. Just looked right through me. Take it from me, that woman has zero class. We see all kinds of millionaires up here, heads of big corporations. The ones who have real class treat our staff with respect. They treat everyone that way." Jory glanced at Des uncertainly. "You must know what I mean, being resident trooper in a snooty place like Dorset, and a woman. And, well, you know . . ."

"Black? I absolutely do know what you mean." Des was starting to like Jory Hearn. She was frank. She had brains. She had pride.

"Aaron told me that he and Carly have an open marriage," Hannah blurted out suddenly. "That she's cool with him seeing other women."

"That's sure not what I was hearing from her last night," Des said. "She was talking divorce."

"Carly's going to *divorce* him?" Hannah's tongue darted out of her mouth, wetting her flaky lips. "Man, I really stepped in something smelly, didn't I?"

"That all depends on how you want things to turn out," Des said.

"More than anything in the world, I care about getting Ada Geiger down on film," Hannah said firmly. "And that's the truth. But she doesn't seem at all interested, and it's pretty obvious that Aaron doesn't have much influence with her. It's dawning on me that this may not pan out for me professionally. And that really, really bites, because it's awful tough out there right now in the cold cruel world."

"I sure don't know what *we'll* do," Jory chimed in gloomily, stirring the oatmeal with a wooden spoon. "This place has always been home for both of us. Norma treated us like we were her own children. Now what? Who knows what'll happen to the castle? I'll get by, I guess. But Jase has a hard time in the outside world. The poor thing's so quiet."

"I'm sure you'll both have a place here with Les," Des said.

"But what if Les decides to sell out?"

"Then you'll move on, and survive."

Jory folded her arms in front of her chest, hugging herself tightly.

"Sorry, I don't mean to whimper. I just feel like my whole world is falling apart."

"It's changing," Des said. "And you'll keep changing with it. The day you stop doing that is the day you end up like that nice lady in bed upstairs."

"It's a little scary," Jory confessed.

"Get used to it," Hannah said. "I'm scared every minute of every day."

"You are?" Jory looked at her in surprise. "How do you deal with it?"

"Not very well, apparently. But I keep on going."

"Just forget about the big questions for now, Jory," Des urged her. "Focus on small steps. Right now, we're making breakfast. Later on, we'll do lunch."

"That reminds me," Jory said, nodding her head. "When Mitch was getting his coffee he started talking about making us a giant vat of something called American chop suey."

"That's my doughboy." Des smiled.

"I'm not even sure what that is. Any idea what's in it?"

"Trust me, girl. You don't ever want to know."

Compared to the kitchen, it felt practically tropical in the taproom. A kerosene space heater was putting out genuine warmth, and a fire was crackling in the fireplace. Les and Ada were seated at a table before the fire with Aaron and Carly. Teddy was off by himself in the Sunset Lounge, playing a slow, painfully heartfelt rendition of "More Than You Know."

"Breakfast will be ready soon," Des announced softly.

"Thanks, Des," Les said distractedly, running a hand through his uncombed hair.

"Does Teddy *have* to keep playing that same damned song?" demanded Aaron, the only one of them who was not clad in something warm and fuzzy. He was dressed as he'd been last night, in a crisp dress shirt, bow tie and blazer. Apparently, he never wore anything else. Aaron's unshaven face offered the only hint that this was not a totally normal morning. His stubble was white, in sharp contrast to his jet-black hair and eyebrows. Des couldn't help wondering if he dyed them. "He's been playing it over and over again."

"Leave him be," commanded Ada, who still had on her wool robe. "The music soothes Teddy."

"Well, it's driving *me* nuts. And it's *my* mother who's dead and I think I deserve a little consideration."

"Acky, shut up," snapped Carly. She wore her mink over a bulky white sweater and stirrup pants. Her long blond hair was pulled back into a tight pony tail, and she had on no makeup. Compared to the blond bombshell of last night, Carly looked not only older but surprisingly plain.

Aaron glared across the table at her, his nose twitching. "What did you say to me?"

"She said shut up." Ada calmly sipped her herbal tea. "And that goes double for me. Show some consideration."

"For what?"

"Other people's feelings," she replied, her eyes glinting at him like hard, precious gems.

Des stood there thinking that this shrewd old lady did know about Norma and Teddy.

"Why don't you join us, dear?" she asked Des graciously. "It's so nice and toasty here by the fire."

"Thanks, I think I will." Des pulled up a chair and sat, her muscles feeling stiff and shivery from the cold. The bright morning sunlight had dimmed. The storm clouds were moving in.

"Aaron, there's something serious we need to discuss," Les said uneasily. "It has to do with how Norma wanted to leave things."

"Do you mean her estate?" Aaron arched his eyebrow at him.

Les nodded. "Our attorney here in town, Whit Conover, drew up an agreement when she and I got married. Did Norma ever discuss it with you?"

Aaron shot a curious glance over at Carly before he said, "Why, no." His manner was very guarded now. "Why, Les, was she supposed to?"

"She was, yes." Les sipped at the dregs of his coffee. "She promised me she would. I'm surprised she didn't, given the state of her health. Then again, I guess she didn't want to think about it. We never do, do we? I feel I ought to fill you in now—in my capacity as executor of her estate."

"*You're* the executor?" Aaron appeared thrown by this. "How can you be? Surely you're the beneficiary."

Les shook his head at him. "Six years ago, when things were starting to get serious between us, Norma sat me down in this very room, poured me a Scotch, and said, 'Lester, you may want out when I tell you what I'm about to tell you.' Christ, I thought she was going to tell me she had incurable insanity in her family."

"Oh, she does," Ada said. "Most assuredly."

"She simply wanted me to know that when she died, Astrid's Castle would pass to you, Aaron. She and her brother, Herbert, agreed ages ago that that's how it would be—they'd leave it to their children. Herbert never had any. She had you. Therefore, you now are the sole proprietor of Astrid's Castle."

"Oh my God," Carly whispered, flabbergasted. Des would have paid cash money to see the expression on her face. Too bad Carly couldn't formulate one. All she could manage was a stricken blank.

As for Aaron, he was goggle-eyed, his face drained of color.

"This was understood between us from the get-go," Les explained. "Whit drew up a pre-nuptual agreement specifying it, and I was happy to sign it. It didn't matter to me. *She* mattered." He glanced at Aaron curiously. "You didn't know this?"

"Les, she never said one word to me about it," Aaron said huskily. "I just . . . I assumed you would be taking over. Frankly, I thought that's why you married her."

Les bristled, greatly offended. "Thanks a lot, pal. It's nice to know what you think of me after all of these years."

"Forgive me for being honest, Les," Aaron said. "If you'd rather I lie to you, I certainly will."

"I'd *rather* you go screw yourself."

"Look, I am aware that you were very fond of Mother," Aaron

acknowledged, retreating somewhere over near the neighborhood of an apology. "I didn't mean for that to sound so harsh."

"No, I'm sure you did," Les said angrily. "You're known for choosing your words carefully. Hell, you're goddamned famous for it." Les got up and went over to the window, his shoulders noticeably hunched. In mourning, the ruddy innkeeper seemed older and frailer. "I simply wanted you to know that I'd be happy to stay on in an employee capacity, if you wish," he said, gazing out at the frozen river and the snow-capped hills of Essex beyond. "I'm sure Jory and Jase would like to stay on, too."

"Les, it'll be months before Norma's estate is settled," Carly pointed out. "Aren't we getting a bit ahead of ourselves?"

"Not if Aaron wants to keep the inn open while we're in probate," he replied. "Our food and liquor suppliers will have to be taken care of, our kitchen staff paid. We're running a business here."

"Well, I certainly don't wish to run it," Aaron said loftily.

"Like I said, I'm happy to stay on," Les persisted. "But I can't access the inn's accounts without some form of temporary legal authority. We have to sit down with Whit and draw up an agreement."

"Les, my mother is dead upstairs," Aaron said frostily. "I don't wish to talk about food and liquor suppliers right now, okay?"

Les held up his hands in a gesture of surrender. "Fine, some other time. But if it's not soon then I'll have to contact the guests who've booked reservations and tell them we're shutting down."

"Do not try to strong-arm me," Aaron warned him.

"I'm not trying to strong-arm you, Aaron. I'm simply explaining the reality of our situation to you so we can deal with it responsibly. This mattered to Norma. It mattered a great deal."

"Relax, Acky." Carly reached over and patted Aaron's hand. "Les is just as upset as you are."

"I should think more so," Ada said. "After all, he's the one whose life has been turned completely upside down."

"Wait one second . . ." Aaron said suddenly, his eyes narrowing at Les. "It just occurred to me what this is all about. You're afraid I'm going to sell this place to some big hotel chain, aren't you? And then you'll be out of a job and a home. That's what this is really about, am I right, Les? Tell me I'm right."

Les refused to respond. Just moseyed over to the pool table and rolled a ball against a cushion, watching as it caromed back toward him.

"I have no intention of selling Astrid's Castle," Aaron assured him. "Mother would want it to stay in the family. As far as I'm concerned, you can continue to run it for as long as you choose."

"Thank you, Aaron," Les said faintly. "That's good to know."

"After all, I happen to enjoy a seven-figure income," Aaron boasted. "It's not as if I'll need the money anytime soon—or ever, for that matter."

Ada let out a heavy sigh. "Dear Norma was right. You *are* very young, Aaron."

"What's that supposed to mean?" he demanded.

"It means, dear boy, that it is always a mistake to predict one's own future. Because if you can imagine it happening, if it is rational and makes good sound sense to you, then that is not what will happen."

Aaron frowned at her. "What will?"

"*Life* will."

A life, Des reflected, in which Carly might very well decide to hire herself that shark lawyer and divorce him, in which case *she* could end up with the seven-figure income he so enjoyed. Hell, she might even end up with Astrid's Castle.

Des heard some polite throat clearing and turned to find Jory standing there in the taproom doorway, an ingratiating smile on her face. Des wondered if she'd been there long enough to overhear that Aaron would be the new lord and master of Astrid's Castle.

"Les, I'll be plating breakfast in five minutes," she informed him, her pink-cheeked face betraying not a thing. "And, believe me, the food won't stay hot for long."

"Thank you, Jory. You'd best let the boys know, too."

"Hannah's outside fetching them."

Now Des heard the stamping of feet out in the entry hall and the resounding echo of husky male voices.

Hannah appeared behind Jory in the doorway. "I encountered very little resistance when I said the words 'hot' and 'food,'" she reported.

"I believe I shall dress," Ada announced, getting slowly to her feet. "I can't stand to eat in my bathrobe. It's a detestable habit."

"Don't take too long, Ada," warned Jory as the old lady wafted past her. "Or your food will be ice cold."

"Feel free to start without me," Ada said with a dismissive wave.

The rest of them started out of the taproom in the direction of the dining hall, where the lumberjacks were trying to warm themselves before a roaring fire, all three of them looking frozen and starved. With his full beard and stocking cap, Jase looked as if he'd just wandered in from the Great North Woods. He also gave off a noticeably gamy odor.

"Hey, Master Sergeant," Mitch exclaimed, his frigid hands held out toward the flames.

"Back at you, Mr. Bunyan."

Teddy wandered in as well, furrows etching his long thin face. He seemed lost in his grief, very far away.

"I think I'll go upstairs for a minute, too," Hannah decided. "Try and do something about my face."

"Good," barked Ada, who was gliding toward the stairs. "Without your makeup on, you look as if you belong behind the counter of the Burger King."

Hannah immediately rolled her eyes at Jory.

"I saw that, Hannah," Ada snapped at her.

"Aha, so you *do* know my name," Hannah said, pursuing Ada to the stairs.

"Of course I do. What I don't know is why the hell you were hired. Pick up your feet when you walk, girl. You tromp around the house like an army of Huns."

"Yes, Ada."

"And stop crowding me, will you? I cannot abide hoverers."

"Think I'll clean up myself," said Spence, following them up the stairs.

"*You* I don't like, period, Mr. New York Office," Ada growled at him.

"What on earth did I do?" wondered Spence, bewildered.

"You smile too much," she told him as they disappeared upstairs. "Every studio man who ever stole money from me just smiled and smiled."

Aaron stood there in the dining hall doorway, shaking his large head. "I would not have thought this possible, but I swear she's getting nastier."

"That's just her grief talking," Teddy said quietly. "The old girl doesn't mean one word of it. Just give her some space."

"Fine by me," Aaron said. "She can have as much space as she wants."

Jase moved over next to Jory and spoke to her, his voice a faint murmur, his eyes cast shyly down at the floor.

Jory listened to him intently before she turned to Les and said, "Do you mind if I serve Jase, too? Our stove out in the cottage is electric, and the poor thing's famished. He can eat out in the kitchen with me."

"Nonsense," Les said. "He'll eat with us in the dining room. You both will. You're family."

"That's very kind of you, Les," she said. "Sweetie, could you maybe wash up a bit? There are some Handi Wipes out in the mudroom. I'll show you, okay?"

Jase nodded and started for the kitchen, rolling up his sleeves. Jory followed him.

"Do you suppose he eats with his hands or with his feet?" Carly wondered aloud, her voice dripping with sarcasm.

Des wasn't sure if Jase heard the nasty little crack, but Jory sure as hell did—she shot a poisonous look at Carly as she passed through the kitchen door.

"Cut him some slack," Mitch spoke up in Jase's defense. "He's a good guy."

"He smells like an animal at the zoo," Carly pointed out. "Believe me, when I was growing up in Virginia we had a name for people like that."

"And believe me, we really don't want to hear what it was," Les said coldly. "So kindly spare us."

Carly went ballistic in response: "You were right last night, Acky," she hissed, seething. "We shouldn't have come here. No one wants us here. They hate us. They all hate us!" She turned on her heel and stormed off in the direction of the main stairs.

"Carly, where are you going?" Aaron called after her. "*Carly . . . !*"

"No, let her go." Les took Aaron by the arm, holding him there. "It's a stressful time for all of us."

"Carly happens to be *my* wife, Les. I'll thank you to stay out of my marriage."

"You could use some help, my boy," Teddy advised. "You've pretty much made a mess of it."

"And how would *you* know? Have you ever even been in a relationship that's lasted for longer than seven minutes in the front seat of a car?"

Teddy stiffened but didn't respond. Which made him a true gentleman in Des's book.

Les turned to Mitch and said, "I'm sorry I've been of no help to you guys out there. I feel pretty darned useless."

"As do I," Teddy said. "Mind you, I haven't done any serious physical work in ages. You'd probably have to carry me inside on a stretcher within a half hour."

"Not to worry," Mitch assured them both. "The three of us are making excellent progress. At the rate we're going, we should have those sycamores completely cleared away by the end of March."

Les let out a halfhearted chuckle. "The power crews will dig us out before you know it."

"The sooner the better," Aaron grumbled. "All I want is to get Mother in the ground and me and Carly the hell out of here."

"Believe me, we all want that," Teddy concurred.

Aaron arched his brow at him. "I know you think you're being terribly amusing, Uncle Teddy, but I will not take this crap from you. I'll have you know that there are plenty of people—influential, powerful people—who actually respect me."

"Only because they don't know you as well as we do," Teddy said. "But give them time, my boy. They'll come around."

"Where *did* Carly go?" Aaron wondered, ignoring him now. Or at least pretending to. "I'll bet she's sneaking a cigarette." He started toward the stairs after her. "*Carly . . . ?*"

"I'm going to help Jory with the serving, if you'll excuse me," Les said. "Would you folks care to listen to the news or some music? The batteries on the sound system are good and charged."

"I'd rather listen to the wind," responded Teddy.

"Sure, whatever you want." Les headed off to the kitchen.

Teddy lingered there before the fire with Des and Mitch. "Seriously, what kind of progress are you boys making out there?"

"Seriously? We might be here for a couple of days."

"Damn."

"Somewhere you need to be?" Des asked Teddy.

"Sig Klein's," he replied glumly. "I don't get paid if I don't sell clothes. And this weekend is a total washout as far as my Jazzmen gig is concerned. Not that I mean to sound petty. It's just that we all have our lives to lead, and mine isn't particularly well-funded right now, sad to say. I have to think about these things. I have to . . ." Teddy trailed off mid-sentence and went over toward the windows to look out at the darkening clouds.

Mitch and Des were alone now before the fire. He immediately put his arms around her and hugged her tightly, his unshaven cheek rough and cold against hers.

"Are you happy to see me or are you just looking for a warm-up?" she wondered, hugging him back.

"Does it matter?" he murmured, his mouth finding hers, kissing hers.

"Not one bit."

"Des, you're putting me on another diet when we get out of here. I don't ever want to end up like Norma—wheezing, laboring, *dead*."

"That's good, baby. I don't want you to either."

"But is there any way we can work just a single glass of chocolate milk per day into this one? Along with the skinless chicken breasts and all of that leafy stuff, I mean."

"I'll do some research and get back to you," she said, unable to keep a silly smile off her face.

"It's snowing again," Teddy declared from the windows.

They joined him, gazing out at the wet snowflakes that were beginning to fall on top of the hard coating of ice.

"Ain't it lovely?" Teddy cracked.

"Yeah, it's a winter wonderland, all right," Mitch responded.

Their table was all set for breakfast. Jory emerged from the kitchen lugging the oatmeal in a big serving tureen. Les followed her a few seconds later with covered platters of eggs and bacon.

"Don't wait for the others," Les urged them as Jory bustled back into the kitchen. "Dig right in. This stuff's no good cold."

"You got that right," Mitch concurred, taking the same seat he'd had at dinner. "If there's one thing I can't abide, it is cold scrambled eggs. In my opinion, if they aren't piping hot they taste exactly like yellow rubber that's been vulcanized and then subjected to high-level centrifugal—"

Unfortunately, Mitch never got to finish sharing his strongly held personal philosophy on non-hot scrambled eggs with Les and Teddy.

Because now was when they heard the scream.

CHAPTER 9

ADA GEIGER'S KILLER USED her bedside telephone.

The phone cord was wrapped so tightly around the old lady's throat that it had become embedded deep in her flesh. The receiver on the floor next to her was bloodied. So was the back of her head. The Queen of the B's lay on her side next to the bed, half-dressed. She wore a long-sleeved undershirt and unbuttoned wool trousers. A heavy wool cardigan was strewn across the bed, as if she'd been about to put it on when she'd been rudely interrupted.

Very rudely interrupted, Mitch thought as he stood watching Des examine her.

The others were gathered outside the open door in the hallway in horrified silence. They were all out there. Hannah, whose screams had brought them running. Aaron and Carly, Les, Teddy, Spence, Jory and Jase. The scene was almost an exact replay of earlier that morning, when they'd been gathered outside of the room right next door. No one was saying a word. Partly out of shock. Partly because Des had asked them not to until she'd taken their individual statements—each was a potential witness to Ada's killing and she did not want them coloring each other's recollections. But mostly, they were hushed by the reality of what they all knew:

One of them had murdered Ada Geiger in cold blood within the past five minutes.

It had to be one of them. No one else was around, not unless somebody was hiding there in the castle's deepest recesses, unbeknownst to all of them. Actually, this nutty notion did trigger a fleeting recollection of something that had happened to Mitch in the night. But the memory vanished before he could fully summon it, shoved aside by the overwhelming revulsion and sorrow he felt as he gazed down upon this gifted, indomitable woman lying there dead on the carpet.

Des crouched over Ada, studying the phone cord around her throat, the bloody wound to her head. She opened an eyelid and examined the pupil. "We have hemorrhaging in the eyes," she told Mitch, keeping her voice very low.

"What does that tell you?" he croaked. He had a hot, bilious taste in the back of his throat.

"It points to strangulation, not the head wound, as cause of death. The small blood vessels in the eyes tend to burst under extreme pressure. Plus her head's still bleeding. She was struck with that receiver before she died."

"How do you know that?"

"The heart's no longer pumping blood after someone's gone. So there's little or no blood. If it bleeds it leads—that's our old crime scene saying."

"I thought journalists owned that expression, vis-à-vis our news priorities, or total lack thereof. We tend to be drawn to the gory, as you may have noticed if you've ever picked up a newspaper, turned on a television or . . ." He was starting to blather. He knew this. He was shaken.

Not Des. She seemed cool, alert and focused. She had, after all, spent years working violent deaths for a living. But on the inside she wasn't calm at all, and Mitch knew that. Because it was precisely this kind of hideous, gut-wrenching violence that had driven her to the drawing pad.

"Most likely," she concluded, "the killer dazed her with the phone receiver, then used the cord to finish the job. Quick and quiet. See those scratches there under the cord?"

Mitch forced himself to look. There were bloody scratch marks on Ada's neck. Many bloody scratch marks. "What do those tell you?"

"That she was still conscious." Des studied Ada's hands. "See this blood and tissue under her nails? I'm guessing it's her own. She made those scratches herself, Mitch. The old girl put up a fight." Now Des stood back up and moved away from Ada over to the window. Outside, the snow was falling heavier, the wind gusting hard enough to rattle the glass.

Mitch joined her there, keeping his voice low. "Let's say she did struggle—could a woman have done this to her? Or are we strictly looking at a man?"

"I don't see why it couldn't have been a woman, provided she's reasonably strong. Ada may have been full of piss and vinegar, but she was still ninety-four years old. Straight up, I don't believe we can rule out anyone yet," she said, letting out a sigh.

Mitch looked at her. "Are you okay, Des?"

"Good. I'm good. But I can't say a whole lot for our situation. We've got us two murders, and until this damned weather eases off I can't dial up any backup. We're strictly on our own here."

"Okay, I have to ask you to hit your rewind button."

"Why?"

"You just said we have *two* murders."

"Well, yeah. A mother and daughter dying within hours of each other this way—you don't think it's a coincidence, do you? The very first thing I learned on the job, boyfriend, is that there's no such as thing as coincidences. Someone wanted both Ada and Norma dead."

"But I thought Norma died of a heart attack."

"An *apparent* heart attack. That's what it was meant to look like. But I guarantee you she was murdered."

"How?"

"Can't answer that yet. We may not know until we get the results of her autopsy. We know very little right now, I'm sorry to say. Except we do know this: We know that no one can get in or out of this place. And we know that one of the people who we're trapped with up here is a murderer."

Mitch puffed out his cheeks, exhaling slowly. "I hate to be the bearer of bad news, but I've seen this movie before," he said grimly. "Except it took place on a remote island instead of a mountaintop. And everyone, not just Norma, had a British accent."

"Mitch . . . ?"

"And there was no such thing as cell phones back then, which changes the dynamics rather dramatically, don't you think? Because they couldn't call out and you can. You *can* call out, can't you?"

"For as long as my charge lasts. So far, so good."

"Plus you have the two-way radio in your cruiser."

"True again," she acknowledged patiently. "Only, Mitch . . . ?"

"Yes, Des?"

"This is not a freakin' movie!"

"Hey, I'm totally aware of that."

"Good, because there's no one else I can count on. There's you and, well, there's you."

"I'm all yours, Des. But you do realize that this sort of thing never happened to me before you came into my life, don't you?"

Right away Des Mitry stiffened and made with her Wary, Scary Look, those pale green almond-shaped eyes of hers searching his face, studying, probing. "Mitch, are you trying to tell me something?" she demanded.

"Like what?"

"Like you're sorry that you met me."

"Not in a million years, slimbo. Where would you get a crazy idea like that?"

"I just can't imagine."

"So where do we start?"

By Des grabbing Ada's room key from the nightstand and heading briskly for the door. "I need to get witness statements from those people, one by one. You need to keep an eye on everyone else while I'm doing it, okay?"

"Let's do it."

They joined the others out in the corridor, Des locking Ada's door behind her and pocketing the key. She glanced from one stricken face to the next, taking the measure of each of them. Mostly, there was a lot of fear. Aaron and Carly were holding hands so tightly that their knuckles were white. Jory and Jase were huddled together like a pair of wide-eyed schoolchildren. Spence and Hannah stood together, too, tight-lipped and tense. Teddy leaned against the wall next to them, looking overwhelmed. Les stood a bit apart from the rest of them with his hands in his pockets, watching Des expectantly. No one spoke. All eyes were fixed on Dorset's resident trooper.

It was Aaron who finally broke the silence. "I demand to know what you are intending to do about this."

"Everything I can. My very best." Des turned to Hannah and said, "You're the one who found her?"

"Yes, that's right," Hannah gulped, shuddering. "I . . . I was just in my room for a minute, putting on my face."

Which she indeed had, Mitch observed. Eye makeup, lipstick, rouge, even those retro round glasses of hers. Mitch had actually preferred how Hannah had looked without all of that on—more serious, less like somebody in costume. But he'd never cared much for makeup on women. Des rarely wore any. Maisie never had.

"You were alone in your room?" Des asked her.

"Well, yeah. Why would anyone be with me?"

"Which one are you in?"

"I'm right here in four," Hannah said, gesturing to the door across the hall from Ada's. Teddy was next door to Hannah in two, directly across from Les and Norma. "I was starting my way back downstairs and I noticed that her door was part open, so I stopped to ask if she was ready to head back down."

"How come you did that?"

"Well, I did work for the woman, in theory. Although she wouldn't let me do a darned thing no matter how hard I tried to . . ." Hannah broke off, wringing her hands. "All I did was find her. She was there on the floor. Really, I have no idea what happened. And I'm sorry I screamed like that. I just couldn't help myself. I mean, I've never seen anyone like that before."

"That's okay, Hannah," Des assured her. "Not to worry. Did you hear any noises coming from her room before you found her?"

Hannah shook her head. "No, nothing."

"These walls are very thick," Les spoke up, his voice strained.

"How about out in the hallway?" Des asked her. "Do you remember hearing any doors open or close, footsteps, anything like that?"

"Well, yeah," Hannah replied, nodding her head convulsively. "All of those things. Everybody was coming and going before breakfast, getting dressed or cleaned up or whatever. Well, not everybody, but lots of people."

Des turned to Les now and said, "I need to seal off rooms one and three. No one goes in or out but me."

"Of course, whatever you say." Les's face dropped. "Wait, what *are* you saying?"

"It's pretty obvious, isn't it?" Teddy said. "She's saying Norma was murdered, too."

"Norma had a heart attack," Les insisted. "Her heart gave out."

"Les, we don't know what happened," Des said evenly. "And under these circumstances, Norma's death now has to be considered suspicious. That makes her room a crime scene just as Ada's is. This is not me passing judgment. It's just me following standard procedure. I need to lock down those rooms, and you need to provide me with every key you have for them. Also your master keys. And Jory, could you please open up—let's see—four more rooms for me?"

Jory had a big jangly key chain stuffed in the pocket of her down vest. She used her master key to unlock the two vacant rooms next to Mitch and Des's, eight and ten. Aaron and Carly were across the hall in five, Spence in seven. Jory unlocked nine and eleven, then handed over her keys to Des. Jase forked over his own large key chain, although very reluctantly, as if he were giving up a piece of himself.

"I've already put Norma's keys in the top drawer of the reception desk," Les said as he gave Des his own set. "There's one more master key down there, plus all of the room keys, of course. If you'd like, I can go fetch them."

"That's okay, I'll take care of that myself in a minute. Right now, I want each of you to hold your hands out like this . . ." Des straightened her arms out before her, palms downward.

"What on earth for?" Carly asked.

Mitch knew what for. He'd seen the claw marks that Ada had made to her own neck when someone was choking the life out of her. It was very possible she'd left her mark on her killer's hands, too.

"Please, just do what I ask," Des said in response.

They all obliged.

Slowly, she went from person to person, studying each pair of hands closely, her own clasped behind her rather like a stern headmistress. "Now palms up, please," she requested, repeating the drill. Des studied their faces and necks as well, making sure she looked each and every one of them right in the eye. Carly seemed to shrink under her steady gaze. Aaron bristled, defiant and twitchy. Hannah shook with fear. Spence acted curious more than anything else. Les responded with placid acceptance. So did Jory. Jase, meanwhile, seemed to have withdrawn inside of himself. His eyes never left the floor. His rough, red hands revealed no fresh scratches, however. Nor did Teddy's hands, which seemed so slim and delicate next to Jase's. Teddy's gaze was that of a man who was hurting more than he could bear.

If Des had been hoping that Ada's strangler would panic and blurt out a guilt-racked confession, well, that wasn't about to happen. Whoever it was, this was not merely a ruthless murderer but a consummate actor. Someone who could stick to the script, play the part, bluff his or her way through.

And Des found no visible scratches on any of them. The killer must have worn gloves and ditched them somewhere, Mitch figured.

"Okay, I need you folks to go your rooms now," Des informed them. "I'll be taking witness statements from each of you. The way this works, it's one person to a room. So Aaron and Carly, you'll have to split up. One of you can have your regular room, the other can take room eight. Les, you're in room ten."

"Des, do we have to split up, too?" Jory asked, meaning her and Jase.

"I'm afraid so. You'll be in nine, Jase in eleven."

"We really shouldn't be separated." Jory glanced over at her brother, whose eyes were still fastened on the carpet. "It's not a good idea."

"Why, what's the problem?" Des asked her, frowning.

"It's not a problem so much as it is a . . ." Jory hesitated, then backed down. "Well, okay. If it's just for a little while."

"Is it just me or does all of this seem a bit extreme?" Spence wondered aloud.

"The word I'm thinking of is cruel," Carly said.

"Outrageous," Aaron concurred, nodding his big meaty head.

"You're absolutely right," Des said. "Murder *is* outrageous."

"Honestly, Des, we're all cold and famished and terribly frightened," Carly said. "And instead of offering us comfort you're banishing us to solitary confinement. Why can't we just gather together in the taproom? There's a fire, food. We can console one another."

"Not just yet," Des replied.

"Well, why not?" Aaron demanded.

"You're witnesses, that's why," Des told him, refusing to be budged. "Look, I know these rooms are unheated. I know you're all hungry and scared. But the simple truth is that two women are dead. My job is to figure out why, and your job is to cooperate with me. If you don't, then you're impeding an official state police investigation. I promise you this won't take long. Besides, it's for your own protection."

"She's right about that part," Hannah allowed. "At least we'll be safe this way. Should we bolt our doors?"

"You can if it will make you feel better. As long as you stay in your rooms, you should be fine. Oh, until we're done, I'll also need your cell phones."

"But I have calls to make," Spence protested.

"No calls. Please hand over your phones to Mitch right now."

Reluctantly, they did so. Although, when Mitch arrived at Aaron, he encountered major resistance.

"Why doesn't *he* have to sit in a cold room by himself?" Aaron groused, refusing to hand over his phone.

"Because he's the only person besides myself who I know for certain is innocent," Des replied.

"And just exactly how do you know that?"

"He and I were together downstairs when Ada was killed, that's how."

Aaron considered this for a moment before he grudgingly shoved his phone at Mitch, who was busy thinking that one other person had in fact been with them at the time of Ada's death: Teddy had been in the dining room that whole time, watching the snow outside the windows. But Teddy was not exactly a bystander to these proceedings. He was a member of the family, and therefore could be a part of whatever, whoever was apparently trying to destroy it, one life at a time.

"Please go to your rooms now," Des said to them. "I'll be in to take your statements soon."

There was some further grumbling, but not much. There was too much fear present. Several of them double-locked their doors behind them. Mitch wasn't sure how many.

Teddy lingered in the doorway of room two. "Des, I wonder if I might have a quick word with you," he said to her in a soft voice.

"What is it, Teddy?"

"Do you remember how I told you I was awake last night, waiting for . . . ?" Teddy glanced at Mitch, coloring slightly. "For Norma to come to me?"

"Yes, I remember."

"At about two-thirty I heard Les and Norma's door open and close, followed by footsteps. I was expecting my own door to open, but that didn't happen . . . She went downstairs instead."

"How do you know this? Did you follow her?"

"I never left my bed. But I could hear her. That old staircase creaks like crazy."

"I see," Des said thoughtfully. "Why didn't you mention this to me earlier?"

"The specifics didn't seem worth mentioning. But things are different now, aren't they?"

"They are."

"Teddy, how can you be sure it was Norma who you heard?" Mitch asked. "How do you know it wasn't Les?"

"You're absolutely right," Teddy admitted. "I don't know that. I'm simply assuming it, since Norma often went downstairs in the night. Les seldom does. But wait, there's more—I also heard another

143

door open and close a few minutes later, followed by more footsteps heading downstairs."

"Whose?" Des asked.

"Ada's."

Des studied him intently. "You're sure about this?"

"Positive." Teddy looked across at room three. "It was her door and her footsteps. The old girl had an unusually light tread. You may have noticed."

"Oh, I noticed," Des said. "You believe Ada followed Norma downstairs, is that it?"

"Yes, I do," Teddy said.

"Did you hear them come back up?"

"After maybe a half hour," he replied, nodding. "Ada came back up first. I could hear her door open and close. I figured Norma would wait awhile downstairs for her to go back to sleep. Then she would, you know, come to me. But that didn't happen. She returned to her own room a moment or two after Ada did and never came back out again. I fell asleep shortly thereafter," Teddy said dejectedly. "May I go down and play now?"

Des frowned at him. "Play?"

"The piano. I get terribly uneasy if I'm away from the keys for long."

"I'm afraid not, Teddy. I need you in your room. But I would like to borrow your desk chair, if you don't mind."

Teddy didn't mind. She took the wooden chair and carried it out into the hall, then closed Teddy in his room. She and Mitch were all alone in the hall now.

"This is for you." She positioned the chair at the top of the stairs, facing the corridor. "I have to go downstairs real quick and radio this in. Can you make sure no one leaves their rooms while I'm gone?"

"Not a problem. If you need it, there's an ice pick under the tarp in the back of my truck. Also a scraper. And, hey, you'd better take this," he offered, fishing his battery-powered lock de-icer from his pocket.

"I'm all set," she said, patting her coat pocket. "What I wish you had on you was a weapon."

"Des, that's just not me."

"There's a couple of hunting rifles in the kitchen."

"No way. I don't believe in guns."

"Mitch, this isn't about guns. It's about protection."

"I'll be fine."

"Okay, suit yourself." She lingered there at the top of the stairs for a moment, furrowing her brow. Mitch knew why. She needed to spitball. When she'd worked Major Crimes she'd had her partner, Soave, to bounce her ideas off. Right now, she had only the lead film critic for the most prestigious of New York City's three daily newspapers. "I'm thinking that more than one person may be behind this," she said to him slowly.

"Why would you think that?"

"Because Ada said *they* to me," she replied. "Last night in the ladies' lounge. We were talking about my work, or so I thought, when out of nowhere she said, 'They will never, ever get it.' Meaning this castle, I think. She was so cryptic about it, I wasn't positive. I even wondered if maybe she wasn't completely together in the head. But now I'm thinking that she *knew* something. Maybe something Norma told her. Something that got both of them killed. Ada wanted to have more words with me this morning. She was quite insistent about it. And whatever those words were, she didn't want to say them in front of Les."

"I wonder how come."

"I wish I knew. I wish I'd managed to get her alone for a few minutes. But I didn't. And that one's on me."

"Don't go blaming yourself for this, girlfriend."

"Mitch, I can't help how I feel."

"If Ada didn't want to speak to you in front of Les, then we have to take a good hard look at him, don't we?"

"For sure. Only, what's his motive?"

"You said it yourself. This place—it's worth millions."

"Not to Les it's not. Aaron gets it all. Les knew that. He's the executor of Norma's estate."

"Then that makes Aaron the prime candidate, no?"

"Aaron has the most to gain from Norma's death," Des acknowledged. "Plus he has a girlfriend and a way pissed-off wife. Hell yeah, he's our early front-runner."

"Do we know exactly where he was when Ada got strangled?"

"He went upstairs looking for Carly is all we know right now." Des started for the stairs, then stopped. "We do know something else—we know that the first murder was planned and the second one wasn't."

"And how do we know that?"

"Because whoever killed Norma would have gotten away with it if they hadn't gone and killed Ada, too. Most likely, there'd have been no autopsy of Norma. Now there will definitely be one. And it will definitely turn something up. Count on it. The only way something this stupid goes down is if the play is blown. I'm talking total desperation, as in Ada accidentally seeing something, maybe. Something so heavy that the risk of her spilling it outweighed the risk of exposing Norma's death to scrutiny. Real world, that is my idea of *beyond* desperation. That is plain, pure loco. Because, damn, we are snowed the hell in up here. No way Ada's murder doesn't fall on *somebody*." Des shook her head disgustedly. "All right, enough of this. I'd better go do what I've got to do. Watch my back, okay?"

"Absolutely. There's nothing in the whole world I enjoy more than watching your back—with the possible exception of watching your front."

She stood there looking at him as if *he* were the loco one.

"Sorry, I blather when I'm knocked out of my comfort zone. I know this about myself." He parked his generous bottom in the chair, facing the hallway.

"You're doing good, baby," she assured him. "It's going to be okay."

"Sure it will."

Des was halfway down the stairs before she abruptly stopped and returned and said, "Okay, I have to know how it turns out."

"How what turns out, Des?"

"This old movie of yours."

"Trust me, you really don't want to know that."

"Yes, I do."

"No, you don't."

"Yes, I do."

"Well, okay, you asked for it," Mitch said, clearing his throat. "No one gets out alive."

"Oh, that's just great."

CHAPTER 10

"WE ARE ALL VICTIMS in the end."

Des photographed Ada Geiger's body from a dozen different angles with the digital camera that she kept in the trunk of her cruiser. She moved nothing as she snapped her pictures, and she touched nothing. That would be a job for the crime scene technicians when they got there—if they got there. For now, her job was to produce photos and protect the scene, even though what she really wanted to do was sit down with her 18-by-24-inch Strathmore 400 drawing pad and a piece of graphite stick. She yearned to capture the spirit of fight that remained in Ada's ancient, intricately lined face. The absence of fear in that face despite the certainty of what was coming.

Acceptance without surrender.

This was the essence of Ada Geiger in death. Yes, there was the unfathomable stillness. But there were also courage, defiance. Even in death, Ada Geiger *spoke*. And Des felt a desperate need to *listen* with her graphite stick. But there was no time for that now. It would have to wait for later, when she could take heed in her studio with these photos pinned to her easel.

Right now, she had a killer to catch.

Des took a quick look around for the gloves that Ada's killer must have worn, taking care not to disturb anything. She found none. She did take the time to glance under the bed for them—a ritual of hers that dated back to one of the first cases she'd caught as a rookie in uniform. She'd found an East Granby woman lying dead on the bedroom floor of her home, stabbed sixteen times in the chest and neck. Des did not see the murder weapon anywhere. She was just about to call it in when, strictly as an afterthought, she'd thought to glance under the bed. That was where she found the bloody knife. If she hadn't done that, she would have looked like a consummate bimbo when the Major Crime Squad people got there and found it. She'd never have lived that down. So she always looked under the bed when she caught a murder. Call it a superstition.

There was nothing under Ada's bed.

Des went back out in the hall now and locked the door behind her. She stretched a length of yellow crime scene tape across the doorframe, sealing it off.

"Find anything?" Mitch asked anxiously from his guard post at the top of the stairs.

"Not so much as a dust bunny."

She unlocked the room next door and went in to photograph Norma, well aware that this crime scene had already been thoroughly compromised. Les had been alone in here with her before he'd called out to them. Hell, he had been in the damned bed with her. Ada had come in to say good-bye to Norma, as had Teddy.

When Des was done snapping her photographs, she slipped on a pair of latex gloves and had herself a closer look at Norma. Opened an eyelid, shining her flashlight into Norma's eye. No hemorrhaging of the blood vessels. This told her that Norma had not been smothered with a pillow. Nor had she been strangled. Not that there was any obvious indication of strangulation. There was no bruising on her neck—or at least none that was visible to Des's naked eye. An autopsy might prove otherwise, of course. She examined Norma's scalp for wounds. Gently lifted her heavy head, fingering the back of it for welts or bruises. Nothing. There was no broken skin, no trace of blood on the pillow underneath. She examined the surface of the quilt that Norma lay under, searching for any hairs or fibers that might be foreign to her person. Nothing obvious jumped out at her. Carefully, she pulled the quilt back, followed by the blanket and sheet. Les had not neatened Norma's flannel nightshirt when he'd tidied her. It was all bunched up around her thighs. Des pulled it up toward Norma's neck, shining the light around on her mammoth, fleshy nakedness. A gross violation of the lady's dignity, to be sure.

But there was absolutely no way to be delicate when it came to examining the dead. Des found no obvious bruises or welts or cuts. The sheet underneath Norma appeared to be free of bloodstains. Also semen stains.

If the medical examiner and crime scene technicians had been standing right there alongside of her, Des would have flopped Norma over onto her stomach now and proceeded to check out her backside. But she was alone, and didn't want to disturb the crime scene any further. So she stretched the quilt back over Norma, knowing full well that she'd already done quite a bit more than a first responder was typically supposed to do. There were two reasons for this. One was that she didn't know when the crime scene technicians would get there. The other was that Des had been in the game. Once you have, it's damned hard to pull yourself back.

Especially when it's not in your nature to pull back

There was the half-empty water glass on Norma's nightstand. Des bent down and sniffed at it. No odor. Not chlorine, not sulphur, not anything. And there was no mineral residue in the bottom of the glass. Still, she carefully bagged and tagged it. Norma's copy of *Ten North Frederick,* the one that Teddy had given her, lay there on the nightstand, too. Recalling just how anxious he'd been to get it back, Des picked it up and flipped through the pages. About a third of the way in she found an Astrid's Castle bookmark. Nothing else. Not until she glanced at the title page and found this inscription written lightly in pencil:

TO N——MTYK——T

Which explained why he wanted the book back. Because here it was for anyone, specifically Les, to see. Written proof of their secret love, signified by the initials of that song of theirs, "More Than You Know." As Des stood there studying the inscription, she found herself wondering just how deeply Teddy might be involved in these deaths. She knew he had loved Norma. She knew he needed money. How did these two facts fit together? *Did* they fit together?

The nightstand had one drawer. She slid it open, found an assortment of hand creams inside, also Vaseline, Vicks VapoRub, nasal spray, a couple of old wristwatches, spare eyeglasses, key chains, a deck of playing cards. Nothing, in other words.

Norma's prescription bottles were on the bottom shelf of the medicine chest over the bathroom sink. Here Des found the bottle of Synthroid tablets that Les had told her Norma took for her underactive thyroid. Also Norma's two hormone-replacement drugs, Prometrium and Premarin. And her heart medication, digoxin, which was marketed under the brand name Lanoxicap. This prescription, like the others, had been filled at Dorset Pharmacy. It also came with a red flag of a warning label:

Be sure you understand how and when to take this medication. Do not change your dosage unless your doctor tells you to do so.

According to the label, Norma's prescribed dosage of Lanoxicap was two capsules twice a day. The bottle had contained 120 capsules when it was full—a thirty-day supply. The label was dated twelve days ago. Therefore, Des figured, it should contain no less than seventy-two capsules. She opened the lid, poured the capsules out into her hand and counted them out, returning them to the bottle one by one. She arrived at a total of eighty capsules. Nothing out of the ordinary there.

Still, she bagged and tagged all of Norma's meds, then went and asked Mitch to fetch Les from room ten. Quickly, she closed the door and scampered over to the bed and listened closely. From there, she could hear Mitch's footsteps creak on the floorboards. Hear him tap on Les's door. Hear the door open, the low murmur of voices, the door close, footsteps approach. She could hear it all, just as Teddy had told her he had heard it all in the night.

Les Josephson was continuing to diminish right before her eyes. The hale and hearty innkeeper looked positively ashen, his posture hunched, his movements slow and unsure as he shut the door behind him. It was beginning to dawn on Des just how much of his usual robust chestiness was sheer willpower on his part. Minus that willpower, he was rapidly turning into a sad little old man.

"How may I help you, Des?" he asked softly, his eyes carefully avoiding the bed.

"By telling me why you rearranged her, Les," Des said to him, not unkindly.

"I told you, I wanted her to look nice."

"And how did she look? What position did you find her lying in?"

Les considered this carefully, his eyes continuing to steer clear of Norma. He absolutely wouldn't look at her. "She was on her side, kind of."

"You mean like a prenatal position?"

"No, it was more like she was on her back with one leg thrown over the other. And her hair was quite messy and, well, clammy. So I combed it."

"Which comb did you use?"

"The one that's there on her dressing table," he said, pointing to the small mirrored table by the bathroom door.

She went over to it and said, "This wooden comb?"

"Yes."

Des bagged and tagged it and set it on the mantel next to Norma's pills and water glass. She took her time doing this, watching Les shift his weight from one foot to the other, growing steadily more uncomfortable in the presence of his cold dead wife. This was not a very nice thing for her to do, but hers was not always a very nice job.

"Is there anything else I should know about, Les? Besides you rearranging her and combing her hair, I mean."

"I don't believe so, no."

"You didn't dispose of anything or pocket anything?"

Les frowned. "Such as what?"

"That's what I'm asking you."

"No, I didn't," he said distractedly, running a hand through his hair. "Look, could we talk about this somewhere else?"

"Les, I know you've suffered a real blow today, but this is official business. Questions need to be asked. And you need to answer them, okay?"

Les turned to face the windows, his back to the bed. "Okay," he said dully.

"Are you sticking to your story that you slept straight through the night? Because if you want to change it, now is the time."

"It's not a story," he protested. "It's the truth."

"You honestly didn't hear Norma go downstairs in the middle of the night?"

"I honestly didn't, I swear."

"Take a minute, Les," she cautioned him. "It's possible that you remember something without realizing it. Like, say, Norma getting back into bed with you, snuggling up close. She would have been real cold from being downstairs, in need of warming up."

"I don't remember anything like that," Les insisted, watching the swirling, windblown snowflakes smack against the window. Des was tired of looking out at the snow herself. In fact, she'd be happy if it never snowed again for as long as she lived. "And, quite frankly, I don't see the point of this," he added reproachfully.

"I'm trying to figure out what happened."

"We know what happened. Norma's heart gave out. There's nothing complicated or sinister about it. To suggest otherwise is a real reach. And I resent it."

"Les, how much do you know about Ada's finances?"

"I know the old girl never really cared much about money," he answered. "She gave away most of her father's fortune to various political causes over the years. She owned her villa in Italy, the townhouse in London. And she still had a pretty steady royalty income. Those old plays of Luther's are considered classics. They still study them in drama classes."

"What about this remake of *Ten Cent Dreams*? How was she going to make out from that?"

"Quite well. It's based on her original work, so they had to pay her a decent sum."

"Are we talking six figures?"

"I'd imagine so, plus a percentage of the profits. Plus they're reissuing the original. There's a book of her photos coming out, too. There's no question that Ada was looking at a lot of new income. I can't tell you how much because I genuinely don't know. But Ada did raise the subject with us the very first night she got here. She'd already been in contact with Bruce Nadel about it."

"And Bruce Nadel is . . . ?"

"The fellow in New York who handled her legal affairs. He's on West Fifty-sixth Street. His father, Bert, was Ada's lawyer before him. She wanted us to know that she was leaving her entire estate to the American Civil Liberties Union. She claimed that the ACLU needed the money because our government was no longer protecting the rights of individuals, only those of corporations. Her words, not mine."

"How was Norma with this news?"

"Fine. She certainly wasn't surprised."

"And Aaron, how was he?"

"Predictably furious. Not because she was giving it away, but because she was giving it to a gang of failed paleo-socialists. His words, not mine. My own view was that it was her money and she could do as she wished with it."

"You weren't worried?"

Les frowned at her. "What about?"

"Keeping this place afloat."

"When you run a big place like Astrid's, you never come out ahead," he answered carefully. "Your profits, assuming you have any, get plowed right back into the business. Something always needs repairing or replacing. It's a lot like running a farm, in that sense. But we've been keeping our heads above water. We do okay."

"I know that Aaron comes into the castle now that Norma is gone," Des stated. "As her executor, you're in a position to know if she provided for anyone else, am I right?"

"You are. And she did. She made provisions in her will for several others."

"Such as who?"

"Well, there's Teddy. And the kids, Jory and Jase."

"You didn't mention that to Aaron this morning."

"I know I didn't. It's none of his damned business."

"May I ask you how much money we're talking about?"

"Actually, I don't think you have a right to ask me that. The terms of Norma's will are confidential until it's been filed with the Court of Probate."

"I have every right to ask. Just as you have every right to not answer. You're not obligated to, but if you want to help me . . ."

"I do want to help. Really, I do." Les fell silent a moment, making up his mind. "Strictly between us, Norma left fifty thousand apiece to Jory and Jase. Seed money, so they can start up a small business or buy a home or whatever. She wanted them to be provided for."

"Are the two of them aware of this?"

"Norma asked me to keep it between us. She may have told them. I didn't."

"And Teddy?"

"The same amount, fifty thousand. The poor guy is always scuffing. She took pity on him. Norma had a soft heart. Too soft, if you ask me."

"And what did she leave you?"

Les coughed uneasily. "She'd earmarked the money from Paul's life insurance policy for me. She'd never touched it. It amounted to two hundred thousand."

"A man can do a lot with that kind of money. What are your plans?"

"My *plans*?" he shot back incredulously. "I'm just trying to figure out how to get through this day. My entire life is in ruins."

"Believe me, I understand." Des counted to three, then squeezed a little harder. "How's your personal debt situation, Les? Do you owe anyone a lot of money?"

Les didn't respond. Just clenched his jaw muscles.

"If you do, I'll find out. You may as well tell me now."

"Tell you *what*? This is outrageous! First you drag me in here in front of my poor dead wife. Now you so much as accuse me of lying to you. How dare you? What do you think you are doing?"

155

"My job. I have to ask pretty harsh questions sometimes."

"I noticed."

"Les, you've been married before, am I right?"

"Twice," he answered coldly. "And in answer to what is no doubt your next harsh question: *Yes,* I do still pay alimony and child support to my second wife, Janice, thereby leaving me penniless. I don't even own the car I drive. The castle leases it for me."

"How were you and Norma getting along?"

"We were happy together. I told you that this morning."

"True enough," she acknowledged. "But you didn't tell me that you're involved with another woman. Who is she, Les?"

Again, he fell silent. But this was not an angry silence. This was the last of his manly resolve leaking slowly out of him, like the air out of a worn-out radial tire. She could practically hear the hiss. And the physical change in the man was really quite startling. His skeletal structure seemed to give way from within, leaving behind only a limp, quivering meat sack. "You actually think I *killed* Norma, don't you?" he said to her forlornly. "Well, I didn't. And shame on you for even thinking it. Maybe I wasn't altogether happy, but so what? Most of us aren't altogether happy. That doesn't make us killers. It just makes us *normal.*"

As Des studied Les's sagging self there at the window, it occurred to her that he had not denied having a girlfriend. In fact, he had managed to avoid the question entirely. All of which translated to this: She could easily like him for plotting to kill Norma, and then killing Ada because she'd somehow stumbled upon what he'd done. Des could like him a lot. After all, $200,000 could buy a lot of happiness. And yet she also could not help shaking the nagging feeling that Les had been much better off with Norma alive than dead.

Her cell phone squawked now.

She thanked Les and asked him to return to his room. He did not pause on his way out to take one last look at Norma. Just oozed on out the door, shutting it softly behind him. He had not been able to look at her the whole time he was in there.

"Resident Trooper Mitry," she said into her phone.

"Yo, Master Sergeant," a voice exclaimed in her ear, the connection crackly but plenty audible. "I understand you've got yourself a situation."

"You understand right, wow man," Des responded, smiling. The voice belonged to Lieutenant Rico "Soave" Tedone, the stumpy young bodybuilder who had been her sergeant back when she was a lieutenant on the Major Crime Squad.

"If I didn't know you better, I'd swear you're glad to hear my voice."

"Ultra-glad, Rico," she said. Which, for a time, had not been true. They'd had their difficulties. But Soave had grown up a lot since then. They both had. "Is this your case?"

"Just got the call," he confirmed. "Not that I can *get* to the damned case. What have you got for me, Des?"

"Two dead, Rico. A mother and daughter. One's a strangulation, the other's an I-don't-know-what. But she was helped along, I'm sure of it." Des walked him though the details, keeping her comments brief and precise. "I've got the situation under control. Witnesses are separated. I'm in the process of taking their statements now."

"And maybe doing a little bit more, if I know you."

"For backup, I've got Mitch."

"Who, Berger? *He's* up there?"

"He is," she replied, knowing what this was all about. Soave was a happily married man these days—he and his high school sweetheart, Tawny, had finally tied the knot on their epic nine-year courtship. But he had been extremely warm for Des's bootylicious form when they were teamed together, had gotten nowhere, and still could not believe that she had fallen for Mitch.

"And how's that going?" he wondered.

"Why would you ask me that?"

"Because I've heard you sound happier in your day."

"Rico, I've just lost two people I liked. I'm stranded, I'm cold, I could use a hot bath. What's your situation? Where are you?"

"Trapped in fuzzy pink hell, that's where."

"Um, okay, you'll have to translate that."

"I'm home," he said heavily. Home being the vinyl-sided raised ranch in Glastonbury that he and Tawny had just bought. Her parents lived right around the corner.

"And this is bad because . . . ?"

"Tawny was having a baby shower here last night for her cousin Ashley."

"Little Ashley or big Ashley?"

"Big Ashley. Little Ashley wouldn't come. They don't speak. Don't ask me why. Anyway, I'm talking horror show, okay? Tawny's three sisters, her eight cousins, another dozen friends. And about nine o'clock, when they're *deep* into the banana daiquiris, this giant tree comes crashing down at the end of the cul-de-sac, okay? Street's totally blocked off. No power, no heat . . ."

"Yeah, I'm familiar with this phenomenon."

"A few of 'em live close by, thank God. The rest had to bunk here for the night. They're still here, Des. It's like one giant slumber party out there. You've never heard so much giggling and screaming in your life."

"I have, too, Rico. I started out life as a girl, remember?"

"I'm hiding here in my weight room and praying for a break in the weather."

"How about Yolie?" Yolie being Sergeant Yolanda Snipes, his half-black, half-Cuban partner.

"She's at her apartment in Meriden, chewing on her hands and feet. That girl *hates* being on the sideline. We're both raring to go. Soon as the plow comes through, she'll pick me up at the end of my block in her Blazer. Route nine is supposed to be okay. Way slow, but we'll get there. I just can't promise when. We may be talking two, three hours."

"Rico, you may want to rethink this plan."

"Why?"

"For starters, because you'll end up flipped over in a ditch somewhere."

"No way. Yolie's a sweet wheelman."

"And even if you do get here, the private drive up to the castle is blocked off. You'll have to hike three miles up a mountain, climb your way over dozens of downed trees. You're looking at another hour on foot, easy."

"Well, hell, that's no good," he admitted. "Time out, are you thinking what I'm thinking? Of course you are—SP-One, right?"

"Any chance we rate a fly-in?"

"Are you kidding me? The state police spent millions on that damned chopper. They'll be thrilled to have any excuse to use it. Only, it's grounded in this weather."

"True, but if the snow and wind taper off in the next hour or two, you'll still get here faster and safer than you will by car. What is it, a twenty-minute flight from headquarters?"

"Give or take. Is there a place to land up there?"

"A great big beautiful parking lot."

"Excellent. I am on this, Des. I'll find out what they need in terms of weather. But you got to give me something else to do, because I am going crazy here. Is there anyone I can call?"

"There is, Rico. See if you can track down a New Haven cardiologist named Lavin, first name Mark. He was treating Norma Josephson. Find out how serious her heart condition was. And see what you can learn about this digoxin he had her taking. As in what would happen to her if her dosage were dramatically altered without her knowledge. Or with her knowledge, for that matter."

"You saying suicide is a possibility?"

"Rico, it's all in play right now."

"You think the digoxin is what did her in?"

"Call it my best guess, until an autopsy proves otherwise. The only hitch is that her pill intake seems to be right on schedule."

"Maybe someone got a hold of some extra pills. Where did she fill her prescription?"

"Locally, Dorset Pharmacy. It's a one-man operation. Pharmacist's name is Tom Maynard. I doubt he'll be open, but you may be able to reach him by phone. If you do, find out if anything irregular has been going on lately with Norma's prescriptions."

"Des, you know we can't access her medical records without a search warrant. And I can't exactly get to no judge right now."

"I hear you, but this is a small town, Rico. Everybody knows everybody. He might remember something and volunteer it. It's worth a try."

"Consider it done. And I'll call Connecticut Light and Power's war room. Let 'em know you have a police emergency up there. Maybe we can get you bumped up to a higher priority. I'll call you back in a few. Hey, you wouldn't lie to me, would you?"

"About what, Rico?"

"Having the situation under control."

"Why would I do that?"

"You said it yourself—you started out life as a girl. Girls consider it a sign of weakness to ask anyone for help. Guys, we don't have that problem. We need a hand, we say so right up front, on account of how we're more secure about ourselves."

"Wait, could you talk just a little bit slower? I want to make sure I write all of this down."

"Go ahead and laugh. I just want to make sure you're safe."

"Rico, I'm fine."

She flicked off her phone and went back out into the hall, where Mitch glanced up at her alertly from his post. "All quiet?" she asked him.

"It's so quiet I can hear the mice in the walls," he replied, beaming at her.

"Gee, thanks large for sharing that with me, baby."

"I share. That's what I do."

Hannah was in room four, next door to Teddy. She'd double-locked her door from the inside. Des had to wait for her to get up and let her in. After she had, Hannah burrowed back under the quilt on her bed, looking pale, cold and frightened. The large-format paperback she was clutching, *Hollywood Dreams,* was a collection of Ada Geiger's screenplays, with an introduction by one Mitchell Berger.

"I'm still trying to figure that old woman out," Hannah confessed, gazing down at it through her round glasses. "There was just such a difference between her work and *her*. I mean, her movies were so forgiving of human weakness. And Ada herself was just so *not*."

"She was young when she made those movies. Not much older than you and I are now."

"True," Hannah acknowledged. "But she just seemed so intolerant."

"She was ninety-four. Her time was running short, and she didn't want to waste any of it on people who weren't worth the bother. Older people get impatient that way. I've encountered it before." Des sat in the chair by the fireplace, stuffing her hands deep into her coat pockets. "Did you leave this room for any reason last night?"

"Are you kidding me? It was pitch-black, freezing cold. I didn't so much as leave this bed. Why would I?"

"You tell me," Des said, raising her chin at her.

Hannah reddened. "Oh, I see. You're wondering about Aaron and me, aren't you?"

Des didn't answer, just gazed at her intently.

Hannah let her breath out slowly and said, "He told me that Carly is a very light sleeper, so I should just forget about us being together while we're here. Which I am fine with. It would be totally disgusting for us to be doing anything with her right across the hall, don't you think?"

"I wouldn't know. My field is the law, not personal virtue."

"Pretty much one and the same thing, aren't they?"

"So you were alone all night?"

"Unless Danielle counts as company," she replied, tugging a tattered Danielle Steele paperback romance novel out from under her quilt. "She's gotten me through many a cold, lonely night. You're probably surprised that I read her. I could tell you that it's some kind of kitschy, ironic thing on my part, but it's not. I just love her books. They're so visual. I'd give anything to film one someday."

"So why don't you?"

Hannah stared at her. "Do you have *any* idea how much money that would cost? The rights alone would be huge. No one's going to give me a project like that to direct."

Then again, Des reflected, it might be another matter entirely if the young director were able to raise a lot of that money herself.

Which she could do if she had herself a patron like Aaron Ackerman on the hook, a man who it so happened was just about to get way rich. Just exactly how ambitious was Hannah Lane? How hungry to succeed? She had no problem getting freaky for Aaron. Would she have any problem killing for him? "Hannah, did you hear anyone coming or going out in the hall last night?"

"I was asleep."

"You didn't hear any doors open or close?"

"I was asleep." A defensive edge crept into her voice. "I just told you."

"That's right, you did," Des said, wondering whether Hannah was telling her the truth or not. Maybe she and Aaron *were* playing in the dirt together last night. Maybe they were doing a whole lot more than that together.

Des didn't know. Not yet. She thanked Hannah Lane and went back out in the hall and tapped on the door to room nine.

Jory Hearn called out for her to come in. Jory was seated on the bed, propped up against the headboard, wearing the quilt like a poncho. Her arms were folded tightly in front of her chest, her chin stuck out.

Des stood there in the doorway watching her. The grim-faced young redhead wasn't looking back at Des. She was busy gazing around at the room, as if she were trying to memorize every last detail of it while she still had the chance. She reminded Des of a high school girl taking stock of her old bedroom the night before she was to leave for college. Des had certainly done this in her own little bedroom in Kensington the night before she went off to West Point, one part excited, two parts scared to death.

"I understand that Norma was up and down a lot in the night," Des said for starters. "That she didn't sleep well as a rule."

"Yeah, she almost always got up." Jory's voice sounded hollow and rather small. "When I'd come in to start breakfast, I'd often find a list of chores on the kitchen table that she'd left for me at like four in the morning. 'Norma's Little Reminders,' I called them."

"Did she leave you one this morning?"

Jory shook her head.

"Did she leave anything out for you this morning?"

Jory frowned, glancing at Des curiously. "Like what?"

"Like something to indicate that she'd been up in the night. A saucepan, maybe a mug. I'm told she liked to make herself a cup of cocoa."

"It's true, she did."

"Did she make herself any last night?"

"I didn't notice anything. But I'm not positive, in all honesty."

"Let's go down and take a look, okay?"

They took the narrow service stairs down to the mudroom, where the smell of bacon and coffee still lingered in the air. The stove was cluttered with the dirty pots and pans from their uneaten breakfast. The bacon fat had congealed to a waxy consistency in the skillet.

"Can you remember how this kitchen looked when you came in, Jory?"

Jory looked around, considering her answer carefully. "Well, the dishes from last night were all in the dishwasher, and the sink was clear. The counter was clear, too."

"Was there a pot on the stove?"

Jory shook her head.

Des's eyes fell on the box of kitchen matches that they'd used to light the burners for breakfast. "How about spent matches?"

"I don't remember seeing any."

"When Norma made herself cocoa, did she usually clean up afterward?"

"She was an innkeeper. She never left a mess behind. Not in her nature."

"She would have put her dishes in the dishwasher?"

"Most likely."

Des opened it up and looked around inside. There were lots of plates and glasses, the serving dishes from dinner, a roasting pan, several Astrid's Castle mugs. "There's no saucepan in here," she said.

"Actually, this is the one she usually used," Jory said, indicating a one-quart no-stick pan that was hanging from a rack over the stove, clean and dry.

"Did she have a favorite mug?"

"Not really, no."

Des pulled the roll of yellow crime scene tape from her coat pocket and stretched a length of it over the dishwasher door. "I'll need for you to steer clear of this, okay?" We'll want to examine the contents."

"Sure, whatever," Jory said, sighing despondently. It seemed as if the weight of the future had fallen on her like an anvil.

Des glanced out the kitchen windows at the snow that was coming down out in the courtyard. The footpath from the kitchen door across to Jory and Jase's cottage was buried so deep under the fresh snowfall that it was impossible to tell where it even was. "How about you, Jory? Did you get up in the night?"

"I woke up a lot, that's for sure." A strand of red hair had come loose from Jory's topknot. She twirled it around her finger distractedly. "Every time that damned wind brought down another tree, I mean, it sounded like the end of the world, you know? But I didn't get up."

"You can see right in here from your front windows," Des observed.

"Yes, we can."

"You didn't notice a light in here last night, did you? A candle, a flashlight—any sign that Norma or someone else might have been up?"

"Someone else?" Jory peered at her, confused. "Like who?"

"Like Ada."

"No, I didn't see anything."

"Do you have any idea whether Jase was up?"

"I'm not sure. You'd have to ask him."

"Is Jase generally a sound sleeper?"

"Very. He works long, hard days."

"He didn't have any issues with Norma, did he?"

"None. Jase loved her dearly. We both did."

"And both of you were in here when we heard Hannah scream, am I right?"

"Pretty much. I'd just brought out the oatmeal, and I was on my way back in here for a fresh coffeepot. Jase was over there in the mudroom," she said, glancing at the open doorway. "I'd given him some Handi Wipes so he could tidy up, since Carly was being such a—" Jory broke off, curling her lip. "She was not being very kind."

"I forget, was Les in here with you, too?"

"Do you mean when Hannah screamed? No, Les was still out in the dining room with you folks. He was bringing out the eggs, remember?"

"Oh, that's right." This jibed with Des's own recollection. Which, by the way, happened to be perfect. "So in the moments just prior to Hannah's scream, you, Jase and Les were all in here together?"

"Yes."

"Was there any point when Les wasn't in here with you?"

"Not really. He did go down to the laundry room for a few seconds."

"Why did he do that?"

"To fetch a pile of fresh napkins. We were running low."

"How many seconds was he down there?"

Jory shrugged her shoulders helplessly. "Twenty, maybe thirty?"

"And Jase?"

"Jase never left the mudroom."

"You're sure about that?"

"I'm positive. Des, do you mind if I ask you something now?"

"Not at all. Go right ahead."

"I sort of heard you guys talking before in the taproom, but I wanted to make sure I heard it right." Jory hesitated, clearing her throat uneasily. "Aaron's the new boss of us, isn't he?"

"That's something you ought to talk to Les about," Des replied, since the details of Norma's last will and testament were not for public consumption. Then again, she reflected, the future of Astrid's Castle did matter a great deal to this woman. Jory deserved to know the truth sooner rather than later. So the hell with it. "Apparently,

Norma and Les signed a pre-nuptual agreement, whereby Les has no ownership rights to this place. Aaron gets it."

Jory nodded her head glumly. "I guess that means all three of us are out. Aaron and Les can barely tolerate each other. And there's no way Jase or I will ever work a single day for Carly."

"Don't get ahead of yourself. Carly may not be in the picture for long."

"Well, that much is true," Jory agreed, brightening a little.

"Besides, Aaron said he had no intention of making any changes."

Jory let out a short laugh. "Sure, that's what they always say—just before they shut down the factory and move all of the jobs to Malaysia or somewhere."

Des's cell phone squawked again.

She answered it and heard an excited Soave blurt out, "Des, you have not lost your touch."

"What have you got for me, Rico?" she asked him as Jory started for the service stairs. Des didn't want anyone wandering around the castle alone, so she motioned for her to sit. Jory flopped down at the kitchen table, puffing out her cheeks.

"Well, for starters," Soave reported, "Dr. Lavin is in Aruba for two weeks."

"Dumb he's not. And . . . ?"

"And the doctor who's covering for him is going to look into Norma Josephson's records and get back to me."

"And . . . ?"

"And I bounced your theory off of the medical examiner. He said that if somebody ODs on digoxin it can trigger, wait a sec, I wrote all of this down . . . 'Excessive slowing of the pulse, thereby leading to atrio-ventricular blockage. Which, if someone is elderly or has a heart condition, can lead to complete cardiac arrest within a half hour.' That's an induced heart attack, in dumbo English. Which is to say, *ka-ching.*"

"That's good work, Rico," she said, her mind starting to race. Whoever killed Norma had known more than a little about her heart condition. Meaning it was someone close to her as opposed to, say,

Spence or Hannah. Although Hannah could have known about it by way of Aaron.

"Yolie's reaching out to your local pharmacist. And I just spoke to the Connecticut Light and Power people."

"This news is not so good. I hear it in your voice, Rico."

"Hey, I got you bumped to a high priority, right behind the hospitals, schools and the governor's mother's house. But they still can't promise anything before the end of tomorrow."

"*Tomorrow?* Rico, we will freeze to death by then."

At the table, Jory nodded her head solemnly.

"Hey, at my house we're looking at seventy-two hours," he complained. "So consider yourself lucky."

"What did the SP-One people say?"

"According to the latest forecast, the snow and wind are supposed to taper off early this afternoon. They think we might be able to land up there maybe one, two o'clock. I've got the authorization."

Des glanced at her watch. It was not quite eleven now.

"Des, I'm still willing to do it the old-fashioned way. Just say the word and me and Yolie will be on the road in ten minutes."

"No, take the chopper, Rico. You're a bigger help to me right where you are. And you'll get here faster."

"Deal. Back at you when I know more."

Des rang off and she and Jory started back upstairs.

"Would it be okay if we looked in on Jase?" Jory asked her as they climbed. "I want to make sure he's okay."

"Any reason he wouldn't be?"

"He doesn't do well under certain circumstances."

"None of us are doing particularly well right now."

"I know, but he's real sensitive, and he can get kind of . . ."

"Kind of what, Jory?"

"Upset," she said quietly.

"Sure, okay," Des said, pushing open the steel door to the second-floor corridor. Mitch was still at his post at the top of the main stairs. "I need to talk to him anyway."

"Can I come in with you?" Jory asked, somewhat pleadingly.

"I'm afraid not."

"Then I'll wait right out here in the hallway, if you don't mind. Just in case you need me."

"That'll be fine." Des tapped on the door to room eleven. It wasn't bolted. She opened it and went inside, shutting it behind her.

Jase sat hunched on the edge of the bed, facing the windows. The unheated room was beginning to smell of his unwashed presence.

"How's it going, Jase?" she asked, starting toward him.

He didn't respond. Didn't so much as acknowledge her presence.

When she made her way around the bed to face him, Des found Jase Hearn to be perspiring heavily despite the chill. He was nodding his head up and down, wringing his hands, jiggling his knee.

Jory knew her brother, all right. He was definitely upset.

"It won't open," he said suddenly. "The window won't open."

Indeed not. The deep granite sill was heavily encrusted with ice, frozen solidly shut.

"Are you going somewhere, Jase?" she asked him, keeping her voice low.

"I have to work on the driveway," he replied, his voice rising with urgency. "Trees are down."

"In a while, Jase."

"No, that's no good," he protested. "I take care of things. I'm supposed to be out there, not sitting here doing nothing."

"Soon, okay?" Des perched on the bed next to him. "And you're not here doing nothing. You're helping me out."

He turned and looked at her blankly. "I am?"

"Absolutely. I need to ask you some questions about last night, okay?"

"I guess," he said, relaxing a little. "I mean, sure."

"Did you get up at all during the night? I'm wondering if you might have seen anything going on downstairs in the kitchen."

Jase cocked his head at her curiously. "Like what?"

"Somebody's flashlight. Somebody moving around in there."

Jase shook his head. "Jory gave me my pill."

"What pill is that, Jase?"

"So I can sleep."

"You take one every night?"

"I do," he said, scratching at his beard. "If I don't I can't stop thinking about stuff."

"What stuff?"

"Stuff I need to do. There's just so much stuff."

"Okay, sure," she said easily. "Jase, I'd like to go over what happened this morning. Where were you when Ada got strangled?"

"I don't know," he answered flatly.

Des frowned at him. "What do you mean?"

"I don't know when it happened. I only know when I heard that girl scream."

"You're right. That wasn't a very precise question. My bad. Where were you when you heard Hannah scream?"

"Washing my hands," he said, staring down at them as if they belonged to someone else. "In the mudroom."

"And Jory was in the kitchen?"

"Yeah."

"And where was Les?"

"With her, serving breakfast."

"Okay, that's good. Very good." Des stood back up, her hamstrings and calves starting to ache from the cold. "Thank you, Jase."

"Can I go outside now?" he asked her.

"I'm afraid you'll have to stay put."

"How much longer?" he wondered, squirming around on the edge of the bed.

"A little while. Can you do that for me?"

"Sure. I'll stay right here," he promised, nodding his head—up, down, up, down.

Des went back out in the hallway, closing the door softly behind her.

A very anxious Jory stood right there before her, eyes searching Des's face. "Is he okay?"

"A little twitchy, but hanging in there," Des replied. "Tell me, what's his story?"

"He doesn't like to be cooped up. It makes him very uncomfortable."

"I noticed." Des also noticed that Jory was highly protective of her brother. This was to be expected. She was several years older than he. Their mother had died giving birth to him. So Jory had had to raise him herself, with an assist from Norma. Still, she seemed particularly worried. Des wondered if she had a reason to be. "He's not going to throw a chair through the window or anything, is he?"

"No, nothing like that. He's a good, sweet boy. Just emotionally fragile."

"I told him to stay put."

"If that's what you told him, that's what he'll do."

"He said you gave him a sleeping pill last night."

"I did," Jory admitted. "He has nightmares. They're anxiety-related. His doctor at the family practice here in town prescribed a mild sedative called diazepam a couple of years ago."

"His name is . . . ?"

"Dr. Dillon," Jory replied. "Why?"

"Just being thorough."

"Honestly, Jase is fine. It's not like he's seeing a shrink or anything."

"I understand. Except for one thing, Jory. When we were downstairs just now, you told me he slept well because he worked so hard. You didn't say anything about meds."

"I know I didn't. And I'm sorry. I was afraid that, see, if Aaron thinks Jase is drug-dependent, that would give him just the excuse he needs to get rid of us."

"*Is* Jase drug-dependent?"

"Totally not. Dr. Dillon said it isn't strong or habit-forming or . . ." Jory trailed off, scrunching her mouth nervously. "Des, does Aaron have to know about this?"

"He won't hear about it from me," Des promised her.

Jory's face broke into a dimply, pink-cheeked smile. "Thanks. You're a real friend."

Mitch moseyed toward them from the top of the stairs and said, "Les wants to know if he can go down and stoke the fires."

"Not now," Des replied. "I want everyone right where they are."

"He needs to keep those fireplaces going, Des," Mitch pointed out. "Otherwise the pipes might freeze."

"You do have a point there," she conceded, shoving her heavy horn-rimmed glasses up her nose. "Okay, go ahead and take him downstairs. Feed the fires—and yourselves while you're at it."

"I am liking this plan," he said, grinning at her.

"Somehow I thought you would. And take Teddy, why don't you?"

"Safety in numbers?"

"Something like that."

"May I join them, too?" Jory asked.

"I may need to ask you some more questions."

"But I don't know anything else."

"Jory, please return to your room."

Sullenly the housekeeper went back into room nine, closing the door behind her.

"How will you keep tabs on everyone while I'm downstairs?" Mitch asked.

"I can move a second chair out to your sentry post and conduct my interviews there." Des ducked into their room, grabbed their desk chair and brought it out with her. "Be careful while you're down there. Keep them in front of you at all times."

"Not to worry," he said over the sound of his growling stomach. "You can count on me."

Les was exceedingly grateful to be sprung from his room. "Norma would never, ever forgive me if our pipes froze," he told Des, his eyes moistening. "I may have to go get more firewood from the woodshed. Is that okay?"

"Do what you have to do, Les. Just don't do it alone."

Teddy seemed plenty thrilled himself. "I'm so hungry I'm ready to start gnawing on the wallpaper," he exulted.

The three of them started down the center stairs immediately, Mitch bringing up the rear.

Des watched them go, mulling over her next move. She'd made a bit of progress, she believed. She knew what had gone down, and pretty much how. But she still didn't know the why. Or the who. Or what kind of a crowbar would pry this damned thing open. Or how to . . .

Actually, come to think of it, she still didn't know a damned thing.

CHAPTER 11

"WHO GETS REFUELED FIRST?" Mitch asked when the three of them had arrived downstairs. "The fireplaces or us?"

"Well, what's your vote?" Les asked him.

"I'm definitely going to come down in favor of us. Unless, that is, a few more minutes is critical to the pipes."

"I'll make you a deal," offered Les, ever the good host. "Let me just check the taproom fire real quick. It's the smallest one, and usually goes out first. Then we'll hit the kitchen. Sound good to you, Teddy?"

"Whatever you'd like," Teddy responded. "I'm not very hungry, actually."

"You just told Des you were starved," Mitch pointed out.

"Sure, I did. I wanted to get the hell out of that room."

The fire in the taproom fireplace had burned down to hot, glowing coals. There were three logs left in the wood bin. Les laid them onto the coals and took a bellows to them, pumping vigorously.

"It's important that we keep all of these fires going," he explained, as the logs caught fire, crackling. "Especially in the Sunset Lounge, which has the most windows. Even a few degrees of warmth can make a critical difference."

Les seemed genuinely worried about the castle's pipes, Mitch observed. But he also sensed that the innkeeper was purposely trying to keep busy so he wouldn't have to think about how totally blown to bits his life was. This was something that Mitch could relate to. When he'd lost Maisie, his own method had been to sit in his apartment watching tapes of old Jimmy Cagney movies and eating Krispy Kreme doughnuts. In fact, if his editor, Lacy Nickerson, hadn't shooed him off to Dorset to write a weekend-getaway travel piece, the chances were good that Mitch would still be sitting there watching old Cagney movies, all 495 pounds of him.

"Not that I'm what you would call an ace fire builder," Les confessed as they started toward the dining hall. "Jase is our resident wizard. That kid can start a fire by rubbing two wet sticks together. But I guess Des still has him in isolation. What's the point of that, anyway?"

"What she said. She doesn't want witnesses comparing notes."

"Why not?" Teddy asked.

"I'm sure she has a good reason. Believe me, she knows what she's doing."

"I'm so glad to hear that," Teddy said. "I may not have much in the way of a life, but I'm still not ready to give it up. Not yet."

Their breakfast serving platters had not fared very well in the drafty dining hall. The oatmeal had thickened into a mucilaginous glop that looked far more like mortar than it did something to eat. The scrambled eggs resembled what might be left behind after the explosion of someone's rubber ducky.

"Ordinarily, I'd just zap all of this in the microwave," Les said rather helplessly.

"No problem, I'm the king of the stove-top reheaters," Mitch assured him, snatching up the egg-and-bacon platters. The oatmeal seemed beyond all hope. He left that. "Besides, you've got enough on your mind right now."

"I'll just make do with some bread and jam, methinks," said Teddy, slathering apricot preserves on a hunk of day-old French bread. He started toward the entry hall, chewing on it.

"Wait, where are you going?" Mitch asked him.

"The piano. I've got to play."

"No, no, we're supposed to stick together."

"You'd better join us in the kitchen, Teddy," Les said.

"I'm playing the piano," Teddy insisted. "You'll know where I am—you'll be able to hear me. Hell, *Des* will be able to hear me all the way upstairs. So what the hell difference does it make?"

"Fine, go ahead," Mitch said, because there was no stopping him. Teddy's need to play was too urgent.

He and Les headed into the kitchen, where Les sat at the big trestle table with his shoulders slumped, staring at nothing. Mitch wiped the cold grease out of the bacon skillet with a paper towel, added butter and a little milk to the egg pan. Then he fired up the two burners under them with a kitchen match. While he waited for the pans to heat back up, he chomped on some of the French bread, which was rapidly taking on the character of biscotti.

In the Sunset Lounge, Teddy launched into a slow, heartfelt rendition of "More than You Know," the same song he'd been playing earlier that morning. Mitch felt quite certain that he would never, ever hear that song again without thinking of being stranded up here at Astrid's Castle in the middle of this ice storm with those two dead women.

"That was *their* song," Les mentioned to him quietly.

"Whose?" asked Mitch, gazing out the kitchen windows at the snow. It was coming down so hard he could barely see across the courtyard.

"Teddy and Norma. They loved each other for years and years. They thought I didn't know. But you always know, Mitch. Love can't hide."

The pans were getting good and hot now. Mitch laid the cold cooked bacon strips back in, then went to work on the eggs, stirring them into the sizzling butter and milk. "Yet she married you, Les," he pointed out.

"That's right, she did. And we were happy together. Or as happy as any married couple can ever really be, which is not very."

"Why do you say that?"

"Because the love goes away, that's why. If you're lucky, you can maintain a degree of affection. Not wake up every morning hating each other's guts. But the love can't last. Never has, never will. That's a myth."

"I don't know that I agree, Les. It doesn't stay the same, I'll grant you that. But it can grow." Not that Mitch had ever put this theory to the test. Maisie had died on him before their second anniversary. Maybe her endearing little eccentricities and foibles would have grown to annoy him. Maybe his endless hours in a screening room would have driven her into the arms of some alpha go-getter with wavy blond hair and a functioning set of social skills. Maybe Les was right, and they would have ended up hating each other.

But Mitch refused to believe this.

The bacon was sizzling and the eggs were hot again. Mitch found plates and forks and served them heaping portions. They dived in like starved field hands. It all tasted remarkably like school cafeteria chow, but Mitch was in no mood to be fussy. "If two people end up unhappy," he said, munching, "it simply means they didn't belong with each other in the first place."

"You're still a young man, Mitch," Les responded as he ate. "Listen to someone who has a few years on you: The longer any couple stays together, the worse it gets. You let each other down too many times, shatter each other's dreams. Believe me, I've seen it happen. My first wife, Hildy, dumped me less than three years after we got out of college. That's how long it took her to realize I wasn't going to become the next Stephen Sondheim, just the next Lester Josephson. As for my second wife, Janice, that was my doing."

"What happened?" Mitch asked as Teddy continued to serenade them from the Sunset Lounge.

"Nothing, really. I just woke up one morning and realized that all she and I had to look forward to in life was growing old and sick and scared together. I couldn't deal with it, so I fled. Left her to raise our little boy, Tyler, on her own. Tyler's in his junior year of high school now. Hates my guts even more than Janice does. Never so much as speaks to me. Down the road, when he has kids of his own, he'll never let them meet me. And when I'm lying on my deathbed in some hospital somewhere, tubes sticking out of my nose, he won't come to me. I know this. And I can't blame him. Hell, I abandoned the poor little bastard. But I couldn't help myself, Mitch. You see, I have this crazy idea that I'm supposed to be happy. Spent too damned many years in advertising, I guess. Writing TV commercials about impossibly happy people leading impossibly happy lives—all thanks to that brand of miracle fabric softener or toilet bowl cleaner they're using. If you do that long enough, Mitch, you start to believe in it. Hell, you *have* to believe in it if you want to be good at your job. The downside is that you can't help measuring your own life against the one that you're creating. You start expecting your own forty-two-year-old housewife with her forty-two-year-old butt to look like a twenty-year-old fashion model, because, damn it, that's who plays forty-two-year-old housewives in TV commercials. Everything's enhanced, prettified, *fake*. Mind you, on Madison Avenue, we don't call it *fake*. We call it *aspirational*."

Mitch cleaned his plate with a chunk of bread, studying Les. "What will you do with yourself now—stay here or get back in the game?"

"Short-term, that's Aaron's call," Les replied. "Long-term, I'm a sixty-two-year-old man in a young person's game. They don't want someone like me anymore. They want the MTV crowd. Edgy, outrageous. Kids selling to kids. Being candid, I'm not even sure I understand what they're selling anymore. I saw a commercial on TV the other night for this new palm-sized communication *thing* and I swear I didn't know whether they were pushing the *thing* or the software inside of the *thing* or the satellite provider that hooks your *thing* up with somebody else's *thing*. I've been out of it for too long, Mitch. I'm a dinosaur." Les finished his breakfast and gazed around at the quaint, roomy old kitchen. "My time here with Norma has been like an escape from reality for me. Right now, I can't imagine what I'll do if I have to leave. Maybe I'll just stay right here in Dorset."

"And do what?"

Les didn't say. Instead, he groaned, "*God,* I wish that man would play something else." Teddy was still working his way through a seemingly endless series of riffs on that same song, *their* song. "Have you had enough to eat, Mitch?"

"No, never. But this will hold me."

"We'd better go get that firewood."

Des had put yellow crime tape over the dishwasher, so Mitch made do with putting their dishes in the sink while Les grabbed work gloves and a storm jacket from out of the mudroom. Mitch had stashed his own outer gear in the entry-hall coatroom when he came in from logging duty. Les tagged along with him while he fetched it.

"Teddy had better come with us," Mitch said as he got into his down jacket. Its outer layer was still wet from working out in the ice. The same went for Spence's jacket hanging next to it. "We're supposed to stick together."

They headed into the Sunset Lounge, where Les called out, "Grab your coat, Teddy. We're going out for firewood."

Teddy smiled thinly at them from behind the keyboard, but did not respond. Or stop playing.

"Des wants us to stick together, Teddy," Mitch added. "Let's go."

"This piano is all that stands between me and a total meltdown," Teddy said in a firm, quiet voice. "If you try to pry my fingers from it, I will die. I am not exaggerating."

"You need to come with us, Teddy."

"That's not going to happen, Mitch. Kindly leave me be. I'm not a danger to anyone. I'll be fine right here, just as long as I can keep on playing."

"You know, I really can't deal with this right now," Les huffed impatiently. "Let's just leave him."

"Fair enough," Mitch agreed, because there was truly no point in discussing this any further with Teddy. The man wasn't budging.

He and Les returned to the kitchen and charged out the back door into the stormy outdoors. It was so cold in the castle that it didn't even seem that nasty out, even though the wind was howling and the snow stung their faces. It was a wet, heavy snow. At least four inches had fallen so far on top of last night's ice. The footing was poor, the walking excruciatingly slow. It went something like this: First Mitch's right foot sank down through the fresh snow, then held for a brief moment, then crashed through the icy crust with a *kerchunk* down into the older snow underneath. No sooner would he yank it up and out, then, *kerchunk*, his left foot would crash on through.

The simple act of putting one foot in front of the other had never been so arduous.

The woodshed's barn-style doors opened outward. It took both of them, with an assist from a snow shovel, to horse them open through the crunchy snow cover. Inside, a wheelbarrow sat on the hard dirt floor next to cords of stacked, seasoned hardwood, maple and hickory mostly. Tools hung everywhere from nails driven into the wall joists—an ax and maul, hatchets, pickaxes, shovels, forks, loops of garden hose. A riding mower waited there patiently for spring, which right now seemed so far off into the future as to be unimaginable.

Les immediately started loading up on firewood, the logs landing with a thundering crash in the empty wheelbarrow. "Mitch, you asked me what I'd do with myself if I stayed here in Dorset," he said, sounding a bit uneasy. "Confidentially, I do have something of a romantic attachment. I've been seeing someone else for several months. She's a local woman, married."

Mitch dropped an armload of logs into the wheelbarrow. "Is that right?" he said, keeping his voice neutral.

"I'm afraid so. I wasn't totally candid about it with Des. I should have been, but it was very difficult for me. You see, Norma was right there in the room with us. And I just couldn't make myself say the words out loud. Not in front of Norma. I couldn't betray her to her face that way. I knew, I *know* that she's dead, and couldn't hear me. But I didn't want to admit it to myself—that she wasn't *there* anymore, I mean. I just couldn't. Does this make any damned sense at all to you?"

"Yes, it does."

Les dropped another armload in the wheelbarrow, his chest heaving. "Dumb move on my part, really, because Des is bound to find out the truth once she starts nosing around. In Dorset there's no such thing as a secret. Not when it involves sex between two consenting adults. Would you mind telling her, Mitch? Would you do that for me?"

"If you'd like," Mitch replied, loading more wood. "Mind you, she'll want to know who this other woman is."

"Naturally," Les acknowledged. "But will it be necessary to involve the woman in this? What's your opinion?"

"How should I know, Les? I'm totally in the dark. I don't even know why Des needs to know any of this."

"Because it speaks to motive, that's why."

"*Whose* motive?"

"Mine," Les said replied. "For murdering Norma."

"Are you saying you did?"

"No, of course not. But I do come into a certain amount of money now. Two hundred thousand, to be exact. That's not a fortune, but it's not chopped liver."

"What are you planning to do with it?"

"Set up a trust fund for Tyler, I imagine. But I don't really know for sure. I haven't given it much thought." Les paused from his labors, swiping at his uncombed silver hair with a gloved hand. "Oh, hell, it's Martha Burgess, okay? Martha's who I'm involved with."

Mitch knew the woman. Martha and her husband, Bob, operated Dorset's quaintest little inn, the Frederick House. Mitch had stayed there when he first came to town, as had Des when her house was being renovated. It was a nice place, and the Burgesses seemed like nice, hardworking people. Martha was maybe forty-five, thin, plain, kind of on the mousy side. Hardly Mitch's mental picture of a steamy, two-timing wife, which ran more along the lines of Barbara Stanwyck in *Double Indemnity*.

"The two of us got to know each other through the Chamber of Commerce," Les went on. "Martha and Bob have been having their problems, marital and financial. They're in a real hole. Weekend tourism is way down. People just don't seem to have the money anymore for high-end romantic getaways."

So the high-end innkeepers had the getaways themselves, Mitch concluded, thinking about what Les had just said to him in the kitchen: *I have this crazy idea that I'm supposed to be happy.* And thinking about something else—Norma's $200,000 could go a long way toward helping the Frederick House out of its financial hole. So possibly Les did have an exit strategy. Possibly he was planning to ease Bob Burgess out and move in on Martha, securing himself a new innkeeping berth in the bargain. It sure sounded like a plan to Mitch. He wondered if Bob Burgess had the slightest idea of what might be going on. Or if he cared. Hell, maybe Bob was busy working on an exit strategy of his very own. "Not that it's any of my business, Les," he said, "but did Norma know about you and Martha?"

"If she did, she didn't let on. But my best guess is no. She detested the village hens and their gossip. And Martha and I have been very discreet. We meet up in Higganum at her sister Susie's apartment. Susie's single and travels a lot on business."

"What about Ada? Is there any chance she found out?"

"I can't imagine how," Les replied. "Not unless Norma knew and told her, and she and Ada weren't that kind of tight. The old girl never really felt much love for Norma, in my opinion. She didn't even bother to fly in for our wedding. Can you imagine that? A mother not coming to her own daughter's wedding?"

"Has Martha heard the news yet? Have you phoned her about Norma?"

"I haven't so much as thought about it. Of course, now that I'm a widower, I'll probably scare the poor woman right back into the arms of her husband."

Then again, maybe not. Maybe Martha was already well aware that Norma was dead. Maybe she and Les had joined together to bump Norma off and ease Bob out. Maybe.

They each dumped another armload of wood in the wheelbarrow, nearly filling it.

"We should stop right there," Mitch cautioned. "If it's too heavy, we'll never be able to push it back through that snow."

"Agreed. We'll come back for a second load."

Les started to maneuver the loaded wheelbarrow toward the barn doors. A couple of logs worked loose from the top of the pile and rolled onto the dirt floor. Mitch bent over to pick them up. When he stood back up, he discovered that Les was studying him with a worried look on his face.

"Mitch, I've just told you something in the absolute strictest confidence. I'm counting on you to tell Des and no one else."

"No problem, Les. You can count on me."

"Considering the circumstances, I probably shouldn't have told you this at all," Les added, swallowing. "You see, there's one more little wrinkle that I'm not especially proud of. And I . . . I guess it might be pretty necessary for Des to know about it."

Mitch turned and put the stray logs back on the woodpile. "What is it, Les?"

Les didn't tell him.

Instead, there was a sudden flurry of movement behind Mitch and before Mitch could whirl around to see what it was, he felt a tremendous crack on the back of his head—an awful, blinding blow that sent him pitching forward. And now the cold dirt floor was rushing right up toward him. And now he was smacking face-first right down into that dirt, of that dirt, going, going . . .

Gone.

CHAPTER 12

"I'm so sorry about what's happened this morning," Des said to Aaron Ackerman. "You must be feeling totally blown away."

"I don't know how I'm feeling, quite honestly," Aaron responded softly. "I've had no chance to absorb it yet, let alone grieve. I only know that I've lost the only family I had left in the world."

"You still have Carly," she reminded him, thinking that he hadn't mentioned Teddy either.

Aaron said nothing in response. Not one word.

The two of them sat facing each other at the top of the stairs, Des's chair positioned so that she was able to eyeball the corridor as well as Aaron. No one could leave any of the second-floor rooms without her seeing them.

Downstairs, Teddy had been drawn back to the piano. The sweet, sad strains of "More Than You Know" resonated throughout the castle's cavernous entry hall. Des felt certain that she would never hear that melody again without associating it with Teddy and Norma. She also felt certain that she would not want to hear it again for a really long time.

A bruised quiet had descended upon Aaron. He seemed humbled by the deaths of his mother and grandmother. When Des knocked on his door she'd found him at the desk tapping away at a battery-powered laptop, so lost in thought that he'd scarcely heard her. When she told him she needed to take his statement, his response wasn't the least bit arrogant or petulant.

"Whatever you wish," he sighed defeatedly. "I want to do what I can to help."

Which intrigued Des. Why was Aaron suddenly acting so unlike himself? Was this simply his honest human grief showing itself, or was it something else? Something like, say, guilt? Because Des had by no means forgotten who stood to gain the most from Norma's death. It was this man who sat facing her now.

"I have to ask you some questions that may seem insensitive at a time like this," she began. "Believe me, I'm not trying to cause you any extra pain. But it's important that we go over this while it's still fresh in your memory."

"I understand," Aaron said. "You may begin."

"For starters, let's run through where you were when Ada was attacked. Jory had just come into the taproom to say breakfast was ready. As I recall, Carly took off upstairs, and you went up after her. Is that about right?"

"It is," he said. "She was rather steamed, apparently. I was trying to calm her down."

"And how did that work out for you?"

Aaron fell silent for a moment. "I've been going about things the wrong way," he said, gazing not so much at Des as through her. Briefly, she felt as if she weren't even there. "I should be trying to follow Grandmother's example, I now realize. What I mean to say is, her death has shone a light on my true mission in life."

"Which mission is that, Aaron?"

"Grandmother was going to leave all of her money to the ACLU. Mind you, I happen to think that's akin to pissing down one's own leg. But the pure concept itself, the idea of using one's money for the common good, that is just so noble. I should be doing that, too. And I want to try."

"How would you go about doing it?"

"By selling Astrid's Castle," he replied, nodding his large head up and down. "And using the proceeds to fund a new think tank devoted to political and social reform. Possibly a weekly journal as well. I was just jotting down a few thoughts on the subject. I am talking about minting an entirely new movement to bridge the widening gap between left and right in this nation. There are just so many issues now, whether it be abortion or gun control, the environment, affirmative action . . . we don't debate them intelligently anymore. Simply talk past one another, and then call each other 'idiotic' or 'un-American' or just plain 'evil.' It's as if our lives have turned into one never-ending installment of *Hardball*. For which, I'll be the first to admit, I've been rewarded most handsomely," he allowed, tugging uncomfortably at his bow tie. "But a heavy price has been paid. We can no longer find any common ground. That's what I'd like to call it—Common Ground." Aaron gazed at her beseechingly, hungry for her approval. "What do you think, Des?"

Des studied the man. He seemed genuinely worked up about this. Also terribly needy for approval. Mitch had been right about him, not that she'd ever doubted it. "What I think," she replied, "is that I wouldn't expect you to be very interested in this."

"Oh, I absolutely am," he assured her. "Just look at what's happened here. Look what happens when people don't talk to each other."

"What did happen here, Aaron?"

"A wake-up call, that's what—for me."

Not only needy but so self-centered that from where he sat, these two murders were not about his mother and grandmother, they were about *him*. "And how does Carly fit into your new plans?"

"She's a bright and gifted scholar. I hope she'll contribute."

"And your marriage?"

Aaron drew back a bit. "I don't know what you mean by that."

"Yes, you do. You know perfectly well."

"Hannah shot her mouth off, didn't she?" he said, casting a guilty look down the hallway.

"Hannah didn't have to shoot off anything. You're plenty obvious all by yourself," Des shoved her glasses up her nose and said, "Tell me, were you aware of your mother's heart problems?"

"I knew she was fat," Aaron answered bluntly. "I knew she needed surgery and wouldn't have it."

"Did you know she took heart medication?"

"I assumed she did."

"Any idea what she was taking?"

"I have no idea at all."

"Aaron, did you get up at all last night? Possibly go downstairs?"

"What does *that* have to do with anything?"

"Just answer the question, please."

"I slept very soundly last night. I'd consumed a couple of snifters of single malt before dinner, and a good deal of wine. Carly and I read in bed for a while. We extinguished our lanterns at approximately eleven, then went to sleep."

"Stayed put in your own bed all night, did you?"

"Just exactly what kind of man do you think I am?" Aaron demanded, arching an eyebrow at her.

"A man who cheats on his wife."

"You know what I think?" he shot back defensively. "I think you're predisposed to dislike me. You're blatantly prejudiced against me, in point of fact, because I happen to espouse traditional conservative values. You know nothing about my marriage or my . . . situation."

"So fill me in."

"For starters, I was *not* waiting for Carly to fall asleep so I could tiptoe across the hall and slip into the sack with Hannah. That would be unforgivably cruel, not to mention stupid. Carly happens to be a pathologically light sleeper. If I so much as twitch a finger in the night, she wakes right up to ask me what's wrong. There is no way I could go to Hannah without Carly knowing. I made it abundantly clear to Hannah that nothing could happen between us while we were up here, which Hannah was fine with. And I . . ." Aaron hesitated, his nose beginning to twitch. "I do plan to come clean about this. I decided it just now in my room. I'm going to tell Carly all about Hannah."

"You're a day late and a dollar short, Aaron. Carly already knows."

Aaron's eyes widened at her. "She does?"

"She's known about you and Hannah for weeks."

"So *that's* it," he said, thumbing his white chin stubble thoughtfully. "I had a feeling that something was . . . as I told you last evening, she's been acting rather strange of late."

"I wouldn't call it strange it all. You've brought your mistress to your mother's house for a major family event. How do you think that makes Carly feel? If my man did that to me, I'd be acting a whole lot more than strange."

Aaron grimaced. "I guess I have that coming. I won't try to excuse my behavior."

"Good, because you can't."

"But I would like to explain myself to you, if you don't mind. Because you have no idea what it was like to be me—a chess-club fatty who every boy always picked on and no girl ever wanted. How could someone like you possibly understand what that's like? Just look at you. You're built like a swimsuit model, you're gorgeous, you're—"

"Are you hitting on *me* now?"

"No! I'm simply pointing out that you've doubtless been fighting off guys since you were twelve years old. What you need to realize is that *no one* ever wanted me. Not ever. And now, because I happen to be a television celebrity, women actually do want me. Beautiful women. And, yes, I've succumbed to temptation. How could I not? It would be unnatural to deny myself after so many years of pain and suffering. Surely you can understand that much."

"I absolutely can, Aaron. But I also understand that you took an oath when you got married, and you've violated it. So kindly spare me the boo-hoo, okay? Because I was married to a player myself once, and I've heard all of the excuses, and they all add up to one great big pile of lame."

Aaron looked at her in hurt silence. "You genuinely don't like me, do you?"

"What do you care?"

"I'm not perfect, I freely acknowledge that. But I swear to you, my days as a player, as you call it, are behind me. I am going to end this thing with Hannah. She'll be disappointed, to be sure, principally because she sees me as her career savior. I did what I could for her with Grandmother. In that regard, my conscience is clear. It's not my fault the old girl is dead, is it?"

"I wouldn't know. You didn't exactly answer my question before."

"Regarding what?"

"Regarding Carly. Did you succeed in calming her down when you came up here looking for her?"

Aaron's face dropped. "I can't say I did, no."

"Exactly where was she?"

"You'll have to ask her that. The truth is, I never found her. Not until I heard Hannah scream." Aaron's eyes fell on the door to room three. "I came running out here into the hall, and Carly was standing right there outside of Ada's room with Hannah and Spence."

"Where had you been?"

"In our room."

"Alone?"

"Yes, alone."

"What were you doing in there?"

"Looking for Carly, as I just said. My God, you don't actually believe *I'm* the killer, do you?"

"Aaron, I'm simply asking questions," Des said. All the while thinking that Aaron Ackerman had no one to vouch for him when Ada was strangled. Not a soul.

Downstairs, Teddy finally switched to a new tune—an Ellington number, "Don't Get Around Much Anymore."

"Do you think it's too late?" asked Aaron.

"Too late for what?"

"To save my marriage."

"If the love is still there, it's never too late. But Carly did tell me that she's thinking about divorcing you."

"She would never do that. She didn't mean it."

"She sounded like she meant it, but you know her better than I do."

"I will try to be a better husband from now on," he said with firm resolve. "I just have to figure out how."

"By showing her the love and respect she deserves. By being honest with her. Hell, Aaron, do I have to draw you a picture? You're a smart guy."

"Not when it comes to women I'm not. I'm still that same lonely fat boy sitting all by himself in the cafeteria, wishing that some nice girl would come and sit—"

"Man, if you start in on this chess-club stuff again, I swear I will get ugly."

"You're right, you're right; I'm sorry." Aaron scratched irritably at the stubble on his neck. A rash was forming at the edge of his tightly buttoned shirt collar. "Carly will be fine on her own, if that's the course she decides to take. But I hope that doesn't happen. I'd genuinely like to save our marriage. I mean that."

"I'm sure you do. From where I'm sitting, your future depends on it."

"Why do you say that?"

"Because if Carly decides to get nasty, you can forget all about Common Ground. Also your town house, your farm and your stock portfolio. She'd clean your clock in a divorce court."

"You're not incorrect," he admitted. "I simply have to do a better job. If I don't, I'll lose everything. It starts at home, doesn't it? Learning how to listen to each other, I mean."

"Beats the hell out of *Hardball,* if you ask me. But that's just one girl's opinion."

"Well, from this moment on, it is my top priority. *Carly* is my top priority."

"Glad to hear it," Des said, wondering if he meant one single word of this.

"May I speak with her?" he asked.

"Not just yet. Soon."

Des led Aaron back to his room and went to fetch Carly from room eight, her mind turning it over. Aaron had no one to vouch for him when his grandmother was strangled. This gave him opportunity, and that made him a suspect. But what about his mother's death? Certainly, he had the greatest motive of anyone for killing Norma—becoming lord of Astrid's Castle was one hell of a motive. Only, what about opportunity? Could Aaron have engineered that digoxin overdose in the night? How? Acting alone? Or with some-one else, someone like Hannah, as his accomplice?

Carly was huddled in her mink in a chair before the fireplace, jot-ting down notes on an Astrid's Castle notepad and smoking a ciga-rette. Des still could not get over how much older and plainer she looked with her hair tied back and no makeup on.

"Is it my turn now?" she asked, glancing up at Des a bit skeptically.

Des stayed in the doorway so she could keep an eye on the hall. "If you don't mind."

"Of course not." Carly flicked her cigarette into the fireplace, tore several pages off the notepad and folded them into the pocket of her fur.

"That seems to be contagious today," Des observed as the profes-sor followed her to the chairs at the top of the stairs. "Aaron was making notes just now himself."

"We ought to compare them. That would be good for a laugh." Carly sat in the chair her husband had just vacated, shivering inside her fur. "I was just trying to get some personal priorities straight. I find I think better when I have a pen in my hand."

"I hear you. With me, it's a piece of graphite stick." Des sat back down, gazing at Carly intently.

Carly stared right back at her, her manner not the least bit guarded or uneasy. She was not behaving like someone who had anything to hide from the law. She just seemed cold. "What can I tell you, Des?"

"For starters, where were you when Ada got attacked? Aaron said he came up here looking for you, but you weren't in your room."

"I know." Carly nodded her blond head. "I was having a cigarette out on the observation deck."

Des shot a look at the glass door down at the end of the hall. "Kind of nasty outside, isn't it?"

"I'm a smoker," Carly said. "They shove us out into the rain, the sleet, snow, dark of night—we all ought to just quit our current jobs and become mail carriers. I guess I'm not being very amusing, am I?" She lowered her eyes. "Do you want the real truth?"

"That would be nice."

"I needed some space from Acky. He can make me so crazy, and I hate feeling that way. I don't feel like *me* anymore. Do you know what I mean?"

"I'd like to, Carly."

"I feel like an airhead in a daytime soap opera. Someone who is bovine and clueless and pathetic. I have a doctorate, damn it. How did I end up this way?"

"You fell in love, that's how."

"Never again," Carly vowed. "I will *never* let another man do this to me. I'm going to buy myself a nice little brick Victorian near campus in Staunton. I'll have my books, many comfortable chairs. I'll get myself a half dozen cats—"

"I can help you out in that department."

"And I'll become dear old prune-faced Professor Cade, Mary Baldwin's faculty eccentric. I'll have my students over for tea and spirited political discussions. I'll author a definitive text or two. When I retire, they'll name a building after me. I'll certainly be in a position to leave them a lot of money. Just think how many thousands of dollars a year I will no longer be spending to inject toxins into my face." Carly broke off, her eyes filling with tears. "I'm sorry, you're trying to take my witness statement and I'm carrying on like a lunatic."

"You're not doing anything of the sort. Was anyone else with you out there on the observation deck?"

"Not a soul."

"Do you know where Aaron was at the time?"

"Why, what did he say?"

"Carly, the format we're searching for here is I ask the questions and you answer them, okay?"

"Acky was in our room, I think."

"But you don't know this for sure?"

"I don't know anything. I was coming back inside when I heard Hannah scream. She was standing right here in the hall outside of Ada's room."

"Can you recall exactly where Aaron was at that moment?"

"He was out here in the hall with Hannah and Spence."

"He got here before you?"

"Well, yes."

"Interesting," Des said, because this directly contradicted what Aaron had just told her. One of them was lying. Or, possibly, mistaken. Witnesses often remembered a sequence of events differently. It could mean something. It could mean nothing. "Let's talk about last night, Carly. Can you describe how your night was for me?"

"It was long," she said, letting out a humorless laugh. "Put yourself in my position, Des. My unfaithful husband is lying there next to me. His humid young whore is parked in bed across the hall, waiting for him to make passionate love to her. I didn't drop off for a single second. I was too busy waiting to catch those two in the act."

"And did you?"

"No, I didn't. Aaron stayed in our bed all night. He never got up once."

"What about the other nights since you folks arrived here?"

"He hasn't dared. He grabs what he can when he thinks it's safe, like when I caught the two of them kissing out on the observation deck yesterday. But he's slept straight through the night every night. I can tell by his breathing. It's deep and steady. When he's awake, it's much shallower and more ragged."

"Sounds like you've made a real study of it."

"When you're married to a man like Acky, you become a pulmonary specialist, believe me."

"Oh, I believe you," Des said, wondering if Carly was being even remotely straight with her. Wondering if she'd lie to protect her husband. If she'd kill for him. What if all was not as it appeared to be? What if Aaron's fling with Hannah, Carly's little vanishing act last evening, the ladies' lounge histrionics—what if all of that was a ploy to throw off suspicion? What if Aaron and Carly were, in actuality, doing just fine together? So fine that they'd teamed up to commit these murders? "Last night, Carly, is there any chance that you yourself dropped off for a little while?"

"No chance at all," Carly answered crisply. "I was awake all night hashing over my new life plan. I've come up with my three top priorities. Number one is to rid myself of my humiliating, debasing marriage."

"And the other two?"

"Quit smoking and start researching a new book. I need to sink my teeth into some solid work. Work is the best man cure I know. Other than starting over with another man, of course. And that's not going to happen. Not for a good, long while. This time, I'm taking care of me."

"Carly, did you happen to get up in the night? Perhaps slip out for a quick smoke?"

"Not a chance. I couldn't. I'm afraid of the dark, you see. Always have been."

"Did you hear anyone else slip out? Footsteps out here in the hall? Doors opening or closing? Because if you were awake all night . . ."

"I was, I swear."

"Then you're in a real position to help me. Think hard, please. This is important."

Carly considered this for a moment, her eyes lingering on the sealed doors to rooms one and three. "You're wondering about Norma, I imagine. If Norma got up, I didn't hear her. But her room is right here next to the stairs. We're over in five."

"Ada was right next door to you. Did you hear her get up?"

"I'm sorry, no. I can't help you with that."

Des wasn't sure whether to buy this or not. While it was true that she herself had easily heard Les open and close the door to room ten from room one, it was also true that Les had not been making any effort to keep quiet. In the middle of the night, Norma and Ada doubtless would have.

"But I'll tell you what I did hear." Now Carly lowered her voice. "I heard somebody moving around upstairs."

Des frowned at her. "What do you mean, upstairs?"

"I mean, up on the third floor," she said, gazing up at the ceiling. "I heard the floorboards creak in the night. Someone was up there."

"Doing what?"

"Besides walking around? I truly can't imagine."

"But there's no one staying up on the third floor, is there?"

"Not a soul. During the off-season, they close it off to save on fuel."

"Any idea what time it was when you heard these footsteps?"

"Two, possibly three in the morning."

Des weighed this, baffled. Why would anyone have been wandering around up there in the middle of the night during a power outage? "And you sure you weren't dreaming?"

"Positive," Carly insisted. "My ears could have been playing tricks on me. It was a stormy night, and old places like this creak like crazy in the wind. Maybe that's all it was. Or maybe it was mice. But you asked me what I heard . . ."

"And you heard creaking floorboards." Des glanced up at the ceiling doubtfully. "Anything else?"

"No," said Carly, the tip of her tongue flicking delicately at her lips. "Not unless you count the lovemakers."

Des cleared her throat, well aware that she and Mitch had gotten more than a little bit busy last night. "Which lovemakers?"

"The ones next door in Spence's room."

"Spence had a woman in his room last night?"

"I'm assuming it was a woman. I don't think he's gay. Mind you, one never knows for sure."

"Well, who was she?"

"I have no idea."

Des had very little doubt. It had to have been Hannah. After all, she and Spence had known each other for years from the studio's internship program. The only question was whether they were long-time lovers or if this was something new. And it was a mighty important question, because if the two of them went back a ways, then it was entirely possible that they were the ones who were behind these killings. Only why would *they* take out Norma and Ada? What was in it for them? "Exactly what did you hear, Carly?"

"The usual moaning and panting. I don't have to act it out for you, do I?"

"Not necessary. You're sure this was coming from Spence's room?"

"Positive."

"Had you heard the woman go into his room sometime earlier?"

Carly stared at her blankly. "Now that you mention it, no."

Downstairs, the piano had fallen silent. The sudden quiet that descended upon the castle was almost eerie.

"But she could have gone in there while everyone was getting settled in for the night," Carly suggested. "Plenty of doors were opening and closing, plus the furnace monkey was making firewood deliveries."

"His name is Jase," Des growled at her, hearing raised voices down in the entry hall now. "Did she stay the whole night?"

"Well, I didn't hear her leave."

Des searched her memory of early that morning, when Les found Norma dead in bed beside him and cried out for help. They'd all come spilling out into the hall. Hannah had come out of her own room. Spence had been alone in his. She was quite certain. "Are you sure about that, Carly?"

"I'm sure."

Now Des heard heavy footsteps behind her on the stairs, someone heading back up. "And you're sure you didn't fall asleep for a few minutes?"

"I *told* you, I was awake all night."

"Well, then how on earth did she—?" Des never got the rest of her words out.

It was Carly. Her big blue eyes were bulging with fright. "Oh my lord!" she gasped, gazing over Des's shoulder at the stairs.

And that's when Des whirled and saw him standing there.

CHAPTER 13

LES WAS STUDYING HIM very, very intently.

The innkeeper's face was extremely close to Mitch's. No more than a foot away.

He's checking to see if I'm awake, Mitch supposed.

Although, quite frankly, Mitch was finding it hard to suppose much of anything just yet. He felt dazed and confused, the world around him a vague, befuddling fog. Slowly, as Mitch began to emerge from that fog, he became aware that the back of his head ached. And now he recalled that Les . . . Les had *hit* him, knocked him out cold. That's why he was presently lying on the frigid dirt floor of the woodshed. And that's why Les was watching him.

Not saying anything. Just watching.

With great difficulty, Mitch tried to formulate a coherent sentence out of the words that were tumbling around in the cotton batting inside of his head. He wanted to ask the man a simple, straightforward question: "Why in the hell did you hit me, Les?" But he couldn't seem to get the words out. His vocal chords were too far away. And yet his brain *was* beginning to clear. And it was starting to dawn upon him that Les was lying on the dirt floor, too, one ear pressed to the ground as if he were listening for the thundering onrush of Choo-Choo Cholly. And not so much studying Mitch as he was staring at him. Not even blinking. Just staring and staring and . . .

Les is dead.

This realization came to Mitch like a splash of ice water in the face. When it did, he immediately let out a strangled yelp of shock and scrambled away from the man, the back of his head throbbing.

He put a hand to it and he came way with blood. Someone had definitely hit him. But not Les. It wasn't Les.

Les is dead.

The innkeeper lay on his stomach with a hatchet embedded deep in the back of his skull. Blood and brain matter were splattered everywhere. It was a truly horrible sight to gaze upon. Mitch willed himself to dab a finger in the puddle of blood on the ground next to the man's head. Still warm despite the freezing cold of the woodshed. Les had been dead only a few moments.

No one has come looking for us yet. No one knows.

As he knelt there, the wind and snow swirling outside the open barn doors, it suddenly dawned on Mitch that Les's killer could still be there in the woodshed with him. Drawing his breath in, he flicked his eyes around at the clutter of tools, searching every dimly lit recess. But no one else was there. Just he and Les. The killer had fled.

A hickory log the approximate thickness of a Louisville Slugger lay on the floor at Les's feet. It had blood on it. Mitch guessed that it was his own, that this was the weapon that had knocked him out. Whoever killed Les had wanted him out of the way. And yet, apparently, not dead. *Because I'm not.* Which seemed like a highly selective form of mental processing for someone who had to be a psychopathic crazy. Not that Mitch was complaining. He just didn't get it.

Why am I still alive?

He realized he didn't know. And, as he climbed slowly to his feet, he realized he had spatters of Les's blood and brains all over his Eddie Bauer goose-down jacket. His stomach did an immediate flip-flop and he lost his skillfully reheated breakfast onto the ground. Dizzy and sick, he staggered over to the tool bench, found a rag and swiped at his jacket with it, knowing that he truly did not belong here. He belonged in the Film Forum watching a nice, harmless Martin and Lewis double bill, maybe *The Caddy* and *Jumping Jacks*. With maybe a jumbo-sized box of hot buttered . . . *Okay, forget the hot buttered popcorn,* he commanded himself as his stomach flip-flopped again. *But do what you have to do. Go after Les's killer. He can't have gone far. Les is still warm, remember? Go on, get your plump heinie out of here. . . .*

Mitch's legs felt like a pair of wobbly broomsticks. And he was still as dizzy as hell. But he also felt a focused alertness coming over him. He had a job to do. He made it over to the open doorway, swaying there like a young sapling, and squinted out at the snow, his eyes searching for movement of any kind, a dab of color from someone's jacket. He saw no movement, nothing. Now he turned his faltering attention to the snow. There were no footprints leading from the woodshed off toward the woods or the parking lot. Only the footprints he and Les had made on their way out here from the kitchen, still deep and fresh. But as Mitch studied their prints more closely, he realized that there were in fact *three* sets of prints heading out here—*and* another set that originated in the shed doorway and led back toward the castle's kitchen door. Translation: Whoever killed Les had come and gone from the castle. And was probably back in there right now with Des and the others.

"Des!" Mitch called out, his voice straining against the howling wind. "Desss . . . !"

No use. The looming castle was too far away, its walls made of solid stone. She would never be able to hear him in there.

Flashbulbs suddenly started popping right before his eyes. He felt as if he might pass out again. He dropped to one knee in the shed doorway, breathed deeply in and out. He grabbed a handful of snow and rubbed his face with it, feeling its wet, stinging cold.

Slowly, he got back up and started his way back across the courtyard, making sure to avoid the killer's footprints, his own feet clumsy blocks of wood beneath him in the crunchy ice and snow. With each gust of wind he could feel himself start to pitch over. Twice in the first ten steps he took, Mitch did go down. But he got back up both times, spitting snow out of his mouth. He had to get back up. If he stayed down, he would end up like Les. So he kept walking, one foot in front of the other, left foot, right foot . . . He was going to make it. Mitch knew this. He knew it because he had prepared for it—marched his way across the frozen tundra of Big

Sister each and every morning. He could do this. He *would* do this. Even if he did keep falling over. Even if this was starting to remind him less of his morning rounds than of Omar Sharif's epic trek across Siberia in *Dr. Zhivago* . . . Left foot, right foot . . . Zhivago trying to get back from the front lines to his beloved Lara, to Julie Christie . . . Left foot, right foot . . . Once again, Mitch pitched over into the snow. This time, he really, really wanted to stay down. The snow felt so soft, like a pillow. He could sleep. He wanted to sleep. It was so hard to stay awake. But no, he had to get up. He must get up. Chest heaving, he climbed back onto his feet and resumed . . . Left foot, right foot . . . Left foot, right foot . . .

Now he was closing in on the kitchen porch. He'd nearly made it. It was slushy there under the overhang. Many wet shoe prints, none leading off anywhere else. Les's killer had come this way.

Mitch threw open the door, immediately hearing Teddy and that damned piano. An old Ellington song. The kitchen floor was dry. The killer had taken off his boots before he came in. And done what, hidden them somewhere? Where was the killer now? And how on earth had he gotten in and out when Des was watching the hallway? Was everyone upstairs dead, too? Was *Des* dead?

He called out her name. Once, twice, three times. Heard the piano stop, heard footsteps.

And then Teddy came rushing across the kitchen toward him, looking pale and frightened. "My God, Mitch, what's happened?"

"Des," he groaned. "Have to see Des."

And now he was staggering past Teddy out into the entry hall, groping his way blindly up the stairs, blinking from all of those flashbulbs that kept popping, popping . . . *"I'm ready for my close-up, Mr. DeMille . . ."* Teddy was calling after him, panic in his voice. But he was doing okay. He was making the climb on his legs of Silly Putty, getting there, getting there, almost there . . .

Only it wasn't Des whom he encountered at the top of the stairs. It was Carly. She let out a horrified gasp at the sight of him, and Mitch could feel himself starting to pass out. His head was a balloon on a very long string, bouncing up, up, up against the ceiling. One of the people way, way down below was Des. Alive, thank God. He saw her jump to her feet.

Heard her cry out, "What happened to your head?"

And, *whoosh,* there went the air right out of Mitch's balloon. As he came *zoom-zooming* all the way back down from the ceiling, he croaked, "Les . . . the woodshed . . ." And then the hallway floor suddenly tilted to a forty-five-degree angle and headed right for him and he was gone again.

When he came to this time, Mitch was lying on the hallway floor with everyone standing over him looking terrified. All except for Des, who wasn't around. And Hannah, who was kneeling on the carpet beside him, waving something stinky under his nose. Ammonia. It was ammonia.

"What's your name?" she barked as she shone a flashlight into his eyes.

"I'm Mitch," he replied hoarsely. "We've already met, haven't we?"

"Do you know where you are, Mitch?"

"Uhh . . . on the floor."

"On the floor *where?*"

"Astrid's. Hannah, do you have to shine that light right in my eyes?"

"Mitch, you've taken a blow to the head and you've lost consciousness. I'm checking to see if your pupils are equal and reacting to light—which they are, so there's no indication of brain damage. Good, good." Hannah flicked off the light and gripped his hands tightly with hers. "Can you feel this?"

"Yes."

"And what am I doing now, Mitch?"

"You mean, besides squeezing the hell out of my ankles?"

"Okay, this is all good. Can you sit up?"

"I can try."

"Here, give me your hand, big guy," Spence said, reaching his own hand down to him. The others just stood there, pie-eyed and mute.

Mitch grabbed hold and Spence pulled him up to a sitting position. Hannah pressed something cold against the back of his head. It was a wet washcloth. A bloodied one already lay discarded on the rug next to him.

"Where's Des?" he wanted to know.

"She's checking out the woodshed," Spence said. "She'll be right back."

"You got yourself quite some smack on the bean," Hannah observed, examining his wound. "The bleeding seems to have stopped, but you should keep applying pressure for a little while longer. We can put some gauze over it later if it starts oozing. I don't think you'll need stitches."

Mitch pressed the cold compress against the back of his head, peering at her. "Have you done this before?"

Hannah let out a big bray of a laugh. "When your mom's a nurse you learn first aid before you can read and write."

"Why don't you let me see what I can do with that, Mitch?" Jory offered gently. She meant his blood- and brain-spattered jacket.

Mitch unzipped it and she helped him out of it and took it into one of the rooms.

"How long was I gone?" he wondered.

"Thirty seconds," Carly answered in a trembly voice. "No more than that."

"No, I mean outside. How long were we out there?"

"A few minutes," Teddy said. "Ten, tops. And I was just sitting there playing the piano like a damned fool. I had no idea that anything out of the ordinary was going on, Mitch. I just figured you guys were loading up on wood."

"We were," Mitch said. "Until somebody hit me."

And murdered Les. But Mitch didn't need to say this part out loud. They already knew it. He could tell by the looks on their faces. By how they kept glancing around at each other. They were not safe. None of them was safe. They knew this. Because, somehow, the murderer in their midst had just managed to take out Les despite Des's best efforts.

But how?

Mitch could not imagine. They had all been tucked inside their individual second-floor rooms, hadn't they? Except for Carly, with whom Des had been eyeball to eyeball, and Teddy. But if Teddy had stopped playing the piano for even a few seconds, Des would have noticed that, right? Besides, Teddy's trouser cuffs were dry, Mitch observed. They'd be soaking wet from the snow if he'd plowed his way out there and killed Les, wouldn't they? Mitch's certainly were. And yet Teddy's were dry. Actually, everyone's legs were dry, he realized, looking around at them. No one was wet. And yet one of them had just knocked him unconscious and killed Les.

But how?

Jory returned with his jacket, scrubbed reasonably clean of blood and brains. "Good as new," she said, mustering a faint smile.

Mitch took it from her and thanked her.

Then he heard footsteps on the stairs and Des returned, her hooded shearling coat caked with fresh snow. "Are you okay, baby?" she asked, kneeling next to him with a fretful expression on her lovely face.

"I'm fine, totally okay. In fact, I'm going to get up off this carpet now."

"Careful, you've suffered a concussion," Hannah warned him.

"I don't think so, actually," Mitch said, slowly getting to his feet. "If I had, then I'd be experiencing short-term memory loss, and I'm not. And, believe me, I wish I were."

Des clamped a hand around his arm just in case he felt teetery, which he didn't. She said, "Okay, I'm going to have to ask you all to go back to your rooms."

"What the devil for?" Aaron demanded.

"Because I said so."

Aaron gaped at her, incredulous. "There's a homicidal lunatic loose among us and that's the best you can offer—go to your rooms? What are we, ill-behaved children?"

"He's right," Spence said. "It's not as if we'll be safe in our rooms. Or anywhere else in this damned place."

"Just please go to your rooms." Des kept her voice steady and firm. "You'll all be fine."

"No, we will not," Aaron argued. "It is blatantly obvious that a fresh approach is called for. I say we stay together. As long as we're all together, we're safe."

"I'm with you," said Spence. "Let's stick together in a group."

"Gentlemen, we need to get something straight right damned now," Des responded, drawing herself up to her full six-foot-one-inch height. Make that six-three in her boots. "This is not a consensual type of situation. I am in charge here."

"And you have been a spectacular failure," Aaron informed her. "Three of us have lost our lives so far on your watch. Believe me, when this nightmare is over I shall demand a full investigation of your conduct by the proper state authorities."

"You go right ahead," Des encouraged him, staying remarkably calm.

Which surprised Mitch, who was about ready to stuff his cold compress in Aaron's big mouth. He couldn't believe she was taking this crap from him.

"In the meantime, I still have to take your statements," she went on. "And I still want you in your rooms. So let's get moving."

Aaron stayed right where he was. "I say we arm ourselves."

Teddy let out a mocking laugh. "Oh, *do* you now, you manly man."

"Shut up, Uncle Teddy," Aaron snarled at him. "I'm sick of your sarcasm."

"There are ... couple of deer rifles in the kitchen," Jase murmured. "The gun case."

"Gee, I don't know about that, sweetie," Jory said doubtfully.

"No, no, he's right." Aaron pounced eagerly on the news. "Let's go get them. We can take turns standing guard until the authorities arrive. We *must* protect ourselves."

"I'm with Aaron," said Spence. "Let's arm ourselves."

"Hold on, guys, this is getting way out of hand," warned Mitch, his head throbbing. "What we need to do is relax."

"I'm with Mitch," said Teddy.

"Please, everybody just take it easy," Hannah agreed.

"Yes, kindly cool it with this vigilante business," Carly said. "And no offense, Acky, but when did you suddenly turn into Ollie North?"

"You know, I've had just about enough of *your* cutting little remarks, too," Aaron huffed at her, his nose twitching.

"How's that for a happy coincidence," she retorted sharply. "I've had just about enough of *you*."

Mitch glanced at Des, surprised that she'd let this situation flare up so badly. "What do *you* say, Master Sergeant?"

In response, Des pulled her SIG out of her coat pocket and showed it to all of them. "I say no one is touching those rifles. I say there is one gun and it's in my hand. Anyone who is not on board with that plan, kindly speak up right now, and I will be happy to bind and gag you for the duration. Anyone? How about you, Aaron?"

Aaron lowered his eyes and shook his head, reddening.

"Does anyone else have anything they'd like to say?" Des asked.

Jase cleared his throat and said, "Did Les get around to stoking the fires before he . . ."

"I'm afraid not, Jase," Mitch told him.

"Would it be okay if I . . . ?"

"Now is not a good time, Jase," Des said to him. "Please return to your rooms now, okay? All of you."

They obeyed her, grumbling and mumbling. And double-locking their doors behind them, each and every one of them.

Mitch and Des remained out in the hall, her hand still clamped around his arm.

"Why didn't you just shut that jerk up?" he asked her. "You practically had a mutiny on your hands."

"It's much better if you let people vent," she explained patiently. "That way, they get it out of their systems, and are less likely to actually do anything."

He smiled at her fondly. "Pretty smart, aren't you?"

"Not feeling very smart right now," she confessed, steering him over to the two chairs at the top of the stairs, where they sat. "On a rare positive note, the pilot of SP-One said he may be able to take off within the hour. You wouldn't know it to look outside, but the storm's tapering off. We'll need to plow a section of the parking lot so he can touch down."

"Sure, we can use Jase's truck. So you updated Soave?"

"From the woodshed," she replied, nodding.

"What did you tell him?"

"That I was wrong."

"About what?"

"I *don't* have this situation under control."

Mitch reached for her slender hand and squeezed it. "That's not true. You've done everything you could do."

"Les died on my watch," she said miserably. "That means I screwed the pooch. Aaron's not totally wrong."

"He is, too. There's no way you could have anticipated what happened to Les. How could you? From where I'm sitting it defies any form of logical explanation. It couldn't possibly have happened. And yet it *did* happen. All we have to do now is figure out how, and we will."

"Mitch, I never took my eyes off this hallway," she said as those pale green eyes of hers scanned the corridor. "They were all in their rooms, I swear. How did someone slip out on me, kill Les and then sneak right back in without me so much as catching a glimpse? How did someone do that? Who is he, the Invisible Man?"

"There's Teddy to consider. He was by himself in the Sunset Lounge."

"But I could hear the piano that whole time," Des countered. "Not once did he stop playing. I don't see any possible way he could have gone outside, bopped you on the head and—" She broke off, her eyes flickering.

"Did you just think of something?" Mitch asked her.

"No, not really," she said quietly. "How does your head feel?"

He glanced at the compress he'd been holding against it. Clean. The bleeding had definitely stopped. "Well enough."

"Can you remember how it all went down?"

"Very fast is how it all went down. We were loading up the wheelbarrow. I turned my back for one second and, wham, I was out. Honestly, I thought it was Les who'd hit me. Until I realized he was dead, that is."

"Somebody lost their breakfast out there."

"That was me, after I came to," Mitch said, shuddering. He was back there again, seeing Les lying facedown in the dirt. "Then I came straight in to get you. I didn't see any footprints leading anywhere else in the snow. Did you?"

"I followed two sets back to the kitchen door. I assume one is yours, the other belongs to . . . whoever."

"Can you tell anything from them? What kind of shoe the killer wore, the size?"

"The snow's way too mushy. I can't even tell whether a man or a woman made them."

"Do you think a woman could have done that?"

"Buried a hatchet in Les's head? No problem. I did notice that the kitchen floor was all wet."

"That was me, too. The floor was completely dry when I came in."

"You sure about that?"

"Positive. Whoever did it must have taken off their wet shoes before they came back in and tossed them in the snow or hidden them somewhere. Changed their pants, too, I'm figuring. Look at mine, Des. My cuffs are soaked. So are my gloves and my hat."

"I found one jacket in the coatroom that was plenty damp."

"Spence's, am I right?"

"You are."

"That's from when we were working outside before. Mine was still damp, too."

"And Jase's wool overshirt in the mudroom is damp."

"Same story. Did you find anything else?"

"No wet boots or pants, that's for damned sure. We'll find them eventually, but we can't afford to take the time right now. There are a million hiding places in this castle. Plus they could be out in the snow, like you said." Des stared intently down the hall, shaking her head. "I cannot fathom how someone got past me."

"Could somebody have gone out their window? The sills are pretty wide. Maybe they made it to the observation deck by climbing from window to window, then downstairs from there."

"Mitch, those sills have six solid inches of ice on them. And the windows are frozen shut." On second thought, she got to her feet and said, "I'm not taking anything for granted. Are you up for checking out the observation deck?"

"I sure am."

Des examined everyone's windows while Mitch headed to the end of the hall and pushed open the outside door. The snow was still coming down pretty hard out there. The sky did seem to be brightening a little, but that may just have been wishful thinking on his part. Or his head wound. He studied the snow carefully for fresh footprints, then came back and sat down and waited for Des to return.

"Anything?" he asked her when she did.

She shook her head. "You?"

He started to shake his head, but that only made it throb worse. "Bupkes."

Des lowered herself into her chair and brooded there in silence for a moment. "Okay, let's try going at this another way."

"Which is . . . ?"

"Why Les? Why did someone want to kill Les?"

"For one of two reasons, it seems to me. Either he figured out who killed Norma and Ada, and had to be silenced before he could tell you . . ."

"That plays," she said, nodding. "I'm with you so far."

"*Or* he actually killed them himself, and had to be punished."

"Are you talking about frontier justice? I don't buy that."

"Why not?

"Because that would mean we've got us two different crazies operating in the same physical space at the same exact time. It doesn't happen that way. Not in my experience. Not unless we're dealing with running buddies who've had themselves a nasty falling out."

"Maybe that's it. Ada did tell you *they* wanted this place."

"That she did," Des acknowledged. "What were you and Les talking about before you got knocked out? Did he give you any news we can use?"

"He may have. It turns out he was getting it on with Martha Burgess."

Des raised her eyebrows in surprise. "From the Frederick House? Well, well . . ."

"She doesn't exactly seem like the type, does she?"

"Mitch, there is no type. Wives who sleep around on their husbands are just normal everyday women like Martha. Although she is awful quiet, I'll give you that. Her husband, Bob, is the talker of the pair. A real Mr. Outgoing."

"Somewhat like Les in that regard, don't you think? Not that I mean to speak ill of the dead. He told me he couldn't admit it to you out loud in front of Norma, even if she was dead. He was ashamed, I think."

"Well, I can buy that. Do you think Norma knew who it was?"

"If she did, she never let on. Les did say that they'd been ultra-discreet. If I had to guess, I'd say neither Norma nor Bob knew about the two of them. Actually, Les said maybe he shouldn't have told *me,* under the circumstances."

Des frowned. "What circumstances?"

"Apparently, there's another little wrinkle he thought you should know about."

"*What* little wrinkle?"

"Des, I wish I knew. But that's when everything went black. I'm afraid we'll never find out."

"Oh, we'll find out," she vowed.

"You think so?"

"I do. It may take a while, but we'll get there."

"Des, there's something I've been wondering about."

"And that is . . . ?"

"Why am I still alive? Why didn't Les's killer murder me, too?"

"Didn't need to, didn't want to."

"Why not?"

"I honestly don't know. But it's a mistake to think that what's happening here is some elaborate scheme to do away with all of us, one by one by one. That's strictly out of that old movie you were talking about."

"You mean the one where no one gets out alive?"

"Really wasn't necessary to say that part out loud again."

"Sorry, I have a head wound."

"This is real life, Mitch. If somebody wants a whole bunch of people dead they line them all up in a row and shoot them down like dogs. End of story. Norma's death was planned ahead of time. But I still say everything that's happened since reeks of a busted play—Ada had to die because of what she found out, and so did Les. Now did he tell you anything else? Think hard."

"He said that the Frederick House is having financial problems. It occurred to me that maybe he intended to buy his way in with the two hundred thou Norma left him. Take Martha for his own and shove Bob Burgess out the door."

"Sounds like a plan," Des concurred. "Mind you, that would point the motive finger right at Bob Burgess for killing him. Too bad Bob's not here at the present time."

Which jarred something in Mitch's head. Something significant that he'd forgotten. "Des, how do we know he's *not* here?"

She looked at him closely. "Baby, do you need another hit of ammonia?"

"No, wait, hear me out. I just remembered something. When I got up to feed our fire in the middle of the night, I could have sworn I heard someone walking around up on the third floor. Astrid's Castle is a huge place with millions of nooks and crannies. What if someone else has been hiding up here with us this whole time? Someone like Bob Burgess. That would explain how Les's killer managed to slip out right under your nose—because he *wasn't* under your nose. He was hiding somewhere else in the castle, waiting for his chance to kill Les. Although why Bob would want to kill Norma and Ada, too, I can't possibly . . ." Mitch suddenly realized that Des was staring at him with a really strange look on her face. "You think I've suffered permanent head damage, don't you?"

"Far from it. While you were outside with Les, Carly told me that *she* heard footsteps up on the third floor in the night."

"Well, that settles it then," Mitch said, gazing slowly up at the ceiling. "We've got company."

"Slow down, cowboy. It's very likely that what you two heard was nothing more than the wind."

"Then again, it could have been Astrid."

"You just said *what* to me?"

"There's this thing they do for the tourists every year on Halloween," Mitch explained. "Which is that Astrid, that she, you know . . ."

"Mitch, believe me when I say this—I don't know."

"She haunts the castle. Her ghost, I mean."

"Okay, this is your head trauma talking now," Des said, nodding to herself. "Random gas is emitting from your person."

"Are you trying to tell me you don't believe in ghosts?"

"Are you trying to tell me you *do?*"

"Well, I certainly don't disbelieve in them. How can I? There are just too many things that happen in life which can't be explained."

"Like what, for instance?"

"Like us."

She stiffened at once. "Oh, is that right?"

"I mean this in a good way, Des. Just think about it . . ."

"Oh, I'm thinking about it, boyfriend. I am sitting here, thinking."

"We come from completely different worlds. We share no common experiences and have no earthly business being together, making each other so unbelievably happy. And yet we are happy. And that can't be explained by any conventional wisdom, can it?"

She let this sink in for a moment before she swallowed and said, "Well, no, you're not wrong about that. But, Mitch . . . ?"

"Yes, Des?"

"We are not ghosts!"

"I know this, and I for one am very happy about it."

"Besides which, we are no longer talking about what we need to be talking about."

"Which is . . . ?"

"One of us needs to take a look around upstairs. I can't leave this hallway, because I'm still clinging to the quaint notion that our killer is a corporeal individual, as opposed to Casper, the unfriendly ghost. Do you feel well enough to nose around up there?"

"Try and stop me."

She fished a master key from her coat pocket and tossed it to him. "You'd better take this, too," she said, handing him her heavy black Mag-Lite flashlight. "Bang it on the floor if you need me. I'll come running."

He got up out of his chair and started for the stairs. "Should we establish any kind of code? Say, three knocks means trouble, two knocks means—"

"Just smack the damned floor, will you?" she growled at him. "Hold on, there's something else I want to tell you."

"What is it?"

She came toward him, her eyes shiny and huge, and hugged him tightly. "When I saw you coming upstairs just now, looking the way you did, all of the air went right out of my body. I thought I was going to die. I *know* we can't be explained, and I don't care. I only care about how I feel."

"Back at you, slats," he said, kissing her softly, then not so softly.

Then she gave him a firm shove and up the stairs he went, clutching the Mag-Lite like a billy club. When he reached the top of the stairs, he encountered locked double doors that closed off the third-floor corridor entirely. Mitch used the master key and went in, closing the door behind him.

The third floor was very much like the second. Twenty-four rooms. More photos of famous guests of yesteryear lining the walls. More floral carpeting. That same steel door to the staff stairs halfway down the hall, a "Fire Exit" sign mounted over it. The only obvious difference that struck Mitch was that there was no door out to the observation deck at the end of the hall. Just a window. The air was exceedingly still up there. Freezing cold, too. It couldn't have been more than forty-five degrees. The room doors had all been left wide open, casting shafts of weak winter light out into the hall. Mitch stood still for a long moment, listening. He could hear his heart pounding, blood rushing in his ears. He could hear nothing else.

He began to search, the carpeted floorboards creaking under his feet. He started in the first room on his left, room twenty-five, which was directly above the room where Norma lay dead. He found a bed that had no linens on it. Just a bare mattress. He found a bathroom that had no towels, no soap, no sterilized water glasses. The bathroom door was thrown open wide and held in place with a wastebasket. So was the closet door. Something to do with ventilation, Mitch guessed. When he shone his light around in the closet, he found only empty hangers. He went across to room 26, and found it to be virtually identical.

From the third-floor windows Mitch could make out Big Sister's lighthouse standing tall and proud down at the mouth of the Connecticut River. Mammoth tree trunks and chunks of ice were flowing out into Long Island Sound—the very stuff that he would find washed up on Big Sister's slender beach when he made it back there. *If* he ever made it back there. It seemed as if his life out on Big Sister had been a million years ago. It seemed as if he'd always been here at Astrid's Castle and he always would be here. Time had stopped. Life had stopped.

But Soave hadn't steered Des wrong—the snow really did seem to be letting up.

As he moved on to the next empty room, Mitch thought he sensed movement behind him in the corridor. But when he turned around, there was no one and nothing. Just the deserted hallway. He was spooked, that was all. It couldn't be anything else—anything like, say, Astrid's spirit wafting through the air. Not a chance. No way. Mitch steadied himself, breathing in and out, and continued his search. He found more open doors, more bare mattresses, more nothing. There was no evidence that anyone was hiding up here. He was sure of this.

Until he went in room 31, that is. And once again sensed movement, heard movement—and then Mitch *saw* something out of the corner of his eye and he whirled and an immense pure white Maine coon cat leaped off of the dresser right into his arms, where it began to dig its front paws into Mitch's chest and purr and purr, just as friendly as can be.

"Well, hello there," Mitch said, standing there stroking it while he waited for his resting pulse rate to dip back down below 185. It was a beautiful cat with startlingly bright blue eyes and the longest, softest fur Mitch had ever felt. A she, by the look of things. "What are you doing up here all by yourself, girl? You must be the lonesomest pussy cat around." He put her back down on the dresser. Or tried to. She immediately jumped right back into his arms, scrambling up on top of his shoulder now, with her front paws thrown over onto his back.

Together, they moved deeper into the room. The mattress in here was bare, just as in the other rooms. But there was more than one bed in room 31. On the floor next to the bathroom doorway Mitch found a cat bed lined with blankets and chock-full of rubber mousy toys. The bathroom did not smell particularly fresh—the litter box in there needed emptying. Kibble and water dishes were positioned on a rubber bath mat. There were plastic storage tubs of kibble and kitty litter, a litter scoop.

There were also two hand towels on the towel rack. Both towels were damp, Mitch discovered. Somebody had been up here recently. Somebody had used these towels.

He moved back out into the bedroom with the cat in his arms and his wheels spinning. So this explained the footsteps that he and Carly had heard in the night. Someone must have been up here feeding this cat, which was living up here on the unheated third floor all alone because . . . well, why *was* she living up here all alone?

She was starting to wriggle around in his arms, so he put her down. She promptly began rubbing up against his leg and yowling at him.

"Well, you're quite the little talker, aren't you?"

In response, she darted toward the open closet and went inside. Mitch followed her, shining his flashlight around in there. Nothing. Just another empty closet. And yet the cat kept circling around and around in there, eager with anticipation.

"What is it, girl?"

She let out another yowl and began sharpening her claws on the carpet, her excitement mounting. The carpet in the closet was not the same as in the bedroom. It was newer and cheaper, made of some kind of synthetic material. Something that hadn't been installed particularly well. Sections of it lifted away from the floor as the cat's claws grabbed hold and pulled.

In fact, the far corner over against the wall hadn't even been tacked down at all.

Mitch knelt there with the flashlight for a closer look. Strips of one-inch wooden molding were tacked in where the floor met the walls, anchoring the carpet in place. Or at least in theory. In reality, Mitch discovered that the molding strips were tacked to the wall but *not* to the floor—because the carpet slid right out from under them.

The big white cat was all over him now, most anxious to get into whatever he was getting into.

Mitch turned back enough of the carpet to expose a three-foot-square section of old, unpolished wooden flooring. Here he found a trapdoor with a recessed thumblatch. The trapdoor was about twenty-four inches square and reminded him very much of the one that was in the floor of his sleeping loft at home. His was there for ventilation. Why was this one here?

He grabbed on to the thumblatch and slowly lifted the trapdoor open, revealing utter darkness down below. He pointed his flashlight down there. He was looking into the closet of the room directly below this one. Its door was closed. Whose closet was it? He couldn't tell. He could make out a couple of jackets hanging there, but from this angle he couldn't determine if they belonged to a man or a woman. Briefly, he tried to count out where room 31 was in relation to the occupants of the second-floor rooms, but that just made his head start to throb again. So he flicked off the light and stuffed it in his jacket pocket.

Tongue sticking out of the side of his mouth, Mitch gripped the edge of the floor with both hands and dropped down through the open trapdoor, hanging there in mid-air by his fingers, his legs waving wildly. Now all he had to do was let go. Which had sure looked a lot easier when Burt Lancaster and Nick Cravat did it in *The Crimson Pirate*. Those two had landed with nimble, effortless grace. Just as that damned show-off of a cat proceeded to do while Mitch continued to hang there and hang there, wondering what in the hell he had been thinking. Then he said his silent "Geronimo!" and let go, touching down with a colossal, well-padded thud.

At the sound of him crashing to the closet floor the door immediately flew open, flooding the closet with natural light. Someone stood silhouetted there in the doorway, hands on hips.

Mitch scrambled to his feet and dusted himself off. Checked to see if his head had started to bleed again. It hadn't. Then he smiled and said, "Hey, Spence, how's it going?"

CHAPTER 14

IT WAS THE SOUND of Mitch touching down on the floor of Spence Sibley's closet that brought Des running.

Not that she had even the remotest idea what had happened. Her first thought was that Astrid's Castle had just taken a direct hit from a short-range ballistic missile. It shook the floorboards and sent everyone spilling out of their rooms into the hallway, terrified. Everyone except for Spence, that is. When Des heard two—count 'em, two—male voices coming out of his room, she pounded on Spence's door and was greeted by none other than Mitch. Also by a huge white Maine coon cat that Des hadn't realized was even around until that very second.

How did Mitch and that cat get inside of Spence's locked room?

She didn't know. She only knew that Spence looked very unhappy.

Mitch, meanwhile, was grinning at her like a gleeful, moon-faced boy. "There's a trapdoor," he explained, tugging her toward the closet so she could see for herself.

"Time out. Where did this damned cat come from?" Des demanded, utterly bewildered. She also didn't like to be tugged. Never had.

"That's Isabella," Jory answered from the doorway, where she and the others were clustered. "She's the castle's unofficial mascot. Hey, Izzy. Here, girl . . ."

The big white cat padded right over to Jory, who bent over and picked her up. Isabella scrambled up onto her shoulder and perched there contentedly.

"She patrols the gardens most of the year," Jory said, stroking her. "Just loves being outside, don't you, girl? When it gets cold, she takes up residence on the third floor. We have a problem with mice up there. Plus Les couldn't be around her. He was allergic to cats."

"So she's got food up there?"

"She's got everything up there," Mitch answered. "A bed, a litter box, hot and cold-running mousy toys." He lowered his voice, adding, "The towels in her bathroom are damp, by the way,"

"Who takes care of her?" Des asked Jory.

"Norma did. Izzy was her cat, really."

"Was Norma likely to go up there in the middle of the night?"

"If she was awake, sure."

"Jory, why didn't you mention this to me before?"

"I wouldn't have let her starve or anything." Jory stuck her chin out defensively. "It just seemed like you had more important things to worry about."

"True, that," Des conceded, studying the opening in Spence's closet ceiling. "What can you tell me about this trapdoor?"

"It's a fire escape. Most of the old three-story houses had them. Otherwise, folks could get trapped in their top-floor rooms if a fire broke out during the night. Actually, those trapdoors were the only fire escape system Astrid's had when Jase and I were little. Remember, sweetie?"

Jase nodded his furry head.

"Then the fire code got stricter and they had to install a sprinkler system and fireproof steel doors to the back stairs."

"Are you telling me that all of these second-floor rooms have trapdoors like this?"

"Well, yeah," Jory replied. "They carpeted over them upstairs but the rugs are just kind of toenailed in. In an emergency, there's no harm in having an extra way out."

"I do not believe this," Des fumed, realizing she hadn't gone in their closet last night. Hadn't so much as opened the door. Just thrown her clothes over a chair and jumped into bed, as had Mitch.

"Hey, look at it this way," he said brightly. "We can definitely set aside our ghost theory now."

"Mitch, did you just land on your head?"

"No, I'm fine."

"Can you keep an eye on these folks for me?"

"Absolutely."

Des herded everyone into Spence's room, then unlocked the housekeeping closet out in the hall and fetched a broom. She went from room to room, checking the closet ceilings. Each had a trapdoor, just as Jory had said. With the broom handle, each trapdoor could easily be pushed open under the detachable third-floor rug—including the trapdoor in the very room she and Mitch had slept in. She positioned the dressing table chair underneath theirs. Standing on it, she did not find it particularly hard to pull herself up and into the closet of the third-floor room directly overhead. Admittedly, it was her business to stay fit. But any of these people could have managed the physical part of this, she believed. With the possible exception of Teddy. And Teddy wasn't an issue since he had been downstairs playing the piano, not locked away in his room.

Des nosed her way around the chilly, vacant third floor, her mind quickly playing it out. Once Les's killer had made it up here, he or she could have accessed the staff stairs by means of the third-floor hallway door and taken those stairs straight on down to the kitchen, bypassing her second-floor lookout entirely. After cold-cocking Mitch and killing Les, he or she had then stashed their wet things somewhere and returned to the third floor by those same stairs—using the towels in Isabella's bathroom to dry off before dropping back down into their room, completely undetected. A well-positioned chair would have prevented the seismic disturbance that Mitch had set off when he'd touched down.

Des stretched a length of crime scene tape across the bathroom door, wondering how many sets of fingerprints they would find in there, and to whom they might belong. She also devoted a great deal of energy to beating the living crap out of herself for not hanging up her pants in the damned closet last night. If only she'd gone in there. If only she'd gone in there *and* looked up. If she had, Les Josephson would still be alive right now. This should not have happened. No, it should not. She was off her game. Enraged, she paced the third-floor corridor, calling herself any number of vile, politically incorrect names.

Her cell phone squawked. She went over by the windows in Isabella's room to answer it.

And Soave said to her: "Yo, you are on a roll, Master Sergeant."

"Could have fooled me," she growled back at him.

"Hey, I don't like your tone of voice. You sound down to me. Are you down?"

"Rico, I don't have very much to be up about right now."

"You can't do this to me, Des. I need you to be up."

"Yeah, why is that?"

"You're my mentor, that's why. If a boy sees his mentor falter, it completely wrecks him."

"Rico, maybe the blood to my brain is starting to freeze, but you actually sound serious."

"Des, I totally am."

"In that case, feel free to cheer me up. What do you have? And *please* make it good."

"Yolie got through to Tom Maynard of Dorset Pharmacy."

"What did Tom have to say?"

Des's heart immediately started beating faster as Soave told her.

"So, what, you're not getting anywhere at your end?" he asked when he was done reporting.

"Starting right now I am, Rico," she said, gazing out the window at the frozen outside world. "Believe it or not, the snow has just about stopped here. How is it where you are?"

"Same. The SP-One pilot says he'll be good to go by the time we get there. Yolie's on her way over here right now. I figure we'll be on your doorstep in an hour, maybe ninety minutes. Sound good?"

"Way better than good. See you then, wow man."

After she rang off, Des idled there by the windows for a moment with her engine revving. Then she shook herself and went down through the open trapdoor into Spence's closet, with an assist by Mitch.

"Okay, everyone, new plan," she announced briskly. "We're moving downstairs to the taproom until the Major Crime Squad arrives."

"Oh, thank God," Carly sighed in relief.

"Amen," echoed Teddy.

"Sanity restored," Aaron declared, nodding his large head in agreement. "At long last."

"Is it okay if I make us some sandwiches and coffee?" Jory asked.

"Good idea."

"I'll give you a hand," Hannah said.

"*Now* can I go get some firewood?" Jase asked somewhat woefully.

"I'm afraid not, Jase. The woodshed is a crime scene, off limits." As the young caretaker's face fell, Des added, "But I do have a job for you. The parking lot needs to be plowed. Could you do that for me?"

"You bet." Jase brightened considerably. "Be happy to."

"You'll be needing the keys to your truck." She reached into her pocket for his key ring.

"Naw, I left 'em in the ignition. Always do."

Typical Dorset behavior. Des had never lived in a place where so many drivers left their keys in their cars. In fact, she hadn't known such places still existed. "Mitch can give you a hand," she said, glancing at her doughboy. "If that's okay with you."

"Totally," Mitch assured her. "Let's get cracking, amigo."

They all started out of Spence's room now.

Until, that is, Des put her hand on Spence's arm to stop him. "We need to talk," she told the studio executive.

"Whatever you want," he said readily.

Spence had kept a small fire going in his room. He poked at it and fed it with the last log from his woodpile, then sat in the armchair before it, looking very at ease and preppy in his burgundy crewneck sweater and flannel slacks. He was a handsome, well-put-together man. But he was also the type of man whom Des had never been attracted to. Too much smooth, corporate charm. Too few endearing personal quirks—they'd been bred out of him. Des preferred men who came fully equipped with all of their rough edges and flaws and surprises. Men like Mitch who were, for better or worse, *real*.

"What's that you're working on?" she asked, noticing the Astrid's stationery and ballpoint pen parked on the end table at Spence's elbow.

"A good old-fashioned love letter," he replied.

Des turned the desk chair around and sat, gazing at him. Spence gazed right back at her, unperturbed. He gave every indication of being agreeable, sincere and innocent. If this man was a cold-blooded killer, then he was in the wrong end of the film business—he belonged in front of the cameras.

"I understand from Mitch that you've stayed at Astrid's before."

"Many times, yes. Ever since I was a little boy. We held our Sibley family reunions here."

"Did you know anything about those trapdoors?"

Spence let out a laugh. "Hell, yes. Every red-blooded kid who's ever stayed here knows about them. My cousins and I used to sneak from room to room in the middle of the night. We'd tell ghost stories, smoke cigarettes, major mischief like that. It was great fun."

"What happened to Les wasn't great fun," Des pointed out, knowing that it would be a long time before she forgot the sight of the innkeeper on the woodshed floor with that hatchet stuck in his head. She'd taken photographs, her third set of the day. It would take her months to draw her way out of this particular winter storm. "Someone used their trapdoor to sneak out and kill him."

"I realize that," Spence said somberly, lowering his eyes.

"Why didn't you warn me about them, Spence? Don't you realize you could have prevented his death?"

"You seemed very sure of what you were doing, so I assumed that you knew. Didn't think it through, I guess. I should have spoken up. You're absolutely right." He glanced up at her uncertainly. "You do believe me, don't you?"

"I have no reason not to," she replied, wondering if he was lying to her. But say he was. Say he was behind all of this. How on earth had he been thinking he'd get away with it? He wasn't dumb, and sure didn't seem crazy.

"Do you have any idea who did it?" he asked her.

"It could have been anyone. Anyone who knew about those trap-doors. I assume Aaron does. Hannah I'm not so sure about. What would you say?"

"About Hannah? I wouldn't know. You'd have to ask her."

"Then again, it could have been you."

"Well, it wasn't," he assured her wholeheartedly. "I have nothing to do with any of this. I'm as shocked and horrified as can be. Plus I've just watched a solid month of hard work go right down the drain. I can't begin to tell you how many man-hours I've spent put-ting this damned weekend together. The movie-going public thinks these gala events just happen. That the stars *rush* in to attend every tribute or benefit that comes along. Trust me, they don't. They have to be begged, every last one of them."

"There's something personal I need to ask you about, Spence."

"Absolutely. Fire away."

"Carly told me she heard you entertaining someone in here last night."

Spence reddened, but said nothing.

"The strange part is that she swears she didn't hear anyone come in or out of this room all night long."

"What was she doing, spying on me?" Irritation had crept into his voice.

"No, on her beloved Acky. You just got caught in the crossfire."

"Oh, I see."

"Carly also mentioned hearing footsteps up on the third floor. I didn't know about the trapdoors at the time. But now that I do I'm sitting here thinking *this* must be how your late-night visitor got in and out of here, am I right?"

Spence thumbed the light brown stubble on his square jaw for a long moment before he said, "Look, this is extremely personal . . ."

"I'm well aware of that. I'm also somewhat surprised by your behavior, Spence. What with you telling Mitch how deeply involved you've gotten with a certain unnamed East Coast lady."

"I *am* involved." He glanced at the love letter he'd been writing. "Very involved. It's complicated."

"I'm cool with complicated," she said. "Complicated is fine by me. Just as long as it's the complicated truth. Give it up, Spence. Is she anyone I know?"

Spence got up and held his hands out to the fire for warmth. Then he turned to face her, sighing. "Look, she's Natalie Ochoa, okay?"

Des stared at him blankly. "Okay . . ."

Spence seemed stunned by her response. "You don't live in the New York media market. Her name doesn't actually mean anything to you, does it?"

"I'm afraid not," Des said. Outside, she could hear the harsh scraping of Jase's plow as it cleared the parking lot, his truck's engine roaring. "Give me a boost, will you?"

"Natalie anchors the five-o'clock news on Channel Four. She's rated number one in her time slot. She's so popular that the network is grooming her to take over their morning show. Natalie's the complete package, Des," he exclaimed, a warm glow coming over his face, "she's beautiful, smart, classy. Not to mention Latina, which hooks her up with the fastest-growing demographic base in the nation. She's very, very hot in network news circles right now. She's also very, very *married*."

"Hence your reticence regarding her name?"

Spence nodded. "We've been seeing each other for six months or so. We have to be real careful or it'll end up in the gossip columns, which could really hurt her image. She and her husband are definitely planning to separate. It's over between them. But for now, it's just a real mess. And it's weighing heavily on my mind, what with my own career thing getting thrown into the mix. That's what I was just writing her about. I'm supposed to relocate to the West Coast next month. Natalie's future is here in New York. She has zero interest in moving back to L.A, where she started out. I don't know what we'll do. I just know . . . it can be a real mess sometimes. This whole love thing."

"I'm with you there. Although I'd drop the word *sometimes*."

Spence sat back down in the armchair, studying Des in guarded silence. "You don't actually think I have anything to do with these deaths, do you?"

Des tried a new approach on for size. "Are you kidding me, man? You're my prime suspect."

Spence's eyes widened in dismay. "I'm *what?*"

"Real deal, Spence," she assured him, nodding her head slowly up and down. "I've been waiting and waiting for you to come clean with me about who was in here with you last night, and you're not. Hell, man, Stevie Wonder could see that you're not being straight with me about it. And if you're not being straight about that, then I have to assume you're not being straight about anything else. I've got three people dead, Spence, and you're withholding valuable information. That means you win the grand prize. When the Major Crime Squad folks arrive you get to take the all-expenses-paid trip to Central District Headquarters in Meriden. Congratulations."

Right away, Spence's smooth composure gave way to panic. "You mean I'll be *arrested?*"

"Brought in for formal questioning."

"My God, will I need a lawyer?"

"That's entirely your decision."

"Does the . . . will the news media find out about this?"

"I imagine they'll be all over it, what with Ada being so famous and Astrid's such a landmark. It makes for quite a story."

"Do you have *any* idea what this could do to my career?"

"That's not my concern. The ball's in your court, Spence. If you don't want to talk, I can't force you to. I have to respect your rights." She got to her feet, not particularly fast, and said, "Come on, we may as well join the others until the chopper gets here."

Spence stayed put, his hands clutching the arms of the chair. "Wait, there's more I can tell you. I want to help, okay? I didn't kill anyone, I swear. Why would I? I came up here to *help* Ada, not strangle her with a phone chord. And I hardly knew Norma and Les. I hardly know any of these people."

"You've known Hannah for years," Des said to him sternly.

"Yeah, okay, that's true," he admitted. "We did go through

Panorama's internship program together. But Hannah's strictly a friend. Someone who I have no romantic feelings for whatsoever. Besides, she's with Aaron, as you know perfectly well."

"I do know that. Hannah's gotten herself caught in a messy love triangle. It occurs to me that maybe she was trying to send Aaron a message last night by having herself a visit with some other man. Is that possible?"

"No, it's not possible," Spence insisted. "That didn't happen."

"Well, *someone* dropped in on you last night. Am I at least right about that much?"

Reluctantly, he nodded his head. "She has to be real careful because of Norma's zero-tolerance rule. Any staff member caught fooling around with a guest is automatically gone. Norma was really obsessed about it, I guess because this place used to be known as a cathouse."

Des sat back down, narrowing her eyes at him. "Just for the record, are we talking about Jory?"

"We are. And, believe me, I didn't initiate it. It was all her."

"Spence, I'm not doubting on your animal magnetism, but are you telling me that Jory jumped your bones right out of the blue?"

"Last night she did." Spence shifted uneasily in his chair. "But we're not exactly total strangers. Jory and I go back a few years. Twelve, actually. The summer when I turned sixteen I stayed here with my parents for a couple of weeks. Jory was working as a chambermaid in those days, and I couldn't take my eyes off her. She was an older woman, all of eighteen, and extra-spicy. The girl was hot. Major boobage, if you know what I mean."

"Yeah, I'm catching what you're pitching."

"Anyway, to my great surprise and delight, she was interested in me, too. We ended up having sex together on a blanket in the woods. She was my first, as a matter of fact."

"And were you hers?"

"Not a chance. She could have—and did have—pretty much any guy she wanted. Quite honestly, I was surprised as hell to discover she was still working here when I arrived from New York on Tuesday. I figured she'd be married by now, have her own house, a couple of kids."

"So you two haven't stayed in touch?"

"Well, I did see her occasionally when I was at Yale," he conceded. "A buddy of mine, Pete Willet, sailed out of the Dorset Yacht Club, and we'd come out here every so often to kick back. If Jory was free, she'd scrounge up a girlfriend for Pete and we'd party out on the Sound together. Jory works hard for a living. She likes to rock and roll when she gets the chance."

"So when the college boy got him the itch, he'd give the chamber-maid a call. Does that about cover it?"

"I wouldn't portray it that way at all," Spence said defensively. "Nobody got used. It was a mutual-consent kind of a deal. Good times. Good sex. Well above average, actually. Jory wasn't looking for anything meaningful with me. She was just looking for humpage. She's really a lot like a guy in that regard."

Des smiled at him sweetly. "Is that right?"

"Not that I mean to plunge myself into the quicksand of sexual politics," he added hurriedly. "I'm just trying to give you my sense of things."

"How about giving me your sense of last night, Spence?"

"I couldn't get to sleep," he recalled, letting his breath out slowly. "I was freezing cold, and missing Natalie like crazy, when out of nowhere I hear footsteps and Jory's sliding right into bed next to me, peeling off her clothes, reaching for me. And I'm like, 'Jory, what the hell are you doing?' And she's like, 'Just for old times' sake, okay? I'm so lonesome and blue.' Des, I was totally up-front with her. I told her I'm seriously into somebody. And she said, 'That's okay, so am I.'"

"Who is she seeing?"

"She didn't say."

"You weren't curious?"

"At that particular moment, I couldn't have cared less—not that I'm trying to be offensive."

226

"You're doing fine, Spence. Well above average, actually. How long did she stay with you?"

"A couple of hours."

"And you say this was all her idea?"

"I swear it was. I was swamped with work from the moment I got here. I barely had a chance to say two words to her. I asked her how she'd been, but that's all. I didn't hit on her. And I sure didn't invite her up to my room. I'm involved with Natalie, remember?"

"Right, you're involved with Natalie," Des said back to him. "Did Jory tell you anything at all about this man who she's involved with? What he does for a living? How they met?"

Spence shook his head. "Mostly, she talked about Jase."

"What about Jase?"

"How dependent he is on her. How she feels responsible for him, and frets over him day and night. She keeps hoping he'll meet a girl and settle down on his own. Lately, she's been trying to fix him up with the weekend chambermaids and waitresses. But the guy hasn't so much as gotten out of the batter's box, let alone to first base. I guess he's kind of shy around the ladies. Jory asked me if I'd give him some pointers while I'm here, man-to-man. She's getting kind of anxious, I guess, because if he doesn't break away from her soon, chances are he never will."

"Does Jase know about you and Jory?"

"I think he must. He's always glowering at me. And he was really busting my chops this morning when we were out working in the driveway. My sense of things is that he sees me as some hotshot who's been taking advantage of his sister. Which, as I said before, is not true. Jory is just as responsible as I am. More so, last night."

"You said she left you after a couple of hours."

"Yes."

"By way of the trapdoor again?"

"She seemed pretty familiar with the drill, to tell you the truth. I'm guessing she's dropped in on plenty of guys over the years."

"I see," Des said, figuring that it was most likely she whom Mitch and Carly had heard up there in the night, not Norma. "What did you do after Jory left?"

"Well, I didn't fall asleep, I can tell you that. I felt so incredibly guilty. I still do, because I'm in love with Natalie. Jory and me, that shouldn't have happened. But it did. And I let it. And I liked it. And I . . ." Spence hesitated, his jaw muscles tightening. "I kept thinking, hey, it's not like Natalie *isn't* climbing into bed every night with her husband, Joel, right? And you have to figure *they're* still partaking of the humpage sometimes, don't you? It would be dopey to think otherwise, wouldn't it?"

"I suppose that's one way of looking at it," Des responded, noticing that Spence was digging the fingernails of his right hand so deep into the palm of his left that he was about ready to draw blood. The smooth young studio executive did not have it so totally together after all. When it came to his love life, he was a tortured mess of emotions. Was he in control of these emotions, or were they running the show? She wondered. "After Jory left, did you hear anyone coming or going out in the hall?"

"I didn't hear anybody."

"And where were you this morning when Ada was attacked?"

"Right here," he replied, stabbing the arm of the chair with an index finger for emphasis. "I was talking to Natalie on my cell phone when I heard Hannah scream. Natalie could hear her over the phone. She asked me what was happening. Go ahead and call Natalie if you don't believe me. She'll back me up. I was on the phone with her at the time of Ada's death."

"Okay, that's not actually what I'm hearing from you, Spence."

He frowned. "What are you hearing?"

"That you were on the phone when Hannah found Ada's body. Technically, you could have strangled her before you slipped in here to call Natalie."

"Well, yeah, okay," he allowed readily enough. "I can see your point. But why would I do it? What possible reason would I have for killing Ada Geiger? Or the others? I've just landed a huge promotion. I'm in love with a beautiful woman. Why would I want to get dragged into any of this?"

Des didn't answer Spence, for the simple reason that she didn't have an answer. Not unless, somehow, he'd gotten himself dragged into it against his will. Or unless every single word he'd just told her was a carefully scripted fabrication. Which was certainly possible. But if Spence *was* being reasonably straight with her, then he was right. He had so many positive things going on right now. Why get dragged into this? For Jory, whom he could apparently sleep with anytime he wanted to? Where was his motive? What was in it for him? For that matter, what was in it for Jory? True, she stood to gain fifty thousand dollars from Norma's death. Not exactly chump change, but was it worth murdering the woman for?

No, not a whole lot of sense here. Not yet.

Spence was looking at her searchingly, trying to follow where her mind was going. "Why would I do it?" he repeated.

"I wish I had some answers for you, Spence," she replied quietly. "But I don't. All I have is more questions."

It seemed eerily quiet down in the taproom, considering how many people were crowded in there around the kerosene space heaters. So quiet that Des could hear the tick-tock of the antique wall clock behind the bar, punctuated by the occasional scrape of Jase's plow outside on the pavement of the parking lot. It took Des a moment to realize what was missing.

There was no background music.

Teddy wasn't playing the piano in the Sunset Lounge. He was seated at the bar, sipping a Scotch and looking very sad. Aaron sat on the stool next to him, chewing halfheartedly on a sandwich. Isabella was sprawled on the bar before them with a saucer of milk, offering up her soft white belly for a rub. The big cat was getting no takers. No one was paying any attention to her. No one was saying anything. They were all just sitting there, trying not to go insane with fear.

The three women, Carly, Hannah and Jory, all looked up at Des apprehensively as she and Spence came in the door. Des felt as if she'd just barged into a hospital waiting room with word of whether the patient's cancer had spread or not.

"Jory, I'm going to need to ask you a few more questions," she said, flashing her a reassuring smile. "I have to clarify some things."

"Anything I can do to help, Des." Jory glanced uncertainly over at Spence, whose own eyes were glued to the carpet. "When would you like to do it?"

"Right now, if you don't mind."

"Sure thing." Jory collected the empty sandwich platter and started for the door with it. "Are you hungry, Spence?"

"I sure am," he replied, moving over toward the bar.

"I can make some more sandwiches, if you'd like." Jory's eyes lingered on him.

"That would be great," he said, stubbornly refusing to look at her.

Jory stuck out her bulldog chin and headed for the kitchen. Des followed her, noticing that Jory was one of those women who had two walks—wiggly for when a man was walking behind her, plain vanilla for when a woman was.

There was a loaf of sliced whole wheat bread on the kitchen table, which was crowded with sandwich fixings—a big hunk of baked ham, a wedge of Swiss cheese, sliced radishes, tomatoes, lettuce, pickles, jars of mayonnaise and mustard. Jory went right to work on the ham with a carving knife, shaving off thin slice after thin slice, her movements practiced and skilled.

"It's funny, I was *so* afraid to open the refrigerator this morning," she chattered at Des as she worked. "I didn't want all of the food in there to spoil. But it finally dawned on me that it's the same temperature out here as it is in there—so what's the difference, right?"

The girl was definitely running at the mouth, Des observed, taking a seat at the table. Major ill at ease.

"So how can I help you, Des?" she rattled on, slathering four slices of bread with mayo and mustard. "What else can I tell you?"

"Why you lied to me," Des replied quietly.

"When did I do that?"

"You told me you never left your cottage last night. We both know that's not true. You were in Spence's room."

Jory blushed, her round cheeks mottling. "I suppose he bragged to you all about his great big conquest."

"Actually, he was very reluctant to give it up. I had to squeeze it out of him."

"How did you manage that?"

"By threatening to take him in for questioning."

"That would do it, all right." Jory finished making two ham and cheese sandwiches, passed one over to Des and immediately started building two more. She offered her nothing in the way of information. Not a word.

"Jory, I've got three deaths to account for," Des said, attacking her sandwich. She'd eaten nothing all day, and was famished. "I could care less about you and Spence keeping each other warm in his room last night. But I need the real deal from you. Why you lied to me. What else you didn't tell me. And I need it right now."

"Okay, sure. Whatever." Jory flopped down in the chair directly across from Des, swiping at a strand of hair that had come loose from her topknot. "I was afraid you'd tell Les. That's why I was a bit less than straight with you about it before. If Les had found out I was in Spence's room last night, he would have fired me instantly. Me and Jase both."

"Because of Norma's zero-tolerance rule?"

Jory shook her head. "No."

"Well, then why?"

"Because the old creep was hot for me, that's why," Jory replied wearily. "You should have seen the way that man would stare at me—day after day, night after night. He'd just keep staring at my assorted body parts with those filthy eyes of his. He made me feel crawly all over. Because I'd *never* go with someone that old, for God's sake. Especially *him*. He was just such a lech. I'll bet he told you what a good husband he was. How much he loved Norma. Well, he wasn't and he didn't. He was obsessed with me from the moment he moved in here. He'd get insanely jealous if I showed even the slightest interest in a man—our produce supplier, the Fed Ex guy, *anyone*. Just last month he fired Franz, one of our chefs, because we went to a movie together on my night off. One lousy movie, Des."

"Why didn't you quit?"

"And go where? This is the only job I've ever held."

"They do have such a thing as sexual harassment laws."

"My word against his," Jory said dismissively. "Who do you think they're going to believe, the president of the Chamber of Commerce or the pair of tits who mops the floors?"

"Did Norma know about this?"

"Of course she did. He was so obvious it was painful. She also knew that I did everything I could to discourage him."

"Did she ever confront him about it?"

"She promised me she'd talk to him, but she never did. She was too afraid of antagonizing him. Norma had a lot of insecurities, you see. To do with her weight and all. She couldn't help me, wouldn't help me. So I put up with it. I could deal. I've had horny guests hitting on me ever since I grew breasts. It's an occupational hazard if you're in the hospitality business. I just had to avoid being caught alone in a room with him."

"When the power went out last night, you were alone in the cellar with him."

"I know." Jory's plump lower lip began to quiver. She bit down hard on it.

"Jory, did something happen down there?"

"Not physically, no. He just . . . he told me I was in his dreams every night. And he got kind of specific about those dreams. I'd really rather not go into the details, if you don't mind. Every time I start to think about them I feel like throwing up."

"Mitch told me that Jase seemed worried when he found out Les was down in the cellar with you."

"He knew how Les felt about me," Jory said, nodding. "But I always told him it was okay, I could take care of myself. The old creep was basically harmless."

"Firing a chef for taking you to the movies is not what I'd call harmless," Des said as she devoured her sandwich, which was delicious.

"I'm with you there, Des. All I meant was that he'd never actually try to rape me or whatever. He just wanted to imagine things about me and then . . . say them out loud to me. That's how he got off."

"Did you know that Les was seeing another woman?"

"Martha Burgess, sure. He told me all about her."

"What did he say?"

"That the affair was all my fault. That the only reason he was having sex with Martha was because he was so aroused by me."

"Last night you told Spence that you're involved with someone yourself."

Jory lowered her eyes, gazing down at the sandwiches she'd just made. "I did, that's true."

"May I ask who he is?"

"There's no one," she replied faintly. "I'm not actually seeing anyone."

"You lied to Spence?"

"I did," she admitted.

"Why would you do that?"

Jory shot a glance at the dining room doorway, then leaned across the table toward her. "Des, could we keep this between us?"

"If I can, I will."

"I didn't want to scare him off, okay?"

"Not okay. I'm still not following you."

"God, this is *so* embarrassing to say out loud," Jory confessed, clearing her throat. "The awful truth is that I've been hopelessly in love with Spence Sibley ever since high school. He was my very first, Des. When it happened, I led him to believe I was a woman of vast experience when it came to sex. I wasn't. I've always tried to be the woman he wants me to be. No clinging, no promises. Nothing but good, frisky fun. For *years* I've been telling Spence that I'm not looking for anything serious, when the truth is that all I think about day and night is marrying him and having his babies. For me, there's never been anybody but Spence. Someday, he'll realize he feels the same way about me. I believe that in my bones. But I also believe that if I pursue him too hard, I'll scare him off. So I've been careful to hide my true feelings. And patient. I've been *so* patient."

"And he has no idea how you really feel?"

"He's a man. They never know how we really feel, do they?"

"Girl, you'll get no argument from me there." Des flashed a smile at her. "Only, Spence claims he's mad about someone in New York."

"Who, Natalie? She's *nothing*. A brief infatuation. That'll blow over. Believe me, there's only one woman in this world for Spence, and you're looking at her. When he called me to say that the studio was sending him up here for Ada's tribute, I was ecstatic. We hadn't seen each other since last summer and I've really, really missed him."

"Last summer?"

"Well, yeah. Supposedly, he was coming out to Dorset to sail. But he ended up staying here with me for the whole week instead. Des, that was the most romantic, perfect week of my entire life." Jory studied Des carefully from across the table. "He didn't mention it to you?"

"No, he didn't," Des replied, wondering why Spence had purposely downplayed how deep into Jory he was. Not that she'd expected him to tell her the whole truth. No one ever actually did that. Still, this was an awfully choice morsel to omit from the telling.

"He stayed here with me for a whole week." Jory sounded tremendously hurt now. It bothered her that Spence had neglected to mention their idyllic interlude. "Every morning we woke up in each other's arms."

"How did you manage to pull that off? Without Norma getting hip to it, I mean."

"He slept out in the cottage with me. Norma hadn't a clue. No one did."

As Des thought this through for a moment, she realized that there could actually be *no* doubt in Spence's mind that Jase knew all about him and Jory. Jase did share that cottage with Jory, after all. Again, Spence had been less than straight with her. Why? "How does Jase feel about him?"

"Who, Spence? He's fine about him. He always worries, naturally."

"About what?"

"Losing me. Not that he has any earthly reason to worry. I've told him a million times that no matter who I marry he'll always have a home with us. Jase knows that. It's written in stone. Still, he worries. Do you have a brother or sister?"

"I'm an only child."

"Well, then it's hard to explain. But there's a bond between Jase and me, a blood thing. And that bond can never, ever be broken." Jory stirred herself and transferred the sandwiches from the cutting board to the platter. "I'd better deliver these. Spence seemed awfully hungry."

"Sure. I just have one more question."

"Absolutely. What is it?"

Des polished off the last of her own sandwich, leaned back in her chair and took a deep breath before she said, "Who slipped the digoxin into Norma's cocoa—was it Les or was it you?"

CHAPTER 15

"EIGHT BALL IN THE side pocket," Mitch announced as he proceeded to sink it. "That's game."

"Yet again," Aaron grumbled sourly. "This means I must owe you . . . how much *do* I owe you now?"

"Well, you'd climbed your way up to a hundred sixty dollars. Double or nothing makes it three hundred twenty, unless my basic math skills went out the window when I got whacked on the head." Actually, he felt fine, aside from the steady ache. "Mind you, that's only if we're playing for real money."

"Oh, we are," Aaron assured him, shooting a nervous glance over at Carly and Hannah, who were seated in charged silence together before a kerosene heater. The two women in Aaron Ackerman's life were behaving very snappishly toward each other. Clearly, Aaron was concerned that a full-fledged bitchfest was about to break out.

Spence, seemingly unaware of the tension, sat there with them while he waited hungrily for Jory to bring out a fresh supply of sandwiches from the kitchen. Des was apparently asking her some follow-up questions while she made them. Mitch didn't know what about. He did know that he sure could go for one or more sandwiches himself.

"I pay my honest debts," Aaron insisted, opening his wallet.

"Whatever you say, Aaron."

"*But* I'm afraid I'll have to write you a check," he apologized, beating a hasty retreat. "I don't have nearly that much cash on me."

Over at the bar, Teddy let out a mocking laugh.

"Have you got something on your mind, Teddy?" Aaron demanded.

"Hardly ever," Teddy replied, sipping his Scotch. "And when I do it usually turns out to be a dreadful idea."

"Therein lies the secret to your success, or lack thereof," Aaron said unpleasantly. "How about one more game, Mitch? Double or nothing?"

"Rack 'em up." Mitch moseyed over to the bar, where Isabella lay on her back with her paws in the air, yearning for a belly rub. Mitch complied, missing Clemmie and Quirt.

Over by the window, Jase continued to stare anxiously out at the dozens of trees that had come down. Which was all he'd been doing ever since Mitch had dragged him back in, per Des's orders. Jase hadn't wanted to come back in. There was much work to be done, and he'd been thrilled to be out there, doing some of it. Mitch had never seen anyone have quite so much fun plowing a parking lot before. But standing there now in his wool checked shirt, stocking cap pulled low over his eyebrows, Jase seemed caged and agitated. His right knee was jiggling.

"Your break, Mitch." Aaron had finished racking the balls.

"Blue sky," Jase said suddenly, hunched there at the window.

Mitch went and joined him for a look. In the western sky out beyond the Connecticut River, he could make out breaks in the clouds and actual patches of blue. At long last, the storm was passing. "We did it," he exclaimed. "We survived."

"Oh, thank goodness," exulted Carly. "Maybe we can actually get out of this awful place. I want to be *home*."

"I'd settle for a hot shower," Hannah said, shivering.

"What's that?" Carly snapped at her. "What did you just say?"

"I've never been so cold in my whole life," Hannah answered sharply. "I feel like every bone in my body is about to shatter. I will never be this cold again, I swear. As far as I'm concerned, this settles it."

"Settles what?" asked Aaron, arching an eyebrow at her.

"I'm moving back to Los Angeles."

"Oh, *are* you now?" Carly said, well aware that they were talking about something more than Hannah's weather preferences.

"This is rather sudden, is it not?" Aaron was caught off guard, and flustered.

"I'm making the move." Hannah's voice was filled with resolve.

"I'm packing my bags as fast as I can, gassing up my clunker and *going*."

"What will you do for work out there?" Aaron's own voice had taken on a rather unappealing whiny tone.

"I don't know and I don't care," Hannah replied. "I'll sling beers at a bowling alley in Pacoima if I have to. Just as long as I'm warm. *Anything* is better than this."

"Your mind's objectively made up?" Aaron pressed her, as Carly glared right at him.

"All made up," said Hannah, effectively slamming the door shut on whatever it was that the two of them had together.

"Hannah, I hope you won't give up on your dream to make a film about Ada," Mitch said. "You've got so much talent, and she's such a great subject."

"She's also *dead*," Hannah pointed out. "I needed on-camera face time with her, Mitch. She was the last of her generation. Her contemporaries are all dead and buried. With her gone, I have no one to put on film. Where's my documentary?"

"Who says it has to be a documentary?"

Hannah widened her eyes at him. "I should write her life story as a bio-pic, is that what you're saying?"

"Why not? She led one hell of a life, and it's a great part for the right actress."

"It's an *Oscar* part, are you kidding me?" Hannah said excitedly. "Nicole Kidman could play the hell out of her, or Cate Blanchett or, God, *Streep*. There's Ada young, Ada old. There's triumph, tragedy . . . Wow, Mitch, you've really given me something to think about on my long drive west. Thanks."

"No problem. And if all else fails, you'd make a great nurse."

"Not a chance. I hate hospitals."

"I'm staying right here," Spence announced emphatically. "Not *here* as in Astrid's Castle," he explained, on their blank stares. "Here in New York."

"What about your promotion to the Coast?" Hannah asked him.

"I'm turning it down."

"Spence, what are you talking about?" she demanded. "That job is everything you've been working toward for years. You're about to become a heavy hitter. What are you, crazy?"

"No, totally sane," Spence said, grinning at her. "It just so happens my priorities have come into acute focus over the past twenty-four hours, and Panorama Studios isn't one of them. But, listen, I'll put in a good word for you before my name turns to total poop. If you decide to pitch them that idea about Ada, I mean."

"That would be awfully nice of you, Spence," she said gratefully.

"No problem. Friends help friends out."

Mitch went back over to the pool table and broke, thinking about how bizarre this all seemed—Hannah and Spence sitting there chatting about their futures as if nothing unusual had just happened. As if no one had been murdered. As if no one's future plans actually consisted of life in prison without chance of parole. Because somebody in this castle, in this very room, was a killer.

But who?

Mitch sank the nine ball with his break and went to work on the table as Teddy sat there at the bar, sipping his Scotch, lost in his thoughts.

Aaron was caught up in some thoughts of his own. "Spence, what were you and Des talking about upstairs?"

"Personal things."

"What sort of personal things?"

"The sort that are none of your damned business," Spence said to him abruptly. "That's what makes them personal."

Jase turned away from the window to look at Spence curiously. Actually, they were all looking at Spence curiously. Except for Isabella, who had fallen asleep.

"Spence, it so happens that this *is* my business," Aaron informed him loftily. "It's my family that's dying here. It's my castle."

"Well, *I'm* not yours," Spence shot back. "So shut the hell up before I take a swing at you, you pompous boob."

"I've got twenty bucks on the blond guy," Teddy jumped in eagerly.

"Teddy, you are not helping," Carly chided him. "And neither are you, Acky. Calm down, and kindly lose your new lord-of-the-manor act before I take a swing at you myself."

"You're right, you're right." Aaron immediately backed down, chastened. "I apologize, Spence. I'm merely upset. I want to know what's going on."

"We all do, kiddo," Teddy said.

"Nobody knows," Carly said, swallowing. "Except for the person who did this, that is."

"A condition which I find completely unacceptable," Aaron said.

"It's strictly a temporary condition," Mitch assured him, dropping the eleven ball in a corner pocket. He still hadn't yielded the shot to Aaron yet. If nothing else, this was turning into a very profitable winter storm. "Des will get to the bottom of this soon enough."

"You sound awfully confident," Aaron said.

"I am. I believe in her."

"*How* will Des get to the bottom of this?" Teddy wondered.

"By being smarter than the average bear, that's how," Mitch replied. "She'll lick this. And her reinforcements from the Major Crime Squad will be landing here before you know it. If they have to, they'll analyze every single hair and fiber of clothing in Ada's room until they find what they need. Which they will. Whoever did this can't go anywhere. So just try to relax. Let the professionals handle it."

"Mitch is totally right," Spence said. "And speaking for myself, I am totally starved. I may have to eat my shoe if Jory doesn't get in here soon with those sandwiches."

"She should be back by now," Jase said fretfully. "What's taking her so long?"

"She's talking to Des," Mitch reminded him. "She's okay, Jase."

"What if she's not?" Jase had started pacing around the taproom, scratching furiously at his beard.

"As long as she's with Des, she'll be perfectly safe," Mitch said.

"No, she won't!" Jase moaned. He was over by the fireplace now, wringing his hands, breathing heavily.

And they were all studying him in guarded silence.

"Why not, Jase?" Mitch asked.

Jase didn't answer. Just paced in anxious silence, scratching at his beard so hard it was almost as if he wanted to tear it from his face.

"Jase, is there something you want to tell us?" Mitch pressed him gently. "Do you know something?"

"*She* knows." He was over behind the bar now. "Des knows."

"Knows what, Jase? What does Des know?"

"That . . . that . . ." Jase let out a strangled sob, then lunged suddenly for something that was stashed under the bar.

It was a handgun.

And he was pointing it at them, his eyes bright and wild.

"Oh, I don't believe this," Carly groaned.

"Y-You just shut up!" he stammered, aiming the gun right at her. "I know all about w-what you think of me. And you can just shut up. I . . . I run things now!"

"Sure, you do, Jase." Mitch could feel his heart begin to race. And his mouth was very dry. "Just take it easy. We're all friends here."

"Bullshit!" Jase cried out. "We are *not* friends!"

"Is that thing loaded?" Aaron inquired. "Do we know for an actual fact that it's loaded?"

"It sure is," Teddy said. "No point in keeping it there if it's not."

Mitch frowned at Teddy. "You knew it was there?"

"Les bought it last year after he was held up in here by a pair of drunken louts from Rhode Island. It's a Smith and Wesson, I believe he said. A thirty-eight."

"You *knew* it was there?" Mitch repeated in disbelief. "Why didn't you say something?"

"It's no use, Mitch," Teddy replied with a vague wave of his hand. "I'm no good at the responsibility thing."

"And *that's* supposed to make it okay?" Aaron roared at him. "The fact that you're a nitwit?"

"Why are you yelling at *me*?" Teddy protested. "*He's* the one with the gun."

"God, shut up, shut up, shut up!" Jase screamed at them. "All of you just . . . shut . . . up!"

They went silent, all eyes on the emotionally fragile young caretaker who was standing there behind the bar with the loaded thirty-eight.

"What's going on, Jase?" Mitch asked him, trying to keep his voice calm.

"I'm the boss of you now, that's what," Jase said toughly as he edged his way out from behind the bar, waving the gun at them as if it were something alive, something he could barely restrain. "And I'm tired of being pushed around."

"Nobody's pushing you, man," Spence said. "Just chill out and put down the gun."

"He's right, Jase," Mitch agreed. "Let's not lose our cool here."

"I'm not *losing* anything," Jase argued. "Mitch, put your hands behind your head right now. Go on, do it."

Mitch obliged him, making no sudden moves. He did not want to stampede him into firing that gun.

"Now take me to Jory," Jase ordered him. "Jory needs me."

"I can definitely do that, Jase," Mitch said. "But are you absolutely sure this is what you want to do? Because once we walk out of this room together, there's no going back."

"Hell, yeah, I'm sure." Jase gave him a hard shove toward the tap-room doorway, jabbing him in the back with the nose of the thirty-eight. "I've never been so sure of anything in my life. Let's go."

CHAPTER 16

"*WHAT* DIGOXIN?" JORY GAZED across the kitchen table at Des, mystified. "What do you mean?"

"I mean that a colleague of mine just hooked up by cell phone with Tom Maynard, our friendly home-town pharmacist."

"Sure, I know Tom," Jory said easily. "I went through school with his oldest girl, Tabitha. She got married last summer to Casey Earle. Casey's major dull, but his dad owns Tri-County Paving so who cares, right?" She paused, shaking her head at Des. "What about Tom?"

"He confirmed that Norma recently needed an extra refill of her digoxin prescription. It seems Norma somehow misplaced a nearly full bottle. She searched the castle from top to bottom but couldn't find it anywhere, she told him. Since Norma's health insurer would only cover one refill per month, the extra one had to come out of her own pocket. So she was real mad at herself. That's why Tom remembered it—because Norma was so mad at herself."

Jory let out a soft laugh. "I'll bet she was. Norma hated wasting so much as a nickel. Why are you telling me this, Des?"

"Because I'm almost positive that's how Norma was killed—by an overdose of digoxin dissolved in her late-night cocoa. And because, according to Tom, Norma requested this extra refill a full two weeks ago, Jory. That lets out all of the folks who came here for Ada's tribute. Whoever drugged Norma is someone who is here all of the time. Either you or Les, in other words. It had to be one of you, since I don't peg Jase as any master schemer."

Jory said nothing to this. Just sat there, her pink hands folded before her on the table. At her right elbow was the cutting board with the hunks of ham and cheese on it.

"It took me a good long while to arrive at you, if that's any consolation." Des studied her from across the table. Jory Hearn did not look at all like a bad girl. She was pretty in a wholesome sort of way, hardworking, capable, agreeable. The truth seemed almost impossible to believe. But Des did believe it. "Mostly, I couldn't figure your motive," she went on. "I kept thinking Aaron and Hannah must have cooked up the whole thing. He's the one with the huge financial upside. She's the one whose mom is a nurse. That girl knows her first aid—I figured her for the digoxin idea. It all played. Until Les got himself murdered, that is. Then my attention shifted to him and Teddy. Teddy's strapped for money, as was Les, and Norma had provided for both of them in her will. Being her executor, Les knew all about that. I started thinking that maybe he and Teddy murdered her together, then had themselves a falling-out over Ada. Teddy did appear to have the best opportunity for killing Les. He was downstairs playing the piano when Les and Mitch were out in the woodshed. The rest of you were locked up tight, or so I thought. And Teddy did mention to me that he'd once given Norma a tape of himself playing "More Than You Know." What if he'd slipped that tape of his into the battery-powered sound system in the dining hall and cranked it up good and loud? I'd be sitting there in the upstairs hallway thinking he was in the Sunset Lounge, playing, when he was actually outside murdering Les. It was plausible. Of course, once I found out about the trapdoors, I realized it could have been any of you. And now that we've spoken to Tom Maynard, everyone else is off the hook. Like I said, they weren't here two weeks ago when you stole Norma's pills. And that's where you blew it, girl."

Jory remained stubbornly silent. She wasn't giving an inch.

So Des kept going. "I'm figuring you pretty much had to play it the way you did. You couldn't sneak a few capsules out of the bottle, here and there, because Norma would come up short at the end of the month and notice it. You had to make it look as if she'd misplaced an entire bottle. Also, in fairness to you, you had no way of knowing at the time that you'd need to cover your tracks by killing Ada. The old lady wrecked your whole scheme, didn't she? You would have gotten away with it if it hadn't been for her. I certainly bought that Norma died of natural causes. Her doctor would have verified that she had a serious heart condition. The medical examiner would have likely forgone the autopsy. It was all working for you, Jory. Until you went and killed Ada. That meant we had to take a fresh hard look at Norma. That also meant Les had to die because . . ." Des paused, shoving her heavy horn-rimmed glasses up her nose. "Actually, this part I still don't get. Was Les going to pin it all on you, is that it?"

Jory lowered her eyes, gazing down at her hands folded there on the table. Slowly, her gaze inched over toward the cutting board at her elbow. And to the carving knife that lay there. It was very long and very sharp.

Des watched Jory's eyes carefully. Also her hands. Her own hands were stuffed in the pockets of her coat. "The time for kidding ourselves is long past, Jory. Les is dead, you're alive. That puts it all on you. So start talking. I repeat: Whose idea was it to put the digoxin in the cocoa—was it Les or was it you?"

"Des, I don't know what you mean," she responded finally, her hands edging fractionally closer to that knife. "Really, I don't."

"Sure you do." Des shifted her SIG out of her pocket and into her lap. "But you've got to get off this story about Spence Sibley being the great love of your life. It's sweet, but it's also complete crap. You *did* rock his world last night. That part's real. But the rest of it is straight out of a Harlequin Romance. You don't feel any love for Spence, and we both know it. So show me some respect, Jory. I don't think you're a bad person. But something bad has happened here, and you were involved. You can't get away with it. That's not going to happen. So get out in front while you have the chance. Work with me. Trust me. If you do, I can help you. If you don't, I can't. And, by the way, you should know that my weapon is pointed right at you underneath this table. Move any closer to that carving knife and you're dead."

Jory's froze, her eyes widening. "You'd *shoot* me?"

"Like a rabid raccoon." Des reached over and snatched the knife away from Jory, then sat back, her SIG still trained on her under the table. "I actually felt sorry for you this morning, know that? I sat here at this very table listening to you sob about how Norma was like a mother to you, and I felt bad for you."

"Hey, I feel bad for me, too," Jory said softly, her eyes puddling with tears. "You can't imagine just how much I ... wish I had ... never ..." She let out a huge, ragged sob, the tears spilling down her pink cheeks.

Des waited her out in patient silence. The tears often flowed at this point. They signified nothing. Nothing to do with sorrow or regret, that is. They were strictly about fear.

"God, I want to wake up from this nightmare," Jory sniffled, swiping at her eyes with the back of her hand.

"So wake up and start talking."

"It was all Les's idea," she began, her voice sounding flat and defeated. "He manipulated me, set me up, whatever you want to call it. And I fell for it all the way. I'm a bird-brained fool. I am *so* stupid."

"Exactly how did Les set you up?"

"The bastard promised to marry me, that's how."

"You and he were lovers?"

"I wouldn't call it love," she said bitterly. "But I did lie to you just now about how he was always harassing me. He didn't have to. I gave myself to him willingly. It was easy, really. All I had to do was close my eyes tight, grit my teeth and think about something, any-thing else. I let that man have me again and again and again. I ... I helped him get rid of Norma, too. All because I believed his prom-ises. I should have known better. I *did* know better. But I wanted to believe him. It's all passing me by, Des. I'm closing in on thirty and I'm so miserable. I'm trapped in this place. I'm lonely. I'm poor. And I want more. I want a life for myself. The sad thing is, Les knew all of this. That's what made me his perfect sucker. Can you understand that?"

"Keep talking. I'm listening."

"He told me that when Norma died, this place would be all his. That *he* would inherit Astrid's Castle. And he would marry me and we'd live happily ever after together. God, talk about a fairy tale. But I went for it. After living my whole life in that grubby caretaker's cottage, stripping the soiled sheets off other people's beds, swabbing out their toilets, smiling at them and smiling at them . . . Think of it, *I* would be running the castle. It would be *my* castle. And I wanted that, Des. Not only for me but for Jase."

"Did he know that you and Les were involved?"

"No, never," she replied. "Jase could tell that Les was into me. That much was pretty obvious. He even warned me to watch out for Les. But I shielded him from the ugly truth, which was that I'd been sleeping with the man for months. We'd slip away once or twice a week together. I'd tell Jase I was running errands, or getting my hair cut. You see, I've always tried to shield him from the truth about people and the awful kinds of behavior we're capable of. Jase is really so innocent that way. He can't understand how people will just flat-out lie. That's what Les did to me. He lied. Made the whole story up. I overheard the terrible truth this morning—that the castle didn't pass to him, it passed to Aaron. The bastard knew this all along. He'd signed a pre-nuptual agreement. But he dangled it in front of me anyway, like a pot of gold at the end of the rainbow. And I bought it. And so I slept with him and I killed Norma for him," she confessed, biting the words off angrily. "He *made* me kill Norma for him."

"Exactly how did he do that, Jory?"

"He said that if I didn't kill her he'd tell her all about our affair. That I'd seduced him. That I was a conniving little slut who slept with lots of guests, often for money. Norma would have fired me instantly. Jase, too. We'd have ended up renting some moldy shack up by Uncas Lake. I'd be working as a cashier at Dunkin' Donuts. And God knows what sort of work Jase could get. Les was a cunning old snake, Des. He was probably leading Martha Burgess on, too. Telling that scrawny dishrag he'd marry *her*. Or maybe he really was planning to marry her. Who knows? I sure don't. I thought he loved me and would marry me. And it was never true, Des. I was never anything more to him than a stupid bimbo who he could screw every which way possible." Sunlight broke through the retreating storm clouds now and streamed through the kitchen window, a shaft of it slanting across Jory's face. "I fooled myself, Des. God, how I fooled myself. But I didn't know that until this morning. And by then the whole damned thing had exploded in our faces."

"Walk me through it, Jory. Step by step."

"Sure, I can do that," she said woodenly. "Les decided that last night was the perfect night for us to make our move. A whole lot of stress was piling up on Norma this weekend. Throw in an ice storm, a power outage—it just seemed to him like the ideal night for her heart to give out. He told me this down in the wine cellar, when he came down to fetch me. 'This is our chance,' he said. 'Tonight's the night.' Assuming she got up, of course. But she got up pretty much every night. Made her cocoa and read her John O'Whoever-he-was. I kept an eye out for her in the cottage. When I saw the flicker of her lantern in here, I joined her. Told her I couldn't sleep either. Told her to let me make the cocoa for her. Les was the one who stole her heart medicine. I'd broken a dozen capsules open and poured the powder into a tiny plastic bag. While we were busy girl-talking away in here, I dumped it into her mug. My back was to her. She never saw me." Jory's mouth tightened. "Unfortunately . . ."

"Ada did," Des said.

"The way that old lady glided around this place, I swear it wasn't human," Jory protested angrily. "I didn't see her. I didn't hear her. All I know is she was suddenly standing right in that doorway with her beady eyes trained right on me. She'd heard Norma come downstairs, I guess. Thought she'd join her. I put on water for her herbal tea and kept sneaking looks at her. Des, those eyes of hers just kept boring right back at me. She didn't so much as blink."

"She knew what you'd done?"

"Not at the time, I don't think. Because if she'd suspected anything, she would have told Norma to pour out the cocoa, right? She didn't. She let Norma drink it. What I do think is that Ada was afraid."

"Afraid of what?"

"That Norma's heart condition was much more serious than

248

Norma had been admitting to her. That Norma required heavy doses of medication and it was my job to make sure she got it. I figured she was concerned about her daughter's health. Not that Ada said one word about it. It was like she didn't want to invade Norma's privacy or something. She just drank her tea and went back up to bed. After Norma finished her cocoa, she went back to bed, too."

"Then what happened?"

"I rinsed out the mug and saucepan, dried them and put them away. Then I sneaked into Spence's room and jumped his bones."

"Why did you do that?"

Jory hesitated, shifting uneasily in her chair. "Look, I'm not very proud of this . . ."

"Girl, you're saying that to me like you're proud of any of it."

"Good point," Jory conceded, coloring. "I needed to be with someone at that moment. I didn't want to be alone, knowing what I'd just done. Knowing that Norma was going to die there in her bed in the next few minutes. Knowing that Les was going to be right next to her in that bed, watching her die, letting her die. Can you even get your mind around the horror of that?"

"Les didn't sleep through it. Is that what you're telling me?"

"Of course he didn't. And just the thought of it made me shudder. I . . . I needed to obliterate it from my mind. Spence was there, so I figured why not. It wasn't as if he'd kick me out on a cold winter night. Also, I was concerned about what Ada might or might not know. Spence could vouch for me, if necessary."

"Vouch for you how?"

"Well, think about it, Des. I acted like I was really concerned about waking up Norma. I tiptoed up the third floor, sneaked in and out through his trapdoor. If I'd known she was dead, I wouldn't have bothered to do that, would I?"

"I guess you have a point there," said Des, who suddenly felt very sick inside. It was the careful, calculated evil of it all. A murder of passion she could understand. A woman walking in on her man in bed with another woman, blowing his brains out—that was human. This here, this wasn't human.

249

"You were right about Spence and me," Jory went on. "There was never anything more than sex between us. I could never love a man like Spence. He's way too involved in himself. It sure made a nice fairy tale, though, didn't it?"

"If you believe in fairy tales."

"I never have, actually," Jory said, smiling faintly. "Not even when I was a little girl. I knew there was no Santa Claus. And for sure that there was no Prince Charming. I've always known that."

"And yet you claim you fell for Les's promises."

"I did. I wanted to believe them. I wanted to believe *him*. That was my one big mistake."

"Girl, you made a whole lot more than one," Des told her. "Let's move ahead a few hours. It's dawn now. Les has just pretended to wake up and find Norma dead in bed beside him. I'm there in the bedroom with him when Ada comes in to say good-bye to Norma. Before she leaves, Ada tells me she has to speak to me about something. That's when she wrote her own death sentence, didn't she? Because Les had to figure that the urgency in Ada's voice meant trouble—she was on to what you two had done to Norma's cocoa."

"He came and found me right away," Jory said, nodding. "He was really upset. Said we had to shut Ada up, and fast. I was against the whole idea, honestly. My view? Hey, she's ninety-something years old, grief-stricken, distraught. Somebody like you would just figure she was raving. But Les wasn't buying it. He was absolutely insistent that we could not let her sit down with you. He didn't let her out of his sight after that, just to make sure she didn't. And when she went upstairs to dress for breakfast, he grabbed me in the kitchen and said, 'This is it—we have to make our move.' And so, well, we did."

"It was not a brilliant move," Des informed her. "In fact, I'd go so far as to say it was lame-assed. From that moment on, Norma's death was bound to look suspicious. Didn't you folks realize that?"

"We couldn't afford the luxury of worrying about it. We simply had to make the best of a bad situation. That's what Les kept saying. He panicked. We both did, I guess."

"Who strangled that fine old woman?"

Jory started snuffling again. "I don't w-want to sit here talking about this anymore."

"Hey, I don't want to be sitting here talking about it either," Des said to her roughly. "I'd much rather be sitting at home in a nice hot bubble bath, sipping fine cognac. But I'm not. I'm getting frostbite at Astrid's Castle instead. So keep talking, before I lose my sweet disposition. I repeat: Who strangled her?"

"I sure couldn't do it," Jory said weakly. "And Les was way too chicken."

"So you made Jase do it, didn't you?" Des demanded, scowling at her.

"I did," Jory admitted. "He was in the mudroom, tidying himself up when I went in there and laid it on the line. I told him, 'Look, Ada somehow thinks I've killed Norma, and if we don't head her off right away, she's going to send me off to to jail.' You see—" She broke off, her chest rising and falling. "There's this one thing that Jase totally can't cope with, and that's being separated from me. As long as we're together, he's fine. But he needs me in his life. Otherwise, he's lost."

"So you pushed his hot button, is that what you're saying?"

"Yes."

"And he murdered Ada for you."

"Faced with the prospect of losing me, Jase will do anything I ask him to do," Jory stated matter-of-factly.

"You have an awesome amount of power over him, don't you?"

Jory didn't respond. Just sat there examining the crumbs on the cutting board.

"What's really behind that, Jory?" Des asked, studying her closely. "Is it chemical?"

"I don't know what you mean."

"Sure you do. Those tranks you give him—is he addicted to them? Is that it?"

"Not really," Jory replied, swallowing.

"Then what is it? How do you explain this power you have over him?"

"I just *told* you." Jory's voice rose defensively. "He can't get along without me. The poor thing is just so fragile and innocent. He may seem like an adult to you, but in many ways he's still a child."

"Was he hip to the fact that you and Les *had* killed Norma?"

Jory shook her head. "I hadn't dared tell him."

"You just told him to kill Ada."

"I did," she acknowledged, turning woeful. "I shouldn't have. I know that. Jase's loyalty to me is something I've never, ever abused. But I did abuse it this morning. He . . . took the staff stairs. I told him to make it quick and quiet. And make sure no one saw him."

"Did he wear gloves?"

"He did. Why?"

"He didn't have any scratches on his hands, that's why. Jory, let's talk some more about Les, okay? There's something I'm a bit confused about. You found out this morning that he'd lied to you about inheriting the castle, correct?"

"Correct," Jory replied. "I heard him talking to Aaron about it in the taproom before breakfast. That's when I realized that I'd been totally had."

"And yet you didn't let on to Les about it. Instead, you conspired with him to eliminate Ada. If you were already aware that Les had double-crossed you, how do you explain this?"

"One task at a time," Jory answered simply.

"You just said what to me?"

"You can't tackle every job at once. If you do that, you'll get overwhelmed. That's one of the secrets to running a successful inn. Norma taught it to me, actually. My immediate priority was Ada. *Our* immediate priority was Ada. So I let Les think I was still the stupid little slut he thought I was, and we took care of her."

"*Jase* took care of her."

Jory swallowed, her eyes filling with tears. "Yes."

"And when that odious chore was disposed of, who took care of Les? Jase again?"

"When you banished all of us to solitary confinement, you put Jase and me in adjoining rooms. The bathroom vents connect. We could whisper to each other through them."

"That's when you told him to kill Les?"

"I didn't have to. I just had to tell him how Les had used me. And how, given half a chance, he'd pin both murders on us. Les could, *would* put us away for life. I had no doubt. I made that clear to Jase."

"This sounds a whole lot like you pushing his hot button again."

"I did," Jory admitted. "But this was something that absolutely needed doing. We couldn't let Les destroy us. Jase knew this. Jase felt comfortable with this. Besides, he wanted to teach that disgusting old man a lesson. He was really upset about Les taking advantage of me physically."

"You were with me in the hallway when I decided to let Les go downstairs for firewood with Mitch and Teddy," Des recalled.

"I was, that's right. As soon as you sent me back to my room, I told Jase that now was his chance. He went up to the third floor through his trapdoor and down the staff stairs. When they headed out to the woodshed, he followed them and killed Les."

"Why didn't he kill Mitch, too?"

"He likes Mitch. Mitch has been nice to him."

"That's my doughboy. Where are Jase's wet things? His work boots, pants?"

"In the big freezer," Jory said, glancing over at the walk-in commercial freezer in the new part of the kitchen. "Along with the gloves he had on when he killed Ada. He always keeps an extra pair of jeans and boots in the mudroom in case he needs them. I buy him the same brand of everything—four pairs of jeans at a time whenever they're on sale, two pairs of boots. He jumped right into identical dry things and went back up to the third floor lickety-split. Finished drying off in Izzy's bathroom and dropped back down into his room."

"And now here we are." Des continued to point her gun at Jory under the table.

"Here we are," Jory acknowledged, puffing out her cheeks. "It's too bad, really."

"What is, Jory?"

"I'm thinking about those damned pills of Norma's. Les shouldn't have stolen them when he did. He should have waited until this week, when everyone else was here. If he had, you would never have figured this out."

"Trust me, you would not have gotten away with this. No chance."

Jory gazed at her curiously. "Really, why not?"

"Eventually, we would have brought Jase in for routine questioning, and there's no way he would have held up. Not given how attached he is to you. If we'd played him even a tiny bit, told him that you'd confessed to the whole thing, he'd have caved in a heartbeat."

Jory said nothing to that, just sat back in her chair with her arms crossed, watching Des.

"Jory, I'm curious about your state of mind right now," Des said, studying her. "Because I'm getting such a strange vibe off of you. Are you at all sorry? Do you regret any of this?"

"Not one bit." Jory sounded defiant now. "You try living in my skin for a few days. You'd have no regrets either. You can't imagine with it's like being saddled with him, Des. Having to watch over him every single minute of every single day. That boy can't make up his mind about *anything* without my help. He's a total baby. And ever since I was a teenager, he's been the story of my life twenty-four hours a day, seven days a week. No holidays. No vacations. No relief. No *life*. Not one boy in town would ever go out with me," she complained, her voice rising. "Not if he was a decent, hardworking boy, a boy who was looking to build a life with somebody. Who'd want to take on me *and* that skulky, needy brother of mine? The only ones who'll even look at me are the Spence Sibleys, who figure I'm so lonely and desperate that I'll give it up, no effort required. So I've watched as one after another of those nice boys have hooked up with my girlfriends, gotten serious with them, *married* them—even though not a one of those girls is as good-looking as I am. I'm a pretty girl, Des. I have a terrific figure, a head on my shoulders, a warm and caring heart. Good things are supposed to happen to a girl like me. I'm supposed to be happy. I *deserve* to be happy! Do you have any idea what it's like to wake up one morning and realize that you're *nowhere?* Every single friend I've ever had is married now except for me. God, how I despise going to the market. I *always* run into one of them and she *always* wants to talk about her wonderful baby and the wonderful addition they're building on to their wonderful house and how they're going skiing this year in the wonderful White Mountains and . . . It's *over* for me, Des! I don't get a life. Not Jory. Not me. Uh-uh. I don't get any of that. You know what I *do* get? I get to share that dingy cottage with my stupid little brother until the day I die. And I am so sick of it. So sick of sitting up here in this damned castle watching my life just . . ." She came up for air, her eyes burning at Des across the table. "My life was passing me right on by. That's what I woke up one day and realized. So when that one chance came along, a chance to make something happen, I reached for it and I grabbed hold, even if it did seem a little wrong. It's not like Norma had very long to live, you know. She was genuinely sick. We were just helping her along. That's how I look at it, anyway. Besides, she was a mean old bitch. Treated Jase and me like her personal slaves. Always so patronizing and condescending."

"I thought she seemed pretty nice."

"Yeah? Well, you didn't work for her."

"Jory, let's say Les hadn't turned out to be a two-timing liar. Let's say this hadn't all blown up in your face . . ." Des thought she heard the creak of floorboards in the dining hall. She glanced at the doorway, but there was no one approaching. "Would you have gone through with it?"

"Gone through with what, Des?" asked Jory, frowning at her.

"Would you have married Les?"

"To get Jase out of my life? Oh, absolutely." Jory seemed quite certain of this. Frighteningly so. "I believe that a really strong case can be made that Jase needs serious long-term care in a residential treatment facility."

"By that you mean a mental hospital?"

"Well, yeah. And with the financial resources of Astrid's Castle behind me, I could have done that. Actually put him somewhere. Actually had a life of my own. He'll never be able to function independently, Des. I swore to my dad on his deathbed that I'd take care of him, and I have. I've kept my word. I've been a good daughter and a good sister. But, God, when is it *my* turn? When do I get to take care of *me*?" She sat there in bitter, angry silence for a moment. "You have no idea what it's like being stuck with Jase. No idea just how deeply and intensely I hate him. How much I wish he'd never been born. How much I wish—"

A sudden flurry of sound interrupted her.

It was the sound of Mitch getting shoved through the doorway, looking ashen with fright.

Behind him, Jase stood there with a crazed expression on his face and a thirty-eight pointed at the small of Mitch's back. "You told me you *loved* me!" he sobbed at his sister, utterly freaked out. "No one else, just *me!*"

"I do love you, sweetie," Jory gulped, her eyes bugging with panic.

"You'd better put down that gun, Jase," Des told him quietly, her own weapon still trained on Jory under the table. She did not want to show it to Jase. It might set him off. She did swing it ever so slowly over in his direction. Only, there was a wooden kitchen chair in between them. She had no clear shot at him. Not where he was standing. "Put it down right now. You don't want to make a bad situation any worse, do you?"

"You *lied* to me!" he wailed at Jory, ignoring Des completely. "When we were parked together at the station, you said we'd have everything we ever wanted. That it was all for *us*. And you never meant *any* of it."

"I did, too," Jory swore. "Honest, I did."

"You *hate* me! You want to have me locked up! I just heard you."

"Sweetie, that's just a story I made up," Jory said soothingly. "It's not the real truth, I swear to you."

"Put down that gun, Jase," Des repeated, wondering if she'd ever be able to unravel the real truth. Whose idea it was to bump off Norma. What Les had promised Jory for her help. What she had promised him in return. With Les gone, there was no way to know. "Where did he find that thing, anyhow?" she asked Mitch, her voice low and calm.

"Behind the bar in the taproom," Mitch answered tightly.

"Is everyone okay in there?"

"Everyone's fine," Mitch replied, struggling to keep his own voice steady. "No one's been hurt. Nothing bad has happened. It's not too late to just put the gun down, Jase. We can sit right here and talk, the four of us. We're all friends here."

Jase didn't respond, didn't budge. Just stood right where he was, gun in hand, his eyes bulging with rage and hurt and confusion.

Des couldn't blame him. The only thing he'd been able to count on his whole life was Jory's love. Now he didn't have that. Didn't have anything. "Mitch is right, Jase," she said. "Listen to Mitch. You trust him, don't you? Why don't you sit down with us, and we'll talk this out."

"Please sit, sweetie." Jory managed a coaxing smile, her eyes shining at Jase. "It's going to be okay. You don't have to worry. You know I love you. Everything I do is for us. *All* for us."

Jase considered Jory's plea carefully. For a brief instant, Des thought that he was giving in to her. The gun drooped slightly in his hand, and some of the coiled tension eased out of his shoulders. Until, that is, whatever it was that held Jase Hearn together suddenly snapped deep down inside of him, like a rubber band that has been stretched too tight. And he mouthed these words: "There's no us."

Before he whirled and shot his sister full in the face.

Jory made a single, awful choking noise as she pitched over backward from the table, a gaping hole where her left eye had just been.

Right away, Des was up on her feet, squeezing off a round of her own at Jase. But she was a split second too late. He'd already gotten off another shot—this one at her. She took it in the forearm of her gun hand, sending her own shot harmlessly into the wall. Her right hand went numb instantly, the SIG dropping to the floor with a thunk.

Now Jase was dashing out the kitchen door into the courtyard, still clutching his thirty-eight.

And Mitch was diving to the floor for her SIG and starting out the door after him.

Des cried out, "No, Mitch! Let him go!" Wondering what on earth that sweet, chubby fool could possibly be thinking.

But she was too late. Mitch was already gone.

CHAPTER 17

HERE IS WHAT MITCH was asking himself as he went rushing out the kitchen door after Jase, SIG-Sauer in hand and Des yelling after him to stop:

What in the hell am I doing?

He was a card-carrying creature of the darkened screening room, a wielder of a flashlight pen, a *critic*—not some gun-toting lawman. So why was he doing this? Why was he chasing Jase Hearn across the castle courtyard, tramping his way through deep snow and ice, panting for breath, his chest heaving?

Because there is no one else.

Because he'd just seen Jase murder his own sister and shoot Des's arm to pieces. Because Jase would get away if he didn't go after him. Because he knew this guy and, strangely enough, liked this guy. And because, well, it wasn't coming from his head, this impulse to chase after him. It came from Mitch's hands, which had picked up the gun from the floor without hesitation. It came from his feet, which just kept moving forward as he slip-slided and crashed his way through the snow, the sun breaking out overhead. It came from being cooped up in that cold, dark castle since last night, witnessing one person after another get strangled, hatcheted, shot. And he'd just plain had enough.

So he ran, Des's gun feeling heavy and unfamiliar in his hand.

Jase was sprinting like mad out ahead of him, stumbling, falling, getting back up. He could definitely hear Mitch's footsteps behind him. He kept looking over his shoulder at him, eyes wild with fear. And as Jase neared the drawbridge over the frozen moat, he spun around and opened fire.

Mitch immediately pancaked himself to the snow as two shots

whizzed right over him. He did not return fire. There was no point. No way he could hit Jase Hearn from this distance. Besides, he didn't want to shoot him.

He wanted Jase to surrender.

Now Jase was dashing across the drawbridge. Mitch scrambled back up onto his feet, covered with snow, and lumbered after him, huffing and puffing, seeing his hot breath before him, the winter air a jagged knife deep in his lungs. He didn't have on his jacket or gloves. His hands were wet and numb. The snow that clung to his sweater was quickly beginning to melt from his considerable body heat. He felt like a slow, hairy mastodon. Also a bit dazed from that blow to the head he'd taken.

And he was not exactly used to getting shot at.

When he'd crossed the drawbridge, gasping, he discovered that Jase had vanished. There wasn't so much as a glimpse of him anywhere in the distance. No movement. Nothing but virgin snow-covered meadows and forest. Mitch held his breath, listening. Not a sound.

But he still had Jase's footprints to go by. All Mitch had to do was follow his trail through the snow. Jase could not get away from him. No, he could not.

So Mitch tracked him—in the direction of Choo-Choo Cholly's miniature depot, which still lay crunched under that huge fallen sugar maple. As Jase's footsteps approached the little station, they veered around it and made for a wide, cleared corridor between the trees. The railroad tracks, Mitch realized. Jase was following Cholly's snow-covered narrow-gauge tracks all the way down the mountain to the front gate, to Route 156, *away*.

Mitch pursued him, running hard, the sweat beginning to stream down his face. Jase's footsteps made a clear path before him down the center of the tracks, the cross-ties deep underfoot beneath the snow and ice. Wherever Jase ran, Mitch ran. Around the trees that had come down alongside the tracks. Over the trees that had fallen across them. Mitch ran and ran. Until he could run no farther without his chest exploding. He paused for just a second to catch his breath, his ears straining for a sound, any sound in the frozen winter silence. Crunching. He could hear the definite crunching of footsteps. Not very far away either. He was staying right with Jase. Maybe even gaining on him.

Heartened, Mitch forced himself farther on down the tracks. There was a quaint, hand-painted wooden sign up ahead now—"River Walk Station." And a big bend around an exposed scenic overlook where there were handrails and benches and wonderful river views that Mitch had no time to look at. As he came charging his way around the bend, Jase's footsteps before him veered off the tracks and curled into the woods. Crashing his way in among the fallen trees, Mitch followed Jase's footprints until, suddenly, they stopped entirely right there deep in the woods. No more footprints. Yet, no Jase either. It was as if he'd disappeared into thin air. Either that or Scotty had just beamed him back aboard the *Enterprise*. Mitch stood there, baffled, seeing no sign of Jase, hearing no sound other than his own heavy breathing. How was this possible? How could Jase's footsteps simply halt right here, two feet from the base of a beech tree? Where the devil was he?

Mitch suddenly realized where. And felt like a total moron.

Only, by the time he looked up, Jase was already diving out of the tree right on top of him, knocking him hard to the ground and smashing him across the bridge of the nose with his thirty-eight. The SIG went flying out of Mitch's hand as he found himself flat on his back in the snow, Jase clutching him by the throat with his rough, powerful hands, jabbering at him incoherently, his breath hot and sour in Mitch's face. His eyes were the crazed eyes of one of those unkempt wild men who prowled the streets of Lower Manhattan at four o'clock in the morning, ranting at unseen enemies in no known language.

Mitch fought back with everything he had. Fought for air. Fought for life. His hands clawed at Jase's. But he was no match for Jase's unleashed fury. And he was losing. And Des's gun was gone—Mitch didn't know where. And he was going to die here in the snow, right here, right now . . .

Until Jase suddenly recoiled from him in horror and screamed, "Damn you! *Damn* you!" And scrambled several feet away from Mitch, scratching angrily at his knit cap, yanking it from his head, hurling it off into the snow. His hair underneath was stringy and long. "Stop following me, will you?! Just let . . . me . . . go!"

"I can't," Mitch croaked, blood streaming from his smashed nose. "Come back to the castle with me, Jase."

"You've *got* to let me go!" Jase moaned, staring in apparent disbelief at the thirty-eight he was clutching in his hand. He seemed genuinely repulsed by who and what he'd become. "*You* go back to the castle. Forget about me, *please!*"

"It's no use, Jase." Mitch yanked his handkerchief from the back pocket of his pants, stanching the flow of blood from his nose. "You have to give yourself up."

Jase shook his head at him violently. "Never. No way. No. I can't go back. I just can't."

"You have to," Mitch insisted, wondering whereabouts in the snow Des's SIG had fallen. If he could reach it. If he could use it . . .

"I'll never, ever go back," Jase vowed, staggering his way back through the trees toward the railroad tracks. "Just *forget* that!" Now he took off again down the tracks, running hard, away from Mitch, away from the castle, away. Jase didn't bother to search for Des's weapon in the snow. Didn't so much as look back.

He just ran.

Mitch remained there in the snow for a moment, his nose bleeding, his throat feeling as if it had just been stepped on by someone wearing cleats. Slowly, he got to his knees, fighting off a wave of dizziness. Kneeling there, he groped around in the snow until his numb fingers found the SIG. Weapon in hand, he climbed back up onto his feet, handkerchief pressed to his nose. Then Mitch resumed the chase.

He was an old hand at this now. All he had to do was follow Jase's trail down those tracks. Around a bend. Into a straightaway. Mitch pursued him, step for step, stumbling repeatedly, falling to his knees, but refusing to stay down. As he came around another big bend, Mitch heard a gunshot up ahead in the snowy silence. Now Mitch was streaking his way around that bend, wondering what he would find.

It was Choo-Choo Cholly's House, the bright red railroad barn where the little train was stored for the winter. A spur of track led off the main line straight for it. So did Jase's footprints. One of the sliding barn doors was opened wide. Mitch found the shattered remains of a lock in the barn's doorway. Jase had shot the lock off.

Once inside the doorway, the narrow-gauge railroad tracks emerged from under their snowy blanket and continued their way deep inside the cavernous barn, which smelled moldy and damp. After the bright white glare of the snow, Mitch could barely make out anything inside the unlit barn. Not until his eyes had a chance to adjust to the dim light coming through the open door. Only then could he make out the brave little train, all shiny and clean, waiting there for spring to arrive. In point of fact, Choo-Choo Cholly was a bizarre thing to stumble upon right now. There was something sur-real about Cholly's locomotive "face," with its bulbous red nose, electric-blue eyes and cheerful crooked smile. To Mitch, the little engine looked eerily like W. C. Fields after Fields had just done some-thing especially stinky to Baby LeRoy. Maybe it was just Mitch's head trauma, but he suddenly felt as if he'd wandered into a ride at Disney World while under the influence of a major hallucinogen.

Until, that is, another gunshot rang out, splintering the barn door next to his head. Mitch hit the ground immediately.

"Don't make me do this!" Jase called to him from deep inside the barn.

"You can't get away, Jase!" Mitch called back, edging his way on hands and knees toward Cholly, keeping low to the tracks. "Give yourself up!"

"No way! I won't ever give up! Not ever!"

And yet, as Mitch inched his way deeper inside the barn, it occurred to him that Jase had purposely trapped himself in here. Why had he chosen to do this? Why hadn't he kept on going down the tracks?

As he crept near enough to get a decent look at him, Mitch knew why—Jase was cowering in the corner behind Cholly like a lost, frightened little boy. Melted snow ran from his hair down into his face. He trembled so badly his teeth were chattering.

"She *made* me do it," he cried to him mournfully. "I didn't want to. Honest, I didn't. Jory *made* me."

"How did she *make* you, Jase?" Mitch asked, kneeling there with Des's gun in his hand. "You and I both know you're no fool. You're a smart guy. How did you let this happen?"

Jase watched him in scared silence for a moment. "You're the smart guy. You don't get it?"

"I'm afraid not."

"Because I loved her!" Jase said this as if it were a special secret.

"Well, of course you did," Mitch responded patiently. "She was your sister."

"No, I mean I *loved* her! Jory and me were *together*."

Mitch experienced an involuntary physical reaction to this revelation. He could actually feel his innards shudder, as if someone had just reached in and given his guts a good hard shake. "Since . . . when, Jase?"

"Since we were kids. She was older. She showed me how. She showed me everything."

"She was your sister," he pointed out gently.

"I couldn't help that," Jase moaned, breathing heavily. "She's the only girl I've ever . . . I'll ever love. She was so pretty. The prettiest. And now I haven't got anybody. I know what we . . . that you're not supposed to. That they . . . people . . . think it's wrong. But you can't help how you feel. You can't. You just can't. God, you of all people should get that."

"Me?" Mitch frowned at him. "Why me?"

"You and Des," Jase said, nodding his wet head convulsively. "Lots of people think that's unnatural and wrong, too, don't they?"

"Jase, I think we're getting off the subject here. You said Jory *made* you do this. How?"

"Killing Norma was all her idea," Jase explained. "She planned the whole thing. It wasn't Les. It was her, all her. One day she told me, 'I think Les is into me.' She figured once Norma was gone she could talk him into marrying her and we could take over the whole castle."

"So she seduced Les."

"He was *easy*. That's what she told me after she . . . after they . . . H-He wanted her bad. God, *everyone* did. She was so beautiful." Jase let out a sob. "Wasn't she beautiful?"

"Very beautiful," Mitch said, although he was having trouble picturing Jory right now without the bullet hole Jase had just put in her left eye. "If you felt about Jory the way you say you did, then you must have hated the whole idea—Jory and Les sleeping together, Jory marrying him. Didn't that bother you?"

"She *swore* he meant nothing to her. That she was doing it all for us. So I went along. I didn't want to, but I did. She *made* me."

"Jase, you keep saying that. *How* did she make you? Why didn't you just tell her it was a really sick, bad idea?"

Jase ducked his head miserably. "If I didn't go along, she said she'd find someone else to marry. Move to a new town and leave me behind. Never let me be with her again. It was the only way I could hold on to her. That's how come I did it—killed the old woman, killed Les. Because I . . . loved Jory. And now I haven't got anybody. Nobody at all."

"That's not true, Jase. You have me. I'm on your side." Mitch moved in a bit closer, Des's gun lowered out of sight. "You can trust me. But you need to turn yourself in. It's the smart move. You can explain this to them. They'll understand. People can be surprisingly understanding."

"No way." Jase retreated deeper into the corner, shaking his head. "I won't be locked up. Can't handle it."

"Hey, I don't blame you. And I won't lie to you, Jase. You've got some serious legal problems ahead of you. But I'm your friend, and I promise I'll speak up for you. I'll tell them that you could have killed me just now out there, which makes twice you could have killed me and didn't. That means you're not a dangerous person. It means that a lot of this is on Jory, and they'll understand that. You might not even have to go to jail. You've got . . . mitigating factors in your favor."

"I'm *not* going to no loony bin!" Jase cried out. "You can forget that. Just let me go, okay? I'll live in the bush by myself. I won't bother anyone. Won't hurt anyone. I'll just disappear."

"I can't let you do that, Jase," Mitch said, moving in closer. He was no more than four feet away from him now, close enough to smell Jase's goaty scent even through his bloodied nose. "You have a couple of options, but running isn't one of them. You can't get away."

"I can so," Jase insisted. "There's twenty thousand acres of woods here. Caves no one else knows about. They'll never find me. Soon as I can make it out, I'll catch me a river barge or freight train. Head south to Mexico, find work, keep my head down. I'll be okay, I swear it." Jase ran a hand through his stringy hair, sniffling. "Just let me go. If you're my friend, let me go. I'm *begging* you."

Truly, Mitch felt bad for Jase Hearn. Or as bad as he could feel for someone who had just murdered three human beings. This was an emotionally fragile, vulnerable guy, a trusting guy who had been ill-used by his older, wiser and infinitely more devious sister. Jory had fully understood the sexual power she held over Jase, and she had cruelly exploited him. It was a twisted and very sad situation. And now justice had to be dispensed. Back there in the kitchen, Jory had already paid the price for her own reprehensible behavior. But what price should Jase pay?

As Mitch crouched there in the damp, cold rail barn, thinking it over, he swore he could hear a faint mechanical hum somewhere off in the distance. Had the electrical power come back on? No, that wasn't it. The sound came from overhead. It was the state police helicopter, SP-One, whirring its way toward them. Des's old sergeant, Soave, and his partner Yolie. They were still a couple of miles off, but growing steadily closer.

Jase raised his eyes slowly to the roof, hearing it. Then he let out a low moan of panic, his eyes darting wildly around the barn for a way out. It was almost as if he hadn't realized until this very moment that he'd let Mitch corner him. Now Jase's eyes fell on the .38 he was clutching in his right hand, half forgotten in the telling of his story. The gun that was his only chance at escape. He knew this. They both did.

Which explained why this happened: When Jase raised his gun at Mitch, he discovered that Mitch already had Des's SIG aimed right back at him.

"Don't do it, Jase," Mitch warned him, swallowing. That .38 was trained directly between his eyes.

"You'd better let me go." There was a quiet resolve in Jase's voice now. His mind was made up.

"That's not going to happen, Jase."

"Back away from me right now."

"No."

Jase let out a groan. "Mitch, I'm getting out of here and you can't stop me."

"Yes, I can." He moved in closer, Des's SIG pointed right at Jase. The chopper was hovering directly overhead now. "Just give me the gun, and we'll face this thing together. I'll stay by your side every step of the way. You have my word."

"Back off, man. I *mean* it. I don't want to kill you, but if I have to, I will. I swear."

"Then I guess you'll have to shoot me, Jase, because I'm not backing off. I'm taking you out of here."

"No, you're not! *Please* don't make me do this to you!"

"Oh, okay, this is starting to make some sense," Mitch said, nodding his head. "Now it's *me* who's making you behave so badly. First Jory, now Mitch. Not you, never you. Well, guess what, Jase? It *is* you. It's your decision. It's your life. Either put the gun down or shoot me. You decide. But do it fast, because we're running out of time here." Mitch was less than three feet from him now. Close enough to stare right down the barrel of the .38. Close enough to see just how tightly clenched Jase's trigger finger was. So tight his knuckle was white. "What's it going to be, Jase?" he demanded, sounding very sure of himself even though his heart was pounding and his knees were quivering. Because he wasn't just staring down a gun barrel, he was staring at the ultimate reality.

It was kill or be killed, and Mitch knew it. And he knew something else. Something that they both knew, which was that Jase had already used his gun and Mitch had not. Jase had proved himself capable of killing. Mitch had not. Jase had crossed over to the dark side of human behavior. Mitch had not.

Jase knew from murder. Mitch knew from Rin Tin Tin.

"What's it going to be, Jase?" he repeated, his voice raised over the helicopter, which was whirring louder and louder as it descended on the castle's parking lot. "For once in your life, make up your own goddamned mind, will you?"

"Don't come any closer," warned Jase, his finger squeezing tighter and tighter on that trigger. "Don't do this! Please, don't! I'm *begging* you . . . !"

CHAPTER 18

THERE WASN'T A HUGE amount of blood. This was a good thing.

Which was not to say that Des's forearm wasn't bleeding as she slumped there at the kitchen table, staring at it dumbly. But the entry and exit wounds were seeping, not gushing. That meant the bullet hadn't blown out an artery and she wouldn't bleed to death before the chopper got there.

The bone was definitely broken. It wasn't protruding through the skin or anything, but it was broken. Des knew it because she couldn't move her hand at all—the nerves just plain wouldn't respond. She knew it because of the unbelievably gut-wrenching pain, pain so bad that she felt as if she might pass out. But she could not, must not.

Because as bad as her arm hurt, Des was more concerned about Mitch and what was happening to him out there in the snow. She'd heard a couple of gunshots not long after he'd chased out the door after Jase. Then nothing. She feared the worst. And no matter how hard she tried not to, she kept thinking about that damned old movie of his. About how he'd said it all turned out in the end:

"No one gets out alive."

"Something has happened to Mitch," she declared, struggling to get up out of her chair. "I have to help him."

"You have to sit still is what you have to do," Hannah said firmly, pushing her back down into the chair and holding her there. It was Hannah who had taken charge after they'd all coming rushing in. Hannah who had ordered Aaron, Carly, Spence and Teddy out of the kitchen. Not that they'd seemed any too anxious to stay. "For your information, missy, you have just been shot."

"But Mitch needs me." For some strange reason, Des couldn't manage to struggle out of Hannah's grasp. Which she found totally amazing. It was incredible how strong Hannah was. Jory seemed to agree. Jory who sat there across the table from her, her head listed over to one side, one eye open, the other eye gone. Jory who was . . .

I am going to faint. I must not faint.

Hannah was wrapping a clean dish towel around her right forearm. And she was talking to her. "Do you know where you are?" Hannah's voice seemed very far away and yet very close at the same time. And the light in the kitchen seemed uncommonly bright. "Do you know *who* you are?"

"I totally do. I'm Resident Trooper Desiree Velma Mitry. I live at number seventeen Uncas Lake Road. I am a Virgo. I wear a size twelve and one-half double-A shoe . . ."

"Wow, you're a big girl, Desiree Velma."

"Yeah, I'm all grown up now. And I *have* to go help Mitch."

"Mitch can take care of himself, big girl."

"Hannah, I love that man to death, but he's never squeezed out a round in his life." Again, Des struggled to get up. "I've got to go help him."

"You're not going anywhere," Hannah growled, shoving her back down into her chair again with amazing ease. It had to be the bullet wound. That was it. She wasn't at full strength. "Des, could we cover Jory over or something?"

"We don't want to be going anywhere near her. That's for the Crime Scene people."

"Okay, sure. Whatever you say. Here, can you hold this in place for me?"

Des used her left hand to press the towel against her wounded forearm while Hannah went riffling through the drawers over by the sink. A little blood was starting to ooze through the towel by the time Hannah returned with a pair of wooden cooking spoons.

"We're going to splint this puppy until we can get you to the hospital," she informed Des briskly. "How does that sound to you?"

"Fine, great. Just get it done." Des gazed up at her. "Hey, I owe you one."

"Not a problem. Believe me, my mom will be thrilled that all of my first aid training came in so handy today."

"I'm sure plenty grateful," Des said, hearing another gunshot now, this one from farther away. Much farther. "Especially if you can speed this the hell up."

"Des, I'm doing the best I can," Hannah said patiently. "Could you put your hand out on the table for me, palm up? No, *up*. That's a girl. Good job." Hannah placed the back of one spoon in Des's palm, running the length of it up the inside of her arm toward her elbow. "Okay, go ahead and close your hand around that for me."

Now Des heard a second gunshot in the distance.

Mitch. I have to save Mitch.

"Des, you're not helping me here. Can you close your hand?"

Des really tried to, but her right hand wouldn't respond at all. It did occur to her that this might present a problem. It was kind of an important hand, after all. Her drawing hand.

"Not to worry," Hannah assured her. "Just hold the spoon there for me with your other hand, okay? That's a girl." Quickly, Hannah positioned the second spoon against the back of Des's hand and forearm, and wrapped a second kitchen towel around the two spoons. She secured the improvised splint in place with a pair of cloth napkins, one knotted at Des's wrist, the other at her elbow. Then she folded a checkered tablecloth into a big triangle and fashioned a sling out of it, first cradling Des's wounded arm inside it, then tying the ends together around Des's neck. "Try to keep the arm elevated, okay? And don't eat or drink anything. Not even water. They may want to go in as soon as you're out of X ray."

" 'Go in?' " Des repeated, frowning at her.

"Operate. If there's anything in your stomach, it might delay them. That's why I'm not giving you any Tylenol."

"I just ate a sandwich."

"Okay, be sure they know that."

As Des shifted her arm around inside the sling, wincing from the pain, she became aware of a faint whirring noise. She couldn't tell where it was coming from. It sure wasn't coming from Jory there across the table. Possibly it was inside her own head. Her wheels spinning away as she wondered where Mitch was, how Mitch was. If she could get to him before he got his head blown off. If she could fire one of those deer rifles with only her one good arm. Didn't matter. She had to try. She got up out of her chair now and tottered over toward the gun case on rubber legs, fishing around with her left hand for Les's key ring in the pocket of her beloved shearling coat, ruined now. Two bullet holes, bloodstains. Then again, maybe that all just gave it more character. What would *Vogue* call it, Victim Chic?

"Just exactly what do you think you're doing?" Hannah demanded.

"My job," she replied, wondering which key would open the case. She ought to just smash the glass open with a cast-iron skillet. "I've got to help Mitch."

"Des, you can't! You've go to sit still until . . ." Hannah fell silent, standing there with her ears cocked. She'd heard it, too. The whirring noise. She went over to the window and glanced hopefully up at the bright blue sky. "I think your helicopter's here, Des. I think it wants to land."

Des could hear it loud and clear now, hovering directly overhead. "Come on, we need to be out there in the parking lot when they touch down. There's no time to waste. This is urgent."

"Are you sure you can make it?" Hannah asked her doubtfully.

"If you don't mind me leaning on you."

"Lean away."

Hannah looped Des's good arm over her shoulders and helped her past Jory's body and out the kitchen door. Together, they tramped their way across the courtyard through the snow. Des could not believe how hard it was simply to put one foot in front of the other. Without Hannah, she wouldn't have made it at all. Part of it was how deep the snow was. But most of it was how wobbly she was. She felt as if she'd been laid up in bed for a week with a wicked Asian flu.

Up above, SP-One was still a few hundred feet over the parking lot, descending slowly.

"You're the real deal, aren't you?" she said as they plowed their way through the snow together. "As a director, I mean."

"I think I am." Hannah glanced at her curiously. "But why do you say that?"

"You don't fold under pressure. You get stronger."

"I have to be that way, if I'm going to make it."

"You're going to make it. I have a good feeling about you."

"Thanks," said Hannah, her cheeks flushing from the praise.

Ahead of them in the courtyard, Des could see footprints in the virgin white snow. And a deep depression, as if someone had taken a head-first slide into it. But there was no sign of blood. This was positive. This was good. The footprints continued on across the drawbridge in the direction of Choo-Choo Cholly's flattened depot. As she and Hannah came around to the front of the castle, she spotted the others gathered outside the front door, waiting for the chopper to touch down. They reminded Des of frightened mice the way they were all cowered there together.

SP-One touched down smack-dab in the center of the plowed parking lot, its rotor blades gradually slowing as Des and Hannah reached the cleared pavement. The pilot remained on board as Soave and Yolie climbed out and scooted toward them in heavy-duty black ski parkas, their heads ducked low against the swirling air.

Soave, who was short-legged and bigged-up from weight lifting, looked remarkably like a bowling ball as he scooted toward them in his parka. Yolie, a four-year starter at point guard for Coach Vivian Stringer at Rutgers, moved like a gazelle in comparison. And looked way less street than usual with her braids buried under a black wool skullcap.

A medical examiner's man climbed out of the chopper, too, and started toward them, clutching his gear.

"Yo, what's up with that?" Soave called to Des as soon as they were within earshot. He was eyeballing her slinged arm with great concern. "Are you hit?"

"I'm fine, Rico. Don't worry about me. Our immediate concern is—"

"She's stable, but *not* fine," Hannah interjected. "She's been shot. She's sustained a compound ulnar fracture and there appears to be neurological damage. The bleeding's under control, but she requires immediate medical attention."

"What are you, a doctor?" Soave asked Hannah.

"No, a documentary filmmaker."

"Oh, boy, here we go again," Soave groaned, rolling his eyes. "Already, I can tell this one'll be a trip to unravel. Am I right, Yolie?" He frowned at his silent partner. "Yolie, you okay?"

"Not really," Yolie Snipes replied glumly, a sickly expression on her face. "I left my stomach and toenails somewhere back over East Haddam. Or maybe it was over—"

"Will you all *please* shut up and listen to me!" Des shouted over them. "We've still got us a hot one—white male, early twenties, name of Jase Hearn. He's armed. He's killed three people. And he's running. Mitch took off after him that-a-way," she said, pointing toward Cholly's depot. "We've heard shots fired. Last one was a few minutes ago."

"Is Berger armed?" Soave asked her.

"He has my weapon."

Soave eye's widened at her with surprise. "Who does he think he is, Vin Diesel?"

"God, I hope not." Des let out an involuntary sob that caught her totally by surprise. It was the bullet wound. Had to be. Because she was totally *not* a girlie-girl. And yet here she was, sobbing just like one. "Rico, if *anything* happens to that man, I swear I will just curl up and die."

"Hey, hey, hey." Soave squeezed her good arm reassuringly. "Not to worry. We got your boy covered, right, Yolie?"

"On it," Yolie vowed, striding off toward the depot with her SIG drawn.

"Excuse me, where will I find the bodies?" the medical examiner spoke up.

"There's so many locations to choose from," Des replied, swiping at her teary eyes. "You can start in the kitchen, if you'd like. Or the woodshed . . ."

"There's also two second-floor rooms," Hannah added. "Numbers one and three."

"Jeez, did Charlie Manson bust out?" Soave marveled, shaking his head.

"The mice can show you the way," Des told the ME, indicating the four who were still gathered at the castle's front door. As the ME started toward them, she said, "Rico, you'll want to make sure you seal off that big freezer in the kitchen, okay? Jase threw some bloody clothes in there."

"Gotcha," he said, nodding. "You ready to go?"

"Go?" She looked at him blankly. "Go where?"

"Our pilot's heading back up to Meriden to fetch us a load of tekkies. He'll drop you at the hospital on his way. Hop aboard."

"No way. Not a chance."

"Des, you need emergency medical care right away," Hannah said insistently. "Every minute is precious."

"I'm not going anywhere," Des insisted, her eyes following Yolie as Soave's sergeant marched her way past the toy railroad station and down the snow-covered tracks.

Yolie hadn't quite disappeared from view when they heard another gunshot off in the distance. Just one.

And then there was only silence.

CHAPTER 19

"Don't make me do this to you," Mitch pleaded with Jase Hearn as he crouched there pointing Des's gun right at him, the SIG feeling so unfamiliar and wrong in his hand. "Don't make me shoot you."

"You have to," Jase argued, his own gun trained right back on Mitch. "Or I have to shoot you. I won't come with you. I won't be locked up. I can't be."

"This is no good, Jase," Mitch said, seeing his breath before him in the rail barn's frigid air. Even though he could barely breathe. His heart was pounding faster than it ever had. And the only other time his knees had trembled this badly was that night he'd gone for his first open-mouthed kiss from Emily Rosenzweig in the doorway of her apartment building on Stuyvesant Oval. How old had he been, fifteen? Emily was married to a periodontist now, had two kids, still lived on the Oval, and *why* was he thinking about her at a time like this? "Jase, the law is already here. Can't you hear them?"

The sound of SP-One's whirring blades had built to a thundering crescendo as the chopper had touched down in the castle's parking lot. Gradually, the sound was beginning to taper off. They'd definitely landed.

"Jase, state troopers will be all over this place in a minute. They'll follow our footsteps directly here."

"They'll never find me," Jase promised, sticking out his furry chin. "I'll be gone before they get here."

"You'll be dead is what you'll be—if you don't drop your gun."

Jase shook his head at him. "You're too nice a guy, Mitch. Can't pull the trigger."

"Sure, I can," said Mitch, who had absolutely no doubt. Not after everything he'd been through over the past eighteen hours. He was not the same person who'd driven up here for dinner last evening. He'd seen too much death. And now he was staring it right in the face. And it was staring right back at him. And he was not going to blink. No, he was not. Because he wanted too much to stay alive. It was simple, really. Sometimes, the truth is.

"Maybe you can," Jase allowed, reading the cold certainty in Mitch's eyes. "But that just means we both die. What good does that do?"

"You don't get away, that's what. I won't lie to you, Jase. I'd really rather not die just yet. But if that's what it takes to stop you, so be it."

"Well, okay then," Jase said easily. As if by magic, all of the panic and desperation began to seep right out of him. He became very relaxed. Even seemed at peace with himself, if such a thing was possible. He lowered the .38 into his lap, holding it there loosely. "It's the best thing all around, you know."

"What is?"

"Shoot me," Jase said, incredibly calmly. "Just go ahead and do it, man. You'll be doing me a favor. I haven't got a single damned thing to live for. Go ahead and shoot me. I want you to."

"Jase, this is not going to happen. I won't be your judge, jury and executioner." Mitch edged closer, almost close enough to touch him. He held his left hand out to him. "So why don't you let me have your gun, okay?"

Jase hung his head in defeat, studying the gun in his lap. "If that's how it has to be." He sighed.

"That's how it has to be."

Jase smiled at him fondly now. "You were nice to me from the moment we met. Didn't treat me like some low-class cretin."

"Because you're not one." Mitch was still holding his hand out to him.

"I wouldn't do this for just anyone," he said, hefting the .38 in his hand. "I hope you get that."

"I do, Jase. And I appreciate it. Now please just hand it—"

"You shouldn't *have* to shoot me, you know. If you do something like that, man, you'll be seeing me in your dreams for the rest of your life. And that's not fair to you, is it?"

"No, it's not."

"Mitch, I'm really glad we agree on this."

And with that, Jase Hearn took a deep breath and put a bullet directly through his own right ear.

He did it so fast that Mitch did not have time to react. All he could do was watch it happen, stunned.

Jase toppled over against the wall, the gun falling from his hand. But he didn't die instantly. He was still there with Mitch for a few seconds, reaching out to him as if he wanted to shake hands. Mitch took his hand and squeezed it. For one brief, weird moment, they were like a pair of civilized gentlemen there on the floor of the barn together, saying, "I was pleased to make your acquaintance, kind sir." Then, Jase's hand quivered and jumped in Mitch's, like a live fish, and then, with a quick spasm, it was not a live anything.

Mitch knelt there, holding him in his arms, feeling so unbelievably sorry for him. He could not direct any anger at Jase. That emotion he reserved for Jory. No, Jase had shown him only kindness. In fact, Jase had probably just done Mitch the biggest favor anyone would ever do for him in his entire life. And so he felt grateful. And he knew that in the weeks to come, when he strolled past Jase's headstone at Duck River Cemetery, he would pause to leave him a smooth, polished stone and say, "Hey, Jase, just came by to say thanks again."

But right now, Mitch had to let go of Jase and leave him there on the cold ground. Mitch staggered back out of the rail barn into the snow and retraced their footsteps up the railroad tracks toward the castle. His ears were still ringing from the gunshot. His nose had stopped bleeding, but he couldn't breathe through it at all. He found himself gasping for breath as he plowed his way back up the hill. It was rugged going, and he was tired. He had never been so tired.

As he came around the big bend near where Jase had jumped him, he spotted someone charging down the tracks in a black ski parka. Someone of color. As they drew nearer to each other, he realized it was Yolie Snipes, Soave's half-black, half-Cuban sergeant.

Yolie had her gun drawn. She was pointing it right at him. "Drop your weapon!"

"It's okay, Yolie, it's me!" Mitch called out. He hadn't even realized he was still holding it.

"Mitch, I still want you to drop the weapon!"

And so he did.

She approached him with a guarded look on her face. Snatched Des's SIG up out of the snow and sniffed at it. "This hasn't been fired."

"That wasn't necessary."

She shoved it in her pocket and checked him over, her brown eyes gleaming at him warmly. "How you doing, big fella? You okay?"

"I think my nose is broken, but I'll live."

"What about our shooter?"

"Jase made other arrangements."

"He made what?"

"You'll find him on the floor of the rail barn, behind Choo-Choo Cholly."

"Choo-Choo *who?*" Yolie shook her head at him. "Damn, what kind of place is this anyhow?"

"A real happy place, Yolie. People come from all over the country just to be here. They watch the eagles soar. They hike the trails. And they ride Choo-Choo Cholly up and down the hill, up and down, up and . . ." Mitch smiled at her. "It's nice to see you again, by the way."

"Back at you," she said, reaching her hand around and pressing it against the back of his head. She came away with blood. "You sure you're okay?"

"That's just from this morning, when I had a small concussion. I blacked out twice, but I'm fine. Why, don't I look fine?"

"You look great." Yolie grinned at him hugely. "And I know me a hurting baby girl who's about to get real happy. Come on, let's get you out of here."

She took him by the arm and helped him back up the hill to the clearing where Cholly's little crunched depot was. From there, he could see the helicopter idling in the parking lot, its blades whirring slowly. Several people were standing near it.

One of them started running toward him right away. It was Des, and she ran very strangely. It was partly the deep snow, partly the homemade sling she was wearing on her wounded arm. As she got closer to him, he saw that she was also sobbing uncontrollably, the tears streaming down her face, which was totally not like her. Des absolutely detested girlie-girls.

When she got to him his girlie-girl slammed into him so hard that they both pitched right over into the snow, Des flush on top of him, covering his face with wet, cold kisses. "Baby, I thought you were dead," she blubbered. "I . . . I heard those shots and I thought you were dead!"

"Hey, it's okay, it's okay. You didn't have to worry about me. I'm inflatable. You punch me, I bounce right back up again."

She drew back, studying him with her shiny pale green eyes. "Why does it sound like you have a clothespin on your nose?"

"It's nothing. But tell me about you. How's your wing?"

"Broken," she replied, making a face. "They're talking some fool stuff about airlifting me to the hospital."

"Well, you'd better go, you big doofus."

"Your big doofus wouldn't leave until she found out how you were," Yolie said, helping both of them back onto their feet.

"Well, how about now?" Mitch asked her. "Will you go now?"

"I guess," she grumbled. "If you'll come with me."

"You mean like on a date?"

"Don't make fun of me," she pleaded, starting to sob all over again. It had to be the bullet wound. She was in shock or something.

"Girlfriend, I'm not making fun," he promised, hugging her tightly, kissing her smooth cheek. "Honest, I'm not."

Soave made his way over to them now, looking Mitch up and down with keen-eyed disapproval. The stumpy lieutenant resented Mitch as a presence in Des's life. Regarded him as an unworthy interloper. Mitch had always detected a whiff of smoldering jealousy on him, too. "We heard a single shot, Berger," he said to him rather stiffly. "You took him out?"

Mitch couldn't bring himself to say the words yet. He could feel Des's eyes on him, studying him anxiously.

"Talk to me, Berger," Soave persisted. "What was it, kill or be killed?"

"Yes, it was, Lieutenant."

"And . . . ?"

"And I don't know how I'll ever be able to pay Jase back."

Yolie held Des's gun out to her. "Go ahead, girl. It hasn't been fired."

"What, he shot himself?" Des asked him, pocketing her SIG.

"He did. Then he shook my hand. And then he died."

Soave took all of this in, tugging thoughtfully at his upper lip with a gloved thumb and forefinger. "Jeez, Berger, this is like a whole new world for you, hunh?"

"I sure hope not, Lieutenant. I was still trying to figure out the old one."

He rode along with her in the chopper, which airlifted her directly to Middlesex Hospital up in Middletown, where they had a helipad and fully restored electrical power.

He was by her side when they took her into the emergency room. He was by her side when they wheeled her into surgery. It was only then that Mitch let them perform an X ray and cat scan on his own bean. He was okay—no skull fracture. A nurse tidied his scalp wound for him and dressed it rather elaborately. She also cleaned up his bloodied, swollen nose and gave him a couple of Advil for his headache.

He reached out to Bella on Des's cell phone to let her know what had happened to her roommate. Bella was very upset by the news. For some strange reason, she was also really abrupt with him on the phone, Mitch felt.

Then he sat and waited. They wheeled her out of the operating room four hours later. He was with her when they moved her from the recovery room to a private room, an IV in her good arm, her broken, bandaged arm secured within an external titanium frame. He stayed with her all night, dozing in a chair next to her bed. She finally began stirring at about four in the morning. She came out of her drugged haze slowly, gazing around at her surroundings uncomprehendingly.

"Hey, tiger," he exclaimed, grinning at her. "How are you feeling?"

"All depends . . ." she responded hoarsely, blinking at him. There was hallway light coming through the open door. "You . . . wearing a turban?"

"That's how they dress head wounds. The nurse said I could take it off tomorrow."

"What am *I* wearing?" she wondered, peering at her titanium frame in bewilderment.

"It's the latest thing. All of the chic New York women swear by them."

"Wha . . . ?"

"You actually want a straight answer, don't you? They can't use a plaster cast in a case like yours, where you have deep flesh wounds. No way to tell if they're healing right if your arm's stuffed inside a cast. That's what the nurse told me, anyway."

"Incredibly glad . . ."

"Glad?" He frowned at her. "How come?"

"We're not in that damned castle anymore."

"I'm with you there, Master Sergeant."

The attending physician was an alert young Asian woman. As the sky outside the hospital room window began to fade from black to the purple of pre-dawn, she told Des that the bullet from Jase Hearn's .38 had not only shattered a bone in her right forearm but had torn through the muscles, ligaments and nerves to her hand. The good news was that the orthopedic surgeon and neurosurgeon believed they had successfully put her back together again. Screws had been inserted in the bone, the damaged nerves repaired. She would have to stay in the hospital for a couple of days, hooked up to intravenous antibiotics and painkillers. Once she was sent home, her arm would have to be immobilized for at least ten weeks. Then there would be extensive rehab. But she should fully recover in time, the young doctor said confidently.

"Still can't wiggle my fingers," Des said, the worry showing in her eyes.

"You've sustained serious nerve trauma, Trooper. It takes time for the feeling to come back." The doctor took a safety pin out of her pocket and opened it. "Tell me if you feel anything when I do this . . ."

"Nothing," Des said glumly when she'd been poked in the pinky finger with the pin. "Still nothing," she reported after the doctor tried her ring finger.

"How about this finger . . . ?"

"A tingle, maybe."

"And this one . . . ?"

"Ow!"

"You're doing fine," she assured Des with a brilliant smile.

Relieved, Des immediately fell back to sleep.

Mitch took a cab home—his truck was still up at the castle. The roads from Middletown to Dorset were well plowed and sanded. The driver had heard on the radio that most of the electricity in the state had come back on in the night. A warm front was moving in. It was supposed to be a sunny, balmy forty-five degrees today.

And maybe the weatherman would even be right this time.

Peck's Point had been plowed all the way out to the gate, Mitch was happy to see. He had his driver drop him there. Then he stepped his way carefully across the battered, snow-packed wooden causeway to his island home, feeling as if he'd been away for two months.

Big Sister had taken a definite pounding. A weeping cherry had come down on Bitsy Peck's covered porch. The fine old oak tree out front of Dolly Peck's had split right down the middle, landing this way and that in her driveway. The private dock where Evan Peck kept his J-24 tied up each summer had been smashed to pieces by the floating chunks of ice that the angry surf had brought crashing in.

But no power lines were down and no houses had taken structural hits. It was all damage that could be dealt with in the weeks ahead, just as the causeway could be dealt with. Standard winter wear and tear when you lived out on an island in the Sound.

Although there was one very important lesson that Mitch had learned from this experience: The next time he saw a burnt orange sunrise in February he would not wonder if it was a good omen. Rather, he would bar the door and hide under the bed.

His carriage house had lost several of its roofing shingles to the wind, exposing the reddish, nearly new-looking cedar underneath. The little apple tree he'd planted in the fall had been uprooted. Otherwise, the place looked okay. And Mitch heard absolutely the most wonderful sound when he went in the door—the steady thrum of his furnace. The power was back on. It was still very, very chilly in the house, but his faucets ran normally. He would have to make his rounds later on just to be certain, but if his own pipes were okay, then the chances were that everyone else's would be, too. His house had the least amount of insulation on the entire island.

Clemmie and Quirt were cold, hungry, lonely, indignant, pissed off and terribly in need of petting and snuggling and more snuggling. Not a crumb of kibble was left in their bowls. He put down fresh kibble and treated each cat to an entire jar of their Beechnut Stage 1 strained chicken with broth. According to Des, baby food was much better for them than canned cat food. No artificial ingredients, no additives—just chicken. Clemmie and Quirt couldn't lick their way through enough of it.

He got a big fire going in the fireplace. Cranked up his coffeemaker. Logged on to his computer. Ada Geiger's death had made its way onto the news wires. Mitch's editor at the paper, Lacy Nickerson, had already e-mailed him three times about it. He e-mailed her back, promising her a piece about the legendary director by day's end. A large, comfortably aged pot of American chop suey was waiting for him in his refrigerator. He put it on the stove to warm while he jumped into a scalding-hot shower, a plastic shower cap of Des's carefully positioned over his bandaged head. He shaved off his itchy stubble, climbed gratefully into clean, dry clothes and shoveled down three man-sized portions of his favorite sustenance. Then he poured himself a mug of coffee, topped it off with two fingers of chocolate milk and sat back down at his computer, gathering his thoughts on Ada.

That was when Yolie Snipes phoned to say she was on her way over with something near and dear to him. He hoofed his way across the causeway to meet her at the gate when she buzzed. It was his beloved Studebaker pickup that she'd brought him. His truck and a pair of envelopes—a large manila one for Des, an Astrid's Castle letter-sized envelope for him. Inside his he found a check for $320 made out in his name and signed by Aaron Ackerman. There was a scribbled note enclosed:

I would very much like a chance to win this back the next time you're in D.C.—Aaron

Somehow, Mitch doubted he'd be taking Acky up on the offer any time soon.

"I take it you folks managed to dig your way out," he said as he drove Yolie back toward Astrid's.

"True, that," she confirmed. "But if we'd left it up to the power company, we'd still be stuck up there. Captain Polito strong-armed him a dozen young recruits with chain saws to clear the private drive. Lousy duty, but those boys got it done."

Yolie had a few more questions for Mitch while he steered the truck up Route 156. Also a bit of news—she'd spoken to Martha Burgess, who had told her something very interesting. And then, before he knew it, Mitch was right back at the front gate to Astrid's Castle. As he started his way up the steep, twisting drive, he was hit by this powerful, awful feeling that someone had just hit the rewind button and the whole movie was going to start all over again from the beginning. This time in slo-mo.

Truly, it was a comfort to see so many state police cars and crime scene vans clustered there by the drawbridge when he pulled up.

"This here's a crazy one," Yolie said as she hopped out, her braids glistening in the sunlight. "There's nobody left to charge with anything. Nobody who did anything is still with us. Everybody's dead."

"Except for us," Mitch said quietly.

"You tell my baby girl to take care, hear?"

"Will do," Mitch promised, flooring it the hell out of there. He could not get away from Astrid's Castle fast enough.

He stopped off at Des's house to pick up a few things for her. Round little Bella Tillis was in the kitchen heating up some of her homemade mushroom-barley soup.

"Good, you can take this to her for me," she huffed at Mitch when he came in the door. "I'll go see her later on this afternoon."

"Sure, that sounds fine."

"Would you mind telling me why you're wearing a turban?"

"That's how they dress head wounds. The nurse said I can take it off tomorrow."

"Oh, I'll just bet she did," Bella snapped, slamming her way around the kitchen like an angry bumper car. "Make sure Desiree eats this while it's still hot," she ordered him as she poured the steaming soup into a heavy-duty thermos bottle.

"I'll sure try. But I can't make her do anything she doesn't want to do."

"No, she's stubborn, all right. But I don't have to tell *you* about stubborn, do I?"

"Bella, do we have a problem I don't know about?"

"You tell me," she fired back, standing there with her hands parked on her hips. "How are you feeling?"

"I'm fine," he said, fingering his bandage. "Just a little headachy."

"No, I mean how are you *feeling*—as if you didn't know."

"I didn't. I don't. I . . ." Actually, Mitch was starting to feel a bit dizzy again. "What *do* you mean?

"If you break that poor girl's heart, she won't be the only one walking around town with a broken arm, that's what," Bella answered, stabbing Mitch in the chest with her stubby index finger.

"You'll still have to deal with me, Mr. Hotshot New York Film Critic. And I will never forgive you. *Now* do we understand each other?"

"No, I honestly don't know what you're talking about."

"Tie that bull outside, as we used to say on Nostrand Avenue."

"Bella, I have never understood what that expression means."

"It means, be afraid," she growled at him. "Be very afraid."

"Trust me, I am," he assured her, backing his way slowly out of the kitchen.

When he arrived at the hospital he found the patient sitting up in bed engrossed by an old rerun of *The Loveboat* on television.

"Okay, this must be all of the painkillers they're giving you," he said, kissing her on the cheek.

"Shush!" Des ordered him, her eyes glued to the set. "She's not really in love with the captain after all. She was just trying to make her ex-husband jealous."

"Des, you are sitting here watching Bert Convy and Florence Henderson exchange witty repartee," he pointed out, flicking off the television.

"Hey . . . !" She protested.

"Why don't you try this instead?" he said, presenting her with the envelope of crime scene photographs that Yolie had delivered, along with the sketch pad and graphite sticks that he'd brought from her house.

"Um, okay, you may have noticed my right arm isn't exactly functioning."

"Your life drawing teacher told you he actually preferred your left-handed stuff. He thought it felt less restrained."

"Mitch, do you remember every single word I tell you?"

"Elephants and Jewish men never forget. Girlfriend, you've been through a lot. This is how you deal. So you may as well start dealing. It's not like you've got anything better to do for the next day or two."

"Actually, I've been lying here thinking about what Ada told me," she confessed. "How I shouldn't be taking any more classes. Kind of scary."

"Why scary?"

"Because taking classes is what I'm about right now. That's why I'm doing this resident-trooper thing instead of humping to get back on Major Crimes. If I'm not learning to be an artist, then what *am* I doing?"

"*Being* an artist."

Her eyes widened with fear. "Doughboy, you just sent a cold chill right up and down my spine."

"Nah, that's just your backless hospital gown—your booty's waving in the breeze. Des, I agree with Ada. You're ready to take the next step. You can handle this."

"Sure about that, are you?" she asked him warily.

"I have no doubts. None."

"So what's in the thermos?"

"Mushroom-barley soup, courtesy of your roommate."

"Yum, let me at it."

He poured some of it into a Styrofoam cup for her and set it on her tray table, along with a spoon.

She sampled it eagerly, smacking her lips. "That Jewish mother can make soup."

"Yolie had herself a conversation with Martha Burgess," Mitch announced, flopping down in the chair next to the bed. "Martha cried her poor eyes out about Les. But here comes the weird part—she told Yolie she'd broken it off with him several weeks ago. Decided to give her marriage another chance."

"So she wasn't planning to leave Bob for Les?"

"Apparently not. Which got me to wondering," Mitch said. "What if Les was actually planning to marry Jory after all?"

"Could be he was," Des answered wearily. "There's no telling what he promised Jory, or she promised him. We only have her version, and that girl and the truth were not exactly tight." She set her spoon aside and slumped back against her pillows. She'd barely touched the soup. Her appetite wasn't back yet.

"Are you going to finish that?" he asked her, gazing hungrily at the nearly full cup.

"Knock yourself out."

He was not disappointed. Bella's soup was hearty and flavorful. "We'll never know the whole truth, will we?" he asked, slurping up every last drop.

"We never do," she said. "Not about anyone or anything. The best we can ever do is guess. My guess? Les and Jory were each conning the other. On top of which she was conning Jase."

"At least Les and Jory ended up paying for it. They got punished for what they did to Norma, not to mention Jase."

Des looked at him curiously. "Jase was in on it, Mitch. He murdered three people in cold blood—*and* put me in this bed."

"All true. But I still have to cut him some slack. He was trusting and vulnerable and Jory took full advantage of him. Believe me, I'm genuinely repulsed by the intimate details of their relationship. But Jory's love was the only anchor Jase had. She threatened to take it away from him. That was more than he could handle, and Jory knew it. I put this all on her. She was greedy. She was ruthless. And, considering how easily Les duped her into killing Norma, she was also incredibly stupid."

"She believed in the dream. Not that I'm defending the sick bitch. I'm just saying it, is all."

"Which dream is that?"

"The one where we all live happily ever after. She *deserved* to be happy. That's what she told me."

"She *deserved* to die a horrible death," Mitch argued vehemently. He was still profoundly shaken by Jase's taking of his own life in that rail barn. He'd *felt* Jase's anguish in those final few moments before Jase pulled the trigger. Gazed right into his eyes as Jase chose death over life. And Mitch could not stop thinking about it. He kept feeling as if something truly momentous had happened to him in Choo-Choo Cholly's house.

In the weeks and months ahead, it would finally dawn on him what that something was: He had survived.

"Could you have done it?" Des lay there limply, her eyes searching his face. "Could you have shot Jase?"

"I honestly don't know. I'm just grateful that I didn't have to find out."

"So am I. If you'd killed him, you wouldn't be the same person anymore. Killing changes you. It changes everything."

"How?"

"I hope you never find out how," she said heavily. "What are you doing with yourself? When you're not fussing over me, I mean."

"Working on a piece about Ada."

"How about that book you've been trying to write?"

"You mean my major treatise on Hollywood and the unbearable lightness of contemporary being? Actually, I was giving that a lot of thought last night while I was sitting here in this chair. You may have noticed that I've been—how shall I say?—having a little trouble getting started on it."

"I may have."

"I think I've figured out why. See, what I've been trying to do is tell people what's wrong with American culture, when what I should be doing is simply letting the story of Jory Hearn tell itself."

"Okay, you'd better trot that one by me again."

"You just said it yourself, Des. All of this happened because she believed in the dream. She was searching for that fairy-tale happy ending, the one that Hollywood keeps telling us will eventually come our way. All we have to do is *believe*. Well, Jory did believe. She thought she was going to marry Prince Charming and live happily ever after."

"Les was no Prince Charming. Les was the frog. And all of that's nothing but childish nonsense."

"Which is exactly the point that Ada was making at dinner before the lights went out and people started dying one by one. Hollywood keeps treating us like little children. That's how they rake in the big bucks—by encouraging us to choose storybook fantasy over adult reality. And we're only too happy to comply, because life is just so much easier that way. It's easier to believe in miracle-diet cures than it is to exercise every day and eat right. It's easier to believe you'll win the Powerball Lottery than it is to work hard for a living and pay your bills on time. It's easier to dream about some fairy-tale romance than it is to apply yourself to a real relationship based on commitment and support and trust. And so we *believe*. That way, we're off the hook. We never have to take any responsibility for our own lives. And this is not a healthy thing. This is how we end up with a flesh-eating mutant like Jory Hearn. Don't misunderstand me, Jory was a genuinely evil, screwed-up person. And I'm not blaming the movies for what she did. Movies are my life. I love them. I need them. We all do. They comfort us when we need comforting. But take a good hard look at her, Des. Look at all of those people who died because she *believed*. And tell me that something isn't terribly wrong somewhere." He trailed off now, clearing his throat. "Speaking of which, Bella seems to think there's something wrong between us."

Des raised her chin at him, nostrils flaring. Here it was in full force—her Wary, Scary Look. "Which *us* would you be talking about?"

"You and me us," Mitch replied, swallowing. "She even threatened to break my arm. She's genuinely pissed at me."

"Does she have any reason to be?"

"Not that I'm aware of, no."

"I see . . ." Des stared and stared at him. "Well, *is* there?"

Mitch swallowed again, with great difficulty. "Is there wuh-what, Des?"

"Something wrong between us."

"Actually, there *has* been something on my mind these past few weeks. I've been trying to find the right moment to talk to you about it, because these words are not exactly easy for muh-me to say out loud. Maybe you've . . . I don't know . . . sensed something."

Des said not one word. Just continued to stare and stare at him.

Mitch plowed ahead, his heart pounding. "But after everything that's happened over the past couple of days, things have really crystallized in my mind. And so—"

"And so you want to lay it all on me *now*? While I'm lying here drugged and immobilized with tubes stuck in me?"

"Well, yeah. Unless, are you reasonably coherent right now?"

"Oh, I'm plenty coherent. I can't tell you how reasonable I am."

"You know what? You're right. Maybe we should have this talk another time."

"Like hell we will!" Des erupted. Her chest had begun to rise and fall, as if she was having trouble breathing. On her face was a look of total panic, just as there had been when they were in bed together at Astrid's during the blackout.

"Des, are you okay? Want me to call the doctor?"

"No, I want you to . . . get this . . . *over* with! I have had it up to *here* with you and your Big Fat Nothing Gulps!"

"My Big Fat Nothing *whats*?"

"Just say what you . . . have to say," she gasped, breathing harder and harder. "Say it and then get the . . . hell out of my room!"

"Fair enough. Des, I think something is missing in our relationship."

"Missing," she repeated, her voice filling with dread.

"From where I sit, we need to do something pretty radical about it. You may not like this. In fact, I'm pretty positive you won't. But I think it'll be the best thing for both of us in the long run, even though it means we'll—"

"Mitch, I *swear* if you don't spit this out I am going to take my external titanium whatever it is and break it over your fool—"

"I want to get married."

She absolutely froze, her eyes widening in total shock. Clearly, this was not what she'd been expecting. Although what she *had* been expecting, Mitch could not fathom. And he for sure couldn't imagine what she'd do next.

She breathed in. She breathed out. She breathed in. Out. And then Des Mitry proceeded to let loose with the single loudest hiccup that Mitch had ever witnessed. His ears popped. Medical charts flew. Furniture slammed into walls. Well, not really, but it was monumental.

She immediately clapped her left hand over her mouth, mortified beyond belief. "I haven't done that since high school. It won't happen again, I swear. I . . . I don't know why I . . . Please, excuse me."

"It's quite all right," Mitch assured her, floored. "Only, I don't speak the language. Did that mean yes or did it mean no?"

For a long moment, Des didn't answer him. When at last she did, she said, "Mitch, I thought we weren't going to do this." Her voice was soft and low. "We made a pact, you and I. That very first night in your living room, after you flicked off the lights. We sealed it with a kiss, remember?"

"I do." Mitch grinned at her. "I also remember that's not all we sealed it with."

"Don't you dare get all adorable on me right now. You made me a promise, sir. No dwelling on the meaning of us, or the future of us, or if there even *is* an us. Now did you or did you not promise me that?"

"I absolutely did. And I'm breaking my promise. And I'm sorry. No, actually, I'm not sorry at all. Because I love you, and that's not something I ever want to feel sorry about. But what we have together just isn't enough for me anymore. This is not a real complicated deal, Des. Either we love each other or we don't. We're both grown-ups. We've both been here before."

"Um, okay, teensy-weensy difference," she pointed out. "You had a good marriage. I didn't."

"That's the past, Des. That's Brandon. I don't want to talk about him. I want to talk about us. I need more. I want more. The question is, what do *you* want?"

In response, Des Mitry stared at Mitch intently for a long, long time. Then she turned her head and gazed out the window at the winter sky. She didn't tell him what she wanted. She didn't say anything at all.

After that, there was only silence.